# Reflected Passion

BLUE FEATHER BOOKS, LTD.

# Reflected Passion

A BLUE FEATHER BOOK

*by*

## Erica Lawson

This is a work of fiction. All characters, locales and events are either products of the author's imagination or are used fictitiously.

REFLECTED PASSION

Cover design by Ann Phillips

A Blue Feather Book
Published by Blue Feather Books, Ltd.

www.bluefeatherbooks.com

ISBN: 978-1-935627-62-3

First edition: October, 2013

Printed in the United States of America and in the United Kingdom.

# Acknowledgements

This particular journey has taken eight years. "Reflected Passion" began in 2005 as nothing more than a single thought in a friend's mind. A mirror. To Isabelle, who gave me the inspiration and the help to begin this journey, I give my thanks. A big thanks to her also for all the French translation. While I did French at school, it would not cut it for a novel.

When I tackled the second half of the book, my beta reader was Evelyn. She gave many hours of valuable information and advice, for which I am forever grateful. Sometimes she saw the potential where I couldn't.

Now, the journey moves to a few months ago. To Chris Paynter, who as my editor, worked diligently on the book and streamlined it to a Boeing 767.

To Nann Dunne, one of the sweetest women I know. She got out her polish, rolled up her sleeves and brought the Boeing to such a shine that I could see my face in it.

And finally to Emily Reed, who has been my publisher from the very beginning of my professional writing career. She showed a lot of faith in signing me, and I hope that this book takes off and pays back that faith ten-fold.

ALSO WRITTEN BY ERICA LAWSON AND
AVAILABLE FROM BLUE FEATHER BOOKS:

❖ POSSESSING MORGAN

❖ THE CHRONICLES OF RATHA:
   CHILDREN OF THE NOORTHI

❖ SOULWALKER

www.bluefeatherbooks.com

# Part One: Awakening

# Chapter 1

"Dale, try the basement. Some new stock came in the other day."

"Thanks, Mr. O'Brien," I told the shop owner.

The day started like any other. As usual, I was scouring the local secondhand shops in Boston for furniture. After all, that was my job. So being surrounded by dusty old tables, cupboards, and armoires was nothing new to me.

I knew this particular shop intimately, having nearly lived in it for the past two years. I spent most of my spare time searching the flea markets, waterfront antique shops, and furniture stores like Mr. O'Brien's. Somewhere out there was the piece that would make my career. Don't get me wrong. I loved restoring old furniture, but one day I knew my break would come.

I had worked in one of those larger antique clearinghouses when I graduated, reinforcing my love for all things old. But like any large organization, the clearinghouse was more interested in the politics rather than the preservation of beautiful furniture. It broke my heart to see such callous disregard of history for money.

Now I worked alone but, as they say, I had to "pay my dues." I certainly didn't have the reputation or the finances to play with the big boys. I had to resort to freelancing, like restoring old furniture for those families on fixed incomes who were searching for a piece of "old world" for their new homes. It was my bread and butter, and it paid my bills. *Come on Dale, it's what you chose to do.*

I fumbled around in the dark until I reached the light switch to the basement. The light blinded my eyes for a moment as it cast an eerie glow across the room packed with everything from bookcases, bed headboards, and cupboards, to some things that defied description. I walked gingerly down the stairs and felt the wood creak under my slight weight.

The newest stock was, of course, closest to me. The older pieces had slowly gathered dust and spiders from their long hibernation in the back of the basement. None of these moved unless Mr. O'Brien sold something upstairs.

I was on the hunt for an armoire for a client. Its age wasn't important, but I needed something that didn't look like the modern stuff. Not that I blamed my clients. Today's furniture was all steel and chrome, with nothing like the smell of real wood and old leather that could permeate the room with memories of a long-forgotten age. Maybe to some it smelled like grandma's house, but to me it was history.

This shop was my last port of call before returning to my loft. I'd been wandering around most of the morning without success. I spotted a couple of new armoires in stock and quickly shuffled down the narrow passageway in an attempt to get to them.

One of the armoires was a little too modern, but the other one had possibilities. I quickly checked its condition and tried to look inside through the narrow crack of the open door. There wasn't a ticket on it. I only hoped it was within my price range. While I considered this, I sifted through what was left. I just couldn't help myself. I still hoped that somewhere in this jumble of wood was my future.

I looked through an assortment of old paintings leaning against the wall. I usually steered clear of art, but I used the exercise to think. Could I afford the cupboard? I knew I wouldn't get paid for it until I delivered the restored piece, so the cost would have to come out of my meager savings. I looked through the half dozen frames and didn't like what I saw. My love was furniture, not art.

But tucked away behind the artwork was a mirror... well, its frame anyway. The paint was thick, pock-marked, and a revolting pale blue color—hideous enough to make me cringe. I suspected there were many layers of similarly abusive paint underneath it. I didn't know what attracted me to it, but suddenly I found the frame in my hands. I put it back and tried to walk away, but I couldn't—as if it had some sort of magnetic pull on me. I circled it like a hungry wolf. I quickly formulated what it would take to secure it from Mr. O'Brien.

I climbed the stairs and held on for my life as the wood under my feet bent under my weight once more. How on earth did they get this stuff down here in the first place? Perhaps I didn't want to know.

The portly owner was at his desk, perusing the morning paper with coffee mug in hand, just as I always found him whenever I visited. He watched me over the glasses perched on his nose. "See anything you like?"

"Maybe. You have an armoire down there. Not the pink one. I'm talking about the other one with the small carved panel in the top corner."

"Yeah. That only came in yesterday."

"How much do you want for it?"

"For you, young lady, how about two hundred dollars? You're my best customer."

*Two hundred!* I reviewed my current bank balance in my head. I wouldn't get much more than that in profit on the piece if I bought it. Still, it would fit the bill, and he usually didn't charge for delivery. Did I want to spend any more time looking? Not really. I was way behind on my work already.

I hesitated before agreeing to the amount. I didn't want to seem too eager about what I really wanted to ask him. "I see you also have an old mirror frame down there. What do you want for it?"

"Old mirror frame? I don't remember it."

"It's sitting behind the paintings against the wall. Big ugly thing painted a repulsive pale blue."

"Oh, that. It came in a lot sale. Why? Are you interested?"

"I'm looking for something for my home." I tried not to sound too eager.

"Yeah?" Unfortunately, he picked up on my interest.

"If the price is right…"

He studied me for a small hint that would give away how much I wanted it. He had me mentally jumping around on hot coals waiting for his answer. This guy should have been a cop. I would have signed any confession he shoved under my nose.

A huge grin split his chubby face as he leaned over and ruffled my hair. "Just razzing you, Dale. You're so easy."

I couldn't help myself. I let out a huge sigh at the relief. "So…"

"I tell you what. You take the armoire, and I'll throw in the mirror for free, okay?"

"Okay, you old rascal."

"Can I deliver on Monday?"

"Sure, no problem."

I handed over my credit card and felt the agony of the money slipping through my fingers like I was giving blood.

Mr. O'Brien laughed. "The look on your face…"

I sighed. "Yeah, I know. Spending the money is positively painful." I left the shop to the echoes of his laughter.

* * *

I had a lot of work to do, but the weekend still dragged by. For some reason, I was eager to see that mirror frame again. The truck arrived mid-morning, and the men deposited my purchases in the middle of my work area. The loft was formerly a dance studio located on the top floor of a small office block, so I had plenty of room to spread out to work, while the bedroom, kitchen, and bathroom occupied the far end of the floor space. I checked the armoire and realized it would be fine for my client. Now it was just a matter of stripping it back to bare wood and applying some oil into its surface.

I turned my attention to what I'd been eagerly waiting on for the past two days. I carried the frame to the large window and examined it in the daylight. The piece was massive and quite heavy for a mirror, and it would cost a pretty penny for the replacement glass. The color was truly horrific—that sickly baby blue, which probably meant it had hung in a child's room at some point.

I tried to look past the paint color and concentrated hard to take in the lines of the wood. The simple frame was ridged around three sides and decorated with a huge scrollwork panel across the top. It would've been quite elegant in its day and would be again if I had anything to do with it. I was eager to start restoring it, but my paying work came first. I put it aside for later and turned my attention to the armoire.

My cell rang. "Wincott Restoration."

"Why do you have to keep up with this silly obsession of yours?"

My mother. Many times I'd had this conversation with her, and all we'd agreed upon was to disagree. "Hello, Mother," I said flatly, already knowing this conversation would cut into my work.

"Don't sound like that, dear. We haven't heard from you in quite a while."

"I've been busy." But she already knew that. "I'm way behind on my work."

"I don't see why you have to work, Dale. Your trust fund—"

"My trust fund can stay untouched. I'm doing fine by myself." My definition of "fine" was that I was *just* paying the bills. No way would I admit that to my mother, though.

"But you don't need to work."

"I suppose I don't, but I love it and don't see it as a job." I tried to end the conversation. "What do you want?"

"Can't I call my only daughter because I want to hear her voice?"

I remained silent.

"Fine. There's a society ball coming up. Young Robert Claridge has asked me for your number. Please don't embarrass the family by saying no."

"If I say no, it's not to embarrass the family."

"Moving to Boston hasn't improved your disposition, I see."

This conversation was going nowhere. I knew very well what she wanted, and I wasn't about to give up where and how I lived just because she said so. "I'll wait for Robert's call then. It's good to hear from you, Mother. Bye."

"But—"

I disconnected the call before she could get another word in. I would probably pay for that at some later date.

Finally, I got some peace and quiet. Inhaling deeply, I let my irritation bleed away as I put on my mask and picked up the stripping gel. For the next few hours, I could immerse myself in the feel of carved wood under my gloved fingertips.

* * *

It had been six weeks since I stripped back the mirror frame to its grain. I was pleased to find that the wood was still sound and would come up to a nice mahogany color when I finished with it. I had treated the dried wood with tung oil, and now I was ready for waxing before ordering the mirror. I took special care with this piece, taking my time to ensure it was done right.

Over the intervening weeks, I'd done a little research to try to find the history of the mirror, but there was nothing definitive about it to pin it down. It might have been eighteenth century, but I couldn't be sure, or maybe someone had made a good replica of one. At that point, its lineage wasn't of primary concern. Even if it was a fake, it would look beautiful in my bedroom.

This particular night was especially dark. The low moonlight from the first-quarter moon infused my loft in a gentle glow through the skylight. I ran my fingers over the soft, clean lines of the wood, my fingertips learning every contour and dip on this beautiful creation.

Closing my eyes, I gently caressed the frame and let the history in it sweep over me. I inhaled deeply and could nearly smell a faint scent—not turpentine, tung oil, or beeswax, but a woman's scent. I continued to daydream as my hand swept over the swirls and valleys in the wood, the surface soft as a woman's skin. Now why did I think of a woman? I'd never touched a woman's skin this way except my own. Had the scent influenced my conclusion?

It had been a while, a long while, since I'd had any sort of physical relationship. Why? I was a normal twenty-seven-year-old female. Why didn't I have a boyfriend? I had to admit my experience had been limited and rather unsatisfying, which was probably why I hadn't actively found a boyfriend. I shook it off by telling myself I was too busy with work. The other possibility scared me.

My attention turned back to the wood as I slid my hands over the frame. Images flashed into my mind of a raven-haired woman. Her piercing dark eyes looked into my very soul to extract each and every secret I had hidden, even from myself. *"Viens à moi, ma chérie..."*

Now I really started to worry. Not only was I having delusions, but she was beckoning to me in French. I couldn't even hallucinate in my native tongue. Maybe it was all that turpentine. I was lucky my hair hadn't fallen out yet from the stuff.

Despite this feeling of detachment, I could sense a tickling in the pit of my stomach, something I hadn't felt in a long time. Would it hurt? It'd been a while since I'd satisfied myself.

The sound and smell left me once I took my hands off the frame. I lay on my bed and searched for a fantasy to arouse me. Where were those images that used to sate me? I struggled because each time I found those fantasy images, they were overridden by a face with deep brown eyes and flying dark hair. Defeated, I turned to the face that refused to leave me.

Behind closed eyelids, I searched for her and listened for that deep, dark voice that, in a few words, flowed over me like molten honey. It shook me to the core. Despite my denial, I was taken with a woman who, for all intents and purposes, came from my fertile imagination. The harder I tried to fantasize, the more I subconsciously blocked her image. I was a heterosexual woman. That's what I'd been brought up to believe, so why should I believe anything else?

My fantasy evaded me, and I struggled on without it to reach for that elusive completion. My fingers went through the motions mechanically, but I knew it wouldn't happen. The harder I tried, the more frustrated I became, and the farther away I got from what I so desperately wanted. I lay there panting, knowing that there was only one way I was going to reach my goal, but was I ready for that revelation?

I pounded the bed in defeat. I couldn't even get satisfaction by my own hand. I had to do something about this before it became a real problem. My gaze wandered over to the frame leaning against the far wall. These new feelings that bombarded me had all started with the mirror…

* * *

The mirror was now on the wall, and it had turned out exceptionally well. It had taken another week before it was complete. Handing over the mirror to get the glass fitted felt like I had given away my child. Earlier in the afternoon, the glaziers delivered the final piece, and because of its heaviness, they were nice enough to hang it for me.

I had difficulty deciding where to put it. The loft had an open-plan living space, so I placed it where I could take advantage of some reflected light. It wasn't quite in my bedroom, but it was close enough for me to see it.

I worked through to early evening, but I couldn't stop looking at the mirror. In desperation, I threw a blanket over it so I could finally concentrate on the job at hand. This time I was restoring an old kitchen cabinet. Maybe I was distracted because the work was laborious, or maybe it was the mirror.

I cleaned up around nine o'clock, and my appetite had waned. This would be my first night alone with the newly completed mirror, and I felt a swelling of pride. Finally, here was something of great beauty that I'd brought back to life. I tugged on the blanket, and it fell away. The muted light of the bedside lamp flowed over the frame, filling the hills and valleys with light and dark. I lay in bed watching it and slowly drifted off to contented sleep.

Later that night, something woke me and I was on instant alert. I grabbed the baseball bat near my bed and went in search of the sound. It was soft at first, like whispering. I moved around the loft to check the doors and windows. Everything was as I'd left it, but I still heard the sound. The low moaning then changed to a soft guttural sound that seemed vaguely familiar to me. I moved around the room to track the noise, but it seemed to be coming from my bedroom… no, from the mirror.

Feeling the coolness of the wooden floor on the soles of my feet, I moved closer, and the moaning became more animated. A low voice spoke softly in French. My phantom woman had returned. I would know that voice anywhere.

I gazed at the mirror and all I saw was what I saw every morning. My image. Looking back at me was a young woman with mousy brown hair and eye color of indeterminate shade. My mother said my eyes were a steel blue, like my temperament, but I always thought the color looked washed out. It wasn't a vibrant blue like I'd wanted as a kid, but more of a blend of blue and gray.

As I stared at my reflection, an image emerged underneath it. Seated on a large bed was a nude woman. I closed my eyes to try and clear my mind of any thought and reopened them. The image was still there. My raven-haired woman perched on the edge of her bed while another woman knelt between her spread legs.

I couldn't help myself. I gasped. Rather loudly, it seemed, because the woman opened her eyes and stared directly at me. Embarrassed, I backed away and out of sight. This couldn't be happening. Was it my mind telling me something I didn't want to know? Why was it happening now? I would see a doctor tomorrow… or visit a lesbian bar tomorrow night.

The sounds continued to emanate from the glass, and I again found myself drawn to them. Hallucination or no, I was curious, as a previously unknown voyeuristic tendency showed itself. I felt like I was on a balcony, looking down onto a stage as the play unfolded. The woman's eyes were closed and a beguiling smile graced her full lips as the woman kneeling in front of her pleasured her. I couldn't see exactly what was going on because her tiny body blocked my view, but my mind filled in the visual gaps. I might not be gay, but I knew enough to know what was happening.

I felt that tingling in my stomach again. It gnawed at me as I watched them together. Those dark eyes opened and met mine, her excitement rising with every second. She didn't acknowledge her companion because her eyes were solely on me. I felt a light sweat break out on my skin, flushed with a rush of adrenaline, as she drew me in to feel her pleasure as my own. I wasn't aware that my own hands had wandered to imitate her stimulation, until I was slowly climbing along with her.

Her passion-filled eyes moved from me to the kneeling woman. She demanded more in a deep, smoky voice that touched something very basic in me. *"Oui, Madeleine… comme ça…"* I didn't need to translate her French to know she was enjoying what the woman was doing to her. She looked back up at me for a moment before a strong pulse of excitement caused her head to roll back to draw an anguished cry and expose her swan-like neck to me. Her pale skin was slick with perspiration, which trickled down her drenched body. I watched a bead roll down to her breast and hang for a moment on a perfect nipple before it dripped to her thigh.

My eyes were now riveted on the rest of her body. I had ignored it before because I could not see past the intensity in her eyes. Perfect. Absolutely perfect. Each part of her was like finely crafted porcelain, pale but combined in perfect harmony to present a very enticing picture.

I couldn't deny what I felt right then. It wasn't the act that excited me, but the woman in the throes of that act. It was to her that I was drawn. Her eyes captured mine once more, and I smiled. She smiled back as we shared the moment.

I suppose I'd always known who I was inside, but family and society had demanded my compliance. The only reason I ever had boyfriends was to please my family. Now, I finally understood that.

My mind mulled over this new revelation as I watched her. She was still babbling in French, but I knew what she said. Her excitement was my own, and I couldn't help it as a whimper escaped me. My fingers found those places that stimulated me as I watched her hips move in that ancient rhythm that would bring her completion. She watched me as I watched her. We reached for that pinnacle and simultaneously slid over the edge into oblivion as it took us both. We cried out in unison as pure sensation rushed through us, joined together in mutual pleasure.

I stood there stunned and panting. Did I see it or was it all in my imagination? My fantasy female took a moment before standing, walking over on unsteady legs toward the mirror. I saw her body in full view for the first time.

My eyes scanned the room, noting the antiques liberally scattered around. I spotted the discarded clothing, and it looked old, perhaps a century or two ago. Looking back at my phantom woman, she was in surprisingly good health for a woman of leisure. Drawing my eyes over her from her feet, I took in the shapely legs, the flat, well-toned stomach, full rounded breasts, and a beautiful aristocratic face. She still had on makeup—heavy pancake with dark outlined eyes and ruby-red lips—as if she had come from a ball or other function. Her cheekbones were long and even, her forehead high.

But most of all, those eyes, now closer to me, were dark as the night, glistening in the muted light. Exquisite.

We stood there looking at each other, possibly wondering if we were imagining what had just happened. She turned away and walked to her companion on the bed. She cast one final glance over her shoulder before turning her attention back to reciprocating the pleasure. I waited a moment longer to grace her with a smile and turned away. My brain had taken in enough for the night. Maybe after a good night's sleep, it would seem clearer in the light of day. Perhaps I'd find it had only been a dream…

# Chapter 2

I woke the next morning, lying on the rumpled ruins of my bed sheets. I contemplated what happened last night. Was it real? Or was it just a fantastic creation of my fevered imagination? Did I want it to be real? Or was this my mind trying to accept my sexuality?

Half an hour later, I was no clearer on any of the questions I posed to myself. Was this a sign? I convinced myself that it was all a dream—a wild fantastic dream—and this was the end of it. Then why did I feel like the woman in the mirror wasn't through with me yet?

I went to the mirror, but I only saw what I should have seen—my reflection and nothing more. I looked closely into the depths of the glass for any trick of light or perhaps some flaw in the mirror, but there appeared to be none. I was baffled. My life of solitude was finally catching up with me.

The frame was cool but warmed to my touch as I ran my fingers around the edges. I felt nothing. Not a tremor. In the light of day, my thoughts seemed silly and frivolous, expressing my own inner desires for the love and comfort that had been absent from my life of late.

I started my work for the day and tried not to ruminate over the previous night, and for a while, I managed to lose myself in the craft. Despite my inner turmoil, the time flew by and I was pleased with what progress I had made.

There was a knock on the door. It could only be one of two people. I was praying it was the second one. The visitor knocked again. I took a deep breath before opening the door. I let out the breath I'd been holding when I saw it was my father.

"Hey there, pumpkin."

"Hey, Daddy. Come in." I stepped aside. "Mother sent you here?"

"I don't need your mother to tell me to visit my only daughter." That meant yes. "She mentioned something about you hanging up on her awhile back." He kissed me on the cheek and moved to the kitchen table to sit down in one of my two chairs. He waited for me to take a seat in the other one. "Can't you just talk to her?"

I reached across the table to grab his hand. "I've tried to talk to her, but she won't listen. I need this work."

"But, sugar…"

"No, Daddy. You, of all people, know that I have to find myself. It's a matter of self-esteem."

He squeezed my hand. "I understand."

"Good, then you can explain it to Mother."

"I'll see what I can do."

"Are you staying for lunch?"

"I suppose I can. What are you offering?"

I opened the refrigerator to see what I had, which wasn't much. "How about a ham and cheese sandwich?" I grabbed a loaf of bread before he even answered.

"That's fine."

"Coffee?"

"Two sugars."

"When did that happen?" The kettle was in my hand and hovered over the stove.

"When what?"

"Didn't you used to have one sugar?"

"A couple of months, I suppose."

It was then that I realized I had lost touch with my family. So many small things had probably changed since I actually took notice of what my parents did. I collected the ham and cheese out of the fridge. "How's the banking business?"

"Booming, as usual. How about you?"

"I'd like to say booming, as usual."

"Things slow?"

"No, I have plenty of work, but there's only one of me. I won't grow rich from this, but I can live on it." He frowned, and I waited for the words to tumble out of his mouth.

"Are you going to accept the Claridge boy's invitation?"

"I haven't decided yet." I let him stew while I sat down. "Are you waiting for a grandchild?"

He coughed discreetly. "What makes you think that?"

"Why else would you be pushing me into this?"

"Is he so bad?"

I looked into the eyes that mirrored my own color. "What if I don't have children?"

His mouth gaped open. "What?"

"I didn't say I wouldn't… or couldn't. It was just a question. What if I don't find my soul mate? Do I then accept someone you approve of?"

"Whoa!" He held up his hands. "Where'd this come from?"

The kettle whistled, and I moved to the bench to make coffee. "I don't know. It's… everything." I didn't know what I meant. "It's Mother phoning every second day to ask about the dance. She's pushing pretty hard." I brought the two coffees to the table and sat down. "I'm twenty-seven years old, Daddy. What should I be expecting from my life?"

He leaned on the table and reached across to grab my hand. "You'll find your own way, honey. If I know anything about you, it's that you are a very determined young woman."

"I got that from you."

He chuckled. "No, you got that from your mother."

"Does she always win the arguments?"

He picked up his coffee and took a sip. "Just the ones in public."

I made him a sandwich and pushed the plate over. "Some important decisions were made in public."

There was a glint in his eye. "That's what you saw. We go home after that."

I sprayed my sip of coffee over the table and coughed loudly. "You wily old fox."

"I didn't get to where I am on looks alone." He took a healthy bite of his sandwich, and I waited while he chewed and swallowed. "I don't like making a scene in front of people who aren't family."

We continued our lunch mostly in silence. We talked about mundane things like the weather and when I would visit next. When it looked like he wouldn't give up easily, I reluctantly agreed to visit Saturday. He glanced at his watch once or twice, so I pushed him out the door. I had a busy afternoon.

I learned two things about my father. He now took two sugars with his coffee, and he wasn't the lamb I thought he was.

But now that he'd left, I had a more immediate problem. Evening was approaching, and I was filled with trepidation about what the night would bring. On the one hand, I was terrified that I'd imagined it all, but on the other, what if I hadn't? I realized I didn't want either scenario to happen.

* * *

As expected, sleep escaped me. I was wound up like a finely coiled spring, and nothing would ease the tension. The bedside clock ticked slowly. Its sound was deafening in the quiet of the loft. I strained to hear any sound from the mirror, but there hadn't been as much as a squeak.

I was so exhausted that my eyes closed despite my apprehension. I finally felt that creeping lethargy that would lead to sleep. I dozed off with a vague awareness of voices murmuring in the distance.

It only seemed like minutes later that I woke to hear that sound, fresh in my mind from the night before. Again? This woman was insatiable.

This time I didn't waste my time looking for the source of the noise. Cautiously, I approached the mirror, as I didn't want to give away my presence. I suspected she would know anyway. As I faced them, she looked up the moment I arrived. A slow, sexy, half-smile crossed those full lips, exuding a sensuality that extended to her eyes as they watched me watching her.

I was so lost in the intense gaze that she pinned me to where I stood. I was helpless but to watch as she took her pleasure and tortured me with images that I knew would haunt me long afterward. Tonight's companion wasn't a small woman but a man. Was he her husband? Her lover? A total stranger?

They were both nude on the bed. She straddled his lap as his hands on her hips urged her on. Their slow torturous rhythm alerted me to what they were doing. Her gentle whimpering was all I needed to hear to know what she was feeling, perhaps not as intensely as the night before, but pleasure just the same.

I was a voyeur, not that it stopped me from watching them. No, watching her. There was no one else as she gazed at me. My whole world had narrowed to one exotically beautiful woman who, in passion's embrace, was showing me everything she felt in that one look. It was breathtaking.

By force of will, I kept my hands at my sides, as I steadfastly refused to fall into this vortex of spiraling emotions again. She increased her pace on the man's lap by using the long, lean muscles in her thighs to raise and lower herself. Helplessly, I watched those muscles bunch and flex as she worked her body into a frenzy, her soft skin sliding over taut muscle and tendon. The light sheen covering her skin radiated in the candlelight and leant a heavenly glow to her body.

She leaned back and extended her arms to brace herself on the bed, knowing full well that she presented herself to me. I placed my hands on either side of the mirror and hung my head in defeat. I couldn't watch any longer. Walking away didn't silence her cries, and I was broken as I listened to her fulfilling her desire. When there was nothing but silence, I left, not looking once to see her reaction. I was tempted to find my baseball bat.

I returned to my bed, but sleep was the last thing on my mind. This woman had stirred up so many emotions. This had to be a dream. A terrifying, sensual dream. Was it time to finally admit what was worrying me?

"Fine!" I yelled. "I'm gay! Are you happy now?" There was no answer. Was I expecting some sort of fanfare for the declaration? Tomorrow night I would have my answer.

* * *

I suppose I shouldn't have been surprised when the sounds returned the following night. Obviously, my mind didn't think I was being sincere enough in my claim. "Please don't do this to me," I whispered. "I can't take it anymore."

"Then surrender to me." The words were laced with a heavy French accent.

"You've got to be kidding." My hallucination had changed tactics and was asking me to join in… in English. I rolled over on the bed and buried my face in my pillow. "I'm gay," I muttered. Then I did the only thing I could do at a time like that. I cried.

"Do not cry, *chérie.*"

"Go away." My voice cracked and broke, just like my spirit. How was I going to tell my parents?

*"Bonne nuit."* The words were low and sweet and acted as a balm to my tortured soul.

"Good night," I answered without thinking.

I covered my head with the pillow because I expected the tirade to start, but it was quiet. Had she covered her mirror? Out of curiosity, I got out of bed and approached the glass.

"What am I doing?" I questioned myself as I peeked around the edge of the frame. If she was waiting, I didn't want to her to see me. The scene before me was as before, except that there was no woman and no sex. The bedroom rested quietly, illuminated by a candelabra holding three lit candles that sat on a bedside table. The whole point of the hallucination was to act as an epiphany. I had discovered that epiphany, so why was her bedroom still in my reflection? I threw a blanket over it and went back to bed.

I was so tired. There was nothing but restless sleep the last few nights, and all I wanted was an undisturbed night's sleep. Suddenly, the normal sounds around me were loud and intrusive, keeping me awake half the night.

* * *

A week had passed since my declaration. That night was my last good night's sleep.

Daddy sent a car to pick me up on Saturday, and in a way, I was glad to escape the loft for a while. That positive turned into a negative very quickly once Mother greeted me. I tried to be civil, I really did, but she was in rare form. It wasn't until Daddy interceded that I had a chance to breathe. When the woman wanted something, she wanted it now. I suspected she was worrying about an heir to the fortune. After all, tick tock, tick tock. If I didn't have a child, the fortune would go to Uncle Harry who, according to my mother, was a "lazy good-for-nothing." Of course, no mention was made of my brother, Marcus, who had already suffered the wrath of mother and been disowned.

I finally acquiesced and said yes to the dance, so long as Mother didn't give out wedding invitations after it. I was extremely glad to get back to my loft after that, even if the woman in the mirror was howling like a banshee. I stayed away from showing myself, but after three days of every imaginable sound that could be made while making love, I was ready to kill myself, metaphorically speaking.

But I couldn't stay away any longer. She'd teased and tortured me, shamelessly flaunting her sexuality. She knew full well that I had to hear her. Those bedroom eyes and that "come hither" voice, low and hypnotic, called to me.

This particular night, I stood before the mirror and watched her sleep. The curtains of the canopy bed were drawn aside, and her lithe body lay in quiet repose. I was spellbound. I had seen her body, for she had shown it to me many times. Tonight, there was an almost innocence in her relaxed posture.

My fingers reached out to touch the glass, the barrier that separated me from her. To my shock, it gave way to allow my hand to slip through. My thoughts had now moved from dream to reality, and the ramifications were staggering. I pulled out my hand and examined it. I saw no ill effects of the experiment.

I considered my next move. Until then, I'd thought of her as only a figment of my imagination. Now, it seemed there was a reality side to this hallucination. Was she the "one" I'd spoken to my father about?

Did I go to her and risk not being able to return, or did I stay behind this mirror, forever wanting what I'd forbidden myself to have? I was contemplating giving her what I'd given no other woman in my life. I knew this was a life-defining moment.

I went to the kitchen for coffee while my mind presented its case like a well-oiled debate, each side marshalling arguments for and against such a move. In a trance, I watched the clock slowly tick by, unable to decide who to award the win to. Perhaps that was my problem. I was thinking too much with my head and not enough with my heart.

The circles under my eyes, which had deepened with every night's missed rest, attested to my lack of sleep. I was anxious, irritable, and preoccupied with her. There was no choice in this. For my sanity, I had to go. I washed my coffee mug and returned to the mirror.

I knew that she saw me in the mirror as I saw her. She had brazenly moved the mirror so that I had an unobstructed view of her, or perhaps it was so she could watch me. I gathered my courage and without another thought stepped through the glass with a certain amount of hope that I could return.

* * *

The room was in semi-darkness, lit only by the dying fire in the fireplace. I was cold. I looked down at my body and found I was naked. I peeked back through the mirror and saw my clothes scattered in a pile on the floor. Then it dawned on me. Only I could come through, nothing else.

I placed a couple of logs on the fire to try to warm up my chilled skin. The embers burst into flame with the addition of fuel and cast flickering shadows around the high walls. I walked toward the bed and stopped, afraid of coming closer. Her dressing gown was draped over a nearby chair. I reverently lifted it to my nose and smelled a scent I'd only dreamed of in my fevered imagination.

I put the gown on to cover my nakedness. As it slid over my skin, the scent wafted around me in a sweet smell that drifted up to my nostrils. Slowly, my body warmed to the feel of the soft lace, which took away the goose bumps that dotted my skin.

I stood there mesmerized. Now that I was in the same room with her, I could see clearly every line and curve of her, her soft skin unblemished by makeup. She was much younger than I had anticipated, perhaps no more than twenty-five to thirty years old.

She shifted in the bed. Her body rolled toward me, and I stood still as I tried not to disturb the air flowing around me. She settled, and I released my breath, wisps of air flowing gently over my parted lips. Before I finished that single breath, her eyes opened and her look pinned me in place.

Her gaze slowly skimmed over me, leaving tingles in its wake. I knew the apparel I was wearing wasn't closed. The loose cloth hung from my breasts, acting like a curtain of its own and hiding what I sensed she wanted to see. It seemed as though she was memorizing my body as her mind filled in the details hidden in shadow.

Her gaze returned to my face, not wavering, as she pushed away the covers. A predatory smile spread her lips into full blossom. My lips returned the favor. Her body was covered in soft linen and lace. I wasn't able to see what she was offering me, but my mind could effortlessly fill in the gaps. She knew what I was thinking as if it were imprinted on my forehead.

"Who are you?" That deep, dark voice that had tormented my dreams, spoke. I was surprised that I understood her. Perhaps I wanted to hear her speak French, the language of love, for that was what she spoke to me while in the throes of her passion, her tongue lovingly rolling over every syllable as if caressing it. Oh yes, she may have had sex with someone else, but she was loving me.

I made no reply, but stood there dumbfounded. She sat up, moved her feet to the floor, and lightly perched on the edge of the mattress. "Do you have a name?"

My name? What was my name? All thought had flown under her intense regard of me. Hesitantly, I stepped back as I tried to keep some distance between us. She stood, and I had to look elsewhere. The sheer force of her presence filled every corner of the room.

"Do not be afraid, little one."

Afraid? I was terrified. She swamped my senses. I moved back toward the mirror, as I vainly searched for my identity.

"Do not go," she pleaded.

Not that night, perhaps another. I stepped back through the mirror, safe now that the barrier was between us. She approached the mirror, picked up the discarded gown, and lifted it to her nose. The smell brought a smile to her lips and our eyes met, filled with promise for another day.

Her passionate gaze slowly slid down my now naked body and glided over my skin like a lover's caress. My secret had been revealed. She'd seen me as I had seen her.

# Chapter 3

*"Ma chérie… je t'en prie."*

Two nights had passed since I stood in her room. I had ignored her pleas to talk, but I couldn't take it any longer

I pulled my pillow on top of my head as I tried to block out that wonderfully hypnotic voice. She was like a siren of the sea who called to me to shipwreck myself on her shore. But I knew what she was like. Her appetites were varied and deep, and I couldn't let myself drown in that.

"No. Go away! I don't want to talk to you."

*"Pourquoi?"*

"No."

*"Viens me parler…* Umm, talk to me, *ma chérie."*

"No."

"Why? What have I done?"

She would keep bothering me until I explained. Sighing deeply, I wrestled myself out of bed and approached the mirror. As expected, she was sitting there in her nightgown as she waited patiently for me. Those sad eyes stared back at me and were nearly my undoing, but I stayed strong.

"No more."

"What is your name?"

I stared back unmoved.

"Please, *chérie*, what is your name?"

I relented. "Dale Wincott."

"Dale…" She rolled her tongue over my name, and I melted. This was not going well.

"And your name?"

"Françoise Marie Aurélie de Villerey." *Well, that was a mouthful.* She saw my stunned reaction and gently laughed, a deep throaty chuckle that tickled my senses.

"Please, call me Françoise."

"Françoise." Her eyes widened as I said her name, my own voice rough with emotion. So, she was also vulnerable.

"Why do you dismiss me?"

"Because we are from two different worlds."

"Of course we are, *chérie*. Even I can see that."

"I can't do this. You ask too much."

"I think you can. You only need to come to me."

"I can't. I will not be a one-night stand."

"I do not understand. What is this 'one-night stand'?" She said it with such innocence that I nearly believed she was incapable of such a thing.

I had hoped to end this without explanation, but I'd backed myself into a corner.

"Each night there is someone new. I have seen you with your paramours, and I won't be one of your conquests."

She looked slightly shocked. "Never. They mean nothing, *chérie.*"

"Stop calling me that. I have a name."

She sighed. "Dale…" I couldn't help but shiver every time she said my name in that melodic voice. I should have let her continue to say *"chérie."* It was a lot safer.

*"Mon Dieu*, Dale, since I saw you I have no other paramour. No one else, only you."

I nearly choked on her claim. "Yeah, right," I mumbled.

"Pardon?" She seemed offended that I questioned her sincerity. I shook my head to dismiss her, but she wouldn't take that for an answer. "Tell me, *chérie.*" She seemed to deliberately use that word to irritate me.

"Tell you? All right, I'll tell you. Every night, every single night, you made love to someone knowing very well that I was watching you. It seems that even before me, you were not loyal to one partner. What makes you think I'm going to change that?"

She shifted around on the chair in front of the mirror, as if she were attending to her toilette. *"Chérie*, I am a *veuve*… a 'widow.' I have no husband. What would you have me do?"

I knew I was being unreasonable, but I feared that once I gave myself to her, she'd cast me aside. Maybe I was looking for a fight to justify my need to keep her at arm's distance.

"Why did you do that to me?" I asked. "Tease me."

"Tease?"

"Umm… torment."

"Ahh, *tourment*. I cannot have you. Is it not the next best thing?"

She had a point. It was the best possible solution to an impossible problem. If I was honest, I'd admit she made me feel things I'd never felt before. She eased a tension that had been quietly simmering in the background for some time.

Admittedly, since I had visited her, she'd been quiet. But two nights did not make the woman celibate. I mentally stepped back from this conversation and slapped myself in the head. We hadn't even made love, and I was already possessive. Was I really being fair here?

"I may not like it, but yes it is the next best thing," I said. "I can't let it continue."

"But, Dale, you can stop all this."

"How?"

"All you have to do is come to me." An impish grin crossed her face. She knew she had won this verbal duel.

I gathered what little remaining dignity I had and left. I crawled back into bed to the sound of her gentle laughter.

Later that night, she began making sounds—wild, untamed, and harsh guttural cries screaming out my name. When I could stand it no longer, I got up and went to the kitchen for coffee. I couldn't help but look as I passed the mirror, only to see her smirking at me.

At the table, I held my head in my hands and gazed down into the murky depths of my cup as the screaming continued. I was glad I didn't have neighbors; otherwise, the police would be knocking on my door. Now that would take some explaining.

For half an hour, she continued her tirade, moaning in French and yelling my name frequently. At that point, I had to smile at her ridiculous lengths to get my attention. Should I be flattered that she was still trying to entice me over?

I wandered back to the mirror. I expected to see a mass of bodies in full-fledged animation. But she sat there, as I had found her once before, with a shy smile on her beautiful face. I couldn't help but return that smile, my emotion rising to my eyes. I felt a tear slide down my cheek.

I closed my eyes, unable to look at her, and felt a thumb gently wipe away the moisture. I looked to find her hand through the glass, a sweet, understanding smile on her face. My own hand, of its own volition, cupped hers. We faced each other as we spanned time and space, looking into each other's eyes to acknowledge what was a simple truth.

Despite my reservations, I gave in. Like the Titanic, I was embarking on a voyage to disaster, certain to go down with the ship. She was my iceberg that crashed against me and broke me in two, and she left me to either sink or swim.

I took her hand and stepped through the mirror. There was the familiar coldness as my clothes left my body. I tried to cover myself, but I found my hands held firm by her strong fingers. Françoise guided me toward the fire and wrapped me in her dressing gown. Her body surrounded me in warmth over the soft material. We were touching, and it was heaven. Why had I fought this?

We faced the cheerful fire and watched fiery embers float into the air before they disappeared up the chimney flue. There was no sound but the crackling of the flames and the settling of the house. It was strange not to hear the constant sounds of civilization—traffic, sirens, and far-off voices—which had been a constant presence in my life. The silence was deafening to my ears. A gentle breeze wafted over my hair as Françoise rested her chin on my shoulder.

Her arms encircled me to draw me closer to her body. The flimsy material was no barrier to what I felt pressed into my back, and it was strange. The realization of what was about to happen hit me. I stiffened, not sure if I was prepared for something so foreign to me.

"What?" Her soft, whispered voice sounded concerned.

I didn't want to appear foolish, but what could I do? She would find out sooner or later. Perhaps I needed to tell her before I did something wrong.

"I've never made love to a woman before." I held my breath and awaited her reaction.

Gripping my chin with a strong hand, she pulled my face around to meet hers. She tipped my chin up for our gazes to meet. Her finger gently ran down my nose and stopped at my lips. Unconsciously, I opened my mouth and let her finger slip inside. Those dark eyes watched keenly as my tongue ran enticingly over her skin.

"I never would have known," she whispered, *"ma chérie."* She drew out the endearment, deep, soft, and full of want. I could feel that familiar pull deep down. I was unable to move as she slowly removed her finger and replaced it with her soft lips.

The first touch was electric, and we both withdrew. I'm sure my expression matched her astonished look. This would be something special and profoundly life-altering. Was this our destiny?

She reached behind my neck and pulled me in as her mouth sought out mine in need. Our exploration was slow and purposeful, while our lips and tongues discovered each other for the first time. Françoise was not demanding but very gentle, perhaps because she didn't want to scare me. This woman was very experienced and knowledgeable, and I worried about stumbling in this dance we had embarked on.

Her fingertips slowly slid over my cheeks while her eyes followed their path. This close, her eyes were like the deepest, darkest part of a forest on a cloudy day. Yet, there was also a richness to the dark brown that gave the color depth and clarity. I found her mapping my own face with equal thoroughness. Françoise was truly an extraordinarily beautiful woman.

*"Incroyable,"* I murmured. She giggled. The woman actually giggled. "Did I say it wrong?"

*"Non. Incroyable*, indeed." She pulled me into a hug so that my face rested in the crook of her neck. Instinctively, my tongue darted out and licked the flesh presented to me. The tang of it sat on my tongue and appealed to my taste buds like a rare vintage wine. I had to have more. I nipped and tasted her skin. I finally found her pulse point and concentrated my lips on that spot until she whimpered.

Françoise was content to let me explore, and it was intoxicating. I couldn't help it. I was addicted after one morsel. I moved to the other side of her neck and indulged myself once more on this veritable feast. She was not idle while I fed. Her hands slipped under my dressing gown and moved from one end of my back to the other. Her touch was like fire as she moved across my heated skin.

I was totally swept away by the gamut of emotions running riot through me. Like a bolt of lightning from the sky, I realized this was what has been missing from my life.

The cloth slid from my body with barely a whisper to fall at my feet. The warmth of her hands, moving everywhere, quickly replaced the chill I felt. Her lips returned to mine with more urgency as our passion rose. My mind quickly reached meltdown as she triggered a hunger in me that I thought I'd never attain.

I reached with trembling fingers for the ties on her gown, but I couldn't grasp them firmly. Her hands came up to mine and helped me in my mission to find her skin. I looked up into those eyes and silently thanked her for letting me set the pace, perhaps even giving her permission to slow me down to enjoy the journey first.

I stepped back a moment and took a deep breath. A smile tugged her sensuous lips. I think she was amused at my impetuous nature. I raised my eyebrow at her. Her smile broadened, rising up to reflect in her eyes. She tapped her finger on my nose in delight. I trapped it in my mouth in frustration and sucked furiously.

Little did I know what effect that would have on her as her gaze dropped to my mouth. I watched the turmoil reflected there as her raw sexual energy rose to the surface. Her nightgown quickly discarded, she pulled me to the bed and drew me down with her to the clean sheets. Her hands buried themselves in my hair to massage my scalp, while her lips found mine again. She teased and nipped me. I felt she wanted to ravish me in the worst way possible but summoned restraint to take her time.

She buried her face in my neck, her gasping breath slowing as my hands touched her back to idly trace the defined muscle I found there. Slowly, I ran my fingers up and down and felt the strange sensation of soft, velvety skin.

Her warm lips tickled my neck and I giggled, my body convulsing in reaction. I laughed again at another nip and instinctively clutched at her back. The muscles under my fingers clenched and bunched as Françoise pushed herself up on her hands. Her raven hair acted as a curtain around our faces. Her tongue reached out for mine in a dance for domination.

I didn't intend to dominate her, but I played the game nonetheless and enjoyed the utter freedom of simply being with her. I absorbed each and every emotion she introduced to me. I didn't want to miss a moment of this first time, a time that would remain with me forever.

Those wonderfully soft lips moved down my chin and traversed my neck as she reverently placed mere whispers of kisses across my skin. I was only aware of them because she brushed the fine hairs on my skin. Françoise continued downward, only occasionally stopping on her journey to investigate a specific piece of skin.

She finally approached where I wanted her to go. A slight rasp could be heard over the snap and crackle of the nearby fire as her tongue tasted my breast, slowly circling her target in ever decreasing circles. I entangled my fingers in her hair and tried to bring her down to ease my agony, but she wouldn't allow me to rush her. I growled in frustration. Those tormenting lips smiled against my skin.

"Please…" I wasn't above begging for what I wanted.

*"Non… pas tout de suite, mon amour."* Her voice rumbled against my skin, vibrating into me. "Patience." That French accent, spoken in low sensual tones, was my undoing. I exploded in a flurry of motion and flipped her over so I was on top of her.

"Please," I repeated.

One side of her mouth tipped up in invitation as she spoke her acquiescence, *"D'accord, ma chérie."*

I was beginning to love that endearment.

I slid my body down hers to feel skin against skin, and I shivered with the sensation. I had never expected it to be like this. So gentle, so freeing, so wonderful, so exciting and so… right. Was it because she was a woman or because of her vast experience? Perhaps it was both.

I sat up and her pubic bone rested against me intimately. I looked down at her and drew my fingers down her soft, silky skin to finally rest on her chest. She again smiled that half-smile, so sensuous and beguiling. My gaze tracked down her body, inch by precious inch, to where my fingers caressed her.

I drew a gasp from her, and knew I had my starting point. My lips replaced my fingers. I felt her skin slowly and thoroughly give way under my questing tongue. Her breathing became ragged as I continued to roam, touching, tasting, teasing, and frustrating her like she had me only moments ago.

"Dale, please."

Two could play this game. *"Non."* I continued my discovery of her. My nimble fingers helped as I felt her response to me under their tips. A fine sheen of sweat covered her skin while she writhed under me. She tried valiantly to maneuver me to her advantage. She could easily take what she wanted, but she stayed within the rules of the game.

I was unaware that my own body hadn't been idle while I learned my craft from a very willing teacher. I stopped mid-assault when I found a particularly sensitive area. Without conscious thought, I threw my head back. I swiveled on her and tried to find that elusive spot that would send me over the edge. I was aware of nothing—not the woman underneath me, the air that I breathed, nor the coolness of the room. Only the intense need to climax.

It hit me like a cyclone and swept away my senses, leaving me to flail in the maelstrom. I forgot to breathe as wave after wave of excruciating pleasure flowed through me. Time had no meaning as the pleasure pulsed through me in slowly decreasing intensity until I limply twitched in time to my own heartbeat.

She placed her hand between us. Her thumb stimulated me as no one had before, which sent me into another series of contractions. I had no strength before, but now I was truly exhausted. My body had reacted to her without my permission. My eyelids, so heavy, refused to open. One of her hands rested on my hip and held me in place as she continued to play me.

"No… no more," I begged her as I teetered from exhaustion. I forced my eyes open to look at her. Her pupils were nearly black as she watched me, her sexuality cloaking her like a suit of armor. What was I to do? She'd taken every bit of energy out of me, and I had nothing to give her in return.

Françoise pulled me down into her embrace and cuddled me as I continued to bask in the aftermath of my undoing. She reached down and pulled up the blankets to wrap us in a cocoon of warmth. I felt her watching me as I drifted off to sleep.

# Chapter 4

I had no idea how long I slept, but it wasn't long enough. My body was spent. She had devoured every bit of strength I had, and she wanted more. A gentle brush of her lips on my skin awoke me to her need, and I wondered if I would be able to survive.

The night seemed endless. Just when I thought I could give no more, Françoise demanded it, and I could do nothing but respond.

Despite my happiness, insecurity sat on my shoulder like a little devil, whispering into my ear, "iceberg ahead!" This woman—this vibrant, sensual woman—couldn't possibly be interested in a lonely and love-starved young woman. Françoise made me realize how much more there could be if I would let it, but I was unable to accept that this was nothing more than what I'd feared most—my dreaded "one-night stand." Now that she'd had me, I was convinced she'd move on.

We lay there exhausted as our heart rates returned to normal. I finally looked around the room and noted the beautiful furniture scattered about. I was envious of her lavish décor. In a far corner stood a wooden dummy covered with her panniers and ball gown.

I turned back to Françoise. "What year is this?"

She seemed puzzled at the question. "1789."

Why does that year seem familiar to me? "And are we in France?"

*"Oui, Anjou.* This is the Château de Montreuil-Bellay. Why do you ask?"

"Just curious."

"Dale… What year do you come from?"

"Umm…" I just hoped she didn't have a heart attack. "2011."

*"Mon Dieu!"* Mon Dieu indeed.

We had spanned over 200 years by some magical trick of the mirror. I studied the item in question. It was exactly the same as the one I'd left behind in my time, its mahogany luster glowing in the dying light.

"Come. Let us sleep. We will talk in the morning."

I couldn't summon the energy to argue and started to close my eyes. I watched her do the same as my eyelids drooped those last few millimeters.

It was still dark when I awoke. The fire had burnt down to dying embers. I felt a whisper of a breeze across my shoulder as Françoise slept. The room was silent except for her gentle snore. I lay there for a moment to try to summon the energy and the will to return home.

A chill hit my skin as I slipped out from under the covers. I placed a couple of logs on the fire before I left, and with one last look over to the sleeping figure, I passed through the mirror and into my loft. It was cold, not only from the coolness of the air, but also from the loneliness that greeted me. Even the clothes that I found couldn't warm the emptiness in my heart. I peered back through the mirror at Françoise and silently thanked her for the wonderful memories that would remain with me for the rest of my life.

Sleep had now left me. I went to the kitchen for a hot cup of coffee. While breakfast cooked, I stared into the depths of my cup and contemplated my next move. After I'd finished cooking, I set the food on the table. It was hot and filling, but I had no taste for it. I ate because I had to not because I wanted to. As I watched the early morning sunlight filter in through the skylight, I considered my jobs for the day with little enthusiasm.

I wandered back to the mirror. All I saw was a young woman with mussed brown hair, flushed skin, and a dazed look in her eye. The window of opportunity had apparently gone with the rising of the sun. I knew only too well what—rather *who*—had put that look on her face. I craved that look again. Should I go back to her again, or should I say no and preserve my heart? There was no point in fighting it, for I feared my heart was already hers.

For the first time in my life, I struggled to apply myself to something that I loved. My work was a chore, even though I wished it not to be. After one night, Françoise had turned my life upside down. Did I want to give up everything I'd worked for?

I smiled grimly at a sudden thought. This was a long-distance relationship in the extreme. But much more was involved than mere miles. The sensations she made me feel blew my mind, but was it enough?

If we wanted to be together, one of us had to make a great sacrifice. Could I walk away from my life, my family, and this time? Could she do the same?

Maybe I was reading more into this infatuation than really existed. I'd slept with her once, and maybe that was all there was. I needed a clear head to think, and that wouldn't happen here in the loft. My cell lay invitingly on the kitchen table. I picked it up and pushed eight on the speed dial to call my best friend.

"Jackie? It's Dale. Can I come for a visit?"

"I'd love to have you, honey, but I'll be in Boston for a few days. Maybe we can meet for lunch?"

"Sure, that'd be great." It wasn't ideal, but I needed to talk to someone.

"I'm busy tomorrow. How about the day after that?"

"Come to the loft. We can talk then."

"Okay." I heard the concern in Jackie's voice. "It's nothing serious, is it?"

"No, it's not serious. I just want an opinion on something." But it was very serious indeed. My whole life depended on it.

The cell went dead, and I stared at the wall. Christ, what was I doing? I wondered what Françoise would say if I didn't answer when she beckoned me. I needed to keep away from her to decide my future. She could sway me with a few well-chosen words, and I'd end up in more trouble than I could handle.

I went to the bedroom and fell back on the bed. A few weeks ago, my biggest worry was getting out of a dance. What a mess. I gazed over at the mirror. Even then, I could feel its pull.

* * *

Two days had passed. Two long, lonely days. It had taken everything I had to ignore Françoise's pleas. When she threatened to come after me, I locked myself in the bathroom. She had effectively made me a prisoner in my own home, but it was a prison of my own making. Jackie's visit couldn't come soon enough.

Finally, there was a knock on the door at lunchtime on the second day. I nearly ran to the door to open it.

"Hey, girl!" Jackie said.

"Jackie!" I hugged her tightly. "Great to see you."

"Long time, Dale."

"Yeah, I know. I've been busy."

Jackie entered and sniffed the air. "Still getting high on turpentine?" She thought I did the job to get stoned.

"Oh yeah, high as the International Space Station."

"Come on," Jackie put her hand around my arm and steered me to a seat at the kitchen table. "Now, what's this all about?"

I tucked my bottom lip behind my front teeth and gnawed at it. "I've got a bit of a dilemma, and I need some advice."

"Spill it."

I got up, fussed with the kettle, and put the quiche into the oven. "Coffee?"

"Of course. Luckily, I haven't lost that bad habit." She stood up and hugged me again. "It really *is* great to see you. It's been too long."

"It sure has."

While I prepared the coffee and fixed our lunch, I caught up on the news concerning mutual friends and local society. I paid only cursory attention to what had been happening in that area. It was my mother's lifestyle, not mine. Many names, places, and occasions were of little interest to me.

Finally, we'd run out of casual chat. "Okay, what is so important that you need to consult me?" she asked.

I took a large, careful swallow of my coffee.

"Whoa, girl. What's the problem? It's not your mother again, is it?"

"My mother's always a problem, but no, not this time."

"Is it a man?" Jackie looked at me hopefully.

"It's my love life," I answered. Something made me hesitate from blurting everything out. "I met someone... on a cruise." Okay, that was a lie, but the truth was just plain crazy.

"I didn't hear about you going on a cruise."

"It was a last minute thing. Anyway we had a fling on board."

"Good for you. It's about time you found someone." Jackie reached over and patted my arm. "So, what's the problem?"

"I don't know if I'm reading more into this than there really is. What if it was just a holiday romance?"

"Have you talked about this with him?"

"I don't want to appear foolish."

"So, instead of appearing foolish, you're anxious and nervous because you don't know what's going to happen. Is that it?"

"In a nutshell."

"Why don't you visit him?"

"In France? I don't think so." I didn't correct her about the gender.

"French, huh? You know what they say about those French guys."

*And girls*, I mentally added. "It's... complicated."

"Isn't it always? He's not married, is he?"

"Widower." There. Now I had officially lied.

"Then what's the problem? Any kids?"

"None that I know of." That was something I hadn't even considered. If she had children, it would be up to me to leave everything behind.

"Would it be a problem if there were?"

"I don't think so. Maybe. I don't know." I took another sip of my coffee.

"I suppose the bottom line is do you want to let him get away? Is he everything you're looking for?"

"I asked myself the same questions."

"And?"

"You're here, aren't you?"

"Ah. If you're looking for someone to say 'it's okay,' then it's okay. Life's too short to waste time."

Jackie sat there relaxed as I agonized over an answer.

"So what's he like?"

"Tall, dark... handsome." I had to say something. Average height, dark flashing eyes, midnight hair and a beauty that took my breath away was what I really wanted to say, but that image was mine and mine alone. "And speaks French that makes me quiver." At last I had said something true.

"Sounds like you've already made up your mind."

"It's a big step, but I'm not sure I'm ready to take it."

"Have you talked to him about this?"

"No." This charade had gone on long enough. Sooner or later Jackie was going to find out, and it might as well come from the source. "And it's not a he."

"Not a..." Jackie put down her mug and slumped back in her chair. I watched her carefully while a number of emotions played across her face.

"Say something," I murmured.

"What is there to say? So you're a lesbian now?" Jackie's voice had gone cold.

"It's not all women, Jackie. It's one woman. She has so totally captivated me."

"Captivated? That's a rich word coming from you."

"And what's that supposed to mean? I'm asking you for advice, and you're giving me sarcasm?"

"I'm not the one who has lost her mind. What were you thinking?"

"I was thinking you were my friend and you'd be happy I'd found someone."

"Do you realize what this will do to your family? People will talk."

"My family will understand." But I didn't believe that for one minute.

"I don't think so. Your mother will kill you."

"I can't help who I fall in love with."

"That's not love. That… that's…"

"That's what, Jackie? Come on, spit it out."

"Sick! It's sick, Dale. It's not normal. Your mother has told everyone that you're going to the dance with Claridge. She'll be the laughingstock."

"And since when do you care what my mother thinks? Or is this more about you?"

"Some of the mud will stick. It always does. Tony's up for an executive position. If this gets out, who knows what will happen?"

"You know what? I don't give a flying fuck about Tony and his position. Besides that, I find it hard to believe my sex life will affect your husband's job." I shook my head. "God, Jackie. I thought I knew you, but obviously I was wrong."

Jackie stood and grabbed her bag. "When you've come to your senses, call me."

When hell freezes over, I thought, when the door slammed shut with a bang. I felt a tear slide down my cheek. I'd just ruined my relationship with the closest female friend I had. Was she right? Despite my bravado, was I sacrificing more than just my heart?

\* \* \*

By mid-afternoon, I gave up on trying to get any work done in my loft because my mind was two hundred years away with my dilemma. I focused instead on the date she'd given me, 1789. I went to my PC and did some Internet surfing. My worst fears were realized when I discovered the significance of 1789 in France—the beginning of the French Revolution. A further search of Françoise's name revealed her château had been ransacked during that turbulent time, but no mention was made of the fate of the owners. I didn't need to see that in print. I knew what happened to the French aristocrats in that period of history. Almost all of them met with Madame Guillotine.

My insides churned as I realized Françoise's predicament. Somehow, I had to convince her of the imminent danger. She wouldn't believe me, so I needed to find some evidence. My shaking fingers flew over the keys and transmitted their urgency to the computer. I grabbed my bag and headed downtown to search for a French bookshop—I had to find something that would make her understand.

I was in luck. A couple of bookstores carried French texts. I only hoped I'd find what I was looking for. A French history book. The first shop proved to be useless, and my hope rested with the second. My heart ached with worry and apprehension, not only for her but also for myself.

I entered the second bookshop, and the cool air conditioning hit me like a wall. There was no point in looking, so I approached the man behind the desk.

"Yes? Can I help you?" The tall, thin man looked down at me through his wire-framed glasses perched on his long nose. He even looked like a snob.

"I'm after a history book on France in French."

Without a word, he turned away and headed over to a shelf. He ran his finger along the bindings until he found what he was looking for. He placed the book down on the counter. I looked up.

"Does it have a section on the French Revolution?" I knew I was showing my ignorance, but I had to be sure.

He drew in an audible breath to show his impatience. He opened the book at the appropriate page. "There, madam." Before he closed the book, I made a mental note of the page number.

I paid the ridiculously high price for the book and felt a lot better armed with my evidence. It was mid-afternoon and only a few hours before I would see Françoise again. I considered doing some window shopping, but I had responsibilities. Reluctantly, I returned home to begin work.

I walked into my loft and immediately thought of Jackie. We had separated abruptly, and I hadn't raised an important point with her. Reluctantly, I reached for my cell.

I nearly hung up when I heard the ring. "Hello?"

"Jackie. It's Dale."

"I'm assuming you're calling to say how ridiculous all of this is."

"Sorry to burst your bubble, Jackie, but I'm still g-gay." I stumbled over that word. It was strange coming from my mouth, especially when it referred to me.

"What do you want then?" Jackie still sounded distant.

"Don't tell my mother, okay? I'll do that."

"Too late."

"What the hell did you do that for?" I practically shouted. Jackie was turning out to be a bitch of the first order. I never would have believed it of her. Not only that, she was a homophobe.

"She had a right to know."

"And it was *my* right to tell her, not yours!"

"You or me, it doesn't matter. Now she knows." Although she didn't say it, I could hear her unspoken words in my head—"deal with it."

"Of course it matters. Now she'll... oh God, what's the point." I hung up. I knew if I talked to her any longer, the damage would be irreparable. If I'd been realistic, it was probably way past repairable even then. Only one scenario would satisfy her, and that was my capitulation.

I prowled around the loft. I really wanted to hit something. Before I knew it, the baseball bat was in my hand. I was looking for something suitable to vent my anger on. When I couldn't find anything I could afford to break, I settled for the mattress. "Shit! Shit! Shit!" I swung the bat time and again on the comforter until my strength gave out. I slumped to the floor and remained in that position for quite some time. My life had gone to hell.

It took a great deal of effort on my part to get up and apply myself to the bureau I was preparing. I had promised the delivery in about three weeks, and I'd only stripped it. I picked up the sandpaper block and began the tedious job of removing the imperfections from the timber.

When I couldn't concentrate, I put a small amount of turpentine into a pot. It wasn't necessary, and my nose had probably had more than enough damage from the fumes. But it helped motivate me. The smell filled my lungs and drew my attention to the wood. I placed the face mask on and vigorously rubbed the surface. For a while, I got lost in the feel of sandpaper on wood.

# Chapter 5

"Dale?"

I'd spent a good deal of time left before her arrival thinking about what I'd do. Should I warn her? How would her disappearance affect history? There was no evidence I could find of her after the Revolution. Was that because of my interference? I had to risk it because I couldn't leave her alone to certain death. Just in case, I wrote a note and left it on the kitchen table. If I chose to stay with Françoise, my parents would find it on their next visit. The note was the coward's way out, but I wasn't up to facing my mother just yet.

*"Mon amour?"*

*Oh God, that French. It just goes right through me.*

"Françoise?" I dropped my voice to its lowest register to tease her with my own brand of fire. Her deep moan made me chuckle.

"Do not make me wait. Please come."

"And why should I?"

"Not tonight, please. I need you."

"You do?" I cleared my throat and dropped my voice. "Ah, you do." I stepped through the mirror and my clothes left me. Before I felt the coolness of the room, Françoise had wrapped me in her cloak. Her hands slid around my waist, and the material warmed to my touch.

"I knew you would come," she whispered in my ear. It tickled and I giggled. "Funny, is it?"

Françoise pinned me against a wall. I was begging for mercy before I'd even realized there was a struggle.

"My love, please." There was a hesitation as I whispered the words, but she didn't loosen her hold.

Her piercing eyes bore into mine. "Yes... my love." The sweetest smile crossed her full lips and melted my heart. I caressed her soft cheek so close to my own.

She began to move her hands and claim areas no longer forbidden to them. She latched onto my throat and laved the area thoroughly. I couldn't help but moan under the onslaught. I was a quivering mass under her talented hands as she branded me as her own. I no longer fought what was inevitable. I ran my hands up her back to pull her in tightly as she took me.

We were so lost in the pleasure that I hadn't noticed another person in the room. I opened my eyes. Standing there was the woman who'd been with Françoise that first night I saw her in the mirror, the young woman called Madeleine. Françoise continued to ravish me, and I barely acknowledged Madeleine's presence.

Madeleine watched us. I took in the gathering storm clouds on her brow, but I couldn't stop the flood of sensations exploding through me. Cries filled the room as Françoise brought me to completion. Madeleine abruptly left, but I was speechless.

Panting, it took me a few moments to get my breath back.

"What is wrong?"

"That woman you were with the first night... Madeleine... she saw us."

"My maid? This is none of her concern."

I held my tongue for the moment. I'd wait to see what happened in the next couple of days, but I feared that the time was fast approaching where waiting would no longer be an option.

I drew Françoise to the bed and quickly stripped off her nightgown. She'd accommodated me by at least getting rid of all her various undergarments before I had arrived. Perhaps she didn't wish to waste any time, either.

Since I'd already decided not to leave in the morning, I had all night to find out all her secret desires and passions. I was intent on discovering everything I needed to know to keep her happy.

Françoise's finger tipped my face to meet her gaze, merriment dancing in those limitless depths. She pulled me into a hug and briskly rubbed my back in comfort and affection. Thirty seconds. I had lasted thirty seconds before she'd distracted me.

"You really need to get some sleep," I said, even as my own eyes drooped with exhaustion.

"Why? We have plenty of time."

"I would've thought that with life at court, you wouldn't have much time for me."

"Court bores me. That is why I live here."

I felt there was more to this. "And?"

"No, nothing else." Her lips said one thing, but her eyes told a completely different tale.

"Yes, there's something else." I lowered my voice, keeping it loving and nurturing. "Tell me."

She wrinkled her brow and pursed her lips. It took a moment or two before she answered. "Well, look at me." I did as she asked and was sure my eyes reflected desire. An affectionate smile crossed her lips at the compliment.

"I don't see any problem."

"I am a woman."

"No… really?"

"Do you know what it is like to be a *veuve* at court? It is only because of my husband's position that they tolerate me at all. I may as well be bald."

"Why are you worried about being a widow when you're so beautiful?"

"*Merci*, but I am not interested in court gossip about myself. I feel very naked."

My lips broke into a lascivious grin. A mental image of her standing in the midst of all that pomp and ceremony in nothing more than a smile made me sweat. No wonder she had paramours lined up at her door. My jealousy reared its ugly head at the thought.

"You have nothing to worry about, Dale. There is only you." I looked at her quizzically. Had she become a mind reader? "Your brow has a wrinkle in it." To illustrate the point, her thumb rubbed over the spot to smooth the crease out of my skin.

"So, you're saying you hate court, and you're hiding out here in the country?" I felt Françoise's body heave with laughter.

"I would not have put it so, but yes."

"And you can get away with it?"

"For now, I can. I have to give a ball here at the château tomorrow night. I am sorry, but they are my husband's friends, not mine. I am bound to keep up appearances, even if it is only in his memory. However, I would like it if you could come as my guest."

A ball! To experience something only found in the history books would be something, that's for sure.

"I don't speak French. That could be a problem."

We snuggled, as Françoise seemed to ponder how to solve the problem. A minute or two passed before she answered. "I have a solution, but you may not like it."

"Let me hear it."

"I want you by my side, so would you be… my manservant?" My expression must have told her I didn't quite understand. "You will be dressed in men's clothes, and you will be by my side all night. No one will talk to you unless I wish them to."

*Ahh… she would parade me as her sexual plaything.* A woman in men's clothes in her time was considered a perversion, unless, of course, it had sexual undertones. Could I put up with all the snickering and staring?

"Never mind," she murmured. She sounded disappointed that I wouldn't agree to the game.

"Is it that important to you?"

"Yes, it is. I want you with me. If I have to go alone, you will leave again. Please." Her voice was barely a whisper. "Do not leave me alone."

She rolled me over so I was underneath her. We lay in bed, her head resting on my chest, and didn't pursue anything more than silent comfort. She idly caressed my stomach, while I buried my fingers in her thick hair to massage her scalp. We both were lost in thought to make sense of all this mayhem.

Her voice carried over the cooling air. "Will you stay with me tonight?"

"Yes, sweetheart, I will stay all night."

"And tomorrow? Will you stay tomorrow?"

"Yes, I will stay tomorrow."

Françoise nodded and we drifted off to troubled sleep.

\* \* \*

I woke in the early hours and felt the pull of the mirror, but I chose to ignore it. Françoise needed me, and I would stay with her for as long as it took. She tightened her arms around me to pull me back into slumber.

I woke much later when the sun streamed in through the large leaded glass window. Daylight… and I was still here. The bed was empty and decidedly lonely without Françoise. Panicked, I gazed around the room and finally found her sitting in a far chair watching me. My heart thudded in my throat, and I tried to quell my dizziness. I'd had a panic attack because I couldn't find her.

Françoise rushed over to the bed and grasped my hand. "Are you all right?" I couldn't answer but managed a weak nod. My gaze riveted on her as my breathing calmed. I didn't want to let her out of my sight.

"I am sorry if my absence in bed frightened you. Come. Have something to eat." She pulled a tray of food toward me and fluffed up the pillow behind my head so I could sit up. No one had ever pampered me before, and I enjoyed the attention very much. She watched as I had my fill, even quietly accepting the offer of food from my fingers.

"Will you ride with me this morning?"

"You mean I get a chance to ride?"

A wicked grin crossed her lips at my double entendre. "You can ride all you want."

My heartbeat picked up with the image in my head. "And am I riding with you naked?"

"As much as that thought is appealing, no. Madeleine has left some clothes that I hope will fit."

Madeleine… there was another problem. Using the maid's clothes would add fuel to the jealousy burning within her.

"Françoise, what day is this?"

"Day?"

"The date."

"Ah, *Jeudi… Jeudi* 16 *Juillet.*"

Thursday, July 16. My mind raced in an effort to put all the pieces together. Two days ago, the French people had stormed the gates of the Bastille. News of the revolt would've filtered out to the rest of the country. Tonight there was a ball and most of the aristocracy in the general area would attend. Added to this was one furious maid who might be looking for a little revenge. I now knew when the attack would come.

"Sweetheart, I'll come with you to the ball tonight."

A quiet glow of joy lit up her eyes with my acceptance. She leapt out of bed and disappeared out the door. It was some time before she returned.

"Here, find one that fits." She threw me a pile of clothes and shoes and left again. There were dresses of varying sizes and lengths, all sturdily made of coarse cotton. They appeared to be servants' clothing.

As I struggled to get a dress over my head, it startled me when a pair of hands descended on my body. It took a few seconds before I recognized the fingers that squeezed me through the material.

"Where did you disappear to?" I asked Françoise.

"I had to arrange some clothes for tonight." I didn't need to see her face to know she was happy. I heard it in her voice. It warmed my heart that I was having as much effect on her as she had on me.

I stood still as she patiently buttoned up the back of the dress. Before my brain stopped me, I muttered, "How on earth do you get out of this in a hurry?"

Her chuckle filled the air. "You do not. You need great patience or you rip all the buttons off." She hesitated for a moment then added, "Perhaps I should find some more dresses."

I felt my face warm with her comment. She faced me with that sexy half-smile of hers, reflecting my own thoughts as if they were tattooed on my forehead.

I finally took note of what she was wearing and gasped. Françoise was dressed in men's clothes... and she was gorgeous. I drooled at the thought of her in skin-tight jeans. Better still, skin-tight leather on the back of a large, powerful bike. Perfect.

She stood at ease and let me look my fill. I think she was quietly enjoying the undisguised lust in my eyes. She had a body built for pants and shirt. The image before me was spectacular, and I couldn't stop staring as my gaze swept from her feet to the top of her head and everything in between.

She'd tucked the fine cotton and lace shirt into her breeches while the flounces lay on her breast from the open collar. The soft brown breeches fit like a second skin, showing her shapely legs to great advantage. She'd somehow squeezed the breeches into knee-length boots. She wore no other adornment and her hair flew free. Simple but elegant.

"Wow," I said.

"Wow, indeed." I felt her own gaze sweep over me, doing exactly what I had done to her moments before.

A familiar tickling started in the pit of my stomach. I dragged her to the door. "Let's go before those buttons go flying."

She took my hand in hers and led me out into the world beyond her bedroom doors.

The château was so beautiful... and enormous. Françoise insisted on giving me a tour. I took in the majestic marble staircase as we descended to the massive foyer. The impossibly high ceiling loomed overhead, elaborately decorated and very impressive. But it didn't seem like a place that Françoise would've picked to live.

"This is my husband's château." She'd read my mind again. "Come." She led me outside toward the stables. I felt the stares of her staff as we made our way across the gravel courtyard to the distant buildings. The enormity of the situation hit me as we strolled across the grass verge. If she came forward in time with me, she would be giving up all of this. I could barely support myself. How would I support her as well?

Françoise's hand tightened around mine in comfort. Did she sense my unease? I shook my head to dismiss the worries for the moment. I was content to enjoy the sun, the warmth, and to watch Françoise tend to her horse. Leaning against the doorjamb to the stables, I watched her muscles flex under her shirt as she lifted herself into the saddle. My heart beat a little bit faster at the scene.

I turned away to look over the expanse of land that comprised Françoise's estate. It was an impressive piece of realty, and I felt a deep sadness for what was about to transpire. A movement at the house drew my attention. Madeleine stood in the shadows watching us. I was certain Françoise's dismissal of Madeleine's affections would have ramifications. As to what those ramifications would entail, only time would tell. I planned to stay close to Françoise for as long as it took me to ensure her safety.

"Dale." The low murmur caused a shudder to run through me. Françoise reached down to lift me into her lap. After she'd wrapped me in her secure arms, she nudged the horse into a gentle walk out of the stables, through the back gate, and to the meadows beyond. I glanced over my shoulder to see Madeleine turn and enter the kitchen door.

The beautiful steed moved to a slow canter, his gentle rolling run shifting me into Françoise's chest with each heave. The slow, hypnotic rhythm sent me off into a pleasant lethargy. My hands rested on her muscled thighs, and I felt them shift with each movement. I couldn't help but idly caress them. My mind wandered back to the bedroom when I felt those thighs wrapped around me, gently holding me in place as she made love to me.

I wasn't aware what effect my idle exploration had on Françoise seated behind me, but I soon found out. The horse abruptly changed direction and picked up speed as it bee-lined for a distant building. I turned to gaze at Françoise and read her intention in those near-black depths.

The battered building turned out to be a disused barn. The lathered horse pulled up and Françoise dismounted before the poor animal had a chance to stop completely. She lifted me off the saddle. She purposefully strode inside and threw me onto a pile of hay. Her chest rose and fell, and a soft moan escaped her lips. She stood there like every secret fantasy I hadn't acknowledged. Her sexuality drew me in with every breath.

"Please, try to save the buttons," I teased. "I have to wear this back to the house."

She gave me a wicked smile. That was the last coherent thought I had for some time.

"Tell me about your time." She panted softly from exertion as she awaited my reply.

I barely heard Françoise's voice over my thundering heart. After our frolic in the hay, she insisted we climb up to the loft for some more fun.

"I live in Boston."

"Ahh, I have heard of that place." She rolled over onto her stomach and leaned on her elbows. "What is it like?"

Where did I begin? "It's not like it is now. Our carriages no longer move by horses. They move on their own."

"Really?" One elegant eyebrow rose. "I would like to see that."

"You would?" I turned to look at her.

"Of course," she said as she lightly brushed my skin.

I seriously doubted her. I imagined she envisaged her own carriage rolling on its own volition down a cobble-stoned road.

"We can travel from Paris to Boston in eight hours."

"Eight? You must be mistaken."

"We can fly." I pointed upwards.

"*Non*, that is impossible. We are not able to fly."

"We can in a thing called an airplane."

"An air-plan? I do not think I would like such a thing."

"It takes some getting used to." I chuckled at her perplexed expression.

Françoise rolled over and pinned me down. "You are teasing me, Dale."

"Fine. If you don't believe me…"

It was obvious she wouldn't take me on my word alone. Could I convince her of the up-coming catastrophe about to befall her?

"While we're talking, I need to warn you." I hesitated for a moment and prayed that I didn't destroy everything with what I was about to tell her. "Have you heard news about Paris?"

"Paris?" She stopped stroking my skin. "What news?"

"About the storming of the Bastille."

"Oh, that. It is but a minor disturbance."

"Françoise, listen to me. It's no minor disturbance. It's the beginning of the end for the aristocracy in France."

"You place too much faith in idle gossip." She dismissed the news with a flick of her wrist.

"I come from the future, remember? I know what will happen."

"They would not dare strike at the very heart of France."

"They did, and they will. They hunted down the aristocracy and killed them, one by one. I don't want to see it happen to you." *There.* Had I altered history by telling her?

Françoise looked up through a hole in the roof. The sky had darkened. "It is late. We must prepare for the ball."

"Didn't you hear a word I said? You will die unless you take action now."

"We will discuss this later."

"There won't be time later." Maybe her destiny would play out as it should whether I warned her or not. "Fine."

While we lay there, I heard a faint noise outside. Not natural, but a random pattern. "Shh. I think there's someone outside."

The sound stopped for a moment, then resumed. We both scrambled over to the edge of the loft and looked down.

"Where are my clothes?" I frantically scanned the hay below, but they were nowhere to be found.

"Probably the same place as mine."

The ladder shook under the strain of both of us trying to get down as quickly as possible.

"Perhaps a friendly squirrel?" she said, gracing me with that annoying smile of hers. "No?"

Despite a thorough search, we couldn't find our clothes. I could think of only one person who'd do such a thing out of spite. I looked over at Françoise to see the gathering storm clouds in her eyes. She was pissed… really pissed.

I felt the anger roll off her. The energy skittered across my skin and let off tiny electrical charges in their wake. I sensed the menace rising in her, and it affected me in a way I never would've expected.

She stalked from one end of the barn to the other, barely keeping her simmering anger in check. This element of danger in her had me excited, and I couldn't help my reaction to it.

Fortunately, the horse was still tied up outside, but I suspected it was all part of the plan designed for maximum embarrassment. What our saboteur hadn't counted on was the sheer torture of the ride back to the château.

I felt the entire length of her along my back. Her skin rubbed against me with every jolt of the ride. I sensed she felt the torture as much as I, because her hands restlessly slid over me. By the time we arrived back at the stables, I was a bundle of nervous energy looking for anything to ease my desire.

We dismounted at the stables, but Françoise ignored the horse. Instead, she strode toward her staff, obviously intent on confronting the person who played the petty trick.

The staff watched our approach. I felt Françoise's ire rise again as if to keep pace with purposeful strides. I walked a few steps behind her to allow her to take care of the matter without interruption. Her nakedness didn't seem to bother her as she stared down each of the servants standing in front of her. One by one their heads lowered. Even Madeleine backed down and dropped her eyes.

Françoise's outburst was harsh and demanding... and in French. I didn't understand her words, but her intonation made it clear that she was accusing someone at the château. I put my money on Madeleine. Muted silence met her tirade, and the servants filed back into the house, not once looking back.

As I watched her verbally dress down the servants, my sexual excitement reached fever pitch. She turned around and walked toward me. I was certain she saw what I tried to hide.

"Oh, for God's sake, Dale. Stop it!" But she couldn't help a sly smile at my predicament. Her edginess and my ardor cooled at her approach. "You have a problem, little one?"

I was ashamed of myself and on the verge of tears at my total loss of control.

Françoise took my hand and led my trembling body up the stairs to our bedroom hideaway. She tucked me into bed like a lost, forlorn child. Perhaps I was. I heard her speak to someone before she joined me in bed, the curtains drawn to preserve our privacy. Visibly calm, she turned to me. Mortified, I ducked my head.

"No?" she said.

No. I couldn't start this conversation.

She lifted my chin. "First of all, do not be ashamed. I am flattered that you want me that much."

Through my tears, I could barely see her beautiful face. With her fingertips, she wiped away my wetness. Her hand remained there to caress my skin in silent comfort.

Finally, she put me out of my misery and continued. "Do you remember when you first saw me? And how you reacted to me having sex?" I noticed she said "having sex" and not "making love." I nodded. "What was it like then? It was not gentle was it, my sweet? It was rough and demanding. Satisfying my animal instincts, *n'est-ce pas?*" Yes, it had definitely been primal. That was why I had touched myself in front of her.

I'm sure she could see my mind slowly putting the puzzle together to fit into the bigger picture.

"I think, *mon amour*, you are just reacting with plain old animal lust to my own heightened emotions."

I struggled for my own words. "It's just... just... when you're all worked up, I go crazy." I stopped. "Now that I think of it, you've never directed that anger toward me. I must get excited by your dark fire." I look up into her eyes. "Where do we go from here?"

"You understand you have done nothing wrong?"

I nodded.

"Good. Now, I think a bath is in order." Françoise pulled the curtains aside to reveal what I definitely wouldn't consider a bathtub. It was more like a huge ceramic bowl.

But something was amiss. It was then that I noticed the mirror. "Someone moved the mirror?"

"I asked for it to be replaced on the wall. There is no need to have it near the bed." Françoise said. "I no longer have to find the reflection. I have you."

Before we went any further, I grabbed her arm. "Can I ask something of you?"

"Of course."

"Tonight, at the ball?"

"Yes?"

"If I ask you to take me upstairs, you'll come without questions?" I knew her mind was on the bed again. That wasn't why I asked. But it was probably easier to let her think that to avoid an explanation.

"You are insatiable, my dear."

I smiled in reply. "Is that a yes?" I batted my eyelashes at her in mock invitation and a laugh erupted from her chest. "Yes?"

"Yes." She swatted my backside as she left the bed.

\* \* \*

My ass sat in about a foot of water in the "bath," barely covering anything. It had a backrest but my legs dangled out onto the floor. Despite the cheerful fire next to me, the water cooled rapidly. I scrubbed within an inch of my life so I could get out and get warm.

So engrossed was I in my washing that I didn't hear the door open and close. I nearly jumped out of my skin when a hand landed on my shoulder. I fell into those warm eyes that knew my very soul.

"*Ma petite sauvage*, I quite like what you are wearing." Those intelligent eyes scanned me as I sat awkwardly in the tub. I handed her the cloth I used in the bath.

"Can you wash my back, please?" I wouldn't pass up this opportunity to soak up her attention, and neither would she, judging by her swift effort to comply with my request. Her hands were strong, yet gentle, and flowed over my skin in a slow, sensual massage. Her soothing touch allowed my body to float in a pleasant haze of lassitude.

I glanced over my shoulder to look at her face. I wondered if my own expression reflected the same contentment. A slight blush colored her features when she realized I'd caught her daydreaming.

A shiver passed through me, and I could stand the cold water no longer. "Sorry, the water's cold."

Françoise stood and offered her hand in assistance. I found it difficult to get any leverage to rise out of the tub because the rim hampered my legs. After much huffing and puffing, I extricated myself, sloshing water onto the carpet in the process. "Sorry."

"Never mind." She moved to the door and pulled the dangling tassel. Madeleine arrived, hostility written on her young features. "*Madeleine. Viens éponger l'eau, je te prie.*"

Although I didn't understand French, I thought I heard something that sounded like "sponge." I didn't want Madeleine to see me naked. Françoise stepped between us and held up her nightgown as a barrier while I dried myself beside the fire. I watched Madeleine clean up the mess, but she occasionally threw me a dirty look.

"*Merci, Madeleine. Tu peux disposer.*" My adversary left, but not before she offered one last parting glare in my direction.

"She hates me."

"Why? You have done nothing to her."

"Oh, yes I have. I've taken you away from her."

"She is but a servant, Dale. She does not matter."

*And that is the reason for the downfall of you all, Françoise. That aristocratic attitude is setting events in motion even now.*

It wasn't the time to discuss the political machinations currently ruling France. Perhaps later, when we were safe, we could look back at these turbulent days with a certain amount of detachment and hindsight. Maybe then, Françoise could see where it all went wrong.

She sat in a nearby chair to watch as I allowed the warm fire to dry my skin. I turned around to face her. It was effortless, this interaction between us. One look, one silent invitation, had us wanting each other again.

"My love…" Her lips turned up in quiet joy at my endearment. "Where did you learn English?" I attempted to divert her away from her lascivious thoughts. The ball was only a few hours away, and soon the room would fill with servants, all primping, pushing, and tucking to ready their mistress for the grand occasion.

"I spent my early years in London, Dale." She watched my reaction as she spoke my name and impudently smiled.

"How so?"

"My family attended court there for a number of years, until I was about fifteen."

"Then what happened?" I was too busy finding the armholes of the dressing gown to think anything of the silence a few feet away.

"Then I was forced to marry my late husband, le Comte de Villerey."

I looked up. "At fifteen?"

"It is common practice, chérie. It was an arranged marriage to a very wealthy man." But I could tell that she harbored great resentment for that act.

I thought I knew the answer before I asked the question. "How old was he?"

"Sixty-three."

Having sex with a man my grandfather's age made me cringe. Françoise sadly acknowledged my reaction. I pulled her head to my breast in comfort. I stroked her hair with my fingers, and a gentle shudder ran through her body. She'd led a tragic life, trapped in a loveless marriage to a man who obviously valued the ownership of a beautiful young girl above all else.

So much of her past contributed to who this woman was today. It also explained the string of sexual conquests left in Françoise's wake. Her family had abandoned her to wallow in a relationship that was physically abhorrent to her and left her to never find love or contentment. Sex became an act to fill her loneliness, not an instrument for love, and her heart cleverly hid from sight.

I grabbed her chin, and her glistening eyes met mine. "I will stay with you until the end of our days, Françoise, in whichever time you desire. I give you my heart as you have given me yours."

A sigh escaped her lips as tears slid down her cheeks unheeded. My thumbs rose to brush them away. She caught them with her hands and softly kissed my palms.

"When did your husband die?" I whispered in deference to the emotion of the conversation.

I noticed Françoise's unease. "Three years ago." Her voice sounded strange, and I was tempted to question her on it, but her expression pleaded with me to let the matter rest.

"And how old are you now?"

"Twenty-eight."

"Ten years?" Ten years of hell, I would imagine, by the look on her face.

"But all his money does not make up for those ten years, *ma petite sauvage*."

"What is this, *'sauvage'?*"

"You are my little, umm… savage cat."

"Do you mean hellcat?"

"What is this 'hellcat'?" Françoise dropped the 'h' on the word, and it was so endearing.

"A hellcat is a woman who's very passionate in the bedroom."

"*Oui*, hellcat. That is what I mean."

"Your hellcat, eh? Hmm, I can live with that. So, you haven't married again?"

"Many have tried, but I am not interested. A lot of them wanted my money. Others wanted the title. None of them wanted me."

"You can keep your money," I said emphatically. "I'm only interested in you."

"I know that, *chérie*. I have known that from the moment I saw you in the mirror." She paused. "What about you, little one? What of your family?"

"I live alone. My parents are still alive."

"Are you not happy with them?"

My troubled expression must have given me away. "My dad and I get along. Mother keeps pushing me to find a man."

"A man?" Françoise grinned. "She does not know?"

"I didn't know myself until I saw you." I dipped my head and blushed. "You were certainly an eye-opener."

"Eye open-er?"

"You opened my eyes to the possibilities. I had wondered what was wrong with me. Now I know."

"*Oui*, now you know." Françoise stood and brushed her hands down her gown. "Will you not be missed?"

"I probably will. My mother and father don't visit much, for which I am eternally grateful. But she recently found out about me—about us. She won't be happy." *That was an understatement.*

"Why is that?"

"My mother is a woman who loves the society lifestyle. Any sort of scandal would anger her greatly."

*"Oui, moi aussi."*

"Our mothers sound alike."

"Except that your mother did not abandon you to a dangerous man."

"True." Would my mother have resorted to such a tactic if it benefitted her? I'd like to think not, but I wouldn't know for sure until I talked to her. "Maybe one day you'll meet her."

Françoise stared at me and raised one eyebrow.

I sighed. "Yeah, I know. And pigs can fly."

"Pigs cannot fly, Dale."

I'd have to abandon my twentieth century colloquialisms. "How about we get you ready for tonight?"

# Chapter 6

I lay on my stomach on the bed. Fascinated, I watched the flurry of activity taking place. A couple of hours had passed. Françoise's hair was piled on her head in a mass of curls. I still couldn't figure out how it stayed put. Poor Françoise. I grimaced in sympathy as her whalebone corset tightened. With a grim expression, she hung onto the bedpost while Madeleine pulled the life out of the ties. The woman had the gall to give me a wicked smile as she looked at me over Françoise's shoulder. *The little witch is enjoying this.*

Françoise's face was beet red with the pressure on her torso.

I could stay silent no longer. "Enough!"

Françoise looked up at the first word I uttered in Madeleine's presence.

*"Cela suffira, Madeleine. Tu peux disposer."* I assumed Françoise had dismissed Madeleine when she abruptly left the room. "What is wrong, Dale?"

"She did that deliberately."

"Of course she did. She has to make it fit."

"But you didn't look at her face. She hurt you."

"Ah, *ma petite sauvage.* Defending me, are you?"

"Against her, yes. She'd better watch it." My ire grew at the nasty little games Madeleine played. I looked up to find Françoise watching me quietly, filled with a mixture of love and hunger. It seemed she felt the same way when I got angry.

"Sorry," I mumbled.

"Please do not be. No one has ever defended me before. I… thank you."

"You're welcome." I looked at her body, and I hurt for her. The corset had pulled in her figure to an impossible degree. I wondered how she could breathe. Her breasts were nearly overflowing the neckline, ready to pop out if she so much as raised her voice. "How do you put up with that?"

"I do not know. I hate wearing this thing, but it is what we have to endure for the sake of fashion."

"I bet a man designed this."

"I am sure you are right, little one." She wriggled around, trying to find a comfortable position in the torture device. "Now, let us get you ready." She held up another corset in my direction, a sly smile plastered on her face.

"Do I have to?"

"I suppose not, but do you not want to know what it feels like? Besides, I want everyone to know that you are a woman... my woman."

That possessive tone sent a chill down my spine. Her woman. Couldn't I do this one little thing for her? I stripped off the dressing gown and turned to face the bedpost muttering, "I hope I don't live to regret this..."

She chuckled as the material encircled my body. Slowly and methodically, Françoise fed the laces through the eyelets and waited until she'd filled all the holes before tightening it. I felt my pulse in my eyeballs as each tug of the ties slowly squeezed the life out of me.

"Holy hell! How do you live with this?" I was nearly in pain with the tightness of the corset as the whalebone inserts dug into my flesh.

"We have been wearing this since we were children, so we have been living with this discomfort for many years."

"Come with me to the future, and you'll no longer need to wear it." I had second thoughts about living in her time, especially if it meant wearing this torturous piece of clothing.

Françoise tied off the corset with a flourish, and I stood up straight. I wriggled around until I could find a position that didn't pinch or jab too much. I tried to stop myself from hyperventilating with shallow gasps. Françoise looked at me highly amused. "Laugh all you want. This is painful."

"Oh, I know, little one, I know."

"Then why wear it?"

"Why do you think I keep to myself? One of the reasons is so I do not have to wear all of this. It is very unhealthy."

"In my time, the underthings are next to nothing. And women wear pants. It's not frowned upon."

"What I would give to move around with that much freedom."

"All you have to do is take my hand, Françoise."

A sad smile crossed her face. "No, Dale. My place is here. I do not belong there."

"What about me? My heart is with you, so where do I belong?"

She couldn't answer that because there was no good outcome. I knew what was best for her, but I walked a fine line between what I wanted and what must be. I only hoped I could seize the moment when it presented itself and save both our souls.

* * *

I was glad I didn't have to make polite conversation to anyone. It allowed me to enjoy the lavishness of the costumes and the setting of the ball unfolding before me. Whatever possessed me to agree to Françoise's request I'll never know, but the sight of me dressed as a male servant was amusing. While I was presentable in my frilled shirt, coat, breeches, hose, and slippers, I didn't compare to the lords and ladies who were Françoise's guests. Still, her staff had worked a miracle to find my clothes in a matter of a few hours.

The pain from the corset kept my mind focused on the comings and goings of the large room and didn't allow me to daydream as I stood next to the hostess. Françoise was conspicuously ignoring me, despite the fact that she kept me close. Her actions lent credence to my position as "her woman," as she put it. Hoarse whispers from behind raised fans reached my ears. For once, I was thankful that I didn't understand a word they said. I didn't want to know the colorful language they used to describe me. One or two brave souls approached Françoise and, judging by their gazes, asked about me. But I had no idea what her answer was, only that she looked my way each time before replying.

I moved to the mirrored wall to study my appearance. Françoise was right. The corset made my figure look fuller, and there was no doubt I was a woman. This strange little game of dressing me as a man piqued my curiosity, but I did it for her and would put up with the snickering.

I smelled her before she appeared behind me. The tall headpiece she wore added another foot to her height, and it made me look like a little mouse next to her. But there was an unmistakable leer about her perusal of me, her eyes following the line of my body from the tip of the powdered wig to my buckled shoes below.

"Incroyable, ma petit sauvage."

"Couldn't find me a dress?"

"Well, first of all, I was not looking for a dress. But I do not think I would have found one to do you justice in such a short time."

"Why am I dressed like this?" Then it hit me. "You're trying to shock all these people, aren't you?" To prove my point, her arm slipped around my waist as she pulled me closer. "You are such a troublemaker."

"I know. *Je t'aime.*" Those two words expressing her love faded off to a whisper as her eyes shone with undisguised affection, while that sexy smile of hers melted me like chocolate in the midday sun.

In the mirror, my gaze sought out her shimmering brown eyes above me, and the emotion flowing between us vibrated in the air. There was something ancient about what existed between us, something that had spanned more than just the two hundred years separating us. She held me in her spell for what seemed a lifetime. Neither of us spoke for fear of breaking the ethereal calm surrounding us. I felt the finality of this moment. Our destiny together was sealed.

The approach of a middle-aged gentleman asking for a dance broke our connection. I could see that she was loathe to reply, but etiquette demanded she be the perfect hostess and accept the invitation. I moved over to a large table laid out with mountains of food to munch on some delicacy, the taste of which I couldn't place. It was such an odd sight to see my lover—a stunningly beautiful woman with impossibly high hair that was the fashion of the day—escorted to the dance floor by a short, stocky middle-aged man. My mood deteriorated as he wooed her, slipping past her closer than the dance required, and whispering to her as he trotted around in an elaborate mating ritual.

I couldn't stand it any longer and moved myself over to the window for some fresh air. I ignored the sly glances from the women and the open ogling from the men. For once, I nearly wished for a dress to cover my legs from the frank perusal. A cool breeze wafted in and slid over the heated skin of my flushed face. I longed to be out in the darkness that would at least give me some anonymity. I saw someone move from the kitchen door toward the front gate. The dark shadows shrouded the identity of the lone figure as he—or she—moved across the lawn.

Françoise was still busy dancing, although her partner now was a portly, balding gentleman whose splendiferous clothing was a sight to behold. He made me think of an ageing peacock spreading his feathers in the hope of finding a mate. As I reached the front door, I glanced back. With a bemused expression, Françoise watched her dance partner huff and puff as he tried to keep up with the lively music. I slipped through the door and scampered across the open ground to the far trees as I made my way silently toward the front gates.

Muted voices forced me to slow my approach. I saw their faces in the light of a lantern. Two rough gentlemen, probably farm workers by the cut of their clothes, were talking to the person from the house… Madeleine.

One of the men spoke to Madeleine, and I heard her say *"Madame de Villerey"*—Françoise's, name.

Another man moved back through the open gate to beyond. The last of the heated conversation ended with *"mort aux aristos!"* Madeleine hurried toward the house.

I didn't need to understand the words. The anger on their faces told me all I needed to know

In the far off distance, bobbing lanterns illuminated the faces of a large group of men as they approached the gate. I didn't wait around to see what they would do, for I knew the outcome. Stumbling in the dark, I tried to move quickly back to the house.

I barged through the front door and locked it behind me. Grabbing a nearby chair, I slipped it up under the handle and wedged it in place. A hand slapped down on my shoulder, and I screamed. My heart throbbed uncontrollably in my throat with the sudden scare.

"Where have you been, and what are you doing?" On any other day, that whisper sent shivers down my spine. Now, it only terrified me.

"I went outside to get some air and thought I heard a prowler."

"Prowler?"

"Umm… someone trying to break in."

"That is a bit foolish I think, Dale. There are forty guests here. He is sadly outnumbered."

"Still, better not take any chances."

I could tell she didn't believe one word I'd spoken. Even to my own ears, it was a weak lie.

"Can you take me upstairs, please?" Squinting her eyes at me, she was clearly skeptical. "I'm feeling a bit dizzy with this corset, and I want to lie down." That she would believe. I guided her hand to my pulse to let her feel the rapid pounding under her fingertips.

*"Chérie*, of course. One moment." Françoise approached her dance partner and excused us. Slowly, we ascended the stairs and

headed toward the door at the end of the hall. We'd almost made it when Madeleine stood in the way.

An argument ensued between Françoise and Madeleine. I could see Françoise was upset because Madeleine refused to budge. There was no time for this confrontation, so I quickly intervened.

"Tell Madeleine that she cannot have you. You are mine."

"What?"

"Please, my love. Just do it."

The young woman looked to her mistress in question. Françoise repeated what I had told her.

Madeleine's features suddenly changed, and she approached me to stand a hair's breadth from my face. She spoke rapidly and with anger.

Françoise was taken aback by whatever Madeleine had said to me.

"Well?" I asked.

"Umm... I was hers before you, and she is not going to let you have me." Françoise was clearly embarrassed at being the object of dispute.

Madeleine's face contorted into rage, and she yelled at me. I didn't need Françoise to tell me what she'd said—jealousy didn't need a translation.

"And you think you're going to stop me?" I let my own anger surface. "I'm prepared to fight for what is mine." She didn't need to understand English. My very posture told her everything.

Loud voices shouted at the front door, followed by the banging of what sounded like a battering ram trying to break the door down. Madeleine smiled grimly at me as if to hide a secret she thought only she knew.

I smiled back in a similar fashion and planted the seed of doubt in her. Madeleine babbled at me, and I knew she was cursing me with every evil word she could muster. The front door began to splinter under the assault. It would be only a matter of a minute or two before they were in the house.

Madeleine frantically gestured at me, and I couldn't wait any longer. "She is mine, you bitch!" I balled my fist and slugged her in the jaw. Françoise watched mutely as her servant staggered and collapsed unconscious to the floor. Her eyes widened and she looked at me slack-jawed.

"Can't explain now." I grabbed Françoise's hand and dragged her through the bedroom door just as the front door gave way. I bolted the door and shoved a chair under the handle.

"Strip." I thought Françoise's brain had seized up because she clearly wasn't listening. I stepped behind her and quickly undid the laces. "Do it! Get your clothes off!"

She dragged the material off her shoulders to pool on the floor. Stepping out of it, she removed the panniers and placed the frame on a nearby chair. I wrestled the laces out of the corset and left her to undress the rest of the way. I grabbed at my own clothes and flung them far and wide around the room.

Faint screaming and yelling emanated from downstairs, followed by the sound of approaching footsteps. A loud bang on the door made us jump, while a deep male voice yelled from the hall.

"Ignore them," I barked at Françoise, who seemed clearly in a daze. In the background, voices shouted, *"Vive la Révolution!"* and *"Mort aux aristos!"* I stripped the bed and tied whatever material I could find together to fashion a makeshift rope. I secured it to a banister and flung it out the window.

The bedroom door started to give way under the constant pushing by the men outside. I grabbed Françoise, hoisted her up onto the bench under the mirror, and shoved her through with little help from her. The chair began to move and the crack in the door widened. I clambered up the bench and pulled myself through as the door opened fully to four burly, unkempt men armed with pitchforks.

I pushed Françoise to the floor and grabbed a blanket. I threw it over the glass and blocked out the light from my side of the mirror. I fell on top of her, placing a hand over her mouth. As we lay there, sounds of destruction traveled through the mirror from cupboards splintering, material tearing, and a final sound of glass breaking.

Silence greeted us for a long time as we lay on the floor. We both shivered as much from fear as from the cold. I stood up and peeked behind the blanket. They'd destroyed Françoise's mirror, severing the connection to the past. For better or worse, she was now living with me in my time.

"What happened?"

"Come, sit." I pulled her to my bed and noticed the perplexed look on her face. I gathered my resolve as I thought to explain what I knew. "You know I'm from the future." She nodded. "So, you know I'm also aware of what has happened in the past... including what just happened then." I jerked my thumb toward the mirror. She nodded again. I was about to repeat what I'd already told her, but she was obviously in shock.

"Three days ago, on the fourteenth of July, a civil war began in France." I could see the incredulity in her eyes. "The people rose up to overthrow the aristocracy." Obviously bewildered as she struggled to understand, I gathered her into my arms in comfort.

*"Pourquoi?"*

"You have so much, and they have so little. It's as simple as that. Well, no, it's more complicated than that, but to the common man, that's all that mattered."

"But why did you bring me here?"

"Because you would have died."

"I think you exaggerate, little one."

"No, most aristocrats that were captured were executed."

"No," her whispered word was lost in her tears. I knew I had gutted her. Her whole world had crumbled, and I was the bearer of the bad news. I covered her with the blankets off the bed and grabbed the extra blanket resting over the mirror to add to the pile.

"Do you want some time alone?" I made a move to leave her, but her hand shot out from under the covers and grabbed my own.

"Please, *chérie,* stay with me."

I pulled her into my embrace and felt the chill not only of her skin but of her heart. My once confident she-demon was an empty shell of herself, her beloved France shattered along with her soul. We lay there quietly for some time before eventually drifting off to troubled sleep.

\* \* \*

I woke to an empty bed and missed her presence immediately. I rolled over to inhale her faint scent off the sheets. "Françoise?" There was no response but the slow tick of the bedside clock. Panic gripped me, and I jumped out of bed. Shafts of sunlight streamed in through the skylight to hit the wooden floor in a random pattern. Dust motes danced in the flickering light and gently floated in the warming air. I called again. "Françoise?" The floor was cool under my feet, but I didn't feel anything but the thudding of my heart and the terror streaking through my soul.

Rounding the corner, I stuttered to a halt. She sat at the kitchen table, her head in her hands and an open book on the table. Red-rimmed eyes greeted me. I could do little but pull her into me and hold her as she wept for her fallen country. Long moments passed as I soothed her tortured soul, knowing that she would have questions.

"What do you want to know?" I whispered. Her head tilted up, and I wiped away the glistening drops sitting on her pale cheeks.

"You knew, and you did not tell me?"

"I tried to tell you in the barn, but you wouldn't listen."

"Did you not know how *incroyable* that sounded?"

"Of course I did. Why did you think I hesitated in telling you? You must have thought I was some sort of mad woman." I looked into her tear-filled eyes. "You never believed anything I told you."

"I know you love me. Is that not all that matters?"

"I suppose it does. But you didn't trust me or trust what I said. I trusted you with my life, but there was much more at stake than my mere mortality." She waited for me to continue. "If I had told you everything and you did one thing differently—one thing, Françoise—it could've changed the whole outcome of history. You couldn't save them, my love. I risked an awful lot by saving you."

Françoise gazed at the book and at the pictures that depicted the grisly truth of the Revolution. "Maybe you should have left me behind as well."

I was shocked. "You would have preferred death to being with me?" It felt like she had stabbed me with her words. Her silence shredded me and left me to bleed slowly. I backed away, crawled to the bed, and rolled into a ball in despair. She didn't follow me, but I could hear her quietly weeping over the book.

I didn't know how long I lay there, trying not to feel anything. She'd lost a lot, but I thought our love would mean something to her. Perhaps I was wrong. The hours slowly drained away as the shifting sunlight crawled across the floor toward the end of the bed. Finally, she came into the bedroom and crossed to the mirror, her hands gliding over its surface as if trying to incant some magical spell to open the door again.

"It's gone." My voice was flat and emotionless, much like how I was feeling.

She shuffled over to the bed and perched on the edge of it. She rested her hand on my leg. "I am sorry, Dale."

I watched her through tear-streaked eyes and waited for something more… something to give me hope.

*"Je t'adore,"* she whispered, and my heart grabbed onto those words like a lifeline. Perhaps my rescue ship had returned to save me after all.

"I'm sorry, too, my love. You've lost everything."

A bittersweet smile crossed her swollen lips. "Not everything, *chérie."* Seeing my questioning look, she stood up and crossed over to the mirror. She pressed her hands around the top of the wood and shifted her fingers in a random pattern until there was a faint click. She pried away the scrollwork panel at the top of the mirror and lifted out a cloth bag before returning to the bed with her prize. She poured out the bag's contents. A pile of very expensive-looking jewelry fell onto the bed.

I stared at the treasure before us. "What…"

"These are the jewels of my husband's family."

"Ahh, the family jewels." Françoise gave me the first genuine smile I'd seen since we left her time.

"They are very…" She wrinkled her nose in distaste.

"Gaudy? Tasteless? Showy?"

"Yes, gaudy. I did not like to wear them, so I hid them here. They are all I have left of my life, but I give them to you. We need to live, do we not?"

We certainly did. I'd been in shock lately, but that thought had crossed my mind earlier. I would have provided for her if I had to. I knew that before I risked everything.

"Understand one thing, Françoise, I don't want your money. I only want you. If we sell your jewelry, yes, at least we can live comfortably, but I can support both of us if I have to."

"I know. That is why I am offering. If I doubted your intentions, I would not have shown you the secret of the mirror." She stood up and went to the mirror. "Perhaps it would be better if these were put in safekeeping." Françoise put the jewels back in the frame and pushed the wood to close the panel.

"I think the first thing I'd better do is buy you some clothes." I grabbed the blanket off the bed and wrapped her in it. I briskly rubbed my hands over her cooling flesh before finally taking refuge under the bedclothes. We lay some moments in the little cocoon of warmth as we soaked in the closeness and hopefully healed our open wounds.

"May I ask you a question?" Her voice was muted in the enclosed space, and her hot breath touched my breast in a most enticing fashion.

"Sure."

"Why did you tie the sheets together when we made our escape?"

"I wanted them to think we had escaped out the window."

"And stripping off of the clothes?"

"For one thing, you'd never have been able to climb through in all the clothes you were wearing. Besides, all that material sitting right under the mirror might have given them a clue as to where we went."

"Why?"

"Because if they knew it was the mirror, they might've been tempted to destroy it completely, and none of this would have happened. No mirror to lead me to you. But since both you and the mirror are still here, somehow it survived. We both heard the glass shatter. Maybe the magic is in the frame." My hand brushed her tear-stained face. "Or maybe the magic is in us."

"Ah... I am sorry, *chérie*. I should not have said that you should have left me behind."

"You were in great pain, Françoise. You couldn't help but lash out."

"But in doing so, I hurt the one thing I had sworn to myself to protect."

"Me?"

"You, *ma petite sauvage.*"

I snuggled into Françoise and used my body heat to warm her. "Welcome to the twenty-first century, my love."

# Part Two: Escape

# Chapter 7

The start of a new day and the start of a new life. Dale lay tucked in beside me, still in blissful slumber, while I could barely hear myself think with all the noise. What was that? *Mon Dieu!* It sounded like a full-fledged battle between the scullery maid and the cook in my kitchen.

Stunned, I contemplated the turn of events. One day, and two centuries ago, we were in my bed. My Dale had gloriously unraveled under my hands as we made love in my château. I had to admit I did like her bed, though. It was a little firmer than I was used to, but it was the right size for a delightful afternoon romp.

This angel stepped through my mirror and stole my heart, saving not only my soul but my life from a peasant uprising. I knew she had said she was from the future, but I was skeptical about her claims. I now know I was wrong.

"How are you doing?" Her soft burr stirred the embers within me and made me ache for her all over again. How could one woman have enchanted me so?

"I am fine. Why do you ask?"

She lifted her hand to my face and gently rubbed the spot between my eyebrows, mimicking my action of a few days ago. *Oh...* I smiled at her touch, which brought back very fond memories of our early forays into lovemaking. It was like seeing the images of our passion as I watched the emotions play across her face. Her eyes slowly darkened and softened with want, while her tongue emerged to lick her lips.

My breath hitched at the sight, and I could not stop my hands from wandering. She rolled over so that her back was against me and allowed me free rein to roam over her velvet skin. Such a wonderfully soft, compact body was at my command. She was truly one of God's better creations. A sigh escaped her as I tenderly drew circles on her abdomen while I brushed my lips against her neck.

Her derrière nudged me as I touched her, and I could not help but react. She shifted so we faced one another. Her fingers ran through my tousled hair, and she allowed the tendrils to slip through her hand. Those eyes, now filled with passion, drew me to her like a thirsting woman to an oasis. I was helpless under the stare of those deep pools. I would walk across broken glass and thank her for it.

She was unaware of the burning sexuality she possessed, untouched and with so much *joie de vivre.* I knew she thought I was the sensual one, but did she not realize she had her own fire—one that lit my soul with one look of those beautiful eyes? She may be inexperienced, but my body was unaware of it. She was enthusiastic, passionate, and truly honest in her feelings that showed me her true essence. How could I not love her?

Our lovemaking progressed at a leisurely pace, and I felt the intensity rise as we reached for the summit. We sought so much more than pleasure. As I loved her, I resisted the urge to open my eyes when a small cry escaped her lips. I did not want to distract myself from the connection of taste, smell, touch, and sound. Bold mental strokes painted a canvas of erotic intensity, emboldened with splashes of vibrant color from her body. It was a masterpiece best viewed with senses other than sight.

Finally, Dale reached her pinnacle. I lay still and placed kisses on her soft skin as her body quaked. She remained quiet. I imagined she was trying to regain control of her thoughts.

*"Chérie."* I whispered the endearment, but I did not think she heard me.

A moment later she replied, "Yes, my sweetness."

My heart melted. "I love you, Dale."

Her eyes, darkened to a deeper blue-gray and still in passion's embrace, looked into mine. "And I love you, too. Come to me, my love."

I willingly crawled into her open arms and allowed her to roll me underneath her. I writhed in ecstasy as she gave me the same pleasure I had given her.

A fine sheen of sweat covered my body as my blood pounded wildly through me—all because of Dale, who sprawled over me as if I were a pillow. We lay quietly for a time, each lost in our own thoughts as a distinctive aroma permeated the air.

"Dale?" There was no response. Dale had worn herself out and had drifted off to sleep. It seemed I would be her pillow for a little while longer…

Rays of sunlight streaked across the end of the bed, and specks of dust playfully chased themselves in the sunbeams. The window in the roof was a delightful idea, and it gave Dale's home a bright cheery interior. Perhaps… I did not complete that thought. I would never return home. That part of my life was over.

Dale snuggled into my breast, her soft skin gliding over my nipple. I bit my tongue so as not to make a sound, and I held my breath until she settled and returned to slumber. I looked around her bed chamber and took in its sparseness. Some items I was familiar with, others I was not.

On the far wall was the mirror—my savior and my judge. I should be happy about this, should I not? Then why at random moments did I feel it was my prison sentence? If something went wrong, I had nowhere else to go. When Dale was with me, she could always retreat to her time if it became too much. Good times or bad, this was all I had. I looked down to the mass of brown hair of my beloved, and I knew I could be happy. After all, she was my love and my life. But…

"Do you want to tell me what's wrong?"

"Nothing, *chérie,* go back to sleep." Her body tensed a moment before she raised her head to look at me. "Really, it is nothing."

"Then why is your heart pounding in my ear?" Those luminous blue-gray eyes watched me patiently, waiting for me to reveal what was wrong. I could not. She would feel guilty for saving me, and I could not make her sad.

"It is my new way of waking you up? Do you like it?"

She raised an eyebrow at the quip, and we both knew it for the withdrawal it was. "How about we have some breakfast?"

"Where is your cook?"

"I don't have a cook. Around here, we make our own meals." She pointedly looked at me, the meaning becoming increasingly clear.

"You expect me to cook? I do not think so."

"Now is as good a time as any."

"I barely know what a kitchen looks like. Do not expect this of me."

She pulled me to my feet. We wandered naked from the bed chamber to the kitchen. Sunlight filtered in from the huge windows and across the length of the room. I stood back to watch her move around with confidence as she pulled things out of a large cupboard.

"I don't have any tea, but I have some milk." She poured the white liquid into a glass and placed it on the solid wooden table.

I looked around expectantly. "And where do you keep the cow?" She snickered. "What? Does the milkmaid deliver the milk to you?"

She held up the square container filled with the liquid and handed it to me to feel the coolness of it. I could not see the milk, yet the box, or whatever it was, held something inside. I looked in through the top and saw it.

Dale grabbed my hand and led me to the cupboard she had removed it from. She opened the door and showed me inside. It felt like a cellar deep in the ground as the cool air slipped over my skin. Inside this cupboard was a variety of vegetables and some cheese. "No meat?"

She opened an even smaller door at the top of the cupboard, packed with ice and meat. I poked my finger at it and found the food solid.

"It's called a freezer, because that's what it does. It freezes things like meat to keep them fresh for a long period. This," she said and waved her hand at the cupboard, "is a fridge, and it keeps things like milk, eggs, cheese, and vegetables cool and fresh."

"And what is that?" The cupboard had a lantern inside.

"It's like a candle to give us light." To illustrate her point, she stepped over to the wall and touched something on it. Another torch illuminated overhead as if by magic. I felt no heat from it and yet it gave light… amazing. I shook my head in disbelief.

Dale smiled at me in understanding. I had barely moved from one room to another, and I was totally out of my depth of comprehension. She grasped my hand and drew me to the table to eat breakfast. At least the furniture was still shaped the same.

I watched as Dale moved around the room swiftly. A loaf of bread sat on the table as well as a cup of milk. The bread was an odd shape and was already sliced.

"Would you like a coffee?"

*"Non*, milk will suffice." I had never liked the taste of coffee because it reminded me of my husband. He would drink it often.

When Dale brought things to the table, I lifted them to my nose to sniff. I recognized the smell of strawberries and the soft white butter that she called "marg-rin." Finally, the arrival of toasted bread on a white plate signaled I could begin to eat. I dared not ask how that little box had turned the bread to toast. Dale took her seat as she held her large cup of hot coffee. The aroma made me shiver.

Dale had just finished her coffee when there was a shrill noise. Its suddenness startled me. Dale held up her hand and reached for a small box on the sideboard.

"Hello?" She said into it as if greeting someone. She rolled her eyes. "Hello, Mother."

I looked around but there was no one there. Who was she talking to?

"What are you talking about?"

I heard a faint noise, although I was unable to discern what it was. It was familiar, like a person talking far away, but I could barely hear the words.

"A woman?" Dale looked nervously at me. I suspected that her mother had found out about us. It made me wonder what my mother would have thought of my choices in life. Since she had sold me, I decided she had no right to judge.

"Where did you hear that?" Sweat broke out on Dale's forehead. "Jackie? Well, yes, I saw Jackie recently."

The faint noise grew a little louder, as if the voice had moved closer to my ear.

"Yes, I told her I met someone on a cruise." Dale stood and paced. "It was a sudden thing. I didn't tell you because I wanted to find out first if there was something between us." She paused in her pacing. "When did I go?" She lifted her finger to her mouth and tapped on her teeth. "Remember when you went to Europe last year? I decided to take a short cruise then. We've been corresponding since then."

I smiled. I knew she was lying. Did her mother think the same?

"Look, I've got to go. I'll call you soon." Dale pushed her thumb on the box and put it down.

"What is that?"

"It's called a cell."

"That looks nothing like a cell. Where are the bars?" I lifted the box and studied it. It had numbers on it, and when I pressed them, each number made a sound. Dale snatched it away and ran her thumb over the surface.

"It's a communication device." She sighed and started again. "I can talk to people hundreds of miles away."

"*Non.* Do not be silly."

"Françoise, remember you're now two hundred years in the future. We can talk to anyone in the world with one of these." She held up the box. "Life is nothing like it was in your time."

Suddenly, I yearned for my home. There I felt secure in my knowledge of the world, and my place in it. "That was your mother?"

"Yes, and she's not happy."

"Who is this Jackie?"

"She is… was a friend of mine. I needed someone to talk to so I met with her. She didn't like what I told her."

"About us?"

"Yeah. I still can't believe she would do this to me."

*"Chérie,* there will always be people who are narrow-minded fools."

"I expected my mother to not be happy, but Jackie?"

"What did you tell her?" I was fearful that she had given intimate details about us.

"Are you jealous?" Dale slyly smiled at me.

"Of course not. Why do you ask?"

"You are jealous." She laughed at me.

"I am not." I stood and turned around to leave her.

"Whoa. I was joking. Please, Françoise, don't be upset." She grabbed my arm.

I faced her. "I am sorry, *chérie.* All of this is…" I waved my hand in the air as I searched for a word.

"Unnerving? Scary? Unbelievable?"

*"Oui,* that and more."

"Not an auspicious beginning, huh?"

I did not know this word, but I believed she understood me. I took a deep breath and sat down once more. Dale knelt in front of me and settled back on her heels. She reached for my hands.

"Everything will work out, Françoise. Despite what my mother and Jackie say, I'll look after you."

"I am not used to being looked after in this way."

"What about your husband?"

I did not want to think about him. It was a time in my life that held only pain, humiliation, and sorrow. Dale would not know my story.

"He was not as loving as you." I would not say more. "And now your mother knows."

"She's going to kill me."

"I will protect you. No one will harm you." I was horrified that Dale's mother would kill her own daughter, but then again, my own mother was not above earning a few coins for me.

"She won't literally kill me, Françoise, but she'll make my life miserable because of this."

"Should she not be happy that you have found someone?"

"This definitely isn't in her plans. She wants me to marry a nice, well-connected boy and give her lots and lots of heirs for the family business."

"You are not interested?"

"I think you know the answer to that." Dale squeezed my hands. "Do you honestly think I'm interested in what my mother wants?"

"I would hope not."

She rose to her knees. "I know I'm not. Didn't you feel it when our eyes met? It was like… like…" Dale stared at the wall as if searching for the word. Then, her eyes met mine. "Destiny. It was meant to be, Françoise. Can't you see that? We both know that the mirror isn't supposed to allow us to shift back and forth in time. There are bigger things at work here than mere love."

"Or lust?" I inquired.

"Oh, yes. There's plenty of that. But underneath everything, there's some divine purpose for us. As to what that is, I don't know yet. But I don't think you'd be here unless it's for something important."

The moment I saw her in the mirror, I was awestruck. At the time, I thought of her as my angel sent to watch over me. When she cried, I reached out for her. To me, she was an illusion. I had expected to touch the glass, not to go into it. I was stunned. It could not be true, for it meant that dark forces were at work. Was the mirror cursed? Was I also cursed for using its black magic for my own selfish desires?

Dale silently awaited my answer.

"Then you should tell your mother everything."

"Right." Dale laughed. "My mother would have me committed."

"Committed to what?"

"She would put me in an asylum. It sounds crazy, and yet here you are."

"*Oui*, here I am." I felt I would have to remind myself of this fact often.

*  *  *

I stood wrapped in one of Dale's robes. It was either this or be naked all together. She had left me to my own inclinations while she went in search of some clothes for me.

Earlier that morning, she showed me her bathing chamber and, *incroyable!* It was nothing like I had ever imagined. Standing under that gentle rain to wash was divine. Watching Dale bathe herself under the "shower" was the most sensual thing I had ever seen, and my mind exploded with possibilities. It took all my willpower to let her leave.

The thing that puzzled me the most was the toilet. I did not understand. I could barely grasp the concept of something that removed bodily wastes. And where did it go? The habits of my fellow countrymen and women irritated me. Perhaps I was ahead of my time, and Dale's bathing chamber attested to that, but I felt my fellow citizens did not take care of themselves very well. I laughed and laughed as I pushed the handle time and again, watching the water swirl around the bowl before disappearing down the hole. A child's toy, that was for sure.

But now I was alone. In my hand sat a small box with what she called "buttons." In the far corner of the room was a bigger box, and the cacophony of sound emanating from it assaulted my senses. It was a "teevee." After my initial disgust at all those poor people locked away in such a small prison, Dale told me they were not captive. She said the teevee was another marvel of this world where the pictures moved. I pushed the buttons as she had shown me and switched from image to image, in shock at the things that I saw.

I felt that urge again to return home, to crawl into my own bed and curl up in a ball to hide from this new world. Despite her assurances, I did not think I could cope with all of this. It was too much. I was fearful of stepping out into the real world.

I put the box down and walked into the larger room that had some old furniture at one end. The shiny wood floor caressed the soles of my feet, and I was glad to feel something solid against my skin. I approached the armoire and ran my hands over the familiar object as I took in the fresh lines of the carved wood. It was much older than anything I had seen in this world, and its presence allowed me a moment to forget the span of time.

I lay my cheek against it to seek some solace from its smell and feel. This was a little of what I remembered. The wood dredged up images of a crackling fire in the fireplace and the peace and quiet of an afternoon's respite in my bedroom. Comfort... home.

I returned to the bed chamber, faced the mirror on the wall, and placed my hands on either side of it. This accursed thing had thrown me forward to a time and place where I did not belong. If it were not for my beloved Dale, it would be hell itself.

# Chapter 8

I made the decision that I would shake my sadness before Dale returned. I knew I could not dwell on this, or it would slowly eat away at me and become a wedge between us. This was meant to be. The magic of the mirror was proof of that.

I heard a noise at the door and decided I needed a little playfulness to cheer me up. I discarded the robe and draped myself over the bed, seductively posing in blatant invitation. The door opened and closed, and moments passed. There was a quiet clack of shoes crossing the wooden floor. "Ah, *chérie,* where have you been? I have been waiting all afternoon for you."

Two elderly people stood there openly staring at me. More to the point, the woman stared and the man ogled. "Er, er… *excusez-moi!"* Frantically I grabbed for the bed linen, but I knew it was rather pointless and way too late. At least the motion covered my embarrassment at being caught in such a position. Once I was covered, common sense prevailed. *"Madame… monsieur.* Are you in the correct house?"

"Yes. We are. And who, may I ask, is inquiring?" That voice spoke of aristocratic breeding. I had been around enough of the upper class to know a snob when I heard one.

"She's a friend of mine, Mother." I looked up to a face that was stricken. I could see her mind frantically trying to find a story to appease these two people. I knew they probably thought I was the woman that Dale had refused to mention. "Mother, this is Françoise Marie Aurélie de Villerey. Françoise, these are my parents, Martha and Joseph Wincott."

I was met with a polite nod. I could only nod in return. I was too busy gathering the rumpled linen around my naked body. Dale put down a number of packages on the bed and motioned me to take them. She grabbed her parents' arms and steered them into the kitchen while I dressed. As they left, I heard Dale ask what would have been my first question. "Why are you here?"

"You hung up on me yesterday, Dale. I can now see why." I heard Dale's intake of breath even from where I sat.

I moved to the edge of the bed, wrapped in the bed linen, while I tried to draw my dignity around me to cover my nakedness. *Mon Dieu. What was I thinking?* Reaching for the bags she left, I looked in them and found the clothes she had bought for me to wear.

I stood and moved to the bathing chamber to get dressed. Any more exposure to her mother or father would be my undoing. The quiet depression I had fleetingly kept at bay crept up on me again, and my head started to pound. It had not been a good day

I sat down on the toilet and pulled out each item from the bag for my inspection. The pants and shirt I recognized, but the other things, well… I could not even begin to guess.

Many colored pieces of material sat inside another parcel, held in by something that I could see through and was shiny. What was this? It was like soft glass. My frustration increased because I could not get inside. I… I… I hated this thing. The material refused to break, and I could not gain access. I became more frantic with each moment.

This was the final thing that broke me. I howled in frustration and bowed my head in defeat, while the packet lay crushed between my shaking hands.

"Honey, are you all right?" Dale's silken voice rolled over me to fill the aching cracks in my psyche, soft and soothing as an ointment to my battered skin. I looked up to see her looking at me with concern. She lowered herself to her knees in front of me. "Why are you crying?"

"I never cry."

In answer to my statement, she lifted her finger to my cheek to wipe away a tear and held it up for me to see. She took the parcel away and broke it easily to pull out one piece. "Here let me help you," she whispered.

"What about your parents?"

"I've sent them away. We'll have dinner with them later."

"But why, Dale?"

"Because you need me."

"I do?"

She grasped my hands in her own. "Yes, you do. I know it's hard for you to accept all of this, but I will be here for you, my love. I will take care of you."

I could not help it. For the first time since my family left me, I cried… really cried. These were not tears for my beloved France but tears for my soul. Dale pulled me to her chest and offered her strength and compassion to me to take as my own. I knew not how long I sought solace in her embrace, but finally there were no more tears.

"Come. Let's get you dressed." Suddenly, I felt like that seven-year-old dressed by my mother to be a "big girl." The linen was stripped away, and I felt a chill, probably as much from my emotional turmoil as from the cool air of the room. Still kneeling, Dale held up the piece of material that until now had eluded me. "These are underpants, Françoise. You wear them under the pants."

She held up the lacy piece of material for me to inspect. She lowered it and tapped each foot for me to lift while she slipped the material over my skin. Her hands skimmed lightly over me as she raised the pants to my hips. She leaned in and placed a soft kiss on my stomach. It was nothing more than a gentle affirmation, and it touched me so in its simplicity and purity

Dale retrieved another piece of material and undid the hooks on it. Her arms lifted toward my breasts, and my mind quickly shifted to more basic urges. I could not help it. Whenever she was close to me, my body reacted to her. I stood quietly while she slipped the straps of this particular piece of cloth up my arms, allowing the two pieces to cup my breasts.

"This is a bra, and we use it to protect our breasts. While your corsets would push the breasts up, the bra is mainly used for giving them shape and support when we move." I understood her explanation and enjoyed the relative freedom and nonexistent pain from wearing them. She stepped up behind me and pulled on it until I felt the pressure from the material as it drew my breasts in toward my chest.

I tried to watch her over my shoulder, but I had to use the mirror instead to study her nimble fingers drawing the closures together. How did she do that? I watched her work, and my heart fluttered under her close attention.

As if she sensed my hesitation, her eyes lifted to mine. The warmth in her smile rose to her eyes. She had done it again, giving me her strength and quiet determination to continue for one more minute, one more hour, one more day. The beast within me was but a tame plaything under her gentle guidance, and I cared none that she controlled my raging spirit. I finally understood that there would be times, like now, when she must lead and I must follow, just as there would be other times when I must lead and I would expect her to trust my judgment.

While I contemplated all this, Dale laid out the pants and patiently waited for me to lift my leg. I looked down at her amused expression and finally did as she silently asked. The cool material dragged along my legs and set my senses aflame. To allow the one person who held my heart unreservedly to dress me was humbling, comforting, and extremely sensual, all rolled into one. The heavy cloth continued to rise up my body until finally, I stood up and let the pants sit on my hips. I looked down at the material.

"What is this?" I pointed at my crotch. "Where are the buttons?" She studied where my finger pointed. Dale stood and stopped inches from my face. Her hand dropped to the pants and gently touched the material between my legs. Suddenly, I felt hot, and my pulse rate rose at the thought of her hand so close to me.

"It's a zipper. It replaces the buttons. You pull it so..." There was a strange sound as her hand moved. I looked down as she pulled the small tag in an upward motion, and the jagged opening closed. She whispered to me, "To open it, you just pull it down." Those eyes looked into mine, as if begging me to remember this vital piece of information.

My breathing quickened with her standing so close and her hand between my legs. For a moment, she hesitated to absorb my reaction. "Dale, please." Her heated breath tormented me as it fanned the fine hair on my face. I was so close to ending this tease, but I reined in my desire. This scene had been a gift to me. I would not spoil it by giving into my baser instincts.

Finally, she picked up the blouse and slid the soft material up my arms and over my body, quickly threading the buttons through the eyelets. Her hands wound around my waist so she could turn me around to face the mirror.

I looked at what I wore. "And you want me to wear this out in public?"

"Most women wear jeans these days, Françoise. It's quite acceptable."

"Jeans?" Dale tugged at the pants I wore. "Not in my time, Dale."

"But you have worn pants, my love. I've seen you in pants before."

"*Chérie*, if I had been caught out in public in those clothes I would have been ostracized for my obvious flaunting of what was socially acceptable."

"And that's precisely why you did it. You just love shocking people. I just wished it wasn't my parents that were on the receiving end of your flair for the dramatic."

"I am so sorry. I thought it was you."

"I was going to introduce you to my parents sooner or later, but not this way. Never mind. It's done now. I'll live."

"It is that bad?"

"I suppose I'll find out in the next few days."

"I am sorry if I embarrassed you. I was missing home and had hoped that you would make me forget such things."

"I would have been more than happy to ease your ache. It was just bad timing."

"But there is something more, *n'est-ce pas?*"

"My mother is… is…" She struggled with a word.

"Dangerous?" The word "snob" was there also, but I doubted she wished to hear that.

"A snob."

I smiled. It seemed we had the same thought.

"She believes in a man and a woman being married," Dale said. "Anything other than that is abhorrent."

"Ab-hor…?"

"Let's just say she thinks it's wrong. If they had walked in on a man lying in my bed, this wouldn't even be a problem." She sighed. "But it's not wrong."

Dale used words that I barely understood. There were so many new things to learn. She tightened her arms around my waist and rested her chin on my shoulder. I could see her face in the mirror, yet she did not smile at me. I turned to face her. Her eyes dropped shyly to the floor, but I tipped up her chin with a touch of my finger. Our eyes met. A look of worry crossed her face. I grabbed her hand and ran my thumb over her wrist in comforting circles. "Everything will be fine. Do not worry."

"But you don't know my mother."

"My mother abandoned me as soon as the deal had been struck with *le Comte de Villerey*. I have not seen her since. How bad can your mother be?" The look on her face made me wonder. What had I gotten myself into?

There was a long moment of contact between us, perhaps too long. She stepped away from me, quietly sniffling. "What?"

"My mother will not let this matter rest, Françoise."

"Be strong. Worse than her have tried to deter me from what I want. I am still here, and I will never leave you… unless you ask me to."

I looked for that answering glow. I hoped she would not disappoint me. Perhaps there was still doubt that she would tire of me and cast me adrift on that sea that was her soul. I was not disappointed. Dale's eyes were full of passion, commitment, and everlasting love for me, which solemnly promised that what we had would last for forever.

\* \* \*

After a leisurely afternoon of our indulging in one another, Dale insisted on showing me how to cook.

"You are wasting your time," I grumbled. This was one duty I did not wish to partake in.

"Look, what's so hard about it?" Dale waved a knife in my direction.

"Could you put that down?" The constant jerking of the knife made me nervous.

"Is something as simple as this too hard for you?"

"Do not play that game with me!" Now she had made me mad.

"Come on, Françoise. What if something happened to me—if I was home late or whatever—are you going to sit there and not eat because it's too hard?"

"I will eat an apple or a piece of bread. I have done that before, and I can do it again."

"Can you at least indulge me by coming over here and watching me?"

Dale was like a hound worrying at a scavenged bone. She would not give up until I relented. I rose and went to the box in the corner. Dale snorted at me from the kitchen.

"I am not your slave, Françoise."

"*Non*? Are you not a slave to my heart?" I smiled at her as she approached, moments before she threw a dishrag at my face.

"You are on dish duty."

"What is this, dish… duty?"

"You will wash and dry the dishes. There's your tea towel."

Dish duty? Tea towel? It was like she spoke another language. "I do not work in the kitchen."

"While you're in this century, yes, you will." Her voice was firm, but bemusement sparkled in her eyes. "That's if you want to eat."

I dropped the cloth and strode over to her, intent on kissing her senseless. I twisted her around to face me. My hand grabbed her wrist as the knife moved toward my chest. "Ah ah," I whispered.

"Oh, Lord. I didn't mean to—"

"It was my fault to scare you like that." I took the knife out of her hand and put it on the bench. My lips sought hers, and I plundered her mouth until she surrendered.

Dale pulled her lips away from me. "You don't play fair."

"I have to use everything I know." My lips moved to her neck, and I nibbled on the flesh there.

"If you let me take you outside tonight, you can have your way with me."

I barely heard the words over the pounding of my own heart. *"Oui,"* I said before I realized what she had said. "Pardon? Outside? Out... there?"

"You said yes."

"It was a mistake. You do not play fair. You distracted me."

"I have to use everything I know." She smiled in triumph as she repeated my words.

"I cannot. Do not ask that of me."

"Don't be afraid. I'll be with you all the way."

I wanted to be a petulant child and refuse to go, but Dale's sad face made me smile. How could I not do what she asked?

"Let's get some dinner," Dale said.

I let the matter rest, at least until after our meal.

After we ate, she took my hand and tugged me toward the door "Come on, let me show you my world."

I did not want to go and pulled back. "Not tonight, please, *chérie.*"

Her lips tipped up into a shy, sensual smile. She extended her hand to mine, "Come on, my love. One step at a time."

Gentle laughter escaped her. "What?" I asked. She turned me toward the mirror, and I looked. I was pouting. I never pouted. Dale stood behind me and looked over my shoulder at the image in the mirror. Her hand came up to slowly rub my stomach, making hypnotic circles in an effort to settle my inner turmoil.

"You are dressed up with nowhere to go. Come on."

"You could always help me take them off." I stared into Dale's eyes reflected in the mirror. I rested my hand over the top of hers and crushed it against the top of my pants.

"You have to go out sometime, Françoise. Now is as good a time as any."

"I do not want to go."

Dale grasped my chin and pulled it around to face her. "Now you listen to me, young lady. You can't keep putting this off." I watched her as she thought for a moment. "Besides, didn't I promise to let you have your wicked way with me afterwards?"

"That you did." She had found my weakness and shamelessly used it to her advantage.

As if she sensed my indecision, she slipped her hand into my pants and slid her fingers slowly down.

"Anything you want…" This was not fair.

"Come on. Trust me," she whispered. I knew I could not refuse despite the agreement. Trust? Had I not contemplated that very thought only moments before? Dale would look after me.

"Fine. But after that you are mine. Anything, you said."

"Anything your heart desires, my sweetness."

Sighing deeply, I relented. "Lead on."

# Chapter 9

One step at a time she had said. One more step down a staircase to what awaited me outside. Dale held my hand tightly, as if she expected me to flee. Images of what we would do later in the night were all that held me to my course.

Finally, we reached the door, and I had run out of excuses. As if through water, her hand reached for the door handle, twisted it, and pulled. Her gaze met mine, and I knew what she saw there... fear. Fear was foreign to me. I knew that I was confident— overconfident, some might say to the point of arrogance. But fear? Perhaps at one time. Now I lived and loved aggressively. But I had always known my world and my place in it.

Gently, Dale tugged me outside, her hand still holding firmly onto mine as it acted as my anchor to our reality. We emerged onto an alleyway of cobblestones and familiar lampposts. I had stepped into my own time in Paris—or at least it appeared to be the Paris I was familiar with.

"Come." Dale's voice sounded low and soothing. She tugged me toward the street. I walked as if I had been in my sickbed for weeks. My legs were slow to respond as I moved in the direction my Dale led me.

As soon as we reached the end of the alleyway, it was like I had stepped across a secret barrier to move from the known world straight into the world of dreams. Lanterns were scattered everywhere, peeking out of empty windows and lining the street, to bring light to the darkness of night.

I jumped back in fright as a noisy metal beast passed. "Wha... what is that?" Somehow, my voice had risen to a tight squeak while I watched its passing. A touch on my arm sent a jolt through me, and I flinched. My blood pumped loudly in my ears, while my breath came in shallow gasps.

"Honey, relax. It's the horseless carriage I told you about. We call it a car." I looked into Dale's eyes for the truth. She was so calm about this, and I felt so out of control. "Come on." My faith in her helped me to follow.

Now I knew why I was fearful of everything. Oh yes, I knew. It was him. I was thinking as a child back to a time when my life was out of control thirteen long years ago. The last time I had felt this lost and abandoned was when I became married to a man who changed my life… and not for the better.

Dale said something, but I could not hear her over the thumping of my heart.

"Françoise!" I jumped at the harsh bark. My terrified gaze moved to her.

She looked disappointed. "Let's go home."

"No, I can do this. Just give me *un moment.*" Hope sparked in her eyes, and it fed me. "Lead on, woman." We walked down the street hand in hand toward a promenade, the trees silhouetted in the far-off darkness.

For a moment, she stopped at a small shop and led me inside. "Let's get some ice cream."

Ice cream? I looked through the glass to the tins of color. Ah, *crème glacée.*

"What flavor do you want?" she asked.

"You choose. We only ever had one choice."

"Two strawberry swirls please." I watched as the merchant scooped out the confection.

"And what is that below it?"

"It's called a 'cone.' You can eat it." She kept her voice low, I am sure in an effort not to draw the merchant's attention to my ignorance.

We walked out of the shop into the night air, and I was glad to feel the cool ice slide down my dry throat. My world slowly righted itself. With an ice cream in one hand and Dale's hand in the other, I strolled down the path that dissolved into the creeping darkness of the nearby promenade.

I looked up, puzzled. "Dale, where are the stars?"

"There're still there. It's just all the lights in the city block them out."

"Lights?" She pointed to the lanterns.

As we moved a little farther past the trees, the sight before me opened up, and I gasped. It was like the stars in the heavens had come down to earth to hang suspended on tall invisible mountains. It was so beautiful.

"Wow," Dale said beside me.

"What?"

"The look on your face is just so amazing."

"Why?"

"This is what I was looking for—that look of wonderment. Françoise, all I ever wanted was for you to be happy, to make you feel at ease here." Her eyes were a deep hazel in the low light, lit by the full smile that crossed her face. She pulled me over to a bench, and we sat down to finish eating the cone.

"Now, will you tell me the truth?"

"Hmm?"

"Why are you so scared here? Don't think I didn't notice that panic attack when we left the apartment."

"It is nothing, little one." Her hand withdrew from mine as she sought solace within herself. She knew I was not telling the truth. I would have expected an answer to such a question if I had asked it. Sighing deeply, I reached once more for her hand. "I do not know where to start. I am lost here, Dale. It brings back many memories, and none of them good." She sat quietly while I talked. Perhaps I needed this to cleanse my soul. The truth had been buried inside me for too long.

Her body snuggled up to mine, and I lifted my arm over her shoulder to pull her in against my side. "This feeling is so close to what I felt back then, thirteen years ago." She stiffened. "Yes, when I was forced to marry him. *Mon Dieu*, what hell were those ten years. The day he died I laughed and cried, from relief." Her hand caressed my skin, slowly and gently in sympathy. "His last days were in great pain, for which I thanked God."

Dale looked at me, puzzled.

"What?" I asked.

"You don't strike me as someone who would wish torment on another."

I smiled at her. "I torment you, do I not?"

"But this is not the same."

"No," I said quietly, "not the same."

I looked into those eyes studying me. "In the beginning, I had no control over my life. I was forced to travel a road that had no escape. Either side was a sheer drop that would lead to my death. I had to stay on the path chosen for me or die."

"Why didn't you run away? Seek a life elsewhere."

"He owned me. It might have been a marriage, but it was nothing more than a sale of a human life. Mine. My family had run into serious financial loss. Mother saw this as a means to an end.

And Father? Well, he was a weak-minded fool who did anything she asked of him, even the selling of his daughter to the Devil. So, I am sorry, *chérie,* if my reaction has not been favorable to your world. It is an instinct long ingrained in me. Please. Just give me time to get used to all of… this." My hand swept the air to take in the grand scheme of everything.

"Take all the time you need."

Good. She understood. I breathed deeply and felt the cool air fill my lungs. I felt better. Someone knew my story—at least part of it—and she was still here. "It is very pretty, you know. All of those lights. Beautiful."

"I'm glad you like it."

"How do they hang there?"

"They don't. Those are buildings. Like the one I live in but stacked on top of one another, making it taller and taller until it reaches into the sky. All of the lights are on so that people can clean them. During the day, other people work there—merchants, laborers, workers. This is enough for tonight. You ready to go home?"

"Home?"

"You filled your end of the agreement. Now it's time for me to do the same."

"You do not have to do that. I am content to just hold you."

"So, you don't want me then?" I could hear the hint of playfulness in her voice.

I turned myself to her to let her see the answer in my eyes. I grabbed her roughly to seek out her lips and claim them. "Take me home, *chérie.*" Her smile widened and tiny wrinkles spread across the bridge of her nose. I felt that ache in my heart again as she pulled me to my feet to return home to fulfill a promise made.

* * *

As soon as we walked in the door, she turned to me. "What did you have in mind?" It appeared that she was as eager as I was. Without a word, I led her to the mirror and turned her to face our image.

"Watch," I whispered, "I know you can do that." Her image smiled at me, but her smile faltered as my hand slid up her body. I stood behind her to get the perfect position to watch her watch us.

"What are you doing, Françoise?"

*"Ma chérie*, if you do not know by now, then I am doing it wrong." Her chuckle vibrated through her slim body. "This," I said and nodded toward the mirror, "is where it all started. You watching me in the mirror. Is it not fitting that you and I watch ourselves in the very thing that brought us together?"

She leaned back against me, and her head rested in the hollow of my neck. I found the buttons on her shirt and slowly fed each one through the eyelets. My gaze never left hers as her blue-gray eyes glistened with unfulfilled passion. I whispered naughty, forbidden things into her ear and watched her fingers twitch in response to my vulgar entreaties.

Her hand shook as she reached for the metal tab of her jeans. I lost my patience as her escalating need drove her to find my hand and place it where she needed me the most.

I withdrew my hand and she whimpered. "No, I must see it all. Naked, Dale, I want you naked." A growl escaped her as her clothes flew around us. Her hand disappeared behind her back and she slipped off her bra in rapid fashion. How did she do that? But she was not content to finish there. She turned her attention to me and nearly ripped the buttons off in her eagerness to find my skin. In desperation, I sought some self-control because I wanted to finish this scene before we completely gave ourselves over to our hunger.

"Steady, we have all night." But her eyes told me different. Her patience was gone and her need all-consuming. I turned her back to face the mirror and allowed her to feel me slide along her back.

Her eyes stared into mine and begged me to continue. She once again found my hand, and she returned it to where it had been moments before. This time her own hand rested there and allowed me to lead her to her passion. I watched her body writhe against mine. Her muscles rippled, bunched, and flexed as she shifted against me, while she vainly tried to find that elusive pinnacle to ease her ache.

I realized that this is what Dale saw that first time. I watched, like a voyeur, two people in the throes of passion and felt their ecstasy as my own even as I was a participant in it. It was exciting, shocking, and so erotic to see this, to be a part of it. I saw my Dale so deep in her own pleasure that she was oblivious to all but her own completion.

No sooner had her peak hit than she turned around and pushed me hard to collapse on the bed. She lay on top of me, and her fingers delved into me without a moment's thought. *Sainte Mère de Dieu!* Here was my little hellcat in full-fledged fury, tearing at my flesh in sweet, sweet agony, and devouring the very heart of me in an orgy of passion.

I was barely aware of anything around me except the eager body over mine and the fingers gliding over me demanding my response. My young, sweet Dale showed me another facet to her that I had not even considered, and it was an unexpected and welcome addition to our bed. With that last thought, she sent me into oblivion. My body sank into a raging pool of utter pleasure and pulsed in ecstasy with every beat of my heart.

After I descended from the dizzying heights where she had taken me, Dale pulled me into her welcoming embrace. As I slid into a contented slumber, she promised to take me shopping tomorrow. That would mean my first day out of her house and in the bright sunlight. My first real day in her world.

\* \* \*

We finally left the sanctuary of her house at mid-morning. Before we left, that sound came from Dale's little box again. She talked into it and was not pleased. Reluctantly, she told me we were to have dinner with her parents that night. While I had some concerns regarding the meeting, she wished to be somewhere else. We talked for a while over tea, and she expressed her concerns. I did not think she was convinced that I would brook no disapproval from her mother regarding our relationship.

That first step past the front door had been the hardest step I had ever taken into a world I was not sure I could survive in. Yes, last night had helped to some degree, but in the light of day, my confidence faltered. Dale wrapped her fingers around my hand and squeezed. She gave me a sympathetic look, while a small smile graced her lips. Then she nodded.

I sighed deeply and straightened my shoulders to brace myself for the trial ahead. Gently, Dale tugged me in the direction of the big city. We entered a building, the stonework close to what I remembered of my own time, and its coolness was a testament to the age of the craftwork invested in its construction. The brass plate announced it was "Community" and nothing more, which left me no clearer to its purpose. Dale exchanged a large pile of paper between herself and a man behind a desk. She put the papers away in her purse, and we left.

"What did he just give you?"

"It's money, and this is a bank, Françoise." She handed over a sample. I studied it with great interest.

"What is this worth?"

"That's twenty dollars. We also have coins, but the paper money is worth more than the coin. It makes it easier to carry and certainly less heavy. Rather than having all this money lying around, we use a bank to look after it for us. Didn't you have banks in your time?"

"I had heard of them in London and Italia, but we would never have used it. My husband preferred to hide his money. I did the same, as you saw with the mirror. But you told me you have little money."

"That's not quite true. I have money, and today, I feel in the mood to spend some of it." Her face lit up with excitement. "Let's go shopping."

We wandered the streets and observed the different people move about their business. My nose twitched at the air. "What is that smell? It is terrible."

"I'm sorry, Françoise, it's from those." She pointed to the horseless carriages I had come to detest.

"So these metal beasts pass wind, *n'est-ce pas*?" She chuckled at my expense. "Well?"

"Yes, Françoise, they pass wind, and that's what you smell."

"Stop feeding them hay then."

"Fine. I'll be sure to tell the manufacturers." She tipped her head back and laughed. I allowed her to delight in my ignorance for the moment, but anyone else would have had hell to pay for belittling me so.

Despite my apprehension, I enjoyed my time with Dale. We strolled along the streets and entered various establishments to try on clothes and shoes. I quickly learned about women's fashion and what suited me and what did not.

Dale found an inn. We sat outside at a table, and a nice gentleman took our order. With the bright sun shining above, the occasional trilling of a nearby bird, and my beautiful Dale sitting opposite me, I felt a bit more confident about life outside her home. Silently, we ate our lunch of sandwiches.

During the afternoon, we walked back toward her apartment, content mostly to just enjoy the warming sun on our backs, the cool breeze in our faces, and the intimacy of each other's company. Something caught Dale's attention, and she directed me into a store.

"We cannot possibly carry any more clothes…" My words faded as we stepped through the sliding door into a quiet environment, the cooling air gliding over our sweat-slicked skin.

Dale approached the merchant and spoke low so I could not hear what she said. With a nod, she led me into a tiny room and gave me a pair of pants that felt heavy and smelled of leather. I held them up to the lantern to see that they were, in fact, leather. I opened the curtain, but Dale pushed me back in.

"Try them on."

I did as she asked, but I had to tug and pull to get the offending garment on. I was about to ask for help when the leather gave way to slide those last few inches up my legs. Remembering Dale's instruction, I found the small tab, pulled it up, and heard the satisfying crunch as the hole closed.

I could barely move in these pants and wondered if certain body parts would fall off if I tried to crouch down in them. I grabbed at the crotch to try and find room in a space where there was none. And that was how Dale found me—my hand stuck between my legs as I tried to pull the leather away from my body. I looked up at her and felt a deep blush travel slowly up my torso. Lately, she seemed to discover me at my most vulnerable moments.

Intent on wiping away the image from the moment before, I stood up and rested a hand on one hip and tried for a dominant and imposing pose. Her gaze traveled from my feet to my waist. She grabbed me and turned me around. I could feel her heated gaze on my derrière, burning a hole right through the leather to the skin below. In the mirror, her eyes looked into mine, smoldering and hungry.

Her wandering hands cupped my cheeks and kneaded me through the leather, pushing my excitement to an accelerated rate.

"You keep doing that, Dale, and the lady will get a show."

"Maybe I don't care."

"Ah, *chérie,* if I truly believed that, you would have no clothes on right now. Come on, let us go home and surrender to each other."

Dale turned me to face her. She dropped her hand and lowered the zipper. She stood so close to me I could smell her. She shifted to the button and deftly fed it through the eyelet. She left those agile fingers hover there to test my control. I was so close to saying "damn to the world" and taking her here, but the woman was standing nearby in anticipation of a sale.

"I will be out in moments." My voice had deepened in its timbre. *Damn her. She is going to be the death of me.*

If it was hard to get the pants on, it was even harder to get them off, especially after Dale's little foray with the zipper. It was like the leather had molded itself to my body and refused to set me free from its grasp. Finally, the material gave way, much like peeling off my pants after a long, hot ride. That thought did not help my control as I remembered that fateful day at the barn when we rode back together naked.

I handed the pants to Dale. "Are you able to afford these?" She inspected the paper tag attached to the pants, and her face blanched. *"Non*, we do not want this." I was about to return the pants to the shelf, but she stopped me.

She looked at the woman, "We'll take them." Before I could ask she said, "They're more for me than for you." As the woman left to wrap them, Dale gave me a sly grin. "I had promised myself to see you in leather pants. Now that I have, I can't say no. You have to wear them... often."

We left the shop with another parcel in my hand and her purse considerably lighter for the purchase. "So, where shall we go? Home?" My voice dripped with want at this point because I wished to make use of her large bed in the beckoning sunlight from the window in the roof.

Tiring, we decided to walk back home. We passed shops whose displays shamelessly tried to entice us into buying their wares, but one discreet doorway drew my attention. "What is that?"

She looked up at the sign and blushed. What had I asked that would cause such a reaction? "It's an... um... an adult shop."

"We are adults, are we not?"

"You don't want to go in there, Françoise."

"It certainly has you flustered, *chérie.* What is in there? Is it a house of ill repute?"

"No, there are no prostitutes in there. At least I don't think so. It's a little embarrassing."

"I want to see." She tugged on my hand and tried pull me past the stairs, but I did not move. "You have to tell me why you do not want me to go in there."

"Because..."

"Because why?"

"Because it's a sex shop." She bowed her head.

"I thought you said it was not a house of ill repute."

"It's not. They sell sex aids."

Sex aids? I wanted to see for myself. I started up the staircase to the door at the top.

"Where are you going?" she whispered.

"To see what these sex aids are. You will not tell me, so I will look myself."

"Please, Françoise, don't go. The men in there are…"

"Are what?" She would not answer me. "Have you been in an establishment like this one?"

Her eyes widened. "No, of course not."

"Then, how do you know? Come with me. Together, we will be fine." I could see that she did not want to come, but she did not want to wait outside the shop either. Reluctantly, she took my hand and we ascended the stairs. I opened the door for her but she refused to enter first. Sighing deeply, I stepped inside and found that it was nothing like what I imagined. Dale's reaction made me think it would be fire and brimstone, like Hell itself.

At one end of the establishment, three men looked through shiny papers. They glanced at us to watch our arrival. As I moved farther into the room, I felt Dale's body against my back. We had made it this far, and I could not leave after the fuss I had made about coming inside.

"Haven't you seen enough already?" Dale pleaded.

*"Un moment.* We have made it this far. At least look before you run."

I knew of the Marquis de Sade. His lifestyle had spread wildly throughout the aristocracy. But looking at the things on display here surely surpassed even his wildest dreams. *"Sacrebleu!"*

Some things I could guess by their obvious shape but others left me perplexed. I picked up a packet, unable to see clearly what was inside. I handed it to Dale, who replaced the packet to the shelf. I picked it up again. "Dale, what is this for?"

"It does the same thing as that." She pointed to another object, one which I recognized immediately.

"But why does it not look the same?"

"Because it vibrates."

"Vibrates?" She moved her hand in a rapid motion, and I finally grasped her meaning. "Oh."

"Now can we go?"

*"Un moment.* What makes it vibrate? Why buy this if your hand can do the same thing?"

"Because it will do it by itself so you don't have to use your hand."

"Is that so? And what is it like?"

"I don't know. I haven't used one."

"Never?"

"No, never. I told you I've never been in one of these stores before." I picked one up and carried it with me as I moved around the room. She hurried after me. "What do you think you're doing?"

"Just adding a little excitement, little one."

"And what we have is not exciting enough?"

"Of course it is, but I have to keep surprising you, do I not?" So, my little hellcat was a bit of a prude. To annoy her, I continued to look at the various items on display. She nudged me every so often, I am sure to leave in the hope of escaping the glares of the men present. A couple of other items had possibilities, but I had gone far enough with the "sex aid" in my hand. When I had decided she had suffered enough, I relented and placed the packet back in its place.

"Shall we go?" I said.

She smiled at me in relief. "That was cruel," she muttered.

"And you, my dear Dale, are a prude."

"All right, I'll admit to that. I know nothing, all right?" Dale looked around nervously.

"Dale?" a male voice said behind us.

Dale paled. She looked around to a portly man who had walked in the door. "Shit," she muttered under her breath.

She turned to meet him. He gave her a huge grin, and his chubby cheeks bunched in an exaggerated fashion. He seemed genuinely pleased to see her, but Dale looked uncomfortable. "Hi, Mr. O'Brien."

"*Chérie,* are you not going to introduce us?"

"Um, Françoise, this is Mr. O'Brien. Mr. O'Brien, this is my friend, Françoise de Villerey." I did not question why she had shortened my name for now.

"Pleased to meet you, monsieur."

"The pleasure is all mine, Françoise."

I cringed. Such an intimate address from a stranger would have been met with disdain in my time.

"Mr. O'Brien is the one who sold me the mirror." Dale's voice had dropped low to give me this particular piece of information. Perhaps I should thank the man.

"I haven't seen you in the shop for a while, Dale. Everything all right?"

"Fine thanks. I've just been busy, that's all. Um… I'll see you soon. Bye." She pushed me toward the door in an effort to leave.

As we left, I heard the comments: "See you later, sweetheart." "Oh yeah, what a hottie." "Did you see which magazine she was in?"

When we reached the street, Dale was breathing heavily.

"Are you all right?"

"Why couldn't we just have left when I asked?"

"Because I was curious. Is it not what this visit was for? It is all over now. Let us go home."

"I could have told you what you wanted to know. You didn't have to carry a vibrator around for everyone to see."

"A vib-rator? I must remember this name." Dale blushed. "Ah, I think you have come a long way when you ravish me, and then along comes this vib-rator and you are a like a virgin on her wedding night. Priceless."

"There's a difference between the privacy of the bedroom and a room of perverts."

"Perverts? Those men?"

"What do you think they were doing there?"

"Reading the newspapers I think."

"Those newspapers were filled with pictures of naked women, all doing what you were doing with that man I saw you with not so long ago." I was not surprised. A blind man could see what was in that shop. "Pornography, Françoise, that's what they were looking at."

"So, perverts indeed then, Dale."

We arrived home tired, but pleased with the successful outing. However, I now had a solemn task ahead of me. As much as I wished to have Dale in her bed, we had to attend a dinner with her parents.

# Chapter 10

Dale's parents would arrive soon to take us to an inn. After that ill-fated exposure yesterday, I was hesitant to renew the meeting. Dale tried to get me to wear what she called a "dress," but I refused to wear something that was nothing more than an undergarment to me. Neither of us wished to argue the point and compromised to wear pants.

A long, horseless carriage that Dale called a "lim-o" pulled to a stop in front of her home. Dale's mother greeted us as we entered the horseless carriage. She continued to stare at me during our ride, which was even more terrifying than watching these beasts pass in the street. Where were the horses? I could not ask such questions because the inquiry would only lead to more questions that neither of us was prepared to answer. I sought out Dale's eyes opposite me and begged for some silent comfort in this devil carriage. I buried myself in my reticence and hoped she would reveal all at the end of this long night.

I observed her mother's short dress whose hem ended just below the knee. Her hair fell just to her neck. Everything was so revealing. Where had her long tresses gone? Considered a woman's crowning glory, removing one's hair was either a sign of severe illness or a sudden termination of one's life. Perhaps *madame* was ill?

On the ride, three pairs of eyes watched me—one with animosity, one with mild curiosity, and the third was the one who knew my heart and was full of love and apprehension. I had watched Dale's eyes in that lengthy carriage ride, not wanting to see who resided in the remaining two seats, staring at me intently.

As we alighted from the carriage, I caught a glimpse of myself in the glass facing me. I had been wearing this attire for a day, and it still bothered me. Yet, on my estate, I longed for the days when I could do such a thing. So different. I wore riding pants, jeans as Dale called them, and a tight black shirt. This outfit would have shocked French society because it revealed so much of a woman's figure in public. I had to admit that leaving the house without a corset took a lot of resolve on my part to override all those years of imposed social propriety. I wriggled around in my new clothes, and while I enjoyed the feel of material on skin and the freedom it gave, I pushed my apprehension to the back of my mind.

We entered a building filled with a large number of people. Were we going to a ball? Perhaps I should have agreed to dress more formally for such an occasion. Dale leaned over to me and whispered, "This is a restaurant—an eating house."

"An inn?"

"Yes, a very fancy inn. But there are no prostitutes here." She paused for a moment. "Well, none that I can identify straight away." There was a hint of mischief in Dale's eyes, as if she was daring me to be shocked.

I was so overwhelmed that nothing would shock me, at least not until my mind caught up to my predicament.

After the hostess sat us at our table and handed me a menu, I looked over the top at Dale across the table, my eyebrow raised in question.

"So, Miss... What was your name again?" Dale's mother asked.

"Françoise is acceptable, *madame. Enchantée de faire votre connaissance, Madame Wincott, Monsieur Wincott.* My apologies for the embarrassment of our first meeting."

"Please, Martha and Joseph." Dale's father answered before her mother could reply.

"Yes, that was quite a shock," her mother said.

"If you had called, Mother..." Dale glared at her.

"I shouldn't think I had to call. We're family. However, I can see why you'd want a bit of advance notice."

"Why did you come over?"

"After Jackie's phone call and your refusal to answer my question, I thought it prudent to see you in person."

"And, by the way, the key I gave you was for emergencies only."

"I considered this an emergency."

"Mother, I told you before. I want to make my own decisions."

"Even if they're wrong?"

"Martha, let the girl speak."

"Joseph, surely you don't agree with this, do you?"

The waiter arrived and the conversation stopped. Dale ordered on my behalf, for which I was grateful. While some of the words on the menu I knew, others I did not.

"She is our daughter, Martha."

"Françoise. That's French, isn't it? And your accent is definitely French." Slate blue eyes stared at me in accusation. Now I knew how those poor souls felt at the Spanish Inquisition.

*"Oui, madame,* it is."

"And where do you come from, Françoise?"

"A small town in France near the Loire, *madame."*

"And just what interest do you have in my daughter?"

"Mother!" Dale glanced around her at the diners' turned heads.

"Quiet, Dale. I'm asking your 'friend' here." My hackles rose at the contemptuous tone in Martha's voice. I tried to be polite, but she would have none of it.

*"Madame...* Martha." I saw her bristle at my use of her first name, even though Dale's father had said I could address them so. Good. "I could say that it is between Dale and myself. But as you are her family, and I was raised in a society that considers politeness a virtue, I am in love with your daughter, and she is in love with me."

"No!" Martha nearly jumped out of her seat at my words. The diners around us again looked up at the raised voice. "No." The second word came out as a harsh whisper. "This cannot happen!" Martha grimaced in disgust.

Dale's eyes pooled with tears. What had I done? I had placed her in a position that she might not be ready for. But she surprised me. "She's right, Mother. I do love her."

I glanced at Dale's father who had a gentle smile on his face.

"Joseph?" Martha looked at him.

"She's happy. Don't you see that?"

"But it's wrong."

"How long has it been since you saw her truly happy?"

"This is neither the time nor the place—"

"Answer me. When did you ever see her this happy?"

"At her last birthday, if I recall."

"Do you really think she would suffer your ire if it wasn't love?"

I watched Dale as the conversation took place. A lone tear slid down her cheek as her father spoke.

Martha dismissed Joseph with a wave of her hand and turned back to Dale. "No. You will not embarrass this family. You will stop this nonsense right now. Let me find you some nice young man. How about the Claridge boy? He comes from a respectable Boston family. Yes, a big society wedding to put all this insanity behind us."

"Françoise is my love—my life—she will be living with me for as long as she wishes." Dale was still crying, but she reached deep inside and found courage to oppose her mother. I silently cheered her stand.

Her mother opened her mouth to speak, but her father stopped her. "That's enough. We're here for a nice meal."

"But, Joseph—"

"Enough!" he bellowed. The patrons of the inn stopped their conversation—or an upraised fork—and looked at us again. "Leave it be." He gritted his teeth.

I tried to intervene. *"Madame—"*

Dale held up one hand. "No, Françoise. This has to stop here." Her eyes pleaded for support, and I complied. "Mother, this is who I choose. You have always made my decisions for me, but you never really understood me. This is who I am, who I *really* am."

Tears sprang to my eyes at her declaration.

"She has bewitched you!"

"She certainly has." Dale gazed at me lovingly, and I smiled.

"Think about the family and what this will do to our reputation."

"Not everything is about you. You have hounded me to find someone, and now that I have, you disapprove."

"I more than 'disapprove.' This is abhorrent."

Dale had used that same word not long ago. She knew her mother very well.

I studied Martha and saw in those blue-grey depths the steely resolve of a woman intent on protecting her family. I felt I had made an enemy tonight.

"Can we at least have a civil meal?" Joseph asked as he glared at Martha.

"Fine, have it your own way. This is not the end."

The meal progressed mostly in silence until Martha spoke. "Dale, don't forget the charity ball coming up in two weeks' time. Young Robert will be escorting you. Can you give him a call sometime this week, please, to organize this?"

"I won't be going. Not now."

Martha leaned over and hissed, "You know this has been organized for months. You can't back out now. I'm sure that your 'friend' won't mind you attending the ball with a date."

The challenge was there in her eyes as she threw down the gauntlet for me to pick up. What could I say? I had to graciously let this happen. "Of course not, Martha." I addressed Dale. "You should go. If this has already been arranged, I cannot stand in your way." I thought I heard a gasp of triumph from Martha.

I turned my gaze to my enemy and infused my look with all the determination and strength I could muster. *She is mine, old woman. I will not willingly give her up to you.*

"Robert has been asking after you, Dale. It seems you've been ignoring him of late."

"I'm not interested in him, all right? Stop trying to shamelessly manipulate me into giving you what you want. Can't you for once just be happy for me?" Dale's jaw tightened.

"At least now I understand your disinterest. This all seems rather sudden, don't you think?"

"You may think so, but I haven't been happy for quite a while. Now I am."

"That's your final decision?"

"Yes it is."

"Fine. Then—"

"Then we'll let young Claridge know that you're not available for the dance, won't we Martha?" Joseph once again glared at his wife as if daring her to speak.

A different expression came across Martha's face. I did not like it at all. "Fine. If you'll excuse me, I have to use the ladies' room." She stood, tossed her napkin down on her plate, and strode away.

Joseph watched his wife leave. "This is not good."

"What?" Dale asked.

"She's up to something. I'd suggest you leave town for a couple of days and allow her time to cool off. I'll see if I can find out what she plans to do about you two. In the meantime, I think it's time to call it a night."

Dale stood up and scraped her chair along the floor. She offered her hand to me and invited me to stand with her.

"Françoise. It has been a pleasure." I took her father's hand and waited for him to kiss mine. When he did not, I shook it the way men do.

"*Monsieur...* Joseph. It is a pleasure to meet you, sir. *Au revoir.* Please give our apologies to Martha." I waited patiently

1

while Dale gave her father a hug, but I could not hear the whispered conversation between the two of them.

We stepped out into the night air, and I breathed deeply with relief. It had been an emotional dinner. Dale walked with me to a horseless carriage, but I was loath to get in yet another scary beast.

"Can we walk?" I asked.

Without a word, she led me in the direction of her house, her emotional turmoil clearly visible even to my dulled senses. I so wanted to hold her in my arms and cheer her act of defiance. To do something I never had the chance to do. To make a stand for the one she loved.

"Speak to me, *cherie.*"

"Remember when I said some things hadn't improved in the last two hundred years? Not everyone is accepting of homosexuality. This city houses a lot of old families whose ancestors were part of the first settlers of this country. There are certain standards they live by, but homosexuality isn't one of them."

"What is this ball you had to attend?"

"It was nothing important, just some charity thing mother has organized."

"Charity? I do not understand."

"She's on a committee that raises money for a children's orphanage. They hold a charity ball as one of their major fund-raising events for the year."

"Then, by all means, you should attend."

"No, Françoise. I am *not* going, despite the good the ball does for the orphanage. It's an excuse for my mother to flaunt her influence. Not much fun, I'm afraid."

"Why did you not tell me you were wealthy?"

"It wasn't important."

"Not important? *Chérie*, I was worried about you using all your money to look after me."

"My father is a very successful financier, and my mother… my mother uses her power to indulge in the catty gossip and idle chatter that sometimes exist within these circles." She paused for a moment, as if deciding how much to tell me. "My parents are wealthy. They have a house that is almost as big as your château."

"But you led me to believe you were poor. Did you not trust me?"

"Of course I did."

"You hid it from me. I never hid anything from you. Perhaps you did not trust my intentions." I pulled away, hurt that she felt she could not trust me enough with this information. It was foolish, but my pride did not like the idea of being a "kept" woman. I had already been in that position once, and it pricked me for many a year.

I liked my independence. The thought of Dale controlling this relationship grated on me. I breathed deeply to calm myself.

"Please, my love. Please, don't turn away." Her plea broke my heart. How could I fight her when those guileless eyes looked deep into mine?

I changed the subject. "Why do they allow you to live alone in your house? Should you not have a *chaperon?*"

"A chaperone? Those days are long gone. In this century, a woman can work, live alone, and own a house—all without a man or a chaperone. Or a mother. I have money, but I choose not to touch it."

"But why? If you have it, why not use it?"

"Because it's my parents' money. I need to prove to myself that I can live on my own without help from them." No wonder I loved her. She was nearly as stubbornly independent as I was. "You can see how my mother is. Could you live with that all day, every day?" My nose wrinkled at the thought of being in the presence of that woman for every moment of every day. "I didn't think so."

"May I ask what your father said to you as we left?" When she hesitated, I withdrew. "No, it is obviously a private conversation. You do not have to tell me."

"It's not that. I felt sorry for him because he had to go home with her. She'll probably keep him up all night talking about us. He said that my inheritance was safe, and that he'd be in contact with me soon."

"There. You at least have your father's support, and mine."

"Very true." The conversation drifted off as we wandered down the pathway, and the fading light of day gave way to the dark hue of impending darkness. Lampposts were scattered liberally along our pathway to light the expanse of ground. As we walked, we passed some shops whose glass windows revealed statues dressed in the clothes of the day. I was fascinated with how far women had come, now dressed like the boldest of whores in the seedier streets of Paris in my time. The expanse of flesh exposed would have earned them a pretty *livre* in tips alone.

We continued to wander home and took our time to allow the cooling air and the slowly returning calm to ease the pent-up excitement from the meal. We walked in silence. I knew that my mind had absorbed all it could for one day and could take no more. I was sure Dale felt the same.

When we finally reached the loft, I closed the door softly behind her. I could see that she was conflicted. Now was not the time for love play but for loving support.

"Does her threat carry any strength?"

"I know she has political connections, and I know what she's capable of," Dale said with a sigh. "What I don't know is how far she's prepared to go against her own child."

"What will you do?"

"I suppose all we can do is wait."

We undressed for bed and slipped between the sheets. I pulled her body close to me, spooning her from behind. My hand slipped around her waist and idly brushed her cooling skin. I kissed her gently on her back. "And if she succeeds?"

Dale did not reply.

# Chapter 11

A gentle tugging woke me. As I lay entwined with Dale, a faint whispering started. *What was that?* I got up to investigate. I wandered from room to room but could not find the source of the sound. I checked the front door, but it was locked. I walked back to the bedroom. It was there that the whispering was at its loudest. "Dale?" There was no response from her. I stopped and listened again and realized that the sound came from the mirror.

"Why on earth are you keeping this thing?" A voice could be heard from the other side.

"Because it was hers. I wanted it." *I knew that voice.*

"It is just a mirror, Madeleine. It is useless. Why bother getting it repaired at all?"

"This is a trophy, Marcel. She took my love and betrayed me with that whore of hers. I took her life."

"So?"

"You think I am going live in this hovel all my life? Since they cleared out the aristocracy, that place has been sitting idle. Only a little while longer, and I am moving in. That mirror will sit right over my bed, just as she had done. Each morning and night it will remind me that what was once hers is now mine."

"Remind me never to upset you, woman."

Madeleine not only betrayed me, but she stole from me as well. Dale had been right all along.

Was I really hearing these voices, though, or was I dreaming? Was it my desperate need to go home or just wishful thinking?

I waited for the conversation to end. When I thought there was no motion behind the mirror, I touched its surface. For a moment, nothing happened, but the cool glass heated up under my wandering finger. I was about to lift it when the mirror bent, allowing the tip of my finger to disappear through the surface. My heart beat wildly at the prospect of what I thought had been lost but was now possible.

Without thought, I was ready to step through the mirror there and then.

A deep sigh emanated from the bed. I turned to see Dale's angelic face, so innocent in sleep. My heart broke at my dilemma. The perfect solution would be that she returned with me, but this was her home. I could solve her problem with her mother by stepping through and never returning. I knew, though, both our hearts would never allow such an action.

I leaned against the frame and absorbed the gentle sounds of shifting wood and muted voices as a balm for my restless soul. A hand rested on my shoulder as Dale joined me at the mirror. I wrapped her in my loving arms.

"What?" she whispered.

"Shhh."

The sound of a door opening filled the silence, followed by footsteps on a wooden floor. We were unable to see anything. Perhaps they had covered the mirror.

"Madeleine?" a voice said from the other side.

Dale gasped at the mention of Madeleine's name.

"Yes?"

"Can you bring out some potatoes?" The mirror must be in a storage room. The door closed again, and there was silence.

I drew Dale away from the mirror and moved into the kitchen for some tea and coffee.

"How is that possible?" she asked.

I looked sheepishly at her. "It may be my fault. I had a secret wish to go home." I turned away as I did not want to see the hurt in her eyes.

"You don't want to stay here?" That voice had a lost quality to it. I understood only too well that intonation. "Are you going to leave me?" My heart broke at the little girl crying out in desperation.

I pulled her into my embrace. "I will never leave you, *chérie*, and I will prove my love for you." I returned to the bedroom to seek out the stick of wood beside the bed. Why Dale called it a "bat" I did not know. It had no wings.

I had made up my mind. I could not leave her. As I swung the stick back to break the mirror, Dale grabbed my wrist and stepped in the way.

"Have you lost your mind, Françoise?"

"No, but if it is what you need to see, then I will do it. I am here for only you, Dale—not this world. If you wish to stay here, then so will I."

"Why do you want to go home?"

"When you were in my world, you could return to your home anytime you wished. I cannot. If something happens to you, I have nowhere to go." I thought for a moment. "Of course, if I return, I will be in Madeleine's grasp."

"You won't be returning without me to defend you then."

That brought a smile to my face. *My protector.*

After we climbed back into bed, her warm body squirmed against me. I looked into her dark, blue-gray eyes. "Do you need something?"

"Hmm…" A soft sweet smile crossed her face as she snuggled closer to me, as if trying to climb inside my skin. I pulled her closer still and allowed her head to settle into the hollow of my neck. I felt a gentle waft of air as she exhaled. Despite my apprehension, it was moments like these that I lived for. With that thought, I drifted off to sleep.

\* \* \*

The next morning, I asked her, "What are we doing today?"

"I was thinking of a drive to the country. I know a place where we can ride horses."

The thought of riding a horse again shot a thrill down my spine. "There are trees and grass still? Looking around here, I thought all that existed were these big buildings and horseless carriages."

"I'll have to rent a car to get us there, but there's some lovely country about an hour's drive away."

I was eager to see nature again, perhaps as a visible link to my past. With renewed vigor, I led Dale to the bathing chamber to indulge in a long, leisurely bath.

While Dale dried herself, I picked up a small stick with a brush on one end. "What is this?" I touched something on the other end and it sprang into life. "Ah, it is a vibrator." It moved so quickly that I could barely see it. I brushed the tip against my skin. "It tickles."

"Did you say something?" Dale's voice came from under her towel.

"*Oui*, and you said you did not have a vibrator." I moved it along my skin and the sensation was wonderful. I let the stick drift down my body until it hovered over my crotch.

"What are you doing?" Her head emerged from under the towel, and her eyes were wide with shock.

"I wish to try your vibrator."

"Vibrator? That's not a vibrator. It's my toothbrush!" She snatched it away just as the tip brushed my hairs.

"Please, so close."

"Ew, not with my toothbrush." She pulled the rope out of the wall and put the thing into a drawer. "Now I'll have to get a new head," she muttered.

"I like your head just the way it is."

"It's the… oh, never mind." She left the bathing room, looking disgusted.

*"Chérie?"* I stood and went to the door. "What did I do?" Perhaps it was something that she wanted to experience alone. I would have to see if she would let me watch.

* * *

Before we had a chance to set out for the day, there was a knock at the door. Dale glanced at me with worry. I followed her and waited.

Dale opened the door. "Mother."

"May I come in?" Martha said stiffly. Dale moved aside.

"Françoise."

I nodded my head but refused to say her name.

"May I have a moment alone with my daughter?"

"Stay here. You can hear what she has to say."

"Fine. If that's the way you want it." Martha took a couple of steps toward Dale. "If you are intent on continuing this sick way of living, you leave me with no choice but to take action."

"Don't threaten me, Mother," Dale said with a growl.

"Understand that I'm doing this for your own good."

"My own good? It's been a well-used phrase the last few days. Let's cut through the crap. It's for *your* own good, not mine."

"I can see where you got your stubbornness from."

"Just get to the point."

"You sound like your father."

"Let's keep Daddy out of this. It's between you and me."

"And her. Let's not forget her." Martha thrust her finger at me. "Remember. I have connections in high places. If you don't stop this nonsense right now, you'll force me to use them."

"What are you talking about?"

"Do you really want Françoise to end up in prison?"

"Prison? She hasn't committed any crime."

Martha had a glint in her eye, and she gave Dale a grim smile—one I did not like at all.

"Threats are below you, Mother."

"I will give you two days to end this once and for all." Without another word or farewell, Martha left.

"Perhaps I should leave." I did not want to, but Dale's predicament was about to become impossible.

"Don't you dare!" Dale went to the bedroom and returned with a bag. "Let's go riding."

"But…" The look on Dale's face told me not to argue.

She opened the door and stared at me until I moved. It would be a long day.

* * *

We finally arrived home at sunset after a day of riding. It had taken awhile for Dale to allow the morning's fight with her mother to settle, and the poor horses were exhausted by midday. Dale had found an excellent inn where we had lunch by a river, leaving us both sated and tired. However, my fingers were still numb after the drive home with Dale in her "car." *Mon Dieu!* The horseless carriage was going so fast that the countryside was a blur. I was sure I had left an impression of my fingers in the leather. I held back from kissing the ground as soon as I climbed out of the metal beast.

I went to the cold box to see what there was to drink and secretly wished for some red wine to settle my nerves. Instead, I poured myself some fruit juice.

"How about we go out for dinner?"

"Anything you wish." Perhaps there would be some red wine there. Besides, I really could not accept the idea that I had to cook. That was so… *bourgeois*. And the washing afterwards…

I refused to ride in the car with Dale again, so we walked. We found a quaint little inn a short distance from her home. It was small, but warm and friendly, and I could enjoy a nice claret, full of body and pleasingly relaxing to my unsteady nerves. Somehow, I had to convince her to slow down when she drove, or we would be walking everywhere.

The food was excellent, but the company was better. Dale sat opposite me in a short dress with tiny straps that held it up, leaving her shoulders bare to the evening air. I looked around and wondered if her lack of clothes would cause a shock. Her state of undress barely caused a ripple of concern, except for the occasional glance of admiration from the male diners. I turned my attention back to my dinner companion and looked at the expanse of skin. A hint of makeup covered her face, which accentuated her eyes that sparkled in the low candlelight. I felt that pain in my heart again, one I associated with my feelings for her. She was so beautiful. I was not aware that she was staring at me until I saw my emotion reflected back at me in her own eyes.

"You look very beautiful tonight," she said.

"I do? I am not wearing anything special." I ducked my head, but not before I was sure she saw my blush.

"Well, you look absolutely stunning. *Incroyable.*" Before I said something stupid, I started to eat. Shyly, I watched her from the corner of my eye, and I again felt that tug in my heart.

After dinner, we walked leisurely back home. We stopped often to look in store windows and find the occasional darkened door to stop and kiss. The day that had started so stressful and upsetting had turned into a most pleasant day indeed... one that I would keep close to my heart.

# Chapter 12

It had been a long day for both of us, and I offered my warmth to her in bed. Despite our burning passion for one another, I declined her silent offer.

"You don't want my touch?" Her voice was tentative.

I sighed deeply as I tried to gain some courage for what I wanted to say. I rolled onto my side so that we faced one another. "Dale," my voice rumbled over her name, lovingly caressing it as if it had skin, muscle, and bone. *"Mon coeur*, I love you. What beats in here"—I tapped my chest—"beats only for you, now and always." A lone tear trickled down her cheek. "There is nothing… *nothing*... that I would not do for you. All you have to do is ask."

I touched her cheek and slowly brushed over the fine skin to try to convey my sincerity. I took her fingers with my other hand and gently placed them over my heart. "All that I am is yours, Dale, but why you want this ugly old thing is beyond me." I managed to extract a smile from her that, in turn, caused me to smile.

"You do not have to be afraid of me… of us. There is nothing you can ask of me that I will not give you." Her eyes skittered away from mine as I tried to make her feel at ease with what we had. "Tonight is about enduring love, not lust. We are both tired, Dale. It has been quite an adventure today, has it not? Will you allow me to hold you while we sleep?"

I felt there was no need to ask, but I wanted her to know it was not something she had done wrong. Dale nodded and snuggled into me. She rested her head in the crook of my neck, and we drifted off to sleep.

I was drawn out of my slumber by a frantic knock on the door. I nudged Dale, who gave me a look of bewilderment and fright. *Sacrebleu!*

"Hello?" That familiar voice sent us scrambling to find our clothes.

"Dale, honey? It's me. Let me in."

"Shit!" After she was dressed, Dale reached for the door and opened the metal lock. "Daddy? What's wrong?"

Joseph stepped into her house. He closed the door behind him and relocked it. He was clearly afraid, as if the Devil himself was on his tail.

"Where have you been? I've been trying to contact you all day. Honey, you have to get out of here." He peered out of the window as he spoke, as if searching for the danger.

"What? Slow down. What are you talking about?"

He turned back to us. "Your mother is on the warpath about you and Françoise. I don't know what you said to her this morning, but she made a call or two." He looked at me in sympathy. "I'm sorry, Dale. She's not going to stand for this." He reached into his pocket and removed some paper. "Here. Take this. It's part of your trust fund."

The packet of paper easily filled her hand to the limit. It was full of notes. "But why?"

"Until I can fix this mess she has caused, honey, you and your partner have to disappear for a while." Despite the circumstances, I could not help but smile at the term.

"Tell me why."

"There's no time. You have to go… now!"

There was a loud knock at the door. Dale grabbed her father's arm. "What?"

"Those men at the door I suspect are from the FBI. Your mother phoned an acquaintance at the Bureau to check into Françoise's background, and it seems she doesn't exist." He watched us for a reaction to this piece of news.

"I don't suppose she would."

"Now the FBI is involved. Since there is no record of her existence, they immediately became suspicious. They think she might have ties to terrorists. Will you tell me what's going on?"

Dale glanced at me. "Daddy, if I told you, you wouldn't believe me, but Françoise is not a terrorist." I could tell he was disappointed she did not say more. Dale looked at me again and was about to speak.

Just as her mouth opened, there was another bang on the door. "Open up, Ms. Wincott, FBI!"

"Get out of here. Go!" He shoved us toward the window. How could we flee through there? We were on the fourth floor. "Use the fire escape. I'm so sorry, honey. You know what your mother's like."

Dale pulled to a stop before we got to the window. "Yeah, I know how she is." Sadness tinged her words. We turned our gaze to the mirror. We had only one place to go.

"Daddy, do one thing for me."

"Anything. You know that."

"Please, please take care of this mirror. Keep it safe for me until I can return for it. I'm sorry I can't say more."

The pounding got louder, accompanied by a bang as someone charged the door.

"Now, get out of here and I'll try to delay them." Joseph pushed us toward the balcony again.

"Good bye, Daddy. I love you."

"Good bye, sweetheart. I love you, too."

As Joseph turned to open the door, we rushed toward the mirror and crossed a barrier that we thought had been lost to us. It was so strange to feel that sensation again, like a forgotten dream. I had to push through the material covering the frame on the other side, batting it away in a frantic effort to complete the crossover. We heard loud voices in Dale's house. It sounded like her father had tried in vain to stop them entering. Thinking they could see us, we hid in the shadows quietly while they searched her rooms, our absence frustrating them.

"Dale?" We lifted the cover. Joseph stood in front of the mirror, our clothes in his hands, looking straight at us but not seeing. Was this mirror so special that it was our domain only?

"Daddy?" She sounded lost and bewildered. He did not answer. His hand rose to the glass to touch it, but it did not come through. He again looked at the clothes and smiled knowingly at the mirror.

"I love you, pun'kin. Goodbye." He shook with emotion as he said goodbye to his daughter, possibly for the last time. He threw our clothes on the bed and bent to pick up the discarded packet of bills. He placed it in his pocket before the two burly men returned to the bedroom. "I told you, she's not here." As we watched, his gaze moved to the mirror, probably in the hope of seeing us before he left.

"Check the fire escape," the first man said.

The other man went to the balcony and returned a moment later. "Not there."

"You going to tell us where they've gone?"

"Like I told you, I don't know."

"Then why are you here?"

"My daughter asked me to pick up something for her."

"Like what?" I heard the suspicion in that voice

"Just this mirror. She wanted me to put it into storage for her. She gave me no other instructions."

The man shoved Joseph in an effort to get to the mirror and knocked him over. As we stood there watching in horror, Joseph lost his balance and fell against the wall. The fall dislodged the mirror from the wall, shattering the glass as it hit the floor. Our only way to her home was now lost to us.

"Goodbye, Daddy," Dale whispered. I was all she had now, unless it was possible we could ever take that leap again. But at least we had an ally in her time now, a guardian of the mirror and our secret. We would have to hope against hope that he repaired the glass and gave us a chance for Dale to return to her time.

I found a quiet corner to draw her to me. We lowered ourselves to the ground while she grieved for her loss. Her mother had ruined Dale's chance of happiness, all because it did not fit into her quaint view of the world. She was a sad, sad woman, but I would not voice my opinions to Dale. Despite all that had happened, Martha was still her mother.

\* \* \*

Darkness surrounded us, much like Dale's waning spirit. A faint glow came from a covered window. Shifting slowly in a room filled with potential for danger, I tried to make my way to the muted brightness. I pulled aside the rough-hewn material and more light filled the room with the pre-dawn grayness. I looked around me. So, my maid had been busy indeed. Madeleine had filled the back room of her meager home with my property. She had stolen not only the mirror but also a whole room full of items from throughout the château.

My anger blossomed at this betrayal. I had invited her into my bedroom, a position of trust, and this was how she repaid me. Hell hath no fury like a woman scorned—a rule that Madeleine evidently lived by. Well, I was in the mood for a little revenge of my own, but first things first.

I recognized a pile of my clothes, not worth much to sell. Other things she had collected also had little monetary value but had great worth to me personally. It was like she wanted to possess me which, in her own twisted way, seemed exactly what she was trying to do. I wondered if she realized how precious the mirror was.

Unwittingly, she had performed a great service for us by giving us an avenue of escape when there was none. I shivered at the thought of being stuck in Dale's world, separated from her by prison bars.

I carried over the clothes to the window to get a better look at them in the light. My riding clothes and an old dress should do nicely. I handed over the dress to Dale and put the pants and shirt on, glad to feel a bit of warmth against my chilled skin. The sight of Dale in my dress made me smile.

Before we tried to leave, I found a small sack and filled it with some food. In the light of day, we would not be able to move about much, for I was a hunted woman. I approached the mirror and stripped back the cloth to search for the hidden mechanism to gain access to the jewels. I would be damned if she would get her hands on those. Covering the mirror once more, I quickly checked to see that nothing was out of place. For the present, the mirror was safe enough in Madeleine's hands.

Carefully, I opened the door and held my breath as it creaked in protest. There was still another room to negotiate before we could escape. We waited a moment or two for any disturbance, but all I heard was the settling of the timbers and the loud snore coming from the bed in the far corner. Quickly and quietly, we left the cabin, glad to be out of harm's way for a while.

I did not recognize where we were immediately. At least we were not in the town where we would have had to make our escape through the main street. At the back of the cabin was a wooded area. We hurried there and faded into the gloom of the surrounding trees.

We followed the edge of the wooded area and headed in a direction that was a mystery to us, but I hoped it would ultimately lead to a safe haven. The ground was cold under my feet. I wished for my old riding boots. Perhaps I should have looked harder to find shoes in that pile of booty, but my need not to get caught overrode my need for shoes.

"Where are we going?" Dale's soft, melodious voice carried a nervous quality to it, and it expressed my own fear.

"I have absolutely no idea." I grabbed her chilled hand in mine out of a need to feel her skin against my own. "Let us keep moving."

I was about to give up when we stumbled out onto the extensive grounds of a château that I knew and loved so well. It was my own. It seemed that I was *une comtesse* without a home.

It took us time to cover the open ground between the woods and the château. We had to move quickly to avoid detection. When we reached the outer wall, I touched it and felt its solid strength under my fingers. Home… I was home. I dared not look into Dale's eyes because I knew her pain. Was this not how I felt in her time? Lost and out of place? It seemed that neither of us was completely at ease in the other's time, but one of us would have to compromise if we were to stay together. If? I would never leave her, just as I was sure she would never leave me. Perhaps we would find a time that we could call our own.

We tried the front door and found it locked. "What now?" Dale asked.

"We try the windows and the back door." Our search ended in the same outcome. The château was boarded up tight. I searched my memory for any forgotten entrance that my husband had shown me all those years ago. There was… something. Where was it?

I walked around the house, trying to recall the secret recess in the stonework. It sat in the back corner of the building and fitted into the shadows of the blocks. A few steps away there was a hidden trigger, much like the one on the mirror that required a number of movements before revealing its secret. It was designed so as not to trigger accidentally but to be deliberately opened in a choreographed number of specialized touches. I could not open it on the first attempt and had to try a number of times before my memory returned to fill in the missing pieces.

The passageway was not wide but large enough to let us pass through one by one. I led the way into the darkness and moved forward by feel alone until I reached a solid barrier. I felt for a rope. It was old and in danger of breaking. I pulled steadily as the barrier slid to one side to allow us to emerge through a wooden panel at the back of the kitchen pantry.

My apprehension grew as I watched the panel slide back in place. I had fled this place in a moment of chaos. What of my possessions would remain? We moved through the rooms, and my heart broke at the devastation around us. Anything useful had been stripped. The huge crystal chandelier hanging in the foyer lay shattered on the floor. Pieces of broken furniture were strewn everywhere. Many of the paintings hanging on the walls were either missing or vandalized.

Dale touched my back, gently rubbing in small circles in comfort. She had to know what I was feeling. This madness was born out of anger by people who had no interest in preserving their cultural history. We moved upstairs to my bedroom, finding yet more destruction. My bed was gone, but I knew where that went. A trophy indeed. *May you rot in hell, Madeleine.*

"We will stay here for now," I told her.

"Are you sure?"

"We have nowhere else to go. Perhaps a rest will clear my mind to find something better. Let me give it some thought."

"Françoise, I... I'm sorry."

"So am I. Now we both have something to be sorry for." This was the lowest point in my sad life, when it should have been my happiest, at home with the woman of my dreams in my arms. Instead, my people were hunting me, and Dale's own mother would do anything to ruin her happiness. Where did our fate go so drastically wrong?

*  *  *

My back was stiff from sleeping on the floor. The light of day made the destruction even worse, and I began to question our decision to cross over. But we could not stay in her world either; we were fugitives in both worlds now. I stood and stretched my tight muscles. Dale also stood to stretch after napping in such an awkward position.

Not long ago, we were in this room, and Dale lay on the bed in all her naked splendor awaiting my touch. I sighed and wished for that delightful moment once more.

"What do we do now?"

"First, we will have something to eat." I reached into the dirty sack I found at the cabin, pulled out a piece of fruit, and passed it to Dale.

"Things aren't going well, are they?"

I had to stop myself from snapping at her for such an obvious statement. "No, *chérie,* they are not."

"Any plans?"

I moved over to the now cold fireplace, hunkered down in the ashes, and reached for the back wall. "Remember when I said we did not use a bank?" I shifted a large brick at the bottom of the back wall, slowly eased it out, and reached inside to extract a number of coin sacks.

Moving to Dale, I poured out the contents of one bag into her hands. "I think this should get us out of France. All we have to do is avoid getting caught or killed on the way."

"And how do you plan on doing that?"

"Despite what you may think, I still possess an old friend or two who I am sure will help us." Dale remained silent. I only hoped that these friends still existed in the aftermath of a revolution.

\* \* \*

There was not one scrap of food, one stick of furniture, or one piece of clothing to be had. Curtains had been ripped down and either taken or shredded. I salvaged one square of cloth barely the size of my bed—it was all that was left of my life. Still, this one piece of material would be worth its weight in gold. I extracted a tidy sum of coins from the fireplace and used this cloth as a makeshift sack to carry it all. Let us hope we had the chance to spend it.

We could not stay here. I needed to find out what was happening, who our allies were, and who could no longer be trusted. On top of the list was Madeleine whose betrayal had shaken me to the core. I had thought that my household was a harmonious one, but apparently, I was the only one who believed that.

"Come, we need to leave here."

"But why? It's a roof over our heads."

"Anyone could return at a moment's notice. I have another place in mind that will suffice and should be a lot more comfortable than the wooden floor to sleep on."

Our food would not last forever. There was no water. The door to the secret passageway was about to give out, and using another exit would alert anyone nearby that someone was inside. We had no choice.

It took the rest of the morning to travel the two miles to the abandoned barn that held a very special memory for me. The old building looked the same as that fateful day... which was what? A week ago? Perhaps less. A gentle chuckle escaped my lips as I remembered the embarrassed little girl who showed me a spark of her sexuality.

"What are you laughing at?" I nodded my head in the direction of the barn. "Oh... yeah... that." A light blush traveled up from her chest to her cheeks.

"Ah sweet, sweet Dale. You are so adorable. Still so shy to the world, are you not?" I grabbed her hand in mine and carried the bundle of money over my shoulder.

The building was situated in the far corner of the estate, out of the way and long forgotten. Its position sat halfway between the château and the local village. It was closer to our enemies than I would have liked, but it was also closer to the goods that we needed. I found a suitable hiding place within the barn for the jewels and money and removed one sack of coins to buy some supplies. "Come, I have to see a friend about a way out of here."

On our walk to the village through the forest, I taught Dale a few French words for her to repeat. My face was recognizable, and she would have to make contact for me. Her strange accent made it difficult to understand the words perfectly. She would be identified as a foreigner immediately, but perhaps it would be enough to achieve our purpose.

From the edges of the undergrowth, I watched nervously as she walked across the main street toward the local blacksmith. She was adorable to watch, her hands waving around in an animated fashion as she tried to repeat what I had taught her. She pointed in my direction. I held my breath and waited to see if my faith in this man was warranted.

I exhaled with relief as both of them walked back across the street and entered a dwelling I knew was Gérard's house. I slipped along to the back window, and it opened to reveal my mentor and my friend.

"Françoise, I thought you were dead. My God, child, you survived!"

"Gérard, my friend, how are you keeping? I need help—"

"Say no more. Tell me what you need."

"My friend and I have to get to Nantes and on a ship to England or anywhere other than France."

"It is very dangerous out there, so be careful. There are roving bands of armed thugs, attacking anyone who opposes them, all in the name of freedom."

"I know. I think we will need a disguise and some horses."

"I can get you some clothes, food, and blankets tonight. The horses may take a few days though. Things have gotten even harsher since the overthrow."

"Overthrow?"

"There is no more king, no more parliament, and no more aristocracy." I had read this in Dale's book, but here was the harsh reality.

"How much time has passed since the attack at the château?"

"It has been just over three weeks, you know that." Three weeks? Madeleine had said a few weeks. She could not have gotten the mirror fixed that quickly had it been any sooner.

"I have lost track of time, on the run."

"Let me start getting things together for you. I will leave a package every day before sunset near the old well. About twenty paces away is a hidden cache in a hollowed out tree. It will be safer for you if we do not meet often. If you need me, send your friend to me." He was about to leave, but I stopped him for one more important thing.

"Gérard, please, I have one more favor to ask of you. I have a special package that needs transporting to Nantes for shipping. It is vital that it gets there, my friend, and safeguarded at the other end until our arrival. Can you meet me with your wagon sunset tomorrow at the well to pick it up?" I handed over the sack of coins. "Take this. It will pay for everything."

"Françoise, this is way too much."

"Please, for my sake just take it. You are risking a lot by helping me. Not only do we need horses, but we will also need protection. Please, just accept the coin with my blessing."

I could see that he wanted to argue, but I also knew that he would be suffering in this time of unrest. Any coin would be of great help to him. "For now, Gérard, please take care. I will see you tomorrow then." The window began to close. "Oh, one more thing, can you add some parchment and writing implements in tonight's package as well?" Confusion creased his brow, but he did not question it.

"Farewell, my friend."

"And you, too, my little *coquin.*" I had forgotten that name. So long ago…

Dale emerged from the dwelling, idly standing in the shadows. She made her way behind the building before she slipped back into the undergrowth where I waited for her.

"So now what?"

"Not much more we can do until sunset. Let us go." The sun was shining, the birds were singing, and I had the love of my life holding my hand. It would nearly be perfect, except for the fact that just about every French man and woman in the land wanted me dead. While we made our way back to the barn to take refuge for the rest of the day, I was already thinking of ways to have Dale.

I examined that thought. I knew I had been reckless with past lovers, but Dale was like a fever. It was a dangerous precedent to have someone buried so deep inside you. If something happened to her... a shiver ran through me at the thought.

"You all right?"

"Fine." I looked over and saw concern written on that youthful face. "Truly, *chérie,* everything is fine."

Despite the turbulence of this time, the forest was empty. I imagined that any aristocrat wishing to live had long departed this area, heading to the coast to escape to England, Spain, or perhaps even Rome. Anywhere but here. It was a blessing, therefore, that we had only just arrived. The madness of the last few weeks had subsided, and our presence was not expected, so we were not sought out. Thank goodness for small mercies.

# Chapter 13

We arrived mid-afternoon at the barn and ate from our meager supply. Although the food did not fill us, it did lessen the hunger. Hopefully, Gérard would add to our supply tonight, and we could eat a decent meal.

I looked up to see the sun streaming in through the familiar hole in the roof. Beams of light lanced through the air like lightning bolts out of the sky. I led Dale up the rickety ladder, as she led me not so long ago, and a familiar burning started in the pit of my stomach. I wanted to make my memories real, to once again see her body clothed in rays of light, casting a fiery glow over her.

It was too dangerous to partake of this particular delicacy, but I could not stop myself from sampling it. Slowly, I drew her down to the hay and lovingly brushed her skin with my fingertips. For the next hour, I indulged my senses by nothing more than holding her in my arms. I would never have enough of Dale, but the sun was approaching the tree line, and we had to find the well before dark.

"Come, *mon coeur,* let us go get some food."

"Mmm, food." Her stomach rumbled, which sent us both into peals of laughter.

I patted her stomach. "I agree with her."

We set off for the grove of trees in search of food. Following its line in the direction of the château, we found what I had been searching for—the cabin Madeleine used as her home. I had forgotten that this structure existed, but now its location would be burned forever into my memory as the home of my downfall.

As we neared the shack, Dale asked, "What are we doing here?" I pulled her back into the forest so we could carry on a conversation without being heard.

"I am going to get that mirror."

"This is crazy. Do you want to get caught?"

"Of course not, but I will be damned if she is going to have it."

"It's just a mirror, Françoise. It's not worth your life."

"Just a mirror? How can you say that?" Her head dropped, and she acknowledged what I said was true. I tipped her head up to see her face. "This is our only link, Dale. If I have any chance at all of getting it back, I have to try."

"But what good will it do me if you die in the attempt?"

"It will get you home. You have a father waiting there for you who loves you deeply. I like him. He is a good man, and I am sure he will do everything in his power to protect you."

"If something happens to you, my love, the mirror will be of no use to me. If you die, I will follow you."

"No, please do not make such a decision. You are young and have your whole life ahead of you. You will find someone else..." She touched her finger to my lips to silence me.

"There will be no one else, my love. Only you."

"Very well. As long as you do the same for me." We had made our pact. "Now stay here." I crept up to the window and listened for signs of movement inside.

"You are such a pig, Marcel."

"What are you complaining about now, woman?"

"I suppose you are off to the tavern again tonight then?"

"There is nothing to keep me here."

"If you think you are going alone, forget it. I know all about you and that barmaid, Emilie."

"Jealousy does not become you, Madeleine."

I wondered how long it would be before she turned on him as well. I returned to Dale, and we moved on toward the abandoned well and food. Half an hour later, I felt around in the hollow log for what had been left behind by Gérard, pleased to find some packets of food, blankets, a lantern and flint, a flask for water, and the parchment, quill, and ink I had asked for. Filling the flask at the well, I considered my next move.

We arrived at the barn and feasted on the food, gorging ourselves on the bread, cheese, and cooked meat offered by Gérard. After our hunger subsided, I wasted no time to use the parchment and ink to write a note for my eyes only.

"I suppose asking you to stay here is pointless, is it not?" Dale's pursed lips gave me an answer I already knew. "Come on then." Grabbing her hand, I led her back to the cabin. I was glad to find that the occupants had already left.

Still being careful, I gently lifted the latch to avoid making a sound. The door creaked open, and my breath was in my throat as I eased inside. With some relief, I saw that they had indeed gone, which left me to sort through my belongings in peace.

My most important mission was removing the mirror. I shuffled the heavy object through the mountain of stolen items to the door and stepped outside to face the trees. "Dale, can you help me, please." Like a ghost, she materialized out of the mass of bushes and approached me quickly and quietly. The task was a lot easier with the two of us. We were able to carry the frame quite a distance from the hovel to deep into the bushes. I returned to the shack and sorted through what was left. My anger grew with the amount of thievery that had taken place. I found my riding boots and a smaller pair of shoes for Dale. While it would not be a good fit, it was enough for her to be able to cover her dainty feet.

"We're not going to carry this all the way back to the barn, are we?" Our temporary home was only a mile away, but it would be hard work to get the mirror that far. The well, on the other hand, was about half that distance and Gérard's hiding place.

"No. Gérard will collect this from us tomorrow evening. We will move it to the well and save the extra distance."

The sun had set for the day. Its fading glow barely touched the treetops as we approached the well. I looked for a suitable hiding place to store our precious package and found a low, dense bush that would protect it from the overnight dew. I replaced the jewels in their hiding place and entrusted its safe passage to a beloved friend. We wrapped the mirror in heavy canvas and laid it down before covering it with branches and leaves. I only hoped it would still be there when we returned.

"There is nothing we can do now. Let us go home." Twilight had touched the sky by the time we reached the barn. In the gloom, we could barely see the supplies left by Gérard. I would so love to have lit the lantern, but it would be foolish to have a naked flame in a barn full of hay and straw. We retired early to sleep buried in the straw and under our new blankets.

I woke in the middle of the night and left Dale asleep in the warm nest of blankets. I had someone to visit, and nothing was going to stop me.

* * *

The next evening, Gérard helped me lift the mirror onto his wagon and cover it with a pile of hay.

"You know, a strange thing happened today. Your former maid…"

"Yes?"

"Madeleine. She was arrested today for murdering her lover." He watched me closely as he told me the news.

"I never thought she was capable of that." I feigned innocence.

"It seems it was over a dispute about the sale of a mirror."

I looked at the ground because I did not want to stare into those dark eyes. "Imagine that."

"Yes, that is what I thought." Finally, I looked up, and he held his gaze. "Do you want to tell me what happened?"

"Nothing happened." He lifted the hay and fixed his attention on the frame, before shifting to mine a moment later.

"He sold me the mirror," I said. "That is all. I paid him for it. In fact, I even left a receipt."

"In plain sight, I suppose. You know very well that Madeleine has a fiery temper."

"I cannot help it if he did not remember selling it."

"No?"

"Well, he was asleep at the time of the transaction."

"Why, Françoise?"

It would have been safer to not answer, but I could not help myself. "Why? She betrayed me. She stole from me! This is my mirror. It was hanging in my bedroom. She sleeps in my bed. Her cottage is on my land, and her house is full of property stolen from my home." My voice grew steadily louder as I vented my anger. "How am I supposed to feel?"

"Times have changed, little rascal. You have to let this go and get on with your life."

I sighed deeply. "I know… I know. But I did not put the weapon in her hand." Curiosity got the better of me. "By the way, how did she kill him?"

"With a kitchen knife."

"Probably from my kitchen, I wager," I muttered. "When is the trial?"

"The magistrate will see her in the morning. The hanging will probably take place the day after that. I will try to have the horses ready by then so you can slip away while the town attends the execution. In the meantime, I will send the supplies to you as we had arranged."

"Thank you for the blankets last night, Gérard. They were most welcome."

"What are you going to do until the horses are ready?" He must have noticed my smirk. "Ah, you little rascal, with such a delectable bedmate, I would probably do the same."

I touched his shoulder. "It can still happen. Do not give up."

"No, my time has passed."

"I do not accept that. You are a wonderful man and would make a lucky woman very happy. Please, my father, do not despair." Did I just say father? I smiled at him and patted his muscled shoulder. I could see he was holding back the tears.

"Go on with you now and enjoy your young filly, and let me get on with my work." He shuffled away, but not before I pulled him into a hug. "I love you, child."

"And I, too, Papa." Tears threatened to fall as I bid a final farewell to the only family who ever gave a damn about my well-being. "I will try to get back some day."

"Until that time, Françoise, keep safe."

"You, too, Gérard. You, too."

We had another day to wait before we could leave. Dale tempted me often to indulge my passion, and it took all my willpower to say no. It was far too dangerous. To divert myself from the temptation, I took on the task of teaching Dale to speak French. She would need to learn some basic words so as not to be at a complete disadvantage on our journey. Even with my time occupied, I did not like being a prisoner on my own estate. I was impatient to finally move around in the outside world.

As promised, there were two horses in the stables. Certainly not thoroughbreds, but anything more than the nags we had would draw attention. Sitting on the ground outside the stalls was a pile of clothes with a note sitting on top:

"Welcome, Philippe Théroux, and his daughter, Isabelle!"

A man? It was probably for the best. Two women traveling alone would be dangerous. I picked up one small pile of clothes and handed it to Dale. "There you go, Isabelle."

"Isabelle?"

"For now, you are Isabelle Théroux, daughter of Philippe." I pointed to my chest. I tried not to laugh as she raised an eyebrow.

"Get changed so we can leave here." I reached for my pants and swiftly undid the buttons. As I pulled the shirt over my head, I heard a gentle gasp. I smiled at her reaction, and I looked forward to reciprocating the emotion when she removed her dress. Naked, I turned her around to reach for the buttons and laces. Slowly, her pale skin was revealed to me, and I drew my lips to the expanse of flesh, placing whispers of kisses across her shoulders.

I pulled back suddenly and muttered, "We do not have time for this." She sighed, and I chuckled. It was nice to know that she felt the same way.

We faced away from one another to dress. Otherwise our departure would be delayed by another hour or so. Gérard had included some rather interesting additions to our costumes, and it made me wonder about the man I thought of as my adopted father.

Bracing myself for the obvious comment to come, I turned around to face Dale. She was breathtaking in the peasant dress she wore, simple but elegant, and it outlined her body to perfection. It took me a moment to realize that she was staring at me. More to the point, she was staring at the bulge in my pants.

I waited for her eyes to meet mine, but she seemed focused on it. I cleared my throat. She blushed furiously at being caught looking so blatantly at my crotch.

"Problem?"

"An interesting addition, don't you think?"

I looked down at the lump sitting there. It was... different. "I would say Gérard thought it was essential that I looked in every way a man." I thought for a moment. "These pants are fairly tight. It might be more obvious if there was not a bulge."

I could tell that Dale tried to keep eye contact with me, but her gaze would drop down my body. I wondered...

I moved closer. *Chérie,* " I whispered. I took her hand in mine and drew it down my body to let her feel the small insert that was sewn into the pants. Her breathing picked up as she touched it, but she would not look at me. I grasped her chin and forced her to meet my gaze. "There is nothing I would not do for you, Dale. Even this." I sighed deeply. "But I cannot grant your wish now. Besides, such an *accoutrement* I would have to purchase in London or Paris. I am sorry, but I am not going to Paris for it."

She laughed nervously and took a step back, finally taking in the rest of my costume. "What happened to..." She waved at my chest.

"To?" I waved my hands in a similar fashion over my breasts. "I chopped them off." Her jaw dropped open for a second. I laughed and opened the top two buttons to show the material binding my breasts. "I do not think a man would be so well endowed, my sweet."

"Perhaps, *my* man."

"Your man?"

"Yes, Philippe. I think we are being incestuous here."

"We could always pose as husband and wife." I watched her reaction to my suggestion.

Her eyes widened at my statement. "What are you talking about?"

I took a deep breath and fell to my knees before her. "Will you be my wife?" If the question were not so serious, I would have laughed at her almost comical expression.

"Are you serious?"

"Of course I am serious."

"But why?"

"Because I love you. Why else?"

"But it's so soon."

"We have just made a pact in death. We cannot be any more committed than that. I will never leave you, and I know you will never leave me." She nodded. "It will never be legal, but in my heart and my mind we will be married, if you will have me."

Tears came unbidden to my eyes as I waited for her decision. Moments passed, and still she did not answer. I stood. "Never mind. It was a foolish notion of mine," I muttered and turned away.

She reached for my hand to halt my progress. She lifted her other hand to my cheek and gently stroked it. "Of course I will, my heart. How could you ever doubt it?"

I released a breath. "So, *Madame Théroux.* No more talk of incestuous liaisons."

"Good. I'm not into that kinky stuff anyway."

"Kinky?"

"Sexual acts out of the normally accepted practices."

I looked at my crotch and then back at her, drawing a blush to her pale skin. "Whatever you say, but let anyone stop me from having you and they will have a fight on their hands." I moved inside the stall and pulled out the weapons left tucked away. Another note sat beside the sword—a letter of introduction to our contact in Nantes who would have the mirror. Tucking the parchment away safely, I attached the belt holding the rapier around my waist to let the sword dangle at my side.

I noticed her confusion.

"We are going on a dangerous journey. Our very lives are at stake. We cannot go unarmed."

"But I would be useless with a weapon."

"Then, it is just as well that I know how to use one." I saw the question in her eye. "Gérard taught me how to ride and fight. It is not seemly for a woman to do so, but when have I ever played by the rules?" Gérard had been my redeeming angel in those days married to *le Comte de Villerey*. He came out once a week to attend to the horses but took the time afterwards to teach me all the manly arts. After my husband's death, Gérard visited me often, no longer bound to a weekly visit. We enjoyed each other's company and a good fight. Now, all the hard work would come back to me ten-fold in the coming weeks as I protected us on the dark and dangerous road ahead.

"Let us go." I steered my docile mount out of the stable onto the path leading to the nearby village. Dale followed a few steps behind, her cloak pulled low over her face. I looked at the château, saddened by the circumstance that had forced me to leave it. We made our way to the barn to pick up the rest of the supplies and, of course, the coin. I packed the coin tightly in the bottom of the saddle bags to try to dampen the sound of its movement.

We were back on the road half an hour later, but I steered the horses toward the village. I sensed Dale as she moved her mount up next to me.

"What are you doing? We're heading right for the town, Françoise."

"I know. I have to see this."

"And you're going to risk everything to see Madeleine hang?"

"Everyone will be too focused on the execution to notice me."

"I hope you're right."

"And if not, then you will have to come in and get me."

"Yeah. Right. This is really foolish."

"Do you think I do not know that? It is something I must do." This was one time where my heart overruled my head. As Madeleine took from me, I would take from her.

I left Dale in the company of Gérard to spare her the horror of seeing someone die. I stood in the crowd, hood in place, and gave off an air of negligent menace to those around me. The condemned was dragged through the center of the yelling horde, her once long, dark locks now cut short and her clothes barely more than a rough-hewn shift. Those dark eyes looked around wildly at the pressing crowd, real fear written across her face as the reality of her fate sunk in.

I stepped forward to the front of the crowd to let her see me as she passed. Eyes widened in recognition, and her mouth opened and closed in silent terror.

"An eye for an eye, Madeleine." My voice was dark and low. I wanted this woman to know her accuser and to take that knowledge with her to the grave. I had not thought myself a vengeful woman, but here I was making a liar of myself. I turned away as her cries about my presence went unheeded.

I made my way back through the crowd. Their voices reached a crescendo as Madeleine took the last few steps she would ever take. I reached my horse and turned one final time to watch a woman I had thought I knew cry as the thick rope tightened around her neck. Her head tipped back as if to beg God for salvation. There was a moment of silence before a thud as the block was kicked away, leaving the woman suspended in midair by the rope around her neck. A cheer rose up to the sky.

I jumped into the saddle, glad to be leaving this pitiful, vengeful little town. Dale was my life now. We would travel this road together to find our own home where we could live in peace and happiness. I knew in my heart now that I had changed. I would do anything to protect Dale… anything.

An eye for an eye.

# Part Three: Flight

# Chapter 14

"Are we there yet?"

They had been traveling only a few hours and already Françoise was annoyed. The small leather attachment in her pants was digging into her crotch with every sway of the broken-down horse underneath her. Now, Dale was making inane comments.

"I always wanted to say that," she said cheerfully.

Françoise stared hard at her.

"Sorry," she muttered.

"No, I am sorry, *chérie*. But you do not have to be so gleeful about this."

"You think I don't know what's going on, do you?"

"Then why are you so happy about it?"

"Because I'm here with you."

Françoise smiled. "Ah, Dale, what would I do without you?"

"I'm not going to give you the chance to find out."

"You do not trust me?" Françoise raised an eyebrow.

"Yeah, but…"

Françoise shifted the horse closer to Dale's and leaned over to pat her hand that tightly gripped the reins. "No. There will never be anyone else. You must believe that." The approach of a wagon from the other direction stopped their conversation. "Say nothing, *chérie.*"

Françoise turned toward the shaggy-haired man and old woman on the battered wagon.

"Good day, monsieur. Good day, madame. Do you travel from Nantes?" The man glared at her in obvious suspicion. "What is the road like up ahead?"

"Nantes is a madhouse, monsieur. It is not a wise place to take your young bride right now."

"How so, monsieur?"

"People everywhere are trying to take refuge or seek a berth on one of the ships leaving the port. There are gangs of vigilantes roaming the streets in search of aristocrats and the helpless. Many of them are traveling this road as well. You two could easily fall prey to such bullies." Françoise was sure that in his eyes, he saw a tall young man of sleek build and a young woman whose beauty would mark her for ravishment.

"Nevertheless, we have business there and must go. I thank you for your help." Françoise gently kicked the side of her nag and nudged the horse into motion past the dilapidated wagon.

Dale followed. "What did he say?"

"We have to find another route."

"He said that?"

"No, I said that." It would be hard enough without the worry of armed gangs raping and pillaging as they went. "Not far up ahead is a crossroad. We will take the north road to follow the river. It is a little longer but should be a lot safer."

"How do you know about this road?"

"I have been along these roads many times. I know them intimately." Too intimately for her liking.

"You've been to Nantes before?"

"Yes," Françoise said firmly. She wanted to end Dale's questions. Her memories of Nantes had not been pleasant.

They rode on in silence until the fork in the road appeared. "To the right." Françoise sat up in the saddle and watched for any lurking danger. She had always been so self-assured, confident, and relaxed, but she was none of those things right now. Nantes couldn't come soon enough.

They led the two nags down the smaller road on what was barely more than a walking track toward the Loire. Françoise didn't tell Dale that while this road was quieter, if they got into trouble, there was less chance of someone coming to their aid. What God gave with one hand, the Devil took away with another. She only hoped that what God gave them was enough to hold the Devil at bay.

* * *

It had been a long day in the saddle, and Françoise could see that Dale was sore in places she didn't think possible. They had found the river and followed its course toward the coast, allowing the horses to walk at their own pace. The sun was hanging low in the sky. It was time to find shelter.

Françoise had no idea what she was doing, but she wasn't going to tell Dale that. This was her time and her country and she felt responsible for Dale's safety. Resolve replaced indecision as she alighted from the horse. "We will stay here tonight." She reached for her crotch and shifted the leather piece that had been her nemesis all day.

"Are you trying to say something, honey?"

"Pardon?" Dale dropped her gaze to where Françoise's hand was hovering. "Oh, *non.* It has been... uncomfortable."

"I just bet. If it's anything how my... how I feel, then it's screaming for relief." Dale smiled sweetly. "Are you looking for relief?"

Françoise blinked. Did she mean what she thought she meant? "Not now."

"Why, what a dirty mind you have."

"Only because you put it there." Despite herself, Françoise laughed. "Thank you, *chérie.*"

"For what?"

"For reminding me what was important." Françoise surveyed the scene. "I will find us somewhere to sleep." Before she had finished her sentence, Dale had dismounted and picked up a small, fallen branch. She used it to sweep away dead leaves and undergrowth until there was a bare patch of ground.

"What are you doing?" Françoise tethered her horse to a nearby tree.

"What you should be doing. Now go and collect some dead wood while I prepare a fire pit."

"And how do you know all this?"

"I was a Girl Scout when I was a kid."

"Girl... Scout... Kid? What are you talking about?"

"Kid is another word for a child, and a Girl Scout is a girl who is taught to survive in the wild. I think all that training will come in handy right about now."

*"Bien."* If whatever Dale said was good, then she was happy. Woodsmanship was not something taught to the aristocracy—especially not to the women—so this was one point on which Françoise would happily defer to Dale. She disappeared into the undergrowth to collect wood while Dale prepared the fire.

Dead branches reached for her and tore at her clothes. Maybe she should have sent Dale on this task because it was about to snap Françoise's last nerve.

"Do you need any help?" Dale called out.

Her pride refused to let her say yes. "I am fine. Why do you ask?"

The crunch of dead leaves signaled Dale's approach. "Because you've been muttering and cursing for the last five minutes." Dale, sporting an impish grin, pushed through the undergrowth. "Here, let me give you a hand."

Françoise grabbed her armful of firewood. "Find your own wood. This is mine."

"Aw, come on now, honey."

"Do not 'honey' me. I can look after myself quite well."

"I didn't say you couldn't. I was just offering…"

The pouting lip was her undoing. "Please, Dale. I can do this."

"You did just fine." The cool air sent a shudder through Dale. "Maybe you can help me with the fire before I freeze to death." She picked up some dry sticks as they returned to the cleared area.

Françoise watched as Dale laid out the wood, trying to commit to memory what she had done. Dale set the sticks next to the wood for tinder, stopped, and looked at her expectantly.

"Now, it's your turn."

"*Moi?*"

"Yes, *toi.*" Dale rose and made her way to their meager belongings to extract the tinderbox from the cloth bag. Silently, she handed over the box and nodded in the direction of the pile of wood.

Françoise struck the stone on the metal, and sparks lit the tinder. Dale hunkered down beside her and pushed the glowing tinder toward the wood. Françoise blew on the smoldering specks until the fire burst into life, its heat already evident in those first few moments. *"Voilá,"* she murmured.

"See? We work well as a team." Dale continued to feed the flames until the fire burned brightly and lit up the darkening sky.

After a dinner of cold rations, Dale lay against Françoise, her back snuggled into Françoise's chest. She looked up at the night sky and sighed contentedly. "Just look at all those stars. It's such a beautiful night. Cold, but beautiful." Françoise pulled the blanket up around both of them, making sure that Dale was comfortable and warm. "You know what I think?"

"What is going on in that head of yours?"

Dale tilted her head to peer up at Françoise. "I've been thinking about what's been happening to us." Françoise tightened her arms around Dale. "I think it's a test."

"A… what you say? Test?"

"It's some divine journey to see whether we are worthy of what we've been given. Up until now, our path has been straight and smooth. What if this is to see whether we survive a rocky path, to test our love and resolve?"

Would that explain why she had the urge to step back through the mirror? Françoise pondered the question. "Maybe."

"It can't be any more *incroyable* than how we met, can it?" Françoise smiled as Dale slipped in a word of French. "I mean, why are we here?"

"Because your mother was trying to separate us?"

Dale twisted in Françoise's grasp, and her trusting eyes sought out Françoise's. "You know what I mean."

*"Oui,* I do."

"You can't explain this." Dale laid her hand gently on Françoise's chest and then patted the cotton surface. "No bandage?"

"I was not going to wear that thing or the devil's spawn in my pants any longer than I had to."

"Oh, goody." Dale turned around and wriggled against Françoise. "Better." Françoise encircled Dale's tiny waist with her hands as Dale's agile fingers moved over the rough cotton. "Much, much better." Dale's voice dropped to a seductive whisper. "I know what would make it perfect."

Françoise chuckled.

"What's so funny?"

"You, *chérie.*"

"Me? What did I do now?"

"You have come so far, my sweet Dale. Has it only been a matter of a few weeks since you first saw me in the mirror? Now look at you."

"Well, I can't. We have no mirror, remember?"

Françoise laughed again.

"Now what are you laughing at?"

"Nothing." Françoise dipped her lips to touch Dale's temple. "Nothing at all, but here you are asking for your pleasure." The blush of Dale's skin brought another smile.

"Stop teasing me." Dale snuggled deeper under the blanket.

"Do not be upset. I find it most, um, endearing. *Oui.* Endearing." She kissed the top of Dale's head and pulled her as close as their bodies would allow. "And as much as I would like to show you how endearing you are, I must decline."

"You're saying no? Again?" Dale pouted.

"We are in danger. I must keep a clear head." All of Françoise's good intentions nearly flew out the window when she felt a warm hand wander along her thigh. "Stop that!" Her own hand came down on top of Dale's to stop the seductive motion of Dale's fingertips.

"You're a spoilsport."

"Keep doing that, and when we reach an inn, you will be in trouble." Françoise stared hard at Dale.

"Oh God, when you look at me like that..." The firelight flickered in Dale's eyes, reflecting an answering promise of ravishment at the next appropriate time.

"He will not help you, *chérie*. So, stop this now before I have to go and kill something."

Dale sighed deeply, settled farther into Françoise's arms, and slipped into silence. A few minutes later, she spoke. "I remember a scene like this not so long ago. The smell of smoke, the crackling of a fire, and you behind my back."

"Oh?" But it only took a second for her to remember. "Oh, of course. The crossroad in my life."

"The divine intervention."

"If you say so."

"Fate, divinity, or plain dumb luck, call it what you will. I'm grabbing onto it with both hands and not letting go."

"Mmm." Françoise smiled, letting Dale's warmth seep into her tired body. A creeping lethargy lay over her. She was content to drift along with it as she leaned against a fallen tree trunk. The fire sputtered and danced, tendrils of flame reaching to the night sky. The cinders rose on the heated air, died out once they had reached their zenith, and fell back to earth in the darkness.

"I'll never forget that first night I came to you."

"My scared little rabbit you were."

"In the beginning, yes, but when you touched my skin that first time it was... it was magical."

"*Oui.* That it was."

"Maybe we should mount the mirror on the ceiling when we finally settle down."

"The ceiling? Where did you get an idea like that?"

"Didn't think I had such an imagination, Françoise? Think about it. *Really* think about it."

"Dale," Françoise growled in warning.

"I'm not doing anything, sweetheart."

"Yes, you are, and you know it."

"I was going to tell you a bedtime story."

"It is because I said no, *n'est-ce pas*? You are playing with fire."

"I like playing with fire," Dale murmured quietly, the intonation in her voice confirming her inner desires. "I like playing with *your* fire."

"Where is my sword?" Françoise's temperature rose, not only from the young woman squirming seductively in her lap, but also from her words that held so much promise.

Dale smiled. Leaning forward, she grabbed another piece of wood and threw it on the fire. The flames erupted, and sparks leapt into the night sky.

"So... back to my story." Françoise moaned, and it drew a quiet chuckle from Dale. "Oh, come now. What am I supposed to do?"

"Go to sleep? But that is probably too much to ask for."

"Not quite yet. Now, we can't put the mirror on my bedroom ceiling because there's no room for a mirror. The skylight is there."

"I liked that... how you say? Skylight? *Très bien.* I would not want a mirror there."

"Okay. How about our bedroom? Not *the* mirror. That will hang on the wall because it would be too heavy for the ceiling. Besides, it deserves a better fate." Dale had drawn Françoise in to her tale. "Now for the bed. The four posts have to go. I like to move around, and the last thing I need is to be constantly hitting my shins on the wood." Françoise laughed. "Then again, maybe just two bedposts for when I chain you up and have my wicked way with you."

"Chain me up?" Françoise asked in confusion. Had she misunderstood? "You... you..." She was nearly afraid to ask. "You follow the teachings of..." Françoise took a deep breath loath to say the name. *"Du Marquis de Sade?"* Sweat popped up on her brow, and she shuddered at the thought.

Dale turned in her arms to look her with concern. "The *Marquis de...* of course not! What on earth gave you that idea?"

"The bedpost. The chains... the..."

"Get that out of your head right now. I know of him, but that's from the history books. Anyone who believes in that stuff is sick."

Françoise relaxed as she said the words.

"I was just joking, my love. I would never do anything that you didn't want me to do." Dale smiled impishly over her shoulder. "I was trying to shock you, and it looks like I succeeded."

"That you did, *ma chèrie.*" Françoise stared at the flames, lost in thought.

"What does it mean to you?" It seemed that Dale was very astute and had deduced there was a problem.

"Nothing. Nothing at all. I am not a..."

"Fan?"

"Fan? *Un éventail?* What is that?"

"It means what you think it means, but in my time it also means someone who is an admirer of a person or a thing."

"*Oui.* I am not a fan of *Le Marquis.*"

"I never thought you were." After a few moments of silence Dale spoke. "Do you want to tell me about it?"

Françoise tensed. "*Non.* It is in the past, and that is where it should stay."

"Do you want me to continue my story?" But the enthusiasm had left Dale's voice. Even she had to know the moment was gone.

"Please, *non.* I am tired, as I am sure are you." She pulled Dale and the blanket close to her before she closed her eyes. Dale didn't answer, but she eventually relaxed in her arms, and from her soft breathing, Françoise knew she had fallen asleep.

# Chapter 15

The next morning turned out to be quite pleasant, despite the uneasiness of last night's conversation. The air was brisk until the sun finally peeked through the dense forest. Françoise was comforted by the warm, sleepy cocoon that nuzzled against her. Dale stirred in her arms. "*Bonjour.* Did you sleep well?"

"Scrummy. And you?" Her voice was muffled by the blanket. All Françoise could see was the top of Dale's head.

Françoise chuckled. "You and your quaint American sayings."

"And you don't use quaint French sayings, *chérie?*"

"Do you want me to stop?"

"Don't you dare." Dale snuggled in closer, her nose digging around for warm flesh. "Ah ha! This is more like it."

"*Mon Dieu,* Dale! Stop that!" Françoise tried to back away from the tickling tongue. "We need to start our journey, *chérie.*" Since they had limited food and neither of them was a hunter, they needed to cover a lot of ground in the daylight if they didn't want to starve.

"Fine, fine. You're no fun."

"Your time will come."

"Yeah, yeah. So you keep telling me, and I'm still waiting." Dale pulled her head out of the blanket. "Jesus, that's cold!" She stayed covered, seemingly content to sit there while Françoise poked at the remnants of the fire. After much cajoling, muttering, and swearing from her, the fire relented and burst into flame, greedily eating up the wood she placed on it.

The cold rations for breakfast were not welcome, but the hot tea was. Françoise hoped it would fortify them enough to face the new day. She again got into her disguise before they mounted their horses to continue on their journey.

The sun played hide-and-seek with the clouds. Despite the grayness, it refused to rain. Françoise studied the Loire River as they traveled. The river slowly grew in width as they ate up the miles toward their destination. As she had expected, the path was nearly deserted. They passed only two travelers during the day. She could see that Dale was tired and uncomfortable as she shifted in her saddle. She pushed them on a little farther before finding suitable cover.

"There." She pointed to a break in the tree line. Guiding their horses carefully through the ragged undergrowth, they rode on for a few minutes. Françoise maneuvered along a winding path toward a small rock outcropping. The soil underneath had eroded away to reveal a low cave.

"Did you plan this?" Dale asked.

"I am good, but even I cannot foresee such things." A wide grin touched her lips. "Come. We have things to attend to, *n'est-ce pas?*"

"Indeed we do." Dale slid off the back of the horse. She collapsed onto the ground. "Does this get any easier?"

"Perhaps in a year or two." The answering groan drew a chuckle from her. "You rest, and I will tend to our horses and collect some wood." Françoise tied the horses off to a branch, removed their saddles, and wiped down the lathered beasts. After she finished, she went in search of firewood. She looked over her shoulder and saw Dale gingerly walk around to prepare a fire pit. She winced in sympathy. Maybe later she could give her a massage to ease the ache.

"Well, well, little one. Out in the woods alone?"

Dale looked up from her kneeling position to see two grubby men standing there. She didn't like their lascivious stares one bit.

"Françoise!" She called out urgently, hoping against hope that she was within earshot. She called again, her voice more frantic than before.

"Let us see what you have for us." The bigger of the two moved toward her, a massive club in his large hand. She could not plead with the man, so she screamed and hurriedly backed away in an effort to put space between them. "Now that is not nice. You do not want to go scaring young Gaston here." He grabbed her dress by the bodice. "Well, well, sweet one. I think you may have something for me." Dale couldn't understand his words, but it didn't matter. The younger of the two men scavenged through their belongings, while the older one seemed intent on having his way with her.

The seriousness of their situation hit her like a tornado. She tried to bat away his hand in the hope of escape, but he had a firm hold, steadily pulling her toward his ugly face. She could smell the stale sweat and alcohol-soaked breath from where she knelt. The foul smell grew stronger as he dragged her toward his hulking body. The cloth began to tear and was about to reveal her breasts to the man. Quickly, she grabbed at the tear as she vainly tried to hold the cloth together.

"You make one more move, and I will cut your throat!"

Dale knew that voice. She sought out Françoise's face behind the man.

There she stood, like some Olympian goddess, already in motion to come to her aid. Raven hair fanned out as she sought out her enemies. Her lips curled back to reveal a snarl, and her piercing dark eyes bore into the man.

"Gaston!" He nodded at Françoise, and the wiry young man complied.

Swinging his club with a certain amount of competence, the thug moved in swiftly toward her. Françoise drew her sword as her heart beat frantically in anticipation of her first real fight. Fighting Gérard was one thing, but a real life-or-death battle was another.

The big brute turned his attention back to Dale. His eyes raked over her rapidly exposing flesh. "Now, little one. You will be nice to old Jacques, will you not?"

Françoise looked over to Dale. The fight had to finish fast before it was too late. "Dale!" she screamed. "The pistol! Use the pistol!" The sight of the hulking man towering over Dale galvanized her into action. Françoise's determination doubled in an effort to get to her.

Dale searched for the pistol. With a rough push by the man, she landed hard on the ground. Before she had a chance, the brute was on top of her, searching for a way to get to her. Her hand flew out to land on the gun. Francoise, still fighting off the younger man, saw Dale grab the pistol and shove it in Jacques' face.

He backed up, holding up his hands in supplication. "Now, now, there, girl. There is no need for violence."

Françoise wrestled the young man to a standstill. "Get away from her before she puts a hole in that thick head of yours!" She supplied the words that Dale couldn't. Returning to her own fight, she only hoped that the sight of the gun was enough to hold the older man at bay until she could get to her wife. Her wife. How she wished she could make that come true. She could see that Dale was shaking like a leaf, barely able to hold the pistol still.

"Cock the hammer!" Françoise continued the fight, inflicting a slice across Gaston's abdomen to force him back a step. "Dale! Dale!" Her words weren't getting through to Dale who was obviously frozen with fear. "Pull back the hammer on the top. Pull it back!"

Françoise's blade cut through the air with lethal intensity and forced the young man even farther back. But he was drawing her away from Dale's plight. Without thinking, she reached into her boot and drew out a dagger. She threw it at the larger man's back. She hadn't thrown a knife before, but it was no matter as the steel left Françoise's hand. It twirled through the air, end-over-end and headed toward her intended target.

The large man reached for the pistol. In the instant the blade pierced his back, he lurched forward. He grabbed the gun from Dale's hand, causing it to discharge. The shot exploded into his face. He collapsed to the ground and lay still.

Driven on by fear and a savage need to reach Dale, Françoise brutally plunged her sword into the young man's chest. The sensation of metal sliding along tissue, muscle, and bone was a strange one indeed. She knew it would stay with her for a long time. But not now. There was no time for remorse or celebration. Dale needed her.

Françoise approached cautiously, seeing that Dale was in shock. *"Chérie?"* Vacant eyes met Françoise's gaze. "Are you all right?" When she reached for Dale, Dale shrunk back in obvious fear. She noticed a faint red spatter of blood on her own white shirt. "Come, come." Françoise beckoned to her and welcomed the rush of Dale's body against her own. Wrapping her arms tightly around her, Françoise crooned gently, "It is all over. Everything will be fine."

"No it won't. I… I killed him."

*"Non.* It was the knife in his back that sent him to grab the pistol. It went off when he pulled it out of your hand. It is no one's fault." Françoise tipped up Dale's face. "Do you hear me? You did nothing wrong. If anyone is to blame, it is them. They came here to rob us and…" Her gaze dropped to the torn bodice for a moment and shuddered. It was so close—too close.

"You…" Dale sobbed. "You warned me, and I didn't listen. It's all my fault."

"I told you, it is not your fault. If anyone is to blame, it is me."

Dale sobbed harder. "No!"

"If I had allowed them to capture me in your time, none of this would have happened."

"And I wouldn't let that happen."

"Then stop blaming yourself for something that was out of your control. I told you this would be a dangerous journey. Now you know." She pulled Dale closer into her embrace. "Now you know," she whispered. "Come on. You get the horses ready, and I will finish with these two."

"Why?"

"There is still a little light, and we can find somewhere else to stay."

"We don't have to."

"I can see that you are upset. We do not need to stay here."

Dale didn't argue any further and began collecting their belongings. Françoise searched the men's clothes. She tried to stop the roiling in her stomach as she reached into dirty, smelly pockets for anything of use. She turned to check on Dale a number of times. She tried to feel some sense of remorse at taking two lives. No, she didn't start the fight, but she sure as hell finished it. She looked in her hand at the stash of small coin she'd taken, barely worth the two lives sacrificed.

Despite Dale being upset at the fight, Françoise's body was singing, adrenaline pumping through her like a drug. It had all been almost too easy. The image of her sword piercing the boy played in her mind in slow motion, exaggerating the feeling of victory. It could be addictive, and it was something she knew she would have to control now.

Françoise walked over to help Dale with the saddles. They turned their horses to leave, but not before they cast their eyes over the bloody scene. Dale looked sad, while Françoise still felt the thrill of the fight.

They traveled for another hour as Françoise tried to put as much distance as possible between them and the two bodies left behind before the light gave out. She was worried. Dale had barely spoken a word since the incident, meekly riding along and giving only one- and two-word responses to Françoise's questions.

Françoise spotted a gap in the brush and steered her horse off the road to take cover. "We will stop here tonight."

Dale dismounted and tethered her horse to a nearby bush. Françoise did the same. She led Dale to a nearby tree. She slid down the bark and held Dale in her lap, encircling her in an embrace. "Shh, little one. I am here."

She continued to whisper to her, letting Dale deal with her shock in her own way. But the silence was worrying. "Let it out, Dale. I…" She didn't know if this was the proper time, but she said it anyway. "I love you, my wife." Dale snuggled closer, and Françoise tightened her hold. Her fingertips gently drew circles on Dale's back. "It is all over, my love."

Françoise tilted up Dale's chin and smiled, hoping to encourage a response from her. Ever so slowly, she lowered her mouth to barely touch Dale's lips before pulling back.

"This is a test, this is a test," Dale murmured.

With all this talk about divine intervention, were they going to falter at the first hurdle? In her heart, she knew they were not murderers. But she thought Dale now accepted Françoise would do whatever it took to protect them both.

Françoise lay back against the tree, still feeling the effects of the fight. Her muscles lightly twitched as images of the mêlée flashed across her mind's eye. Gérard had never described fighting like that. She was no stranger to death but this… This was something more exciting, heart thumping…visceral.

* * *

Françoise awoke the next morning with an aching back. Dale was no longer in her arms but poking at the fire in a daze. "Dale?" It took a few moments for Dale to respond. "How are you this morning?"

"Getting there."

"Yes, we are, *chérie*. If we push the horses, we should reach the main road again the day after tomorrow. There is rather a nice inn and I, for one, would welcome a hot bath."

Dale smiled. "No, I meant I'm getting better. I still have some things to work through in my mind though."

"Oh. I am not used to all these words you use."

"In time, my love."

Françoise warmed at the term of endearment. "Ah, little one, it pleases my heart to hear you say those words. I thought I had lost you." She looked into Dale's eyes and saw the sadness there. "I am so sorry I was not there to save you from all of this."

They mounted and Françoise had them push the horses into a steady trot in an attempt to cover as many miles as possible. She kept up a steady stream of chatter as she tried to distract Dale from what dangers might lie ahead.

"Where do you think we'll go?" Dale asked.

"There is England, but France is not a friend of England. Maybe Spain or Rome or… the Colonies."

"America?" Dale's expression was hopeful. "Can we go there?"

"If there is a ship going there, then *oui.*" Dale studied her with interest. "But we may have to go somewhere else first. Not all ships go that far."

"America."

"We may not end up there." Françoise sighed. That wistful look alone made her want to move heaven and earth for Dale. "I will try."

As the journey continued, Dale suggested a search for various herbs that might be needed. "Something I learned from the Girl Scouts." The rest of the journey to the crossroads was uneventful, and for that Françoise was grateful.

Finally, they approached the two-story inn. This would be their first interaction with people as husband and wife. Françoise knew if they could fool them here, then there would be some hope that they could carry off the deception on the rest of the journey. Raucous laughter of drunken men drifted outside. She wanted to enter the building alone, but she was not confident about leaving Dale by herself with the horses. Taking Dale inside was fraught with danger, but there was no way in hell she was going to let her out of her sight again.

They rode their horses to the large barn out back and unpacked their few belongings. Exhausted, they stripped down the animals and led them to the waiting stalls inside.

"Come." Françoise took a deep breath as she strode across the courtyard. She reached for the handle to push the heavy wooden door aside to allow Dale to enter. The noise immediately died down as all eyes watched them crossing the floor to the bar.

Dale drew her cloak tighter around herself and tugged at Françoise's sleeve. Françoise rested her hand on top and gave her a reassuring pat.

"Monsieur, we are in need of a room for the night."

"Top of the stairs, last room on the right. Three *sous.*"

Françoise dipped into her tattered waistband to extract the coins. After paying the man, she steered Dale toward the staircase. The weight of the saddlebag bit deep into her shoulder. The wood underneath her feet creaked ominously as if it felt the extra weight of the gold coin she was carrying.

Their room was bare but livable.

"It'll do," Dale muttered as she pushed down on the straw-filled mattress.

"We deserve better. This is…"

"What we have to get used to from now on," Dale said. "And the sooner you realize that your old life is gone, the better."

Laying her hands on the small sacks of gold coin at the bottom of the saddle bags, Françoise looked around for somewhere to hide them. There was precious little in the room to start with, so finding a hiding spot was near impossible. She crossed to the window and looked out. Their room sat on the first floor at the back of the building, and the window led to a sheer drop to the ground below.

She looked at the only possible option. Removing her dagger from her boot, she sliced open the mattress and slipped the coin bags inside. "Share the rest of our supplies through these bags." Dale did as asked, while Françoise twisted the mattress so the tear faced the wall. She punched the straw a few times to remove the lumps and stood back to look at the disheveled sheets and blanket.

"Let's hope this works." Dale tried to make the bed, but the weight of the mattress made it nearly impossible to lift. "Oh crap." She persisted until she was done.

"I find this thirsty work. Would you like a drink?"

"There's nothing to hang around here for. Why not?" Dale moved toward the door. "Besides, I could use a hot meal right about now."

Françoise settled her hand on the small of Dale's back and steered her through the door. "Your wish is my command, wife." She could feel the laughter ripple through Dale's body. "And maybe later you can continue your bedtime story."

Françoise stopped at the bar. "Monsieur, an ale if you please, and a cool water for my wife." Françoise's lips curled in amusement at the word. She could get used to saying that very easily. She scanned the room and stared down each and every person watching them. Françoise turned her attention back to the barkeep and threw a precious coin on the counter.

"I would also like to arrange for a hot bath for my wife. The road has been long and dusty."

The large innkeeper looked at her a long moment before bursting into laughter. "A bath, monsieur? You are joking, are you not? The best I can do is a bucket of hot water." He sloshed down two full mugs on the top of the counter.

"Then that will do, innkeeper. Thank you." Françoise did not dare to think about how clean the water or the mug was.

"Do you have something hot to eat?"

The bullish man nodded, then indicated a bench against the far wall. Françoise sighed. It looked like they were both going to be the entertainment for a little longer while they ate. Françoise led Dale toward the sturdy wooden benches.

"I don't like it here," Dale said as her gaze darted around the room.

"I have asked for some hot food, as you requested. We can still go…" But she knew very well that Dale would stay. She was hungry, so she would just have to put up with the bawdy conversation. At least Dale had no idea what they were saying.

Two large bowls were unceremoniously dropped onto the table in front of them along with a torn loaf of bread. "Two *sous*." Françoise looked up into the face of a churlish barmaid who must have been, in reality, not much older than her but looked twenty years older. Once more, she reached into the tiny cloth bag, took out the coins, and silently handed them over to the woman.

Françoise looked down into the bowl. She widened her eyes in disgust. "What is this slop?"

"Shh. Cover that aristocratic streak of yours," Dale whispered. "That is your dinner, Philippe." She sniffed the food. "Actually, it doesn't smell too bad." She picked up the crude spoon and dipped it into the bowl. Tentatively, she tasted it. "Not bad." Dale dipped the spoon again, this time taking some meat. "I told you a hot meal was what we needed." Dale reached for the bread. She tore off a small piece and doused it in the gravy before popping it into her mouth.

Françoise poked around the syrupy mixture trying to decide whether to risk her life. She tore off a piece of bread, dunked it in the gravy, and shoved it in her mouth before she could change her mind. It took a moment or two for her taste buds to absorb the new sensation. She finally decided that the stew was not going to kill her. As if emphasizing its point, her stomach rumbled noisily.

"Now if you can get that stubborn head of yours to agree with your stomach, you'll eat the food before it got cold."

Françoise smiled. This was the Dale she knew. Despite herself, Françoise didn't stop eating until she was mopping up the bowl with the last piece of bread. "I must have been hungrier than I thought." There was little coin left, and she couldn't throw around gold coin without arousing suspicion. Françoise patted her stomach. "I am full. Do you wish for some more?"

"No, that was enough. Can we get out of here please? I feel like a piece of meat on display."

"In a way you are." Françoise looked around at the avid eyes watching them. No. Watching Dale. She wasn't surprised. Dale was a stunning woman.

The heavy wooden door swung open and hit the wall with a thud. "Barkeep, eight of your best, if you please!" A man of middling height swaggered in, followed by his seven companions. His muddy brown eyes swept the room. "It is thirsty work ridding the world of aristos." He laughed at his own joke. "Do you not agree, my friends?"

The man and his companions looked around the bar as their hands fell to clubs, pistols, knives, and swords, as if to hope someone would dispute their claim. There was a quiet murmur from the patrons.

While the other seven men went to the bar for their drink, the man who appeared to be the leader wandered around the room. The patrons kept their gaze averted. The man turned his attention to Françoise. "So, citizen, are you not pleased that we are protecting you from those aristocratic scum?"

She bit her tongue until she tasted blood. A bitter remark sat there begging for release.

"What? You have something to say, citizen?"

Dale reached across the table to touch Françoise's clenched fist. She looked up into those hooded eyes and saw the warning there. She nodded slightly at Dale. "No, monsieur. I am sure that you defend the Republic very well."

"I do not like the tone of your voice, monsieur. Are you for or against us?"

"I have always been a friend of France, monsieur. Never doubt that."

"And who is this pretty young thing sitting with you?" Without permission, he grabbed the hood and lifted it off Dale's head. "Well, well, well. You are most fortunate to have such a lovely wench for company."

"I ask you not to insult my wife." A hardened edge tinged Françoise's words.

"Such a beauty should not be owned by just one man, do you not think so?"

"I say again, she is my wife. Step very carefully, monsieur."

"That sounds a bit like a threat to me. Are you challenging the law?"

"This has nothing to do with the law, and you know it." Françoise's voice steadily rose to match her anger.

"Well, lads, maybe this young citizen needs a lesson in manners." The group laughed as they approached the two women.

"Now, now, Justin," the barkeep said. "We do not want a fight here."

"You are a coward, monsieur." Françoise practically spat the words. "You hide behind the name of the Republic to rape, rob, and pillage. You have no honor." A collective gasp echoed around the room.

Dale's eyes widened. "Philippe," she whispered.

"She has the voice of an angel," the man said with a sneer. "I do not think you deserve her, citizen. Maybe I just might take her from you and show her what a real man is like."

Françoise's lips spread into a dangerous smile. "You can try." Her smile widened. He quickly backed down, apparently not prepared to test her. "Just as I thought," she muttered as he turned away.

In an apparent attempt to recover some of his pride, he told his cohorts that Dale was nothing but a whore anyway. It took all of her strength not to go after the man and rip his tongue out. Live to fight another day was what Gérard had taught her.

After the unruly mob had left, they made their way to the bar. "I am sorry, monsieur, for the disruption."

"No need, young man. They come in once every couple of days and cause trouble. You were right. Not that I would tell them to their faces."

They turned and ascended the stairs.

# Chapter 16

The adrenaline once again surfaced after the confrontation, feeding Françoise's already blossoming hunger. She could see why men liked to fight. She had never felt as alive as she had in the heat of danger.

"Do you think they're waiting out there for us?" Dale asked.

"I hope not. They are in for a long wait if they are." Even Françoise could hear the rough timbre in her own voice. She needed Dale and she needed her now. The door closed quietly, and Françoise faced her. "So," she murmured. She grabbed the only chair in the room and wedged it up against the door. If they were going to break in, it was going to take awhile.

"So," Dale repeated, as she rested her hip on the edge of the rough-hewn table. She watched Françoise with interest. "What do we do now?"

"What do you desire, *chérie?*" Françoise poured every ounce of seduction and want into her voice that she felt. Dale was fidgety and nervous.

"You. I desire you."

Françoise smiled. "And I you, but you are not ready for this."

"No, no I am."

Françoise could see the conflict in Dale's eyes. "Perhaps we should get some sleep. Come." She moved to the bed and faced away from Dale to change.

"You don't want to?" Dale sounded hurt.

"Of course I do, little one." Françoise turned and moved to Dale. "I do not doubt you are ready here"—she gently touched the swell of her breast—"but are you ready here?" Françoise moved her hand to Dale's temple.

Dale approached her slowly and reached for the ties on her cloak. A small smile touched her lips as Françoise dropped her gaze to Dale's torn bodice.

"I want you in my body, in my mind, in my heart, and in my soul," Dale said with conviction. "I want you to make me forget everything—my mother, France, and the danger. I want… no, I *need* to know the depth of your love for me."

Françoise understood Dale's request. She too wanted to be swept away. "Your wish is my command."

Françoise started slowly, not wanting to frighten Dale with her hunger. If she had her way, she would already be ravishing Dale's body.

Dale wasted no time in finding the buttons on Françoise's shirt, her own eagerness showing with every frantic movement.

Françoise tipped her chin up with a light touch. "Are you in a hurry, little one?" A lone tear trickled down Dale's cheek. She caught it and presented it to her. "Talk to me. What troubles you?"

"I guess I'm just overwhelmed by all of this."

"Not what you expected?"

"No, not what I expected."

"Are… are you having second thoughts?"

"Of course not." Dale shook her head. "Just give me a minute."

"*Non.* About all of this. About us." Françoise held her breath before continuing. "Perhaps wishing this had never happened at all?"

Dale looked incredulous. "How could you say that? I would never leave you. You do know that, don't you?"

"Yes. As I will never leave you. It just seems all so…"

"Surreal?"

"What? What is this word?"

"It's…" Dale gazed at the ceiling. "It's like living in a dream. Things are not quite real."

"Ah, interesting word. I shall remember it." Françoise's lips gently nipped the pulse point at the base of Dale's neck.

"Never doubt that I love you with everything that I am, my love."

"And I love you, *mon petit cœur.* But I wish—"

"No more 'ifs' or 'buts,' Françoise. We go forward from here together. We do what we have to do to survive. I want a long life with you."

"I will protect you with my life."

"No, that life is mine. You protect me with your strong right arm." Dale smiled. "Just as I will protect you." Dale shoved Françoise against the table while her hands fumbled with the crude buttons on the shabby shirt. "If I remember correctly, you were supposed to grant me my wish." She tore at the bandage around Françoise's chest and drew her lips to the exposed skin. Her lips moved to a breast, encircling the nipple with her tongue before sucking it into her mouth with vigor.

Françoise gasped. "Oh God! How do you do this to me?" The sweet agony Dale inflicted with her lips, tongue, and teeth tore through Françoise's body. "Every time," she whispered. A knock on the door stopped the movement of Dale's lips. "What do you want?" Françoise growled as she stared down at the excited blue eyes watching her.

"Your hot water, monsieur." The voice was that of a young lad.

"Leave it at the door. Thank you." Françoise spared a moment to soften her voice before she returned to the hands roaming down her body. "You are a... *mon Dieu...* a troublemaker." Dale rested her hand on the lump in her pants before caressing it as if it were a part of Françoise. The image it presented was nothing short of salacious. Dale's lips resumed their wandering while her hand never wavered from stroking her.

The fire in the pit of her belly that had been simmering since the fight erupted. Françoise batted away Dale's hand and nearly ripped off the buttons as she attempted to remove the leather blocking Dale's access.

In an instant, Françoise's breeches were around her ankles, her skin laid bare to Dale's advances. Moist lips left a wet trail as they sought her out, finally circling the source of Françoise's need. There was an audible sigh as Dale latched on and drew her in, the suction almost painful as Françoise was swept away. Her passion had been held in check far too long, and now it was like a dam breaking. The sudden rush of completion flowed over her to nearly drown her with its intensity. But it was not enough... not nearly enough.

Before Françoise had a chance to ground herself, Dale had moved, and her fingers slipped into her easily. The table creaked as Françoise gripped the wood tightly. She nearly snapped off splinters as Dale played her. She could barely breathe as Dale's two fingers moved in a constant, driving rhythm.

Françoise tried to watch, but she had very little control over her own body. She tried to spread her legs to gain more purchase, but the breeches pooled around her ankles had her effectively tied.

Dale shifted her stance, and her hip added weight behind her hand. Anchoring one hand to Françoise's hip, Dale rocked steadily against her other hand to make the movement more forceful and increase the gratification ten-fold. The table creaked ominously with each thrust. Dale eyes met hers in question.

"If you stop now I will kill you," Françoise growled. She was finding it difficult to put a sentence together.

For a second Dale blinked in confusion. She increased her tempo slowly and allowed her thumb to come into play.

Françoise slammed her eyes shut, and her bottom lip quivered. Dale slowed down and then stopped. Françoise rested her body against the wood table only long enough to catch her breath.

Françoise ignored her state of undress, except for her pants that she hitched up in order to walk. She slowly backed Dale toward the door. She swept her lips down the twitching skin of Dale's throat and sucked viciously, as if trying to draw her life force to the surface. Dale's hands fumbled for Françoise's waist and gripped her tightly.

*"Mon amour, je t'aime de toutes les fibres de mon âme,"* Françoise murmured in a language that crossed the borders of time and space. *"Je t'aimerai jusqu'à mon dernier souffle de vie, et au-delà."* She glanced up from her work to see the result of her words. A tiny shudder shook Dale's body. Françoise couldn't help but smile.

"Oh God, you know how to drive me crazy." Dale's voice had dropped to a seductive whisper. "Say some more…"

*"La flamme éblouissante de notre amour fait pâlir les étoiles dans le ciel."*

While Dale was wrapped in a verbal haze, Françoise found the edge of her torn bodice and gently pulled it down. It would be so simple to rip the clothes off, but a small kernel of common sense whispered to her that Dale only had one dress.

Françoise reined in her wildly escalating desire and tugged at the neckline to reveal more and more skin until she'd freed Dale's breasts from their cloth prison. The barrier now removed, Françoise was neither gentle nor slow. Her lips slipped downward until she reached Dale's thighs, easing down the dress as she went.

"Oh God." Dale moaned as Françoise's tongue found her. "Make me forget."

Françoise continued her assault with her tongue. She barely held on to Dale's legs as her hips rocked back and forth. When she stiffened, Françoise slowed to a gentle swipe of her tongue.

Dale breathed hard before finally speaking. "Damn."

"What?" Françoise uttered between moist kisses.

"I missed it. I must have passed out." With a shy grin, she met Françoise's eyes. "You did make me forget. Can you do that again?"

*"Certainement."* Dale shivered at the word as Françoise returned her smile. *"Avec plaisir…"*

\* \* \*

*"You dare disobey me?" Le Comte's voice was at odds with his words. While the inflection held menace, his timbre was weak as if a boy were speaking. Françoise cowered back. He was a portly man in his late sixties, but he still commanded fear. He raised his hand to strike a blow, the riding crop in his fist singing through the air as it descended…*

Françoise awoke in a light sweat. It took a moment or two for her to become aware of a loud banging on the door. "Monshhieur!" The incessant thumping reverberated through her brain.

"What… what's going on?" The sleep-tainted voice of Dale drew her attention away from the door.

"Shh. Go back to sleep," she whispered.

"Open up! I wishhh t-to… ummm…" The voice dropped to mumbling before the owner once again pounded on the door. "Come and faaaccee meee, monshhieur." His voice was slurred, the intonation reeking of alcohol.

Annoyed, Françoise arose and quickly donned her disguise. It took a moment to light a candle. The pounding started again. She removed the chair and wrenched the door open, sword in hand, to face the annoying little man from earlier in the evening. Françoise was pleased to see that he was alone, so any violence was only with him. "It is the middle of the night. What do you want?" Maybe she needed to remind him again that Dale belonged to her.

"I am looking for you." He swayed in the dim light and lurched forward.

She raised her hand to his chest to effectively block his entrance. "This bed is taken. Try another room." Françoise looked out the door. "Where are your companions?"

"Out there"—he waved down the hall toward the front door— "somewhere. But I do not sleep with the likesh of them." He closed his eyes for a long moment. Françoise wondered whether the man had fallen asleep where he stood. His bloodshot eyes suddenly popped open. "I am… I do not like the open air and the hard ground."

"I do not care if your life depends on it, you are not crossing this portal." To prove her point, she raised the sword point to sit level with his chest. "Now leave us alone." She enunciated each word.

The man reached for his crotch to give it a scratch. Françoise screwed up her nose in distaste. "Refushing a... a... son of the Republish? You have made a dangeroush enemy tonight, monsheeuurr! You be better to watch your back!"

Françoise had had enough and prodded him with the tip of her sword. "Go away, little man."

The staircase creaked, and the darkness slowly gave way to a lone candle. "Justin?" The deep gruff voice of the barkeep slowly approached them. "Come, back to bed."

"No." The man shook his scraggly head violently, nearly causing him to lose his balance.

"There is no bed here. Marie is waiting for you." Françoise watched the exchange with interest. "Go and sleep it off. There is nothing here for you."

Françoise and the barkeep watched as the tipsy man wandered off. He unsteadily negotiated the staircase to the bottom. There was a thud a moment later, accompanied by a rather virulent curse.

"I am sorry for the disturbance, monsieur. He does not like to be taken down like a stag in the forest, especially in front of a room full of people."

"Then he should not have insulted my wife." Despite the man's pleas, Françoise was still seething at the affront.

"Marie will calm his temper. She always does."

"If he already has a bedmate, why is he seeking out mine?"

"Bedmate?" He chuckled. "No, monsieur. Marie is his sister. My wife."

"Oh. I am sorry."

"No. Justin is a troublemaker. He always has been and always will be. It is only because he is my brother-in-law that I put up with him at all." In the dim light, he gave her an apologetic smile. "I think it would be better if you were not here for breakfast."

"You may be right. I do not want any trouble."

"Goodnight then and safe journey."

"Goodnight." She closed the door, causing Dale to stir. "Back to sleep, Dale."

"What's going on?" Dale asked sleepily.

"It was that troublemaker from earlier in the night. First he wanted you, now he wants our bed."

"Well, it's occupied and I'm not about to give it up."

"I told him that. But he was insistent. Maybe he wanted the one warming the bed rather than the bed itself."

"That weasely little man? He was disgusting. Besides I only have one bed warmer in my bed, and I'm looking at her." Dale snuggled into the tattered blanket for warmth. "Come back to bed, Françoise." She pulled the blanket back with a seductive smile, letting Françoise see her naked body.

Françoise felt Dale's intense gaze as she disrobed, slowly sliding off each piece of clothing. Françoise sauntered toward Dale's waiting arms. When she saw desire flare in Dale's eyes, her own desire spiked through her.

"Do you think he will be a problem?"

"Maybe. If he can remember it after he wakes up." Françoise made a decision. "I do not think we should put off leaving until the morning."

"Then maybe we better stay awake."

A sly smile crossed Françoise's lips. "Absolutely…"

* * *

Despite her best intentions, Dale had fallen asleep, cuddled up in her arms. Françoise lay quietly and idly drew circles on Dale's warm skin. Her mind wandered as she looked out the window at the night sky and contemplated the events of the previous night with a lot of affection and some concern.

Her gaze drifted to the crown of Dale's head. Dale had no idea what a lifesaver she had been to Françoise. Françoise had been living her life with a careless disregard for her own health, and she knew at some point she would fall victim to some disease or other. But she hadn't cared. Her husband had stripped away her dignity, her self-respect, and her will to live, leaving her an empty shell. Until…

Until that night with Madeleine. She didn't know what made her open her eyes at that particular moment, but she did. She looked up into the mirror and expected to see nothing more than the reflection of her having sex with someone. Anyone. It didn't matter anymore. But, as if standing at a window looking in, there was this waif, this angel, watching them. No, watching her as she sought her pleasure. And yet she could feel her, feel her excitement, feel her loneliness, feel her pain. From that very first moment, Dale had stolen her heart.

Now that same woman was fleeing with her from danger. Because of her, Dale had given up her home, her family, and her own time to live in another point in history that was fraught with danger.

Her thoughts returned to the annoying little man who had been bothering them all evening. She couldn't blame him for his need—after all Dale was a very beautiful woman. But his arrogant supposition that all he simply had to do was ask and he would get her made Françoise burn. It was hypocritical of him to claim to be protecting the Republic when he himself acted like a bully. As a member of the aristocracy, she hadn't acted like that, had she?

Here was a man who aggressively sought out power and blatantly used it for his own ends, claiming his rights with intimidation and violence. Were the people any better off with this kind of man protecting them?

As she contemplated the journey ahead and where they would ultimately end up, the sky shifted from pitch black to the grey of pre-dawn. Françoise shook Dale gently. "Time to wake up."

"Huh? I didn't fall asleep, did I?" Bleary blue eyes looked up at her.

"That is fine. We could not move until light anyway."

"I thought we were leaving before now."

"And what? We could not see where we were going," she gently chided her. "Come on. Let us move quickly now before there is any trouble."

They dressed and packed in silence and moved swiftly to the barn to collect the horses. They led their horses down the road for a short distance, mounted the nags, and nudged them into a slow walk until they were a safe distance from the inn.

"If we hurry, we should reach the outskirts of Nantes by nightfall." With that, Françoise kicked her horse into a canter. Dale clicked her tongue to move the second horse.

* * *

The outskirts of Nantes came into view with the last rays of the sun. They stopped the horses at the bridge that crossed the Loire and led into the township. Françoise was nervous. She had sworn she'd never return here, yet here she was. She had so many bad memories of this place.

"Are you all right?"

"*Oui.* Everything is fine. I am tired and this thing is most unpleasant." She grabbed the leather piece in her pants and tried to push it out of the way. Dale would never know what happened here. Never.

"It's been a long day, that's for sure."

Françoise noticed Dale's painful expression as she shifted on her horse. She wondered if she could find a place where they could get a hot bath.

They discovered a comfortable inn in the centre of the city where they could house the horses in a nearby livery. They ate their dinner in silence and without interruption. Finally, they took refuge in their room. A small tub full of steaming water awaited them. Dale bathed first.

Françoise had barely said two words during dinner and now lounged on the bed as she watched her bathe.

"What's going on? Have I done something wrong?" Dale asked.

"No. I am just thinking about what to do next, that is all." Françoise hated lying to Dale.

"Can we try to get some soap tomorrow?" Dale held up the rag she was sponging herself with. "Water can do only so much."

"What about the soap the innkeeper gave you?"

"This thing?" Dale held up the finger of what she thought must have been a bar of soap. "I couldn't wash a cat with this!"

Dale made a good point. It would mean leaving her alone, but Françoise would go. "Is there anything else you need while I am out?"

Dale looked as though she were trying to make a mental shopping list. "Where are we going from here?"

"I will visit the dock tomorrow to find out what ships are there."

"Okay. Let's see. Some needle, thread, and some material. Plain white material is fine."

"Material? What on earth do you need material for?"

"First of all, I'd like a pair of underpants, Françoise. I don't like walking around naked underneath. Also..." Dale nervously cleared her throat. "I need something for my monthly visitor."

"You are expecting someone? We will be on a ship, not at my château."

"No, no." Dale's face reddened. My monthly visitor is my.... oh God.... my period."

"Period?"

"You just want me to say it, don't you?" Dale sighed "My period. My monthly bleeding, all right? How do you cope with it?"

Françoise's lips tightened. "I do not have a problem with that."

"Why?"

"Because… because… I do not. That is all you need to know. Please do not ask any more." She didn't have the energy to tell her tale. Françoise thought she had left it all behind her when her husband died. She knew Dale hadn't meant to open old wounds, but it was a tale she hoped to bury and never speak of again.

\* \* \*

Françoise was floating in that state between sleep and awake when a pounding at the door roused her fully into consciousness. What was it about people waking her at all hours of the night? Sleepily, she got dressed into her disguise before answering the door. There was another loud pounding before she swung the door open. "I do not appreciate my sleep being disturbed—" She stopped speaking at the sight of three brawny men with somber faces. They batted their open palms with small clubs. She addressed the man she thought was the leader. "Monsieur, can I help you?" Françoise voice wavered as she tried to stay composed.

The man looked her up and down. She felt as though he had stripped away her clothes. "Where have you traveled from, citizen?" The deep voice resonated through her, unnerving her.

"Anjou."

"And how are things there?"

Was he seeking a lie? "Many citizens are confused, monsieur. News does not travel quickly to Anjou."

"And where are you going?"

"That is my business."

"Not tonight, citizen. We are the law here, so I ask you again. Where are you traveling to?"

"Home." Françoise felt it best to keep her lies simple. "My wife comes from the Colonies. We were visiting my family here when Paris fell. I am taking her home."

His dark eyes looked past her to a sleeping Dale. His gaze slowly raked over her prone form. Françoise stepped to one side to block his view.

"I do not appreciate you looking at my wife in a state of undress."

At that moment a melodic voice spoke. "Philippe?" Dale at least had the presence of mind to use the right name.

The man's eyes narrowed again for a long moment as he stared intently at Françoise. "Then be on your way quickly, citizen," he finally said. He turned to leave, his men trailing behind him.

Shaking, Françoise closed the door and leaned heavily against it as her insides trembled. She could feel her heartbeat in her throat from the scrutiny.

"What was that all about?"

"We cannot stay here. I have an uneasy feeling about this. I do not wish to be here if he decides to come back. Quickly. Get dressed."

Some minutes later, they left by the available ground floor window to the street. There were men everywhere, some standing around outside the inn drinking, others knocking on all the doors up and down the street, and others simply leaning against walls, watching. The horses were now inaccessible. They had no option but to travel on foot.

Françoise thought fast. It was the middle of the night. They had very little available money. The city was swarming with guards. They had nowhere to go except the one place she wanted to avoid. "Follow me," she whispered as they disappeared into the shadows of the night.

They had to detour many times before eventually reaching the dock area, where they stood in front of a large, scarred, wooden door. Over the portal hung a swinging sign that read, *Le panier fleuri de Lucette.*

"Where are we?"

"Somewhere where I hope someone will help us." Françoise was not sure what reception they would receive, but they had nowhere else to go. She didn't even bother to knock, knowing very well that this particular establishment never closed. They entered.

"May I help you, monsieur?" The young woman who greeted them looked a little surprised to see a young man with a woman behind him.

"I wish to see Madame Didieur, please."

"Is she expecting you?"

"No, but she will want to see me." Françoise's insides were knotted. As expected, when she looked at her hands, they shook slightly. Her chest tightened up at the approach of a woman whom she knew as well as her own mother.

"May I help you, monsieur?" As the older woman said the words, a strange look came over her face.

"Lucette." Françoise spoke normally to the woman, and her hazel eyes widened in recognition.

"Come, come." Lucette quickly ushered them into her room, closing the door behind them. "Françoise! Oh my God! I thought you were dead."

"I had to disguise myself, Tantine. I have run out of places to hide."

*"Tantine?"* Dale said, repeating one of the words she heard.

Françoise answered without taking her gaze from Lucette. "You would say... auntie. Lucette is a close friend. Closer than my mother ever was."

Dale watched with apparent interest as the conversation progressed. The older woman pulled Françoise into a friendly embrace.

"And who is this young woman?" Lucette asked.

"This is Dale. She is my..." What could she say? The love of my life? My lover? She said what she felt in her heart. "My wife."

"Wife?" Lucette studied Dale closely. "So, Dale. I am pleased to meet you."

"She cannot speak French, Tantine. She comes from the Colonies. America."

"Ahh, America. Well." Lucette hesitated and then spoke in broken English, "'allo, Dale. I... am... please... meet you."

*"Moi aussi, madame."* Dale looked over at Françoise. "Did I say it right?"

Lucette went to the door and opened it. The young woman who had first greeted them trotted up to her. "Amélie, prepare the back room for our guests, please." She handed over the key to the locked room. Lucette escorted them down a long hall to the last door.

There was the occasional moan and scream emanating from the various rooms they passed. "What's going on in there?" Dale asked.

Françoise felt the heat rise to her cheeks. "What does it sounds like."

"Oh?" Dale let out a nervous giggle. *"Ohh."* A blush tinged her face.

*"Oui."* Françoise could see Dale's confusion and was surprised when she didn't question the situation.

"You should be safe here," Lucette said.

"What about the others?" Françoise awaited her answer with a little trepidation.

"They can be trusted... monsieur." Lucette smiled. "Now let us all get some sleep and we will talk in the morning." She handed over the key to Françoise. "Secure the room from the inside." She turned to Dale again. *"Bonne nuit."*

*"Bonne nuit, madame."* Her American twang made the French sound foreign.

"Madame? No. It is Lucette... please." A gentle smile touched her lips.

"Then *bonne nuit,* Lucette." Dale graced her with a smile of her own.

After Lucette left, Dale turned to Françoise. "A bordello?"

"There was nowhere else for us to go."

"They know you in a bordello?" Dale awaited an answer, but Françoise ignored the question.

"I am tired, *chérie.* Time for sleep." With those final words, Françoise undressed and climbed into bed. Dale stared at her, obviously waiting for her to respond. Françoise would not oblige her.

# Chapter 17

Dale woke to an empty bed. She slid her hand over the sheet and felt the fading warmth. She looked around the room and saw that their belongings were still there. Maybe Françoise was talking to Lucette. Inhaling the scent that was her lover, Dale smiled.

She rose, dressed, and donned her cloak to cover the rip in her bodice. Opening the door, she walked down the hallway and attempted to close her ears to the sounds emanating from behind closed doors.

The door to one of the front rooms opened. A portly middle-aged man staggered out as he fumbled for the buttons on his pants. "Well, well, well... Lucette. Your quality of women is getting better." He made a grab for Dale's behind.

"Hey!" She swung around to face the man trying to feel her up. She glared at him. "Don't..." She stopped when she remembered about the language barrier.

"What is going on here?" It took a moment for Lucette to assess the situation. "Henri, you have had your fun, now back to your wife." She ushered the man out into the street and then turned her attention to Dale. "Come." Lucette led them into her empty room.

"Where's Françoise?"

Lucette looked thoughtful for a moment. *"Elle est allée au marché...* Err... mar... mark..."

"Market? Françoise has gone to the market?"

"Market. *Oui.*" Lucette studied Dale for a long moment. "You and Françoise..."

"Yes, we are a couple."

"Cup... couple... ah, *oui. Bien.* English not good." Dale suspected that Lucette's exposure to English consisted mainly of British sailors, which would mean that many salty words would liberally spatter her vocabulary.

"How do you know Françoise?"

*"Quoi donc?"*

"You and Françoise..." Dale brought her fingers together and saw the answering understanding in Lucette's eyes. *"S'il vous plait."* Françoise was not going to tell her, but Lucette knew the whole truth.

*"Non."* Lucette shook her head and waved her hands. *"Non, non, non."*

Dale grabbed her hands, holding them gently. "Please. I have to know."

Lucette finally closed her eyes as if making a decision. *"Le Comte."*

"The Count? Françoise's husband? What has he got to do with it?"

"It is none of your business." The deep voice resonated throughout the tiny room.

Dale turned to the door to see Françoise standing there. "Ahh, my handsome husband." But the compliment was not going to get her out of trouble. Françoise put down her basket full of parcels and closed the door.

"I wanted you to leave this matter alone, but you went behind my back."

"That's because I knew you would never tell me."

"Did you ever think it was because I did not want you to know?"

"Enough!" Lucette raised a hand to stop the argument. "What is going on?"

"Why were you going to tell her? She does not need to know."

To Dale's disappointment, they spoke solely in French. With her rudimentary knowledge of the language, she only caught a few words.

"Why not let her be the one to decide that, little one."

"Tantine, I... I..."

"I understand, child, you do not want to appear a fool in front of her."

"It is more than that, Lucette. Terrible things happened here, things that still haunt me."

"And we all live with them."

"I know." Françoise sighed deeply. "I know. I am so sorry for what he did to you and your girls."

"Do not forget to include yourself in that forgiveness, Françoise. You suffered, too."

"Maybe, but I am not the one carrying the visible scars of his tortured preferences."

"But you helped in your own way by sending us money."

"I know, but it is not enough. It will never be enough."

"Put your mind at rest, child. None of us harbors any ill will against you. The money you sent us helped where it was most needed." Lucette's expression softened. "Tell her. She deserves to know."

Dale watched the exchange and caught Lucette's last words. "You don't have to tell me," she said softly. "I'm sorry for asking Lucette, but I could see that you were troubled. I just wanted to help."

Françoise's mind raced in all directions. Should she tell Dale everything about her past? She was worried that the depth of her depravity would be too much of a shock for her young, naïve wife. Françoise looked over the top of Dale's head to Lucette standing behind her. Lucette nodded and gave her an encouraging smile.

"This…" she whispered. "This is my second home. I know this place well."

"You were a prostitute?" She searched Françoise's eyes. "I don't believe it. No." Dale shook her head emphatically. "No. I refuse to believe you were capable of it."

Lucette cleared her throat.

*"Non, mon petit cœur,* for him."

"He brought you here?"

Françoise could only nod in answer.

"Why?"

"Bad man," Lucette spat the words out. "Bad, bad man."

Dale looked back at Françoise.

"Remember when I said he was the devil? It was no idle comment. He was an evil man. His tastes in sex were…" She struggled for the right word.

"Perverse?" Dale offered.

"Yes. Perverse." Françoise looked at Lucette for confirmation and received a nod.

"He…" Françoise's hung her head, only to have Dale tip it up. "He made me," she said and looked again at Lucette, *"us* do unspeakable things, *chérie.* When I say I have done everything, I mean *everything.*" Dale wiped away a stray tear trickling down Françoise's cheek.

The smell of vomit, her hands glistening with her own blood—
Françoise remembered it like it was yesterday. All he did was smile
at her. An evil smile that barely masked his excitement.

"Some of these women were not as lucky as I was." Her voice
was barely a whisper. "At least my scars were on the inside. Now do
you see why I did not want to tell you? He does this to me. I never
feared anything in my life, except him. I could not leave because he
would hunt me down. Out of spite, he would hurt these women
here."

"Honor bound to the last breath, just as I knew you would be."
Dale smiled gently.

"Pardon?"

"Even then you were thinking as much for these women as you
were of yourself. You were in a horrible position, and yet you bore
it to protect them."

"I… I never thought of it that way."

"No. You wouldn't. That's just you. You take responsibility for
everything, even when it's not your fault."

Françoise managed a smile. Maybe Dale was right. It was not
fear that kept her there but a need to protect those around her.

"Are you going to tell her everything, little one?" Lucette
asked. "What about how he died?"

"No, Tantine! She is to never know, do you understand me?
That is for you and me, and we will die with that secret."

"But—"

"I said no!" Françoise tried to rein in her roiling emotions.

"Are you afraid she will think less of you?"

"Of course not." Françoise tried to sound indignant, but they
both knew the truth.

"Please, Françoise," Dale said." I don't know all of what you
said, but I understand enough to know you're struggling with
something in your past. Free yourself and please tell me everything.
Put your husband's memory where it belongs… in the ground."

Lucette made a move toward the door.

"And where are you going, Tantine?"

Lucette jumped at the sound of Françoise's voice. "Do not
scare me like that. I am letting you two have some time alone."

"If we wanted that, our room is only down the hall. Come.
Let's end this serious discussion and enjoy some sweet delicacies."

"But, Francoise—"

*"Non, Dale. Enough!"*

Apparently, her tone let Dale know that now was not the time to reopen the past because she let the matter drop. Françoise moved to the basket and extracted a piece of cloth. "Try one." She offered Lucette a small hand-made pastry nestled in the cloth before offering one to Dale and finally taking one herself. "Mmm... *palets bretons.*"

"What have you been up to?" Dale asked before she took a bite of the pastry.

Françoise heard the disappointment in her voice about being dismissed, but Françoise wouldn't let it deter her. "What you asked me to do." She reached into the basket, extracted two parcels, and tossed them to Dale. "Those herbs you wanted and the cloth. And a few other things that I thought we would need."

"But did you find the soap?"

"It was not easy. It seems that this city does not believe in bathing." She pulled out two waxy bars and passed them over to Dale as well. *"Non.* I could not find the shopkeeper. I had to barter for these, so use them wisely."

Dale held the presents against her chest, as if fearing someone would snatch them away, before placing them back in the basket. "Soap, soap, soap." She sounded like a small child given a shiny new toy.

Françoise laughed at her antics and was pleased to see that look of joy on her face once more. "Come, we will leave Lucette to her business. Tantine, if you need us, we will be in our room."

"I will knock first." Lucette winked.

Françoise winked back. "Good idea."

As they walked down the shadowed corridor, a large hand grabbed Dale's elbow. "Now, here is a willing bedmate." Françoise tried to steer Dale around the man obstructing the hallway.

"You have no other business than to attend to me, wench!" He kicked in the nearest door and pushed Dale inside. Françoise followed closely behind, intent on protecting her. "Now, get those clothes off quickly, woman. I paid good money for some service." He was already reaching for his belt, fumbling with the rough-hewn buckle.

They were cornered. If Françoise caused a scene, the man could look more closely at them and may discover that she was a woman. The walls closed in on her as she realized which room this was.

Dale looked over at her as she backed away from the man. "What's wrong?"

"This room," she mumbled. "No, no, no." Françoise shrank into a corner and wrapped her arms around herself.

"Françoise?" Dale obviously forgot to call her Philippe. She moved toward her, but the man grabbed her arm. "Leave me alone!" She shook free and reached for Françoise.

Françoise flinched and looked at her. "No more. Please! The pain!"

"What is it? I don't understand." Dale tried to pull her into her arms.

"Stay away, please!" Françoise held up her hands and tried to push Dale away.

"What did he do to you?"

There was blood. Too much blood. Françoise looked at her hands and at the floor. The blood was everywhere. She reached for her crotch. "Please, monsieur!" she cried out.

At that moment, the door flew open and half a dozen women rushed in, moved to their customer, and ushered him out the door.

This time, Dale was able to cradle Françoise to her chest. "Let me help you. I'm here for you." She gently stroked her hair. "I love you. Everything will be all right."

Lucette stood in the doorway. "Get her out of here."

Although Françoise knew that Dale didn't understand the words, she must have understood their intent.

"Come on, my love," Dale whispered.

Lucette helped her to get Françoise to her feet and move her to their room at the end of the corridor.

"I am so sorry, little one. He was too quick for me. Are you all right?"

"That room." Françoise took a deep breath and allowed the precious air to flow through her.

Dale looked at Lucette. "Room? The bad man?" Her eyes widened, and she turned to her partner.

Françoise tried to gain control of her emotions as she was held in the grasp of her painful memories. She felt numb. It had been quite a while since she had suffered such a visceral reaction to the past. "I am sorry. The room surprised me."

"You mean it caught you unawares."

"I did not expect that."

"Excuse me." With a final look at Françoise, Lucette left them alone.

"What is so bad that you can't tell me?" Dale reached for Françoise's hand and guided her to their bed. She gently pushed her down to sit on the mattress and sat next to her. Françoise tried to pull free and stand, but Dale held her firmly in place. "No. It stops here. You obviously don't trust me enough to share your pain."

"It is not about trust."

"It has everything to do with trust." Dale lifted her hand and palmed Françoise's cheek. "We're in this together, for better or for worse."

"I am trying to protect you."

Dale dropped her hand. "It sounds more like you're trying to protect yourself."

"That is ridiculous."

"No? What are you afraid of, huh? That I won't love you anymore?" Dale stared hard at Françoise. "That's it, isn't it? You're afraid that your little secret will drive us apart."

Françoise lowered her head. *"Oui,* I know that it will."

Dale touched her cheek. "Please look at me." Françoise met her eyes. "You really don't get it, do you? I left my life behind to be with you."

"So little time…"

"I agree. There has been little time to get to know one another. Well, here's your chance."

Françoise's shoulders slumped as she felt the weight of Dale's words. "I… this is too hard."

"Come on." Dale patted Françoise's hand. "Start at the beginning."

"You know the beginning. My parents agreed to the marriage to *le Comte* in exchange for a large dowry. I did not know him, and at first, the marriage was polite. We knew nothing of one another."

"When did things change?"

"About a season after the marriage." Françoise took a deep breath. "It started at the chateau—first an errant smack, then a riding crop. But it was not enough. He sought out somewhere private to inflict his pain."

"And you ended up here."

"Once a month at the beginning. Toward the end of his life, it was once a week, maybe more if he was well enough to travel."

"That would barely give his victims time to recover."

*"Oui.* Lucette had to find more girls."

"That bastard!"

Françoise looked down at her trembling hands. "Part of his amusement was to make me whip them. I did not want to, but if I did not, I would also be punished and one of the servants who accompanied us would mete out the punishment in my stead."

"Oh, Françoise."

"What could I do? He had all the power and I had none. He…" Françoise struggled to speak.

Dale caressed Françoise's hand. "And I just bet you tried to make the lashes softer than they should have been."

"I tried, but he knew my intentions."

"And he punished you for it."

Françoise's head dropped.

"Come here." Dale pulled Françoise into her arms and hugged her tightly.

"That was not the end." The words Françoise spoke sounded like those of a frightened child. "The whip was never enough. He made more and more wild demands."

"Hence the reference to the Marquis de Sade."

"*Oui.* Even imprisonment in Le Bastille could not quiet that man's disgusting rhetoric."

"Why can't you have children?"

"You know why. Must I say it?" A single tear dropped from Françoise's damp eyelash. It slowly trickled down her cheek and rested on the curve of her jaw.

Dale gently wiped it away. "If you don't want to, no, but I want to know everything. This is all part of who you are, Françoise. This is a side of you that few will get to see, and I hope to be one of that precious few. What did he do?"

"He had more than one use for his whip. There were so many toys at his command and too much blood." Françoise looked at her hands.

"Yet you survived."

"I nearly died. It was after that my menses ceased. The physician informed me that I would not have children." Françoise smiled sadly. "I was glad I could not give him a son."

"And Lucette?"

"These girls bore the scars of his insanity. I tried to help with coin, but it never seemed enough." She shuddered. "Can we talk of something else, *chérie?* Please." Dale smiled. "What?"

"You called me *chérie.*"

"So?"

"That means you haven't drawn away from me." Dale leaned in to press her lips against Françoise's before pulling back. "What happened to him?"

Françoise clenched her jaw.

"I never said this conversation would be easy."

"I killed him."

Dale looked into Françoise's eyes as she obviously waited for her to continue. "Three words. That's it?"

"They are the three words that matter."

"There has to be more. How did you kill him?"

"What does it matter? I committed murder. How do you feel about me now?"

"I still feel the same, Françoise. I know in my heart that you're a good woman, and I will continue to tell you that until you believe me."

"My life, and the lives of these girls, had become a nightmare. I had to do something. I poisoned him."

"Did he know what you did?"

"Not at first. I am not sure he even knew at the end. I put a little into his food every night until he died." Françoise sniffed and another tear tracked down her face.

"I could say good riddance, but I don't think that's what you want to hear." Dale lay back on the bed and pulled Françoise with her. She wrapped her arms around her and snuggled in tightly. "You were wrong."

"I was?"

"You told me, and I'm still here. I love you even more because you trusted me with your secret. Well, your *other* secret." Dale touched her lips to Françoise's forehead. "Besides, I'm sure Lucette and the girls would think you're a hero for what you did. You saved them, and yourself. Don't ever forget that."

"It is the only truth I hold onto, *chérie*. You are right. He is dead." But even from the grave, he had a hold over her. Now, leaving these shores was more important than ever. "We have to get out of here."

"Why?"

"It is too dangerous." Françoise stared at the door, afraid at any moment the past would come bursting through.

"If it's because of him…"

*"Non!"* Françoise said it a little more forcefully than she intended. *"Non.* There will be trouble here. Soon." She stood up and acting quickly, she reached into the bottom of their bag for some coin. "Make your underpants, Dale." She tossed the wrapped packet in Dale's direction. "I will be back soon."

"Where are you going now?"

174

"To find a ship."

* * *

Françoise breathed in the sea air as she stood outside in the street. Dale had given her a lot to think about. Her husband's specter had hovered over her for far too long, and she wished to be rid of it. The trip to the Colonies would put some distance between her and her homeland, but Dale would be the balm for her troubled soul.

With a name from Lucette in her possession, she had searched out a moneylender who would not ask questions about gold coin. The sooner they left this godforsaken country, the better. However, as she stepped onto the wooden pier, things did not look good. There was only one ship moored at the now-deserted waterfront.

"Monsieur." She addressed an aging fisherman sitting on the edge of a pylon. "Where are the ships?"

"All gone. That one is the only one left."

"When are more due?"

"Not for four or five days."

She now had no choice, unless they left Nantes and took to the road once again. Maybe Bordeaux... She took a step toward the lone ship.

"But I would not travel on that one."

"Why?"

"It is a slave ship, or so I have been told."

"Told?"

"I have not seen this ship before. It is smaller than the regular slave ships that stop here, but the ship's sailors claim that it is indeed picking up slaves."

Françoise studied the vessel, noticing the garish silhouette of a fox on the stern. Below it was written, *"Le Renard."* "Where will it be heading?"

"Where they all do. First to Africa, then across the water to the Colonies."

The Colonies? Maybe she could honor her promise to Dale after all. "America?"

"No, monsieur. St. Domingue."

Françoise looked at the ship once more. If it got them partway there, maybe they could find another ship to take them the rest of the way. She ignored the possibility that they could be killed in a slave rebellion or end up stranded in a port that could be even more dangerous than Nantes. She started toward the vessel before she even completed the thought.

"Your need must be great then, monsieur."

She looked over her shoulder to see the old man studying her carefully. "It is. My wife's father is gravely ill, and we need to get to the Colonies as quickly as we can." The intense stare softened a little, but she wasn't sure whether her reason was good enough, at least in this man's eyes. "Thank you for your assistance."

She boldly strode along the pier, the wooden planks vibrating with each sturdy step. Françoise stood at the bottom of the gangway and looked up at the deck. A couple of burly sailors glanced up from their work, their weather-beaten faces scowling at her approach.

"I wish to see the captain." Her voice was deep and strong.

Neither of them spoke, but one dropped his rope and walked off toward the cabins. A moment later another man emerged, dressed in clothes that were more for show than practicality. "Yes?" His voice was heavy and gravelly and spoke of malevolence. "I am Captain Beaudry."

Françoise took an instant dislike to the man. She almost turned away, but a scuffle at the dock front strengthened her resolve. They could not stay here. "I am looking for passage to St. Domingue, Captain."

"I do not take passengers, at least not willing ones." He laughed loudly, showing his stained, decaying teeth. The two sailors joined in the laughter.

"Nevertheless, monsieur, I am asking for passage for myself and my wife."

His demeanor changed. "You are in a hurry to get out of France?" His eyes narrowed as if searching for the truth in Françoise's eyes.

"In a way, Captain. My wife is from the Colonies, and her father is gravely ill. We need to get home as quickly as possible." She kept her expression neutral.

"One hundred *livres*... each."

Françoise tightened her jaw at the outrageous price, but they both knew he had the upper hand.

"And you sleep below deck."

"One hundred more, and we get the captain's cabin."

His eyes widened at the offer. Slowly, a smile crossed his craggy features. "I suppose it would not hurt me to sleep with the crew for one voyage."

"Very well. It is a deal. Let us shake on it, Captain. I would hate to think that the deal would be changed later." She moved toward him when he offered no such courtesy. She didn't hesitate in grabbing his hand, shaking it firmly. "The deal is sealed. When do we sail?"

"Tomorrow morning with the tide. We will sail to Ouidah first before continuing to St. Domingue. I have a package or two to pick up there before we continue." He turned his back and walked away, chuckling at his own joke.

As Françoise left the vessel, she made a mental note to shop for more weapons. She felt they would need them.

Now that she had taken care of the most pressing business, she set off to find the most important one. She drew out the piece of paper Gérard had given her and read the name. Sébastien Baptiste— the man who held Gérard's trust and her future in his hands. Quickly, she negotiated the narrow cobblestone streets as she tried to avoid the groups of armed men where she could. The small livery finally came into view where a brawny middle-aged man was working industriously over his anvil with a large hammer.

When it was safe to do so, Françoise crossed the street and approached the man. "Monsieur!" she shouted, trying to raise her voice over the din of his work.

The palest blue eyes she had ever seen slowly slid over her, as if trying to decide whether she was friend or foe. "Yes?"

"Gérard sent me."

"Gérard?" He looked up and down the street and motioned Françoise to follow him. "You know Gérard?"

Françoise handed over the letter she had been guarding all the way from Anjou. She was almost afraid to ask about the mirror for fear of hearing of its demise. And yet Dale was still here. She didn't understand how the mirror worked, but wouldn't the magic die if the mirror was completely broken?

"Yes, monsieur." Sébastien looked at the paper in the dim light. He moved closer to the open door to read the note. "Philippe Théroux, your property is safe. It arrived yesterday."

"Oh, monsieur, I am indebted to you. Thank you very much." Françoise hadn't realized she'd been holding her breath until the tightness in her chest told her to breathe.

"No need. Gérard asked for a favor, which I gladly give. He is a good man."

"Indeed he is. Indeed he is."

"What do you wish me to do with it now?"

"There is a ship in the harbor, *Le Renard,* leaving on the tide in the morning. Can you arrange delivery first thing?"

"You do not want me to deliver it today?"

"No. I have a feeling Captain Beaudry cannot be trusted. It would be better for me to be there to receive it."

"As you wish."

"I thank you, Sébastien. In these dangerous times, it is hard to find someone to trust."

"Anything for Gérard, Philippe. For him to ask such a favor, he must hold you in high regard."

Françoise smiled. If only he knew the whole story.

"I also need to find some weapons. I fear this journey is not going to be a smooth one."

Sébastien disappeared for a minute. He returned with two daggers and a heavier sword than her rapier. She studied the workmanship. While not finely crafted, they were sturdy, well made and quite serviceable. "Did you make these?"

"It is not common knowledge."

"Are you prepared to sell them?"

"They are a gift to Gérard's friend."

"No. I cannot accept these."

"Philippe, I offer them freely. It sounds like you will be more in need of them than I."

"I do not... it is too..." She stopped herself. "Thank you, Sébastien. That is most generous of you. I am also in need of a pistol."

"Say no more. Two streets that way." His pointed his pudgy finger up the gentle incline. "Look for the shop front of Marcel Jugnon."

"Monsieur, Gérard has chosen his friends wisely." Her words drew a grin from the blacksmith. "Here." She handed over some coin to him. Not gold, but *livres.* Valuable just the same.

"There is no need."

"Take it. Please." He hesitated as his hand hovered over hers. "For taking such good care of my property." A small smile touched her lips. He met her eyes and then dropped his gaze to the coins in her hand. Before he could change his mind, she flipped his hand over and poured the coins onto his palm. She closed his hand into a fist. "Until tomorrow then."

"Until tomorrow."

She left the workshop without another word, her footsteps a little lighter. They had passage, and the mirror was safe.

* * *

Trying to make a pair of underpants was turning out to be quite an undertaking. No scissors to cut the material, and Dale would give her life savings for a sewing machine. She had considered just going without them, but it was more than a matter of clothing. It was a matter of coping in a world without mechanical aids.

She had grown accustomed to the unusual sounds emanating from the other rooms, only because it never stopped. Day and night, all the time. She was living in a bordello. Her mother would have a hissy fit. A *major* hissy fit. Sucking her thumb after another needle prick in a long line of needle pricks, her hearing picked up a new sound. She set the sewing aside before she went to the door, opening it a crack to see what was going on.

"*Madame… s'il vous plait.*"

"*Non.*"

A young girl, seventeen or eighteen years old, was pleading with Lucette. It was desperate and emotional. Lucette was vainly trying to discourage whatever the young woman wanted.

Dale opened the door farther and poked her head out into the hallway. The action stopped the conversation. Lucette looked over her shoulder and motioned for Dale to return to her room. But she never was one to do as she was told. Her heart leapt into her throat as the front door opened, sending her scurrying for the relative safety of their room. She wished for no more confrontations with any customer.

* * *

Françoise felt the tension release in her neck once she walked back through the bordello front door. Things were getting very agitated in the streets. There had been some shoving and swearing among small groups of armed men, but so far, the peace was still intact. As she entered, she encountered a heated discussion between Lucette and a young girl.

"Madame, I have nowhere else to turn. Please…"

"Uh…"

"Rosalie."

"Rosalie, this is no life for you. Do you not understand that?"

"But, madame…"

"No."

A flash of movement caught Françoise's eye. She saw Dale slip back into their room.

"What is going on?" Françoise asked.

"Monsieur, please, this is a conversation between Madame Lucette and myself."

"Girl, this is not a customer. He lives here." Lucette glanced down at the two plump chickens dangling from Françoise's hand.

"This is for dinner." Françoise handed over the poultry, smiling at Lucette's look of gratitude. "I hope you have someone to cook these. You know cooking is not a skill of mine."

"I am sure that is still so, little one." She raised her voice. "Honorine, I have something for you!" A small, middle-aged woman trotted out from the back of the establishment, wiping her hands on a ragged cloth. "Our friend here has donated these to the pot. Treat them well." Almost reverently, Honorine carried the chickens back toward the kitchen, mumbling to herself about how to cook them.

"She is a little cracked, but she can make anything edible." Lucette smiled at the antics of their resident cook. She turned back to Rosalie. Sighing, she looked at Françoise, a silent plea in her eyes.

"Oh, no, no, no, no. Stop looking at me that way, Tantine."

"I have no more room, Philippe. She does not deserve a life here, and you know it."

Rosalie became agitated. "I am not going with him. I am trying to get away from one man. Why would I go to another?"

"And yet you want to work in a bordello," Françoise snapped. "You cannot pick and choose as you like, girl. Especially here. Maybe it would be better if you return home to your husband."

"Husband? Oh no. He is evil. My parents have sold me to marry him, but I will *never* be his bride."

That struck a chord within her. This was her tale all over again. Françoise looked deep into the child's hazel eyes, trying to ascertain the truth within them. *Damn.* Frustrated, she walked away. Why did everyone think she could solve their problems?

Dale went back to her sewing as she awaited Françoise. Moments later, Françoise stepped through the door and threw a couple of parcels into the basket sitting on the floor.

"And what are you doing?"

"Sewing, like you asked me to." Dale tried to put on her best innocent face.

"Then why were you looking out of the room?"

"Asking Lucette for help?"

Françoise pursed her lips at Dale, who sat there batting her eyelashes at her. "I doubt that. And stop trying to distract me. I know you were being curious. That could get you killed."

"It didn't stop you asking questions." Françoise's lips slowly spread into a smile as Dale talked. "What did you find out?"

"We leave in the morning with the mirror."

Dale wondered why Françoise wouldn't meet her eyes. It was as if she was holding something back. "Really? And where are we heading?"

"St. Domingue."

"Where on earth is that?"

"It is a French colony over the sea. Somewhere near America, I believe. I am not sure."

"Home?"

"Not quite, but close enough. From there we will seek passage the rest of the way."

"I knew you could do it." She threw her arms around Françoise and smothered her cheeks in kisses. "I love you."

*"Moi aussi, ma chérie."* Françoise drew Dale's lips to hers. The kiss was passionate and hinted of the pleasure to come. "Now, I have things to do before we sail." Françoise tried to pull away, but Dale wouldn't let her go. "Dale, please. There is not much time."

"There is always time, my love."

"Not now. We sail first thing in the morning, and there are still some things I must try to find."

"I don't need anything but you."

"And I you, but love alone will not sustain our hunger or our safety."

"Oh, I don't know." Dale backed away, letting her eyes slide over Françoise's obvious assets. "I think you could satisfy my hunger."

*"Mon Dieu.* You are going to kill me." Francoise turned on her heel and stalked out of the room.

Dale laughed. "I'll try, my sweet. Maybe I'll finish that bedtime story tonight."

Françoise muttered some expletives as she headed down the hallway.

"Is there a problem?" Lucette asked.

"My partner was trying to convince me to stay."

"Then why are you fighting it?"

"Because we sail in the morning."

"So?"

"It is a slave ship."

"Is that wise?" Concern etched Lucette's face. "What is to stop them robbing and killing you while at sea?"

"This." Françoise grasped the rapier dangling at her side. "I will not give up without a fight."

"Is there no other recourse?"

"The harbor is empty. There will be no ships for another four to five days."

"You can always hide here... Philippe." Lucette stumbled on the name.

"Trouble is coming. We cannot stay and neither should you."

"Leave? I do not think so."

"The streets are full of men—angry, drunken men—and they are all looking for a fight. I do not want you caught in the middle of it."

"Where am I supposed to go, eh? I have lived here most of my life. These girls are in the same predicament. This is all we have."

"But..."

"No. If you have to go, then fine. Do what you have to do. But do not ask me to leave."

"You are the most stubborn..." Francoise rubbed her hand over her face.

"Philippe, I think that finger you are pointing is facing the wrong direction." With that final comment, she turned and walked away.

*Maybe the vendors in the street won't give me as much trouble as this old woman.*

The sun was valiantly trying to shine through the smattering of dark clouds. Françoise looked one way then the other as she tried to decide which way to go. The pistol was her first priority, so she walked in the direction of the livery. She waved at Sébastien as she passed and continued up the hill. As he had directed, she found Monsieur Jugnon's shop two streets away.

The bell above the door announced her arrival, and a slim man with wire-rimmed glasses emerged from the back. "Monsieur? How may I help you?"

"I am in need of a pistol."

"I do not—"

"Sébastien Baptiste directed me to you."

"Our city does not want troublemakers."

"I am leaving in the morning aboard the ship moored in the harbor."

"Oh. One moment." He disappeared through the curtain, leaving Françoise alone to look around the shop. There were no weapons in sight. In their place, trunks, chests, and boxes of varying sizes and quality were on display.

A plain, rough-hewn, but sturdy chest caught her eye. Their supplies were mounting and needed a home. Her mind returned to the captain. The man could not be trusted—that much was obvious. This particular chest took her fancy because of the large lock that hung from the clasp.

"Monsieur." The voice cut through her thoughts as the vendor returned with two identical pistols. "Twenty *livres* each."

"Twenty?"

"I will include a good supply of ammunition for free." Despite his earlier reluctance to sell weapons, his eyes told a different story.

"Fine." Françoise schooled her expression as the man smiled. "I am also interested in that chest." She nodded her head in the direction of the plain chest, unaware that his eyes had landed on the ornate piece sitting next to it.

"Fifty *livres*."

"Fifty? For that?"

"It took many hours to make, monsieur. Surely, you do not begrudge me for the craftsmanship put into its making."

"It is just a box." Craftsmanship? Obviously, what Françoise considered fine craft work was not the same as what this man thought.

"But the carvings alone took me a number of days."

"Carvings? Oh, no. The one next to it. The one with the lock."

"Oh." His forlorn face nearly made her laugh. His precious *livres* were flying out the window. "Fifteen *livres*, but as you can see it is very plain."

"That is all I need. Nothing more." Anything more ornate would only draw the captain's attention. "I will give you twenty if you can deliver it for me."

"Twenty? Of course." His eyes gleamed with greed. "And where would you like it delivered?"

"Lucette's on the waterfront."

"Lucette's?" He looked Françoise up and down.

"Lucette is family, monsieur. Be careful what you say." Françoise was starting to feel sorry for the brothel madam. They all scorned her in public, but behind closed doors, many of them had turned to her establishment for comfort. Hypocrites. "I would like that lock reinforced and two keys please."

"As you wish, monsieur. It will be delivered later today, along with the pistols."

Françoise nodded. The man's face lit up as coin after coin hit his palm.

"I have a dilemma. I wish to block a door without using a lock and key. Do you have any suggestions?"

"Hmm…" He tapped his index finger against his lips. "Stop a door opening… ah. I have it. Give me a moment." He turned and walked out the back, disappearing for a few minutes before returning with several chunks of wood in his hands. He dropped the wood onto the table and sorted through the off-cuts. He found the one he must have thought suitable for the job. He walked over to the door and slipped the wedge underneath, effectively blocking it.

"Simple but effective. Very good. Monsieur, you are a genius." Now, she could get some sleep on the voyage and keep the human hounds at bay.

* * *

It had been a long, long day. Françoise sat at the dinner table and allowed the brisk conversation to flow around her. She had no energy to participate, and she gave up trying to translate the thread of conversation for Dale.

"And where are you from, monsieur?" Edith was the smallest girl in the establishment, her brown curls bouncing merrily. Françoise had seen her earlier escorting a bull of a man into one of the front rooms and wondered how she survived such an encounter.

"Anjou."

"Are you staying in Nantes for long?" Françoise turned to Sabine whose dark looks made her one of the busiest girls in the bordello.

"Just passing through. We're sailing on the tide tomorrow."

"Ooh, travel. I always wanted to travel," Violette said excitedly. She was one of Lucette's longer-serving girls. Françoise remembered she'd been saving her coin to travel. "Maybe England or Portugal. Or maybe Italy."

Françoise's eyes began to droop.

Dale must have noticed. "How about we call it a night?"

"Call it a night?"

"Let's go to bed, my love."

"I do not think…"

"To sleep, Philippe. You are out on your feet."

Françoise did not argue and pushed herself back from the table. "Tantine, I am sorry. I am so tired."

"No need. I was wondering how long it would take you to retire." Lucette smiled. "Your eyes were half-closed."

She summoned the strength to simply say, "Good night."

"Good night." The chorus echoed along the walls as the two women walked down the corridor to their room.

"I'm tired of listening to all of that." Dale waved at the rooms they passed. "All that sex would become tiresome, don't you think?"

"*Oui*, very tiresome."

"Oh, God, Françoise. I'm sorry."

"Do not be. It was my choice, not yours."

"Do you… do you miss it? I mean, they say variety is the spice of life."

Françoise stopped her in the hallway. "I have never regretted my decision. I love you with all my heart."

Dale's eyes welled up. "But I know so little."

"Do you not realize yet that does not matter to me? I have not lost any of the pleasure because you are inexperienced. Matters of the heart and mind are more eternal than fleeting pleasure, my love. I have never been happier."

"Really?" Dale gave her a tentative smile.

"*Oui*, really. I would move heaven and earth for you, *chérie*. You are the only one who ever loved me for who I am. Me. Françoise. I thank God every night for sending you to me."

Dale guided her through the door to their bed and pushed her onto the mattress. "Come on, sleep time for tired aristocrats."

"But… no… aristocrat." Françoise could barely form the words as sleep overtook her. The last thing she remembered was Dale removing her clothes.

# Chapter 18

Françoise slipped out of bed, careful not to disturb her sleeping partner. She had wanted to see Lucette alone before they left and now was as good a time as any, if not better. It was a change of shift, if she could call it that, when some husbands went home to their wives, and other husbands came in on their way to work.

"Tantine," she called quietly as the door to their bedroom clicked closed behind her. "One moment of your time."

"Of course. Let me show my cust… this gentlemen into room two." The older woman gave her a wink. Seconds later, Lucette emerged, looking worn out. She steered Françoise into her own room.

"You should get some rest."

"I did, child, but somehow it never seems enough."

"Maybe you should turn to one of your girls for help."

"No, they are too busy on their backs."

A thought popped into Françoise's head. It seemed like a simple solution. "How about that girl? You know, from yesterday? What was her name?"

"Rosalie."

"Yes. Rosalie. Train her as your assistant. You will get some rest, and it will keep her off the streets and out of beds." Françoise studied Lucette. "You know you are not getting any younger."

"Are you my mother now?"

"No. I am not your mother, but someone has to look out for you." Françoise let her eyes convey her feelings. "I was fearful of coming here. So much pain. But you know that only too well. I am sorry for not coming sooner. I had never forgotten this place and what happened here. Please understand. And it was why I could not return."

Lucette gripped her arm. "There is no need for explanations. I do understand. Things have been busy here anyway, even more so since the unrest. All of this heightened anxiety and fear has driven the men to my door. I can barely keep up with the demand."

"Unrest? Or is it war? Whatever it is always stirs up the emotions and the libido. You are performing a valuable service."

"Valuable service?" Lucette laughed loudly. "Valuable service… I have never been called that before."

"The reason I wanted to see you before I go is to give you this." She handed over a sack. Lucette's eyes widened at the sound of the clinking of coin.

"Oh no. Keep that. You will need it in the New World."

"We are comfortable. Do not worry."

"But business is good, my little heart."

"Then keep it for when you all grow old." Still Lucette hesitated. "Please, for me. Take it." Lucette held onto the sack, her gnarled fingers barely able to cup the money bag.

Her gaze went from Françoise's face on down her body. She paused on the bulge in the pants before continuing. "Well then, I have something for you, Françoise."

"Me?"

"Yes, you." Lucette went to an aged cabinet in the corner and took out something wrapped in cotton. "You are barely a threat with that." She handed over the parcel.

"With what?"

"Just look."

Françoise unwrapped the material. "Oh…" She looked down to her crotch.

"Never fear, Françoise, it has never been used."

"How did you know what I was thinking?"

"Ah, *chérie,* your nose crinkles up right there." Lucette lifted a finger to touch the bridge of Françoise's nose. "On a ship full of men, we cannot have you looking less than impressive, now can we?"

"I suppose not. But you giving it to me is strange."

"Oh, tish tosh. I am sure your little Dale will not object either." With that final word, she gave her a wink and ushered her out the door. "Honorine is serving breakfast now, if you hurry."

\* \* \*

Dale woke to another empty bed. Getting up at daybreak definitely was for the birds. She lay on her stomach. Her blurry eyes fixated on the trunk that now occupied their room. Françoise had been busy yesterday, but the appearance of the trunk lent testament to how much she had accomplished.

"Did I wake you?"

Dale looked toward the door and saw Françoise standing there.

"No," she mumbled, her voice raspy with sleep.

"It is time to rise. The ship will sail soon, and we must not miss it."

"I know, I know." But she couldn't summon up the energy. All she wanted was to drift back to sleep wrapped in Françoise's loving arms. A swat on the backside made her jump. "Hey! I was getting up."

"Uh-huh." Françoise's eyebrow rose. She moved away and propped herself near the door.

"Did you have to buy so much stuff?"

"Stuff?"

"In the trunk. Are we going to need all of that?" Dale rolled onto her back and stretched like a feline.

"Need? Uh..." Françoise stumbled over her words.

Dale knew she was teasing her mercilessly.

"Please do not do that," Françoise said. "Breakfast is waiting."

"Do what?" Dale gave her a sly grin. "Oh. Is what I did so bad?"

"It is when we are in a hurry. Come on, wench. Move."

"But we may not have another chance until we reach land again." Dale's voice dropped to a seductive whisper.

"I know. Believe me I know, but now is not the time."

"But I think it is." Dale slowly pushed aside the blanket to reveal pale skin. She beckoned her with a finger.

A sweat broke out on Françoise's upper lip. "I hope I have some *palets bretons* left."

"*Palets...* what?"

"Those... um... cakes, because there will be no meal for us."

It still took some moments to get undressed, but Dale knew that she could find a shortcut or two to speed things up. She could feel the heat of Françoise's stare as her own gaze slid down her body, resting on the point where her pants hung open. Dale's gaze rose to Françoise's. Her face heated at being caught ogling Françoise so openly.

Françoise wasted no time climbing into bed. While Dale didn't mind the intense attention, Françoise's urgency was blinding her senses. "What's the hurry?"

"We have a boat to catch."

"Oh, yeah. I forgot." Françoise lowered her lips to Dale's throat. "Oh God."

Françoise chuckled at Dale's inability to form words. *"Oui, one of us has to remember, little one."* She gently massaged the soft skin and defined muscle, as if preparing the way for her assault.

"I have an idea," Dale said with some hesitation, unsure how Françoise would react.

Françoise smiled as Dale rolled her over onto her back and descended, turning her body at the last second so that she was facing away.

Dale probed her with her tongue and Françoise knew what she wanted in return. *"Mon Dieu!"*

Françoise laved the moist skin. Dale jumped when she felt her tongue for the first time. Time and again, she teased her, and each time a soft noise escaped Dale's lips.

The temperature in the room rose steadily as their breathing increased. Their bodies broke out in a thin sheen of sweat. For the moment, all was forgotten. Their flight, their danger, and the fall of a dynasty held no meaning, only the fulfillment of their desire. They worked in perfect harmony.

Françoise knew this position well and yet she didn't know how to describe what she was feeling. She of course liked it, not only because it felt so good, but also because she knew Dale was feeling the same sensation. Françoise added a finger and then a thumb. Dale moaned at the move.

She pulled her mouth away. "Ah, *ma chérie...* so..." Françoise's words died on her lips when Dale copied her, vigorously stimulating her. Her orgasm approached suddenly and sent her body into spasms of delight. Dale joined her, crying out as her body stiffened in climax.

As much as she would like to remain in bed with Dale, Françoise knew it wasn't possible. There was precious little time to reach *Le Renard* before it sailed.

"Now, we must move." Françoise stood on shaky legs. She smacked the naked backside next to her. "Now, Dale!"

Dale swung her legs off the bed and stood, swaying slightly. "I hate this crack of dawn shit," she muttered.

"My, my. Such language." Françoise poured a liberal amount of water into the ceramic bowl. "Wash up quickly because we need to leave as soon as we are done."

* * *

Françoise stood at the dock and watched the two young men struggle with the full trunk. As she had predicted, the farewell was awash with tears, more on Lucette's part than her own. She had shed her tears years ago.

Françoise glanced at the dilapidated building that was Lucette's bordello. This would be the last time she'd see the place. She felt ashamed that she had fallen apart in *that* room, but it had caught her off guard.

Beads of sweat dotted the young faces of the men as they struggled under the weight of the trunk. "Up the gangway to the captain's cabin. Thank you." She patted one of them on the shoulder as they passed and felt a certain amount of sympathy as the weight of the box had to have cut deep into their hands. Her gaze fell on the captain. She noted the gleam in his eye. At least the trunk was heavy enough to slow him down in stealing it.

Dale stood patiently by while the men carried the chest into the cabin. Françoise was filled with trepidation about the upcoming voyage. Dale tugged on her sleeve and pointed to a large man driving a wagon along the waterfront.

"The mirror," Françoise murmured, trying not to let her voice carry. "That is Sébastien. It seems he is a good friend of Gérard."

Dale nodded. The wagon changed direction and steered slowly along the pier toward them. The horse's head hung down, as if finding the load too heavy, his legs moving in a shuffling gait.

Françoise paid the two lads the agreed amount, plus a little bit more for their trouble. The burly blacksmith acknowledged the boys as they passed by. He lifted the mirror, and the muscles in his arms bulged as they took its full weight.

"Ah, monsieur." Françoise greeted him jovially. "Sébastien. Good to see you again."

"Ah, Philippe, it is a good morning to sail," he said with a smile. He walked slowly but steadily up the gangplank, the crew parting the way like the Red Sea at his approach.

"Thank you, Sébastien."

"Where do you want me to put it?"

"In the captain's cabin. I will find somewhere to store it." Françoise stared at the captain, trying to impart everything she was not saying. "The gift is not expensive, but it has great sentimental value." Françoise followed Sébastien on board and guided Dale up the gangplank. "Are we ready to sail, Captain?"

"As soon as you have completed your business, monsieur." But she could tell he was impatient.

A few minutes later, Sébastien emerged. "All done, Philippe."

"Thank you, my friend." A noise from the street drew everyone to the railing. Shouts and clanging of metal rang out, but nothing could be seen.

Françoise made a move to run down the gangplank, but Dale grasped her arm. "Where do you think you are going?"

"It is what I feared."

"Feared?"

"Yes…"

"Cast off now!" While Captain Beaudry barked out his order, a group of women exited Lucette's, bundles clutched in their hands.

"Stay!" Françoise shouted.

"This is my ship, monsieur. I give the orders here."

"I said wait." Her eyes were riveted on the one person she knew to be Lucette. "Lucette!" She hoped her voice would carry the distance. "Over here!" She was pleased to see the woman's head turn her direction. "This way!"

"Get us out of here… now!" The crew was slow to respond, looking back and forth between their captain and Françoise.

Before the captain had a moment to think, she held a rapier point to his throat. "You are not going anywhere, Captain."

"I do not have to—"

"Oh, but you do. You are not going anywhere without those women."

"You paid berth for two, not for all of them." He motioned to the women who shoved people out of their way.

"And you would willingly allow them to die in a fight that is not theirs? Innocent women, Captain?" She spat out the last word.

"Innocent? They are just whores from that bordello."

"But they are my responsibility." Françoise paused for effect. "We will wait." The point of the blade touched his skin and pricked it. Françoise smiled with satisfaction as a bead of blood accumulated there. She looked over her shoulder at the women and saw them scurrying along the pier. "Hurry, Lucette!" At that moment, the noise erupted with a cacophony of sound from loud voices, swords clashing, and pistols firing. Two groups of men approaching the waterfront from different streets, merged. While the women had a good lead on the mêlée, someone had spotted them and fired his musket. One woman fell, and the rest of the group stopped to help.

"Oh... *non, non, non.*" Françoise grabbed Dale's arm and pulled her toward the captain. "Take this." She shoved the rapier handle into Dale's hand.

"But..." Before Dale could finish her sentence, Françoise was gone, already flying down the gangplank at breakneck speed and onto the pier, her legs eating up the precious distance between the ship and the women.

Beaudry began to edge closer to Dale.

"One move, Captain, and I will tear off your arm," Sébastien snapped.

"Stay out of this. You have made your delivery. Now leave."

"No."

Dale wasn't sure what had transpired but could see there was a standoff between the two men. She jabbed the point into the captain's expansive waist and returned the end to his throat. "Sebastian." Her American accent changed the pronunciation but she made herself understood as he looked in her direction. She gave him a look of gratitude. He smiled.

"Where is your first mate?" Sébastien asked.

"I will not help you." The captain's chin remained firm, as if begging for the brawny man to hit him.

"Is the first mate here?" Sébastien directed his question to the crew.

"Yes, that would be me," a small, wiry man responded.

"Monsieur..."

"Rumkey."

"Monsieur Rumkey, will you stand by while women are slaughtered needlessly?"

Rumkey hesitated.

"If I leave, who will protect madame here?" Sébastien said. "I am not as fit as some of your crew. Please, monsieur. They are in need of your help."

Rumkey did not ignore the plea. He motioned to two of the younger men. They set off down the gangplank at a fast pace, quickly reaching the struggling group.

"Thank you, Rumkey."

Dale watched as Françoise reached the women and directed them toward the ship. "Come on, come on," she urged quietly. Françoise had saved the women, but had she saved herself?

Françoise reached the distressed women. "Tantine... quickly. There is not much time."

Lucette stared at the fallen woman.

Françoise saw the life leave the woman's vacant eyes. "We cannot help her now. Come." She got behind the women and tried to physically move them toward the ship. Progress was slow. She heard the approach of angry men behind her. "Now, Tantine." She started to push, and fear sent a surge of strength through her body.

"You there. Stop!" Pistol fire broke through the noise. Françoise felt the brush of a lead ball as it whizzed past her head. She looked over her shoulder and saw two men running toward her.

Françoise again shoved the group forward. "Go! Do not look back! Just go!" She turned to face the men and reached for a sword that was no longer in her possession.

Her pursuers slowed to a walk, sly smiles crossing their faces. "You do not need to run, monsieur," one of them said.

"I think I do, since you seem to be shooting at strangers."

"Only those who run."

"We run because you are shooting at us."

"Only our enemies run, monsieur." He aimed his pistol at her chest.

"Enemies? We are all Frenchmen. We get rid of the aristocracy, and now we turn on one another?" Françoise saw the hesitation in their eyes. "Are you all so eager to die? And for what? A little pushing and shoving and now it is war?"

"It is not war. It is a disagreement."

"A disagreement?" Françoise's voice rose in anger, despite the pistol leveled at her. "Look." She pointed to the waterfront and the fighting there. "Go on. Look." Both men turned. "That is a disagreement?" She continued her tirade. "Is this a disagreement?" Françoise pointed to the dead woman lying nearby. "This is not a disagreement. This is madness. I do not want any part of this, messieurs." Françoise turned away and walked slowly toward the vessel, praying they wouldn't shoot her in the back for her trouble. She kept her gait slow and smooth as she ascended the gangplank. Dale flung herself into her arms.

Françoise's insides were shaking. Dale had a tight hold on her and kept her upright. As the ship moved away from the dock, Françoise looked back at the pier to see the two men standing there, stock still. Her eyes met theirs for a moment before they turned and walked back toward the fight raging onshore.

Françoise felt Lucette move next to her and knew what troubled her. "I am sorry for your loss, Tantine ."

"Florette had been with me for many years, my dear."

"I remember her."

"And she remembered you. She will be missed." She and Françoise gazed at her establishment, already in disarray from the scuffle. "Why?"

"Who knows? With the aristocrats gone, maybe their anger needed a scapegoat." Françoise turned away from the carnage. "For now, it is a confrontation here and there. Let us hope it does not escalate to war." Françoise sighed before glancing at Lucette. "I will not be coming back." But Lucette did not reply.

# Part Four: Journey

# Chapter 19

Dale stood apart from Françoise and allowed her the time to say goodbye to her homeland. She studied her strong profile and felt a clutching at her heart. A gentle breeze ruffled Françoise's hair.

*"Madame."* The deep voice of the blacksmith interrupted her thoughts.

"It's Dale, *monsieur."* She would have to see Françoise about more French lessons.

*"Et moi* Sébastien."

"I know."

He continued the conversation, but Dale raised her hand. "Non... no... speak... *français.* Um.... *je ne parle pas français."* Was that right?

Françoise responded on her behalf. She watched with interest as the two engaged in a conversation.

Françoise stepped up behind her and placed her hands on Dale's shoulders. "If you become her friend, Sébastien, you will not be disappointed." She lightly squeezed her shoulders, enjoying the feel of her soft skin. "I am sorry that I have taken you away from your home."

"It could not be helped, Philippe. It just happened."

"It certainly did, but—"

"No, Philippe. Do not start thinking about what might have been. I am here and I am alive. I may or may not have survived that battle onshore. It is all in the past now. We move on."

"How very philosophical of you, my friend." She smiled because it was true—he was now a good friend.

"Yes... friend." He held out his large callused hand and shook hers, her fingers disappearing into the large slab of meat that was his fist.

"How very cozy."

Françoise glanced over Sébastien's shoulder at the captain and gave him a dark look. "How may I help you, Captain?"

"Help? You nearly got us all killed. Rumkey, place Monsieur Théroux under arrest and throw him in the brig."

"Brig, Cap'n? Do you think that is necessary?"

"Are you questioning me, Rumkey?"

"No, Cap'n."

"Then lock him up."

"But Cap'n, we do not have the extra men to take care of a prisoner."

"I do not care if he rots in hell!" The captain took a breath. "Then just get him out of my sight." He looked around the crowded deck. "And get rid of the others." As he turned away, he muttered, "Trouble." Françoise didn't miss the lecherous leer he gave Dale as his eyes skimmed over her body.

"Monsieur, please follow me. I would suggest you stay out of the captain's way until he calms down."

"Sébastien? Would you please remain with the ladies until I have made sleeping arrangements."

"My pleasure, Philippe." He leaned against the railing and watched the small group of women crowd together.

"Monsieur... uh..."

"Rumkey, monsieur."

"Rumkey. That is an unusual name."

"My real name is René but no one uses it. Earlier in my life I earned the reputation of not partaking alcohol, so I was given the key to the crew's rum supplies."

"Ah, Rumkey. Very good."

"Who's that?" Dale asked as he walked in front of them.

"He is the first mate, Rumkey. If something happens to the captain, he is the one we depend upon to get us home."

"And is something going to happen to him?"

"I hope not," Françoise said. By the look that the captain gave her, she was sure he had not finished with them yet.

"The cap'n's cabin, monsieur."

Dale looked around the room. "Not bad."

"Is the captain's cabin always this big?" Françoise asked. "I was led to believe that all available space on a ship was used for cargo."

"This is a small ship, monsieur. It just appears to be bigger than it really is."

But Françoise doubted that. The width of the vessel and half as deep in size, the cabin was spacious. A bunk was recessed into the near wall, which added a small hallway when the door was open. In the center of the cabin sat the captain's desk. Ornate and showy, much like the man himself, charts, an open bottle, and a plate of leftover food covered the surface. Crossing the width of the room at the stern were lead glass windows, currently open to allow a cool sea breeze to enter. In the far corner, under one of the windows, stood their precious mirror, braced upright by their trunk.

"Monsieur, our extra passengers have nowhere else to stay." Rumkey glanced around the quarters. Françoise realized what he was saying.

"Bring them and the smith, here. We will make some sort of arrangement. May I have a few minutes with my wife first?"

"As you wish, monsieur." He gave Françoise a toothy grin before turning and leaving.

"Lucette and her girls will be sharing the cabin with us."

"Aw, man."

"What would you have me do? We have to stay together."

Dale pouted. "No hanky panky?"

"Han… ky?"

"You know… fun."

"Pan… ky?"

Dale stepped into Françoise's personal space. She slipped a finger inside her shirt and teased the skin underneath. "No more lovin', huh?"

Françoise felt the tingle all the way to her toes. "Fun." Dale leaned over and pressed her lips to Françoise's neck. "Hanky panky." Those two words were going to haunt her in the days and weeks to come. *"Non."* Françoise stepped back to put some space between them. "We have things to do before the women arrive."

"Things?"

"The money."

"Why not put it in the chest?" Dale said it as if that was the most obvious solution.

"It is a good idea, but that will be the first place the captain will look."

"He won't touch it."

"Ah, my sweet and innocent Dale. Of course he will try to get it. He will not be able to stop himself. We cannot stay here for the entire voyage guarding it, either." Françoise looked around the room for places to conceal it. "There is nowhere to hide it."

"Well…" Dale gazed around the room. She moved to the bunk, her eyes gliding over the recesses there and the straw mattress pushed to the side.

"That will not work. I am not sleeping on gold coin for weeks on end. It is bad enough I have to put up with these." She waved her hand over her body to indicate the bandage and the phallus.

"No, I wasn't thinking the mattress." Dale tapped the wooden base. "Do you think this might be empty underneath?"

Françoise's eyes lit up. Drawing the dagger from her boot, she pried away one of the boards to find a hollow space. "Dale, you are wonderful." Françoise went to the trunk. With a swift twist of a key, the chest opened. She rifled through the contents.

"What are you doing?"

Françoise drew out a rough blanket from the trunk and placed it in the bottom of the hole. "This will dampen the sound." She reached for the sacks she had carried on board and with great difficulty, lifted out the cloth bags. She placed one after another into the nested blanket. When there were only two bags left, Françoise banged the wood back into place.

"What about those?" Dale nodded toward the other money bags.

"We cannot be penniless. If he does get inside the box, he has to find something. Otherwise, he will know that we have hidden it elsewhere. It is better to lose a little than lose it all."

Dale stood beside Françoise as she put the items back into the box. A spare change of clothes, herbs, dried foods, and flasks nestled inside the trunk. The items must have caught Dale's eye before Françoise slammed the lid. "Where's the kitchen sink?"

"Sink?"

Dale sighed. "Never mind." She pointed to the mirror. "What about that? The jewels are still in there, right?"

"*Oui.* But I will correct that." With one swift twist, a push here and a prod there, the wooden frame gave up its secret. Françoise removed the jewels, lifted off the piece of wood from their hiding place, and carefully wrapped the jewels in the blanket. "That is all we can do. I only hope that will be enough."

Turning back to the frame, she put the panel back in place before walking to the chest again and opening it. She sorted through the contents until she found what she was looking for. She lifted out the leather journal. At first, she intended to write to while away the monotonous days ahead, but maybe Dale needed it more than she did. Her frequent use of expressions that Françoise didn't know frustrated her. She showed the book to Dale. "Maybe you can write the words down."

"Which words?"

"The words that constantly confuse me. I want to understand them."

"Now you know how I feel. All of you talk at a mile a minute, and I am left wondering what the hell is going on."

*"Pardon?"*

"You know what I mean."

*"Non.* I do not know what you mean." Françoise handed her the large bound book. Then she went to the captain's desk and got his quill and ink bottle. "Here." She thrust them at Dale. "Help me to understand."

There was a knock at the door. *"Entrez!"* Before the door opened, Françoise turned to Dale. "Everything will be fine, *chérie."* Lucette and her girls entered the cabin, followed by Sébastien. "Thank you, Monsieur Rumkey." He nodded before leaving the group alone.

Dale stood back while Françoise took control.

"Lucette." What could Françoise say? Things had happened so fast that she didn't have time to consider the consequences.

"I should thank you for saving our lives, my friend."

"I know it was not what you wanted."

"But you were right. As much as I did not want to believe it, you were right."

"My wife and I have paid passage in this cabin. You are all welcome to share it." Françoise looked at Sébastien. "You may look elsewhere if you wish, Sébastien. I am not sure what is available, but you are most welcome to sleep here. It is not so seemly, but I think the women will need our constant protection. We should all stay together on this voyage."

"I will ask, monsieur, but for now I will accept your invitation. I have heard that there is another passenger on board. I will approach him to see if he is prepared to share."

"Good. Let us get some air. We will be spending long hours in here in the weeks to come." Françoise escorted the women out of the cabin. She stopped Sébastien when he passed by. "Do not worry. I will protect you from the women." He laughed as she followed him out of the cabin.

Françoise had been unaware there was another passenger on board. Everything had been in such turmoil that it left her only time to focus solely on her own problems. The young man sat on a small barrel staring out to sea. He was perhaps in his early twenties, of slim build and bordering-on-handsome features. His quiet demeanor spoke of seclusion.

"Monsieur. Excuse my manners. I did not see you arrive on board."

He stared at her before turning his attention back to the sea. "You would not have," he said without facing her.

"My name is Philippe Théroux. Good day." For a moment, Françoise thought he wouldn't respond, but he faced her again and looked her up and down. He extended his hand. "Alain Barbineau, monsieur."

"Barbineau? I know that name." Françoise tried to remember where she'd heard it. "Étienne Barbineau? Do you know him?"

"He is my father." He once again looked her over. Françoise glanced down at her tattered coat and mud-spattered hose and saw her appearance from his perspective. "And you know him?" He sounded incredulous.

"No. I have not met him personally, but I know of him." Her husband had dealings with him concerning some of his more dubious requests. Étienne was a very wealthy and very successful merchant, undeterred by the legality of some of the cargo he carried.

Her eyes dropped to the book resting in Alain's lap. "Ah, Marivaux. Very good."

"You have read Marivaux?"

"I have read many works, monsieur. Do not let the state of my attire deceive you. Le Paysan parvenu. That is one of his better works. Les Fausses Confidences is also very good, but my favorite is Marianne. It is a shame that he never finished them."

"Yes, it is."

"I would have taken you for a reader of Voltaire or Rousseau."

"Considering what has happened to France, monsieur, my heart is not in reading such prose right now. Times are dark enough without reading about their so-called 'enlightenment.'"

"Interesting."

He studied her. "Do you have some complaint, monsieur?" His voice hardened as he asked the question.

"Not at all, Alain." Françoise stopped to gauge his reaction to using his first name. When no objection came, she continued. "It surprises me that someone of your obvious breeding is reading a comedy instead of immersing himself in the ideals of Rousseau. It is a time of upheaval, monsieur, and most young men's minds have turned to politics and freedom."

"And you do not believe in such things, Philippe?" He smiled as he addressed her by her first name.

"I am a merchant. It does not matter to me who is in power. Goods are sold to those with money, despite whatever regime controls it."

"Ah. You sound just like my father."

"I do not mean to do so."

"No. Do not apologize. Successful merchants take advantage of the circumstances presented to them." But there was a tinge of resentment in his voice.

"Well, I am not taking advantage now. My wife and I are returning to America. Her father is gravely ill."

"We are not going to America."

"I am aware of that. We are hoping to find another ship at St. Domingue."

"That may prove difficult. Not many French ships travel to the English Colonies. We are not on good terms with the English."

"Nevertheless, we will try. It is better to be nearly there than not to have left at all." She saw Dale approaching. "There is my wife." Dale strode across the expanse of deck toward them, the gentle sway of her hips under the dress enchanting Françoise. "Monsieur Barbineau, may I present my wife, Madame Isa—" What was the point of hiding Dale's name? "Dale Théroux."

*"Bonjour, madame."*

"Dale, this is Monsieur Alain Barbineau, another passenger."

"Pleased to meet… *bonjour, monsieur,*" Dale said. He took her offered hand and kissed the back of it.

"If you will excuse me, monsieur," he said, "I will adjourn to my room."

"And where is your room? I saw no other cabin."

"It is next to Captain Beaudry's cabin. I believe it used to be a storage room."

"The captain did not offer you his own cabin?"

"Why would he? I am but a paying passenger." He walked off in the direction of the cabin. He turned his head for a moment in the direction of young Rosalie.

"Cupid is busy, I see," Dale murmured.

"Hmm?"

"Never mind." Dale looked toward land. "I thought we were going to America. Why are we sailing along the coast?"

"Ah." Françoise's time had just run out. "We are going somewhere else first."

"You mean a detour?"

*"Oui, un détour,* as you say." She remained quiet, hoping Dale would be satisfied with that answer.

"And..."

"And?"

"What are you not telling me, oh husband of mine?" Dale folded her arms across her chest.

"We are going to Africa first," Françoise mumbled, the words trailing off to nothing.

"Where?"

Rumkey must have overheard their conversation. As he passed them, he said, "We should reach Ouidah in a few days. Once we have picked up our cargo and supplies, we will begin our journey to St. Domingue."

"Thank you, monsieur," Françoise said before Rumkey walked away.

"Fran... uh... Philippe. What's going on?" Françoise was still afraid to tell her everything. "Come on, spit it out."

"I will do no such disgusting thing, Dale."

"Tell me!" Dale all but shouted.

"We are going to Ouidah, the Ivory Coast, to pick up slaves for the west." There. It was said. She herself had never thought about the plight of black slaves. She always thought that the slaves were being taken to a better life. It was not of her concern and therefore not her problem. But Dale... From what she had seen of the future, social propriety had changed. "This is a slave ship, *chérie.*"

Dale said nothing as she gazed at the water.

A long moment passed between them. "Say something, Dale. This silence is maddening." Still nothing. "Slap me, kick me, yell at me. Do something." Dale's eyes looked into hers. "I had no choice. There were no other ships."

"Sorry. You just took me by surprise."

"Maybe I should have looked elsewhere..."

"Don't question your decisions now, Philippe. These women are alive because of you. How I feel about this will just have to be put aside for the moment."

"I know how you feel, little one."

"How could you know? We've never discussed this before."

"I can see it in your eyes."

"And you, Philippe? How do you feel?"

"It does not matter how I feel. I only want to make you happy."

Dale touched her hand. "Tell me."

"I have never really thought about it."

"Did you have any slaves?"

"At first we did. One or two. But that was my husband's doing, not mine."

Dale's gaze returned to the sea. "And after his death?"

"They were gone by then. He was too ill to have his way with them." Dale shivered at her words. "I sold them."

"Why didn't you leave as well?"

Why didn't she? "I had nowhere else to go. My family had disappeared. I had money and a title that was worth something. The cause of my pain was gone. He took everything I had, and I did not care anymore. I stayed because the servants looked after me. They could have left, but I was the source of their wages. We needed each other."

"I'm sorry."

"For what? None of this is your fault."

"Because I made you feel again. I made you take responsibility for your life." Dale rested her chin on her hands that sat on the rail. "Maybe I am a taker as well."

"Maybe, my love." Dale looked surprised. "But then where would I be? At the end of a hangman's noose, perhaps?"

"I sort of got the impression that's where you wanted to be."

"Before... maybe. I was tired of living. But now? Do you not realize how important you are to me? Everything has changed. Everything." She touched Dale's cheek to have Dale turn toward her. "You saved me, Dale."

"And you saved me. This is all part of our destiny, you know."

"Destiny." Françoise peered at the coastline, wondering where this was all going to lead.

"Monsieur, a word with you."

Françoise looked over her shoulder at who had interrupted them. *The captain.* She could smell him even on the gentle breeze. Shuddering, she asked, "What do you want?"

"In my cabin."

"It is our cabin now, Captain."

He bristled. "It will always be *my* cabin, monsieur. You are there only because I agreed to it. Never forget that. Now, in my cabin," he repeated, already swiveling to walk away.

"So what does Mr. Stinky want?" Dale asked.

"I think he wants his thirty pieces of silver." She left Dale on the deck while she attended to the captain's business.

"Where is my money?" He sat in his chair as Françoise entered the room.

"*Your* money, Captain? I thought the fare would go to the owner of this vessel."

"In due course."

Françoise doubted him; otherwise, he would have accepted payment above deck. She unlocked the trunk and searched around for the sack of coins. The bag landed with a clink as it hit the tabletop. "There."

He reached for the bag quickly, his eyes glowing with greed. His bushy eyebrows met in a frown. "Where is the rest of it?"

"You will get it when we reach the New World."

"That was not our agreement."

"We agreed to the amount, not how it would be paid." Françoise smiled. "If the voyage is satisfactory, I will add another one hundred *livres* to the amount for the other passengers."

"One hundred? They are worth ten times that."

"One hundred. That is all I am offering."

"They still have to be fed, to be housed."

"I will arrange for supplies at Ouidah, and they will stay in this cabin with me. Now, if you will get out of my cabin, our business is done."

Angrily, he grabbed his charts and instruments and moved across the room, standing in the doorway as his eyes fixated on the trunk.

"Before you go, Captain, there is nothing of value in that trunk, so do not bother wasting your time trying to open it." Françoise made a show of sitting down in the captain's chair. "By the way," she said, not bothering to look up, "if you are thinking about doing something stupid, remember this. If anything happens to us, there will be no more money. My business partner does not take kindly to harm befalling me or my wife, and as he will be the one paying the rest of the money, I would suggest that you ensure we arrive safely. That includes the other passengers as well. Is that understood?"

"Understood," he growled.

Françoise thought she could hear his teeth grind.

\* \* \*

"What on earth are you doing?" Dale glared at Françoise who was standing at the railing with a clay pipe hanging from her mouth.

"I am blowing bubbles, *chérie,*" she replied sarcastically.

"That is a disgusting habit. How come I never knew you smoked?"

"I do not smoke."

"Looks like you're doing a pretty good imitation of it."

"I am supposed to be a man. I have to do manly things."

"Manly things? That's shaving, scratching your crotch, spitting if necessary, and making love to me standing up. Not smoking." She crinkled her nose at the pipe. "Nope. Uh-uh. No."

"I am not actually smoking it. I am pretending to smoke it."

"So that's pretend smoke coming out the top?"

"Remember this moment in the weeks to come when I do not have a beard. How are we going to explain that?"

"Oh."

"Oh indeed." It was so nice to win an argument against Dale.

Sébastien sidled up alongside Françoise. "I did not imagine that you were a smoker of the weed."

"Do you partake, Sébastien?"

"Not anymore. I lost the taste for it." When Françoise began to put it out, he held up a hand. "Do not stop because of me."

"I am not, my friend, I am stopping because of her." She pointed at Dale. "I want to sleep well tonight." Françoise slipped the pipe into her pocket and rested her arms on the railing while she looked out over the roiling sea. "Will you be staying in the captain's cabin with us?" she asked, wondering if he'd spoken with Alain yet.

"I have not had the chance to ask him."

"Would you like me to do it for you?"

Sébastien lowered his voice. "I am not sure he will say yes to a simple peasant."

"My friend, you are anything but simple."

Françoise pushed herself away from the railing and walked to where Alain sat on a barrel. Without an invitation, she sat down on the small barrel next to him. "Monsieur, I have come to ask you a favor."

Alain looked up from his book. "A favor?"

"As I am sure you know, *Le Renard* gained a few extra passengers when it left Nantes."

"I witnessed it."

"I could not, in all God's graces, allow them to stay behind." Alain nodded but did not offer a reply. "At present, Sébastien is with us in the captain's cabin, but he is not comfortable with this arrangement. I am asking if he could use a small piece of floor in your cabin to sleep."

"Well…"

"I would make payment to you, but I doubt that coin is an issue."

"No, it is not. However, my privacy is."

"Thank you for your time." Françoise stood, disheartened that she was not successful. She took a step toward Sébastien who waited by the railing.

"Philippe."

Françoise stopped but did not turn to face Alain.

"There is nowhere else?" he asked.

"He could sleep in the corridor or on the deck here."

Françoise thought she heard him sigh, but the wind was too loud for her to be sure. "He can sleep with me."

She looked over her shoulder and met his eyes. "Thank you, monsieur."

Françoise walked over to Sébastien. "You have a place to sleep."

Sébastien slapped his large hand down on Françoise's shoulder and nearly sent her to her knees. "Thank you very much."

# Chapter 20

Despite the piece of wood wedged under the door, sleep had been eluding Françoise. Since the beginning of the voyage, the captain had been observing them or, more to the point, observing her. She could almost see his mind working as he plotted out his plan.

She rose from bed and wandered over to the window, trying to avoid the mass of bodies sleeping on the floor. The moonlight cast its ghostly light over the sea and touched the foamy tops in a fluorescent glow. It was as if the sea never slept as it tossed whatever had the impudence to sail on it.

Her gaze slipped to the left to their luggage and the mirror resting behind it. It was barely visible in the dark, but she knew it was there. She could feel it. With one last glance at the darkened waves, she moved to the frame. She ran her index finger over its contours.

The familiarity of it stimulated the dream she'd had last night. It was at the beginning of their romance. She sat at her toilette as she observed Dale through the mirror. She was pleased she'd moved the mirror to a more amenable place, easily visible from her seated position. Dale was asleep as the moon illuminated the bed through the skylight above. The sight of Dale's disheveled state, uncovered from the bedclothes wrapped around her, sorely tested Françoise's resolve. Dale's nightgown had ridden up her body, making her bare legs visible up to mid-thigh. It was a torture that she could no longer endure. She disrobed and stepped through the mirror.

As her mind recounted the dream, Françoise's hands absently caressed the dark wood that warmed to her touch. It was soft and pliable like familiar soft skin… Dale's skin. In her dream, Dale's skin was just as soft as Françoise had imagined it would be, and she was lost in their passion. Dale's sighs of pleasure reached deep inside to a place that Françoise had thought she'd closed off years ago. Yet, here was her salvation. This angel... here in her arms. The night went on and on... and on.

She'd awakened, shaken and exhausted.

Françoise stared blankly at the empty mirror. The dream told her what she already knew—she needed Dale's touch, and soon. Her only course of action was to breathe in some cool sea air and try to calm her raging libido.

She left the cabin and went to the railing to again gaze at the moon-kissed water. How much longer could she last without touching Dale? Looking over her shoulder at the upper deck, she observed the two men on watch, one at the wheel while the other surveyed the horizon for possible danger. It would be so easy to ease her ache.

Silently, Françoise moved farther away to seek the shadows near the bow. She'd already reached for the buttons of her breeches. Trembling, she moved her fingers through the well-worn holes. Her hand hovered there, her mind in conflict over seeking completion and remaining true to Dale.

Françoise felt Dale's presence even before she spoke.

"What are you doing out here?" Dale said in a low voice.

"Getting some fresh air, *ma chérie.*"

"I can see that. Why do you need fresh air? Why didn't you come back to bed?"

Françoise felt that Dale knew. It was a bit unnerving that someone could read her so easily. "I—"

"I know how you feel."

Françoise seriously doubted that. After her dream, she was about to explode. Since Dale was in her presence, any relief was going to have to wait. She tried to look into Dale's eyes hidden by the darkness. "I had a dream..."

Françoise heard the rough edge in her own voice. She knew that Dale would figure out what was bothering her.

"What was it about?"

"You do not want to know. At least, not here."

"Is that all you think about?" Dale teased.

"Is there anything else?"

Dale looked out over the waves before she returned her gaze to Françoise, "I suppose not... at least, in your case." She hesitated before asking, "Do you want to go somewhere?"

Françoise threw caution to the wind and grabbed Dale's hand, sliding it down between her breeches and her heated skin.

Dale looked over her shoulder at the top deck, probably thinking the same thing Françoise had about being seen. She followed Dale's gaze. The two sailors seemed to be ignoring them. She withdrew her hand and turned around so that her back was brushing the railing, effectively changing the angle of her body so that she was facing Françoise. Her right hand took up position where her left hand had been a moment before. "Too hard the other way," she whispered.

Françoise's eyes locked onto Dale's as her hand agonizingly crawled toward her destination. There was an innocence in Dale's eyes, a sensuality in those shadowed lips that curved slightly in invitation. The moonlight bathed her face as her expression softened, and Françoise felt her throat tighten with emotion.

Dale negotiated around the leather fixture in her pants and found the source of Françoise's pleasure. She tightened her grip on the railing as Dale moved subtly to stimulate the nerve endings that jumped to life.

It was harder than she thought possible to keep silent, so Françoise resorted to taking a deep breath and holding it to allow the sweeping pleasure to drown her. She felt herself slip into her orgasm.

Long after she had come back to earth from her climax, Dale continued to caress her and send sparks through her body in an uneven rhythm. Françoise was on the edge of that precipice, ready to jump with a flick of a finger. She felt lightheaded with all the deep breathing, but it kept her from crying out to the heavens. And she wanted to cry out not only her pleasure, but her love for the woman loving her. When she met Dale's gaze, she hoped she conveyed her feelings without saying the words.

"Better?" Dale's voice was sensual. She removed her hand from Françoise's breeches, then raised her fingers to her mouth and sucked them.

*"Mon Dieu."* Françoise moaned softly at the display. She leaned on the railing, her mind reeling and her body still tingling.

"What brought this on?"

"You have to ask?"

Dale didn't answer, not that she expected her to.

"I was reminiscing."

"Anything I should know about?"

"I could not sleep. I was at the window when I saw the mirror. I had to touch it. Maybe it was to remember why we were here, but it brought out a memory in me. Well, more like a fantasy."

Dale shifted closer. "Do you want to tell me?"

"It was just after you came to me. I was watching you sleep in your bed. I was so tempted to come to you that night, but I did not."

"Why?"

"Well, my scared little rabbit, if you woke up in your bed with me standing over you, you would have run away fast. No, *ma petite sauvage.* It was always your decision. I know I sometimes can be…"

"Overwhelming? Dominating? Sex-starved?"

*"Oui,* and more."

"Tell me about this fantasy."

"I think I should save it for another day." She laughed at Dale's pouting lip. "A bedtime story when we have time to investigate it more. Now, back to bed, my sweet." Dale moaned in obvious frustration. "Soon."

"How soon?"

"When I can find somewhere quiet on this vessel that we can hide. As you can see, it is a little crowded. Still, you did very well for your first performance in public."

"My first performance… Oh no, no, no, it's not."

Françoise was sure Dale was blushing. *"Oui,* it is."

"It is only if they know what I was doing to you."

Françoise looked up at the bridge crew as she and Dale entered the hall of the lower deck. She could make out the smirks on their faces. "How silly of me to think such a thing…"

As they passed one door on their way back to their cabin, Françoise thought she'd try it. When she discovered it was a storage room, she pushed Dale inside and hurried to give her relief. Dale bit her hand to stifle her cry as Françoise stroked her.

Once she was happy that Dale had been satisfied, they continued to their cabin. The door opened with a squeak of hinges, which sounded loud against the breaking waves and the occasional snore. They shuffled quietly back to the bunk and shifted around on the lumpy mattress until they were settled.

"Are you happy now… Philippe?" Lucette's voice cut through the darkness, followed by the snickering of females. Françoise suspected it was all of them, but she picked out the distinctive high-pitched giggle of Lisette.

"Oh, Lord," Dale muttered. She slapped Françoise's arm.

"Yes, Tantine." Françoise scratched the storage room off her mental list of possible locations for liaisons.

# Chapter 21

The port of Algiers grew steadily nearer as the ship approached land on the morning of the fourth day they had been at sea. They had been hugging the coastline of Portugal before crossing open water to Africa and following the coast south until they would reach the hub of the African trade. The Ivory Coast. The bulk of African slaves were funneled through this area. English and French sought the valuable cargo here and then would sail to other parts of the world with a labor force to support their burgeoning empires.

"Monsieur Rumkey!" Françoise yelled.

"Yes, monsieur?"

"Why are we stopping here? Should we not be going to Ouidah?"

"Normally we do, but the captain told us to sail to Algiers first."

"Strange…" It was an unscheduled stop, but Françoise was thankful for the shorter voyage. She had spent a considerable amount of that time on deck with a watchful eye on the captain, but she knew she couldn't keep it up forever. It was tiring and stressful.

"Poor Violette." Dale tilted her head toward the young woman heaving over the side.

"You know her name?"

"I may not understand French, but I am not deaf," Dale said in a huff.

"Ah, Dale, you are so delightful." It was nice to have something to laugh about. She wrapped her arms around Dale and held her close while the crew hurried about to trim the sails and prepare for docking.

Françoise breathed deeply. She wondered what Dale was thinking. There were so many sights, sounds, and smells… everything so foreign to her. And two hundred years of history would put a different slant on her perceptions. Dale gripped Françoise's arms and pulled her tighter.

A number of ships were in port, either unloading or loading goods. Françoise watched a crowd of street urchins trying to sell wares, begging for money, or just plain stealing. They danced around two white men who had come off the next ship alongside them. It was like a shell game. Watch one hand while the other robbed you blind.

"Break out the gangplank!" Beaudry's rusty voice yelled over the clatter of winches, the rumble of collapsing sail, and the grunts of tired men.

"So what happens now, Monsieur Rumkey?"

"We will be in port for a few hours to pick up our cargo. We set sail on the evening tide."

"Very well."

"It is not wise to wander too far from the ship." Rumkey's gaze flickered to Dale in warning. She understood the meaning. A white woman in this exotic port, especially one as beautiful as Dale, would be a rare prize.

"I will heed your warning."

"What's going on?" Dale asked.

"He was just suggesting that we stay on board."

"But—"

"I am sorry. It is too dangerous for us to wander about alone. I do not want to have to fight some Arabian prince to get my wife back."

"Oh."

"However…" Françoise loosened her hold of Dale. "Lucette! If you please." She didn't try to move away from Dale, knowing that she hated to be left out of what was going on. "We need more supplies. Are you up to carrying out such a task? Take Honorine with you, as she is the cook. I will ask Monsieur Baptiste to escort you. Perhaps Monsieur Rumkey can spare one or two of the crew to help with the supplies."

\* \* \*

Françoise stood at the top of the gangplank and watched the party leave on their expedition. She had taken Lucette with her to their cabin and had given her the remaining coin sack from the trunk. Something made her show the woman the secret compartment, in case something happened to her. To them. Lucette handed over her own sack of coin for safekeeping. Along with the second pistol in the trunk, Françoise added them to the secret hoard and sealed the hiding place with a swift kick to the wooden board.

The small group reached dry land. They were quickly swallowed up in the swarm of people buzzing around in a hive of activity.

Rumkey moved beside her. "I am surprised, monsieur, that you did not go yourself."

"I was thinking the same thing. But I cannot leave my wife alone. Thank you for sparing a few men to help with supplies."

"My pleasure."

She smiled. She liked this man. "I am sure you were not expecting this many passengers. I feel that we should make amends for that."

"The captain may not think so, but I understand the need to save those women. It is a sad day, monsieur, a sad day."

"Indeed. Who would have thought that one Frenchman would turn on another, eh?" Françoise paused for a moment. "Where do we go now?"

"From here we set sail to Ouidah, then west to St. Domingue. For this time of year, it could take from four to six weeks. But it depends on weather, wind conditions, and currents. We are sailing at the end of the season. Had we waited any longer, the winds would have been unfavorable and the trip would take one to two weeks longer."

"There is that much difference?"

"The winds are seasonal. They blow one way for summer and the other way for winter."

"I did not know that."

"Unless you are a man of the sea, you would have no need to, monsieur."

Françoise watched the slow loading and unloading of vessels. "We are leaving tonight?"

"Yes."

"That is quick, is it not?"

"Yes. Normally we would be in port for two to three days, or even a week or two, to unload and load. The captain's orders were to prepare to set sail on the tide."

"I see. Thank you, Monsieur Rumkey. I will not stop you from your work."

He walked away with a spring to his step. It drew a smile from Françoise. She only hoped that she was full of that much energy when she reached his age. Fatigue crept over her, and she longed for a nap. She watched as Dale tried to communicate with Violette, her hands playing charades in an effort to make her thoughts known.

"Dale."

"Yes, my husband?"

"I will be in our cabin if you need me."

"Sure, no problem."

*Sure...* Françoise wondered if her wife had started that log yet with all those funny words Dale was prone to use. As she approached the door, a sound inside made her stop. She reached for the pistol in her waistband. Her finger twitched over the trigger. Slowly, she opened the door and peered inside for danger. Kneeling on the floor in front of the trunk was one of the crew, one of the two she met that first day she came aboard to arrange passage. She rested her shoulder against the wall and studied him as he clumsily tried to use a knife to pry open the lock.

"A key works better." Her low words cut through the air. Françoise leveled the pistol at the intruder. "Get up," she growled.

"But... but..."

"There is nothing you can say that will satisfy me, monsieur. You are a thief, and I shoot thieves."

"No, no. The captain—"

"The captain was behind this?" He nodded mutely. She was not surprised. Waving him away from the box with the muzzle of the gun, she stepped toward the trunk. She shifted the weapon to her other hand before removing the key from around her neck and opening the lid. She lifted out everything inside for his inspection. "As you can see, there is nothing of value here. I told the captain that, but he obviously did not believe me."

She moved the pistol back to her right hand and pointed it again at his chest. "The captain is so cowardly that he has to send someone else to get caught? Well, you can tell him that there is no money. What coin I had left is being spent as we speak buying food and supplies for the voyage." She pointed to the mirror frame. "That is of sentimental value only. It was a wedding present from my parents. There is nothing there but wood, monsieur. Instead of worrying about the contents of my chest, the captain should be concerned with sailing this ship." She stepped closer until the pistol was touching the smelly sailor's chest. "You tell him that the next person I find in this cabin without my permission will be shot on sight. Do you understand?"

"Yes, monsieur."

"Now get out of here."

The sailor scrambled to the door, his gaze briefly touching hers before he disappeared from sight. Françoise sighed. She was tired. All she wanted was Dale in her arms and a warm comfortable bed.

*   *   *

Dale had tried her best to communicate with the sick woman. Barely taller than herself, Violette was a pretty little thing. When she smiled, her impish face lit up with energy. She wasn't smiling now, however. The pasty color had faded to a pale pink, but it was only a respite before the real voyage began. Maybe there was something that would help in the herbs they had. She sought out Françoise to ask.

One of the sailors rushed by her as she made her way to the cabin. He looked back over his shoulder numerous times as if the devil himself was on his tail. Dale smiled. Or the devil *herself*, in the shape of a luscious, dark-haired vixen who could bewitch anyone she chose.

She slowly opened the door and peered inside. Maybe Françoise was trigger happy, and Dale really wanted to keep her own head on her shoulders. "Hello?" Françoise was perched on the edge of the bunk, her head drooping in exhaustion. Dale stepped farther into the room. "You look tired. You have to get some sleep, my love. The captain be damned."

"I *am* tired."

"Then take a nap."

"I would like to, but—"

"No buts. I tell you what, how about a bedtime story? Come on, off with those boots. That's my girl," she said as Françoise loosened her boots.

"I cannot."

"Yes you can. You can't go on like this, Françoise. You need rest."

"I can think of something better that would cure my tiredness." Françoise reached out and grabbed Dale's arm, her hand sliding seductively up her skin.

"Now stop."

"It is a perfect time."

"I know it is, but how embarrassing would it be to get caught?"

"My sweet Dale, here is another chance to experience the thrill of performing in public, eh?"

"You're can't be serious,"

Françoise laughed. "So innocent. You are a delight." She tugged Dale closer. "Come. Lie with me for a little while."

Dale was reluctant.

"Just hold me, *chérie*. I miss feeling you close to me." Françoise reached under her shirt and loosened the bandage. "That is so much better." Françoise's hand disappeared down her breeches and shifted the attachment that had been her nemesis.

She removed Françoise's boots, took them to the far wall, and opened the window to allow a cool breeze to air the room and her lover's smelly footwear. "Your feet smell."

"That is ridiculous. They do not."

"Oh, yes they do. Either that or your hose need washing. It's probably both."

"I cannot smell them." Françoise sniffed the air. "Well, you *are* closer to the floor."

"Why you..." Dale made a lunge at the bed and wrestled Françoise to the mattress.

"Now I have you where I want you." Françoise lay down flat and pulled Dale toward her. She tucked her under her arm until her head was resting on her shoulder. "I believe you owe me a story."

"A story. Yes. Once upon a time..."

"A time? Not today or tomorrow?"

"No, this is a pretend time. We're swimming in the blue ocean."

"I cannot swim."

"Will you stop interrupting?"

"But you are saying silly things."

"It's a pretend story. I'm allowed to say silly things." She prodded Françoise in the side. "We're shipwrecked on a desert island." Dale could feel the intake of breath and stopped Françoise before she could interrupt. "It's paradise, okay? Just accept it. Sheesh."

"Fine."

Dale felt Françoise's tense body relax.

"We're playing around in the shallows. The sun is out, and the water is clear and cool."

"I have never—"

"No, you haven't, but one day you will."

"*Oui*, one day..." A yawn stopped Françoise's words.

"One day you'll understand all these words. We're naked in the water."

"Now you have my attention." Her eyelids started to droop.

Dale's mind wandered as she told her story, and her hand idly drew circles on Françoise's stomach. She wished for the whole trip to be over. Françoise had checked everywhere, and there seemed to be very little space where they could hide away and enjoy each other's bodies. It was going to be a hell of a long voyage.

Dale looked down at Françoise whose head was in her lap. She smiled at the peaceful expression on her face. She brushed away the dark tendrils framing Françoise's face and caressed her high forehead and long cheek. Dale continued to stroke her hair as Françoise emitted a gentle snore, barely heard over the creaking of the vessel. Everything else faded away as she focused her attention on the two of them. This. This was what was important. Not the captain, not the voyage, nothing else.

"Philippe."

Dale turned at the sound of a voice at the door. Four people loaded down with supplies entered the room. She motioned at them to keep the noise down and allow Françoise to sleep.

"I am sorry, little one," Lucette said.

Françoise groaned. Dale quickly covered her chest with her arm to remind her that the bandage was loose. "You have finished?" Françoise asked.

"Yes, we have. Monsieur Rumkey arranged delivery of more water barrels in our absence. I left the choice of food supplies in Honorine's capable hands."

"And I found very little that I would want to use," Honorine said. "Heathens."

"Honorine. Manners!"

"We should not be here in the first place, Lucette. If he had not pushed us onto this accursed boat—"

"We would be dead. We all know that. The sooner you make the best of our circumstances, the easier this trip will be."

Honorine started to object.

"No, Honorine. It stops here. No more complaining, if you please." Lucette ushered the helpers out the door. "Thank you everyone. Now, we should leave them alone."

"Alone? Do not spoil them," Honorine muttered under her breath.

"Let them be." Lucette gave Dale and Françoise one final look, rolled her eyes in exasperation, and closed the door behind her.

"Thank God for that woman," Françoise said.

"See what would have happened if we'd been fooling around?"

"*Oui.* I would have a smile on my face."

"And I would be embarrassed."

"I could make you forget everything, Dale."

"That's nothing new. You do that on a daily basis." Françoise smiled. "And you know it."

"Of course. I have a reputation to uphold, have I not?"

"You have nothing to prove to me, Françoise. I love all of you, including the troublemaker and the seductress. But," Dale said and nudged her to sit up, "reality awaits."

"Reality?"

"It's another word to add to that list, huh? It means real life. It's time for us to go back on deck and join the others."

Françoise stood and adjusted her accoutrements before pulling on her boots. She took a moment to collect the coin sack sitting on the table, much lighter from its recent use, and place it in the trunk. The empty flasks sat there forgotten. "Damn."

The muttering drew Dale's attention. "What?"

"I had forgotten these." Françoise held up a number of small glass bottles strung together on one tether line. "I meant to ask Lucette to fill them before we sail."

"Maybe the blacksmith would oblige. Why do we need these?"

"If something happens…"

"In case of an emergency?"

"Em-merge?"

"Emergency… if something goes wrong."

"*Oui*, em-merge." Françoise escorted Dale out the door, one hand resting on the small of her back, while the other held the empty bottles.

"Rumkey."

"Yes?"

"When do we sail?"

He looked at the sun's position in the sky. "Mid-afternoon, monsieur."

"Where can I fill these?" Françoise held up the bottles.

"Our supplies are below deck. I can get one of the crew to fill them,"

"No. There will barely be enough for the journey."

"In that case, there is a well near the markets."

"Thank you. Do I have time to carry out such a task?"

"We still have to clear the deck and stow the cargo. There is more than enough time." He turned his back for a moment. "Henri!"

"Wait." She rested her hand on his bony shoulder. "Sébastien."

He walked over to them. "Yes, Philippe?"

"Would you accompany me to the well near the markets?"

"Of course."

Françoise had not planned to leave Dale alone, but she was standing with the other women on the upper deck. While not actively taking part in the conversation, she was in the general vicinity and in relative safety. "Dale!"

"Yes, my husband." Dale moved briskly to the stairs to meet her halfway.

"Sébastien and I are going to the well at the markets. Stay here."

"But you get to see everything." Dale was obviously not happy.

"Please, *chérie*, do not argue with me. Stay here where it is safe."

"This will be my only chance."

*"Non."* The sternness of the word made Dale jump. "It is too dangerous."

"And it isn't for you?"

"I am the man of this family."

"Only by default."

"De-fault." Françoise waved her hand. "Please, do not confuse me now." She was getting a headache. "You do not play fair."

"Well, I'm not the one wearing the pants now, am I?"

"You act indignantly so well, *mon amour.*" She kissed her on the cheek and then whispered in her ear. "Here. Take this." The pistol suddenly materialized in Dale's hand, and she hid it in the folds of her dress. "In case of em-merge."

"Emergency."

*"Oui.* As you say."

Dale sighed deeply. "All right, but just this once. Next time you take me."

"I promise." But she knew that was a promise she could not keep. At least not yet.

Françoise bounded down the stairs to the gangplank. "Sébastien, are you sure you remember the way?"

"Yes. It is just a matter of going down that street. It is no more than a few minutes."

"Good. Rumkey, we will not be long. Perhaps thirty minutes. Do not leave without us." She grinned at him as he organized the men and supplies.

"Very well, monsieur." He grinned back, his yellowing teeth visible except for a missing side tooth.

The wooden plank began to sway as the two of them disembarked, Sébastien's weight lending a bounce to their steps. It felt strange to be on dry land. Françoise felt herself lurch in anticipation of the sway of the ship, but there was nothing there. It took some concentration not to stagger and look like some drunken fop.

She followed Sébastien down the dusty street toward the sounds and smells of the local food market. After much hand signaling, she found her man and politely asked him for water. Obviously touched by her show of respect, he offered not only the water, but some food and tea as well.

They partook of the finger foods, including something their host called *makrout,* a sweet pasty stuffed with figs and honey. Françoise drank her tea in relative silence, enjoying the Arabian flavors that teased her taste buds. Time was short, so she begged to be excused, and detoured to the well to refill the bottles. The precious liquid spilled over, dripping back into the well so that not a drop was wasted.

As they wandered along the stalls, Françoise glanced in fascination at the variety of produce that was available. She wondered what the cook had bought. Her taste buds sharpened at the thought of more exotic meals to come.

As they approached the dock area, it took a moment for the situation to sink in. Beaudry shouted out orders, and she heard the sound of winches shifting.

"Oh no, he would not dare." She sprinted to the ship and felt Sébastien dogging her every step. "That whoreson of a pig!" Dale would be proud of her colorful expletive.

The crew had already hauled the gangplank aboard and removed the docking ropes. The ship had barely moved inches from the dock but it was drifting away with every passing second. "Captain! What are you doing?" she yelled at the figure standing on the upper deck and saw the grin of triumph on his face.

A length of rope appeared over the side, and it swung precariously out from the hull. Sébastien nudged her back. He nodded his head toward the rope. "But I cannot leave you here," she said.

"Go. She needs you more than I do."

"I will return." Before she had time to think, she ran toward the edge of the dock. With a leap of faith, Françoise launched herself off the dock and over the water. She extended her body to gain every inch of air she could to grab the rope. Her forward motion was stopped with a thud when she slammed into the hull. She diverted the pain into her hatred of the captain. He was a dead man.

\* \* \*

Dale had watched Françoise go but already wished that she had returned from her little journey. She was lonely and never felt more out of place than standing near a group of women babbling in French. She turned her attention to the dock but found little comfort in watching the children play.

For some reason, the captain seemed to be in a hurry. He pushed his men into a scrambling run to accomplish his orders. It took her a moment to realize what he was doing. Would he be so foolish as to leave without all the passengers? She got her answer when the gangplank appeared on the deck.

Françoise and Sébastien came into view as the men pulled the ropes on board.

"Captain!" Françoise's voice was strong and clear. "What are you doing?"

Dale had no intention of allowing him to leave Françoise behind. She moved the few feet to where he stood. He overlooked the lower deck imperiously. "Captain!" He laughed at her, but his laugh faded when the pistol in her hand found its way to his temple. She spared a moment to cast a glance sideways, but Françoise had disappeared. A moment later, there was a bang against the ship.

\* \* \*

By no mean feat, Françoise slowly pulled herself up the dangling rope. No one came to her aid, so she hauled herself aboard. Her arms felt like jelly and shook uncontrollably from the strain. It took all her strength to pull herself over the railing, which left her to fall unceremoniously onto the deck and land in a puddle of water. She didn't care.

Once the shaking subsided, Françoise's gaze rose and blazed a path to the source of her ire. There stood her Dale with a pistol at the head of the captain. Her heart burst with pride. "I will assume, Captain, you were unaware that we were not on board. Now, return to the dock and pick up Monsieur Baptiste."

Beaudry yelled out the orders. As the men lowered the plank, she sought out Rumkey. He gave her a friendly wink in acknowledgement. So, he was the one who lowered the rope over the side. She tilted her head in thanks and turned her attention to the arrival of Sébastien. "Welcome aboard, monsieur." She slapped him on the back.

"Good to be back. I did not fancy living in Algiers."

"I am sure, just as you were not expecting to be taking a sea voyage." As the ship slipped away from its berth, Françoise glared at the captain, and she poured every ounce of menace she could into that one look. She sought out Dale, who had backed away and stood near the railing. She dipped her head in thanks. Dale smiled.

"I thought I had lost you there for a moment."

"It would take more than that man to stop me from getting to you, *chérie.*"

"Oh, I know—my very heart knows, my love."

A shiver ran through her soul when Dale spoke, as if someone else had spoken the words. Someone who held their destiny in their capable hands.

"Come." Françoise guided Dale to their cabin in silence.

# Chapter 22

The fort town of Ouidah came into view, but there appeared to be no docks. The anchor hit the water with a harsh splash.

"Monsieur Rumkey!"

"Yes, monsieur?" The wiry man looked up from his work.

"Why are we stopped here?"

"As you can see, there are no docks. We weigh anchor here, and the cargo is transported to us by rowboat."

The bustle of activity continued on the deck. The existing cargo was shifted around to make room for what they were about to accept. Cargo. It was such a cold word for humans. Françoise took a moment at the railing to look at the rowboats slowly coming into view. Huddled in a group were the slaves. If she had to guess from the number of boats, there were perhaps forty to fifty people of all ages, male and female, and more adults than children. A white woman with a baby sitting on her lap drew her attention.

The slaves climbed aboard the vessel. They appeared dazed but not confused about what was expected of them. They stood on the deck listlessly. Françoise had heard stories of slave ships. It was common for vessels to lose one third of their human cargo to malnutrition, disease, and rebellion. Now she could see why. Fifty humans would be stored in what was nothing more than a hole. Knowing the captain as she did, the slaves would more likely die of mistreatment. He did not care one way or the other how they arrived at St. Domingue.

"Come on you lot!"

The crack of the whip cut through her, the closeness of it screeching in her ears. Françoise instinctively reacted to the sound, her body cringing as if the whip had touched her back.

"Move, or I will flay the skin off your bodies!"

The captain grinned wickedly. The slaves might not understand the words, but they understood the whip. Françoise suspected it was a lesson learned with great pain and suffering.

The woman and child passed by her on their way below. She was definitely pale, but she looked odd for a white woman, possessing the broad nose and slightly pronounced brow ridge of her fellow slaves. It led Françoise to believe that she was, in fact, partially black. She would have to ask Rumkey the next chance she had.

Françoise felt her anger rise, and she let it show in her eyes as she met those of the captain. The smile slowly slipped from his face as she glared at him.

"Rumkey!" he bellowed. "Set sail!"

"Aye, Cap'n."

Six weeks on a small vessel with nearly one hundred people on it. Françoise wondered if they would survive.

\* \* \*

Dale stared at the scrawling mess that sat on the sheet of paper. It looked like two chickens had danced across the page in some manic mating ritual. She twirled the quill idly in her hand while she considered her options. Writing with pen and ink was a lot harder than she imagined. It would take some practice to avoid dropping liberal blobs of ink in the future.

She had second thoughts about her twenty-first-century dictionary for Françoise. What if it fell into someone else's hands? What would history make of that discovery? No, it was probably better that this particular lesson be learnt verbally. Instead, she would put her writing toward a more cathartic use.

Ripping out the damaged page, she bent her head over the paper and applied the nib lightly. She stuck out her tongue and twisted the side of her lips upward while she wrote.

Dale looked over the words on the page with disgust. The words sprawled across it with a sharp slant upward. "Damn it!" A large drop of ink landed in the middle of her work. She raised her head at Françoise's arrival.

"Do you have that list yet?" Françoise looked over her shoulder to study the words. "That does not look like a list. It looks more like a diary."

"I'm not used to pen and ink."

"I can see that."

"Stop it. I'm doing the best I can."

"Come." Françoise nudged Dale out of her seat and sat there herself. "You must allow the ink to flow."

"I've been doing that. In fact, it flowed all over the page." Dale showed Françoise her previous attempt at writing.

*"Non, non, non.* You push too hard." Françoise demonstrated and wrote *'Je t'aime'* in a very lyrical script.

"I love you too, but that doesn't solve my problem."

*"Non?"* Françoise looked up at her.

"It solves one of my problems, but not the writing one. You know what I mean."

*"Oui,* I do. It is all practice."

"Practice, yeah. I hate practice."

"And yet you practice very well with me." Françoise grinned at her.

"I don't consider that practice. That is perfect." Dale caressed Françoise's shoulder.

"Ah, little one. If you keep doing that, I will forget all about the letters."

"I don't mind."

"Please. We know that it is not possible for such activity."

"God, I wish it were."

*"Moi aussi,"* Françoise growled and dipped the pen into the ink bottle. She started to write words on the torn page—erotic words that Dale recognized and made her sweat. She snatched the page and crumpled it in her hands.

"Why did you do that?"

"Because you are a troublemaker. Now, are you going to show me how to use this thing properly or not?"

Françoise spent the rest of the day instructing Dale in the use of the quill, made even harder by the sway of the ship. Eventually, Françoise told her she had learned well and left her to her writing.

As the light faded in the cabin, Dale gave up any further attempts at her journal and joined Françoise on the deck to watch the sunset.

\* \* \*

The next morning, Dale found Françoise standing at the railing staring out to sea. She handed over a couple of sea biscuits to Françoise for breakfast, now the standard fare once the fresh food ran out. Honorine was preparing some *gruau* as well, but these hard bricks of wheat were the basis of meals on the high seas.

"These have got to be the most tasteless things I have ever eaten." Dale wrinkled up her nose in distaste.

"You say that every morning."

"And until we reach land, I will probably continue to say it. These are hard as rock." Dale struck the biscuit against the railing to illustrate her point. "That's if I can get my teeth into it."

"You cannot eat it."

"But I'm hungry." Françoise raised a dark eyebrow. "All right, all right. I know. Shut up and eat."

"I would never say such a thing."

"It looks like it'll be another nice day, thank goodness." Dale looked past her to Violette hanging over the railing. "Those herbs don't look like they helped."

Françoise looked over her shoulder at the young woman. "What do you suggest?"

"I don't know a lot about herbal remedies. Maybe we could try a combination."

"Let us hope we do not make her sicker."

"Hmm." A deep frown crossed Françoise's brow. Dale turned to see the captain on the deck above. "Just ignore him."

"I cannot. He… he…"

"He pisses you off, I know."

"Peesses?"

"Pisses you off. Makes you angry. Another one of those annoying twenty-first-century sayings you need to learn." Dale smiled.

"How is your journal writing?" Something in Françoise's voice sounded almost wistful.

"Fine. Why?"

"No reason. I was just curious."

"You can read it if you want to."

"You do not mind?"

"No. There's nothing in there to hide from you." Dale looked up shyly. "You know, you can write in it, too. There are plenty of pages to spare."

Françoise appeared to think about it. *"Non.* I gave the book to you."

"Please. This is our journey, so it will be our journal. I want to know all about you. Who you are. What you think. What you feel."

Françoise leaned on the rail, her attention returning to the sea. "I…"

"What?" Dale could see that she wanted to ask something.

"You know all my secrets." Dale laid her hand on top of her arm and patted her gently. "But I know nothing about you."

"You met my parents."

"Which only left more questions than answers," Françoise said.

"All right. What do you want to know?"

"Where does your family come from?"

"From Boston, but you know that."

*"Non,* before."

"You mean, in the beginning?" Françoise nodded. "Back when I was a kid—a child—our family history became a daily ritual. The bottom line was that my mother was a first-class snob, which was ironic because it was Daddy's heritage, not her own, that she so jealously guarded. My mother's heritage was formidable in its own right, but the Wincotts were thoroughbreds through and through. At least according to her. My family came to America around this time, in fact. Strange. Maybe I should look them up when we reach Boston."

"That may not be wise."

"Why not? A chance to see my ancestors? Then why am I here?" The words tumbled out of Dale's mouth without thought. "I mean, besides finding the love of my life."

"Is that not enough?"

"It's enough for me, my love. But still…"

*"Non.* Leave it alone."

"Why? Why are you so intent on stopping me?"

"I…"

"Françoise?"

"Because I am afraid it will undo all of this. Maybe this is not in God's plan for us."

"But maybe it is." Dale saw the disappointment in the stance of her partner. "Anyway." She changed the subject. "They arrived in Boston around 1790 from England. Elizabeth and Joshua Wincott. Their home still stands. In fact, we live in it. What else… Joshua made his wealth in shipping."

"Anything else?" Françoise chuckled. "Your mother thinks she is descended from the King of England, and you are barely aware of who started the empire?"

"Yeah, I know. My mother lives in a dream world."

"You could not trace your family back any farther?"

"No." Dale sighed as she took in the expanse of water. "Strange, isn't it? You would think there would be some evidence of Wincotts in England prior to their arrival in America."

"Maybe their name changed."

"I was thinking that, too, but from what?"

"I do not know. Only they could answer that."

The breeze blew the tendrils hanging around Dale's face. "My mother would have a fit if they turned out to be thieves or something." Dale laughed loudly. "I would love to be there if she found out that were true." She suddenly sobered. "Probably not going to happen now."

"You never know." Silence settled over the two of them, as they were content to stand at the railing and absorb the majesty of the open sea. Françoise's fingers entwined with hers, and Dale took comfort from the simple contact. They were together. That was all that mattered.

*   *   *

Lucette and the girls had managed to keep out of Françoise's way, which was curious considering the ship was barely over one hundred feet long. But this morning she decided to make a point to seek them out. She inwardly laughed. Seek them out. She only had to take half a dozen steps. The women stood in a circle around a lone crewman sitting at an empty barrel. He was playing some game with cards and amusing his observers. They clucked and shifted around the cards like a gaggle of hens waiting to catch the first worm of the day.

Françoise sidled up next to Lucette and murmured in her ear, "What has you all so amused?"

Lucette jumped, her hand resting over her heart. "Do not do that! You will kill me."

"I have not talked to you recently."

"Well, you and your wife seemed busy, my dear."

"Not too busy for you." Françoise smiled at her.

"Ah, I see. Then I could enter the captain's cabin whenever I choose, eh?"

"Most of the time, yes." The smile widened to a full grin. "What sort of example would we set for your girls if we were there all the time?"

"My girls?"

"Tantine." Now that she'd broached the subject, it was time for a serious discussion. "I…" Françoise gulped loudly. It was not her place to tell the madam how to run her business, but some restraint was needed to avoid conflict. "It is probably best for your girls not to—"

"Look for work?" Lucette laughed as Françoise shifted uncomfortably.

"Yes. We want to avoid any more trouble."

"Philippe, I think the captain is more worried about you than he is about us."

"But we do not want any fights on board."

"You think that will happen?"

"Men and women together and sex as well? It is a certainty."

"Some may not like it."

"I am sure. That is why Dale and I have agreed to show some restraint."

"Restraint?" Lucette laughed long and hard. "Is that what it is called these days?"

"Tantine, please. We need to agree upon this."

"It may already be too late, little one. One or two of them have already struck up a friendship."

Françoise inwardly cursed for not keeping a closer eye on her charges. She had meant to approach Lucette about the matter earlier, but her own problems had consumed her. Maybe it was already too late. "All we can do is ask them to refrain from… you know."

"Yes, I know. Even if you cannot say it."

"I can say it. I just choose not to."

"Fine, my little lamb." Lucette smiled as Françoise bit her lower lip in worry.

"I can. It does not frighten me."

"I did not say that it did."

"Tantine. It is not something one discusses with one's family." Lucette raised a wrinkled hand to touch her cheek. Françoise dropped her head to shift her gaze from the eyes boring into her soul. "You were more of a mother than my own ever was."

"I know. We have been through a lot together, you and me. Most of it was bad, but we survived it. It made us stronger. It bonded us together. It made us a family."

"That it did."

* * *

Françoise's blood was boiling.

"Why do you torment yourself like this?" Dale asked.

"Where else do I have to go? It is either here or the cabin. I cannot help where my eyes wander."

"Yeah, you can. They are your own mind and eyes. You can tell them to go to hell if you want."

To Françoise it was like a toothache. She had to worry at it even though it was painful to do so. "But look at him."

"Philippe, I don't wish to. He's a piece of shit, and I'd rather look at my own mother. That's how bad I don't want to look at him."

Beaudry stood arrogantly on the upper deck and stared down at the crowded area overflowing with slaves and crew. For a short while each day, the slaves were allowed to stand on deck, one small group at a time, and get some fresh air—a much needed respite from the fetid smell below.

Françoise studied them. Most of them had huddled against the hull. The gruel they had been fed had been eagerly consumed as if it were their last meal. Maybe it was. Knowing the captain, he could kill them on a whim if he so desired. With what she had seen of him so far, it was a distinct possibility.

She shifted her attention to the one person who sat away from the group—the white woman and her child. "Monsieur Rumkey." Françoise called the first mate away from his meal.

He walked over. "Yes, monsieur? What may I do for you?"

"That woman," she said and indicated the young girl, "why do they treat her so?"

"Because the blacks claim that she is white and the whites claim that she is black. She is neither one nor the other."

"How so?"

"Cross-breeding, monsieur. Black mother and a white father. After two or three generations of that, the child is almost white. Not quite, but almost."

"That is a sad tale."

"I suppose so, monsieur."

"What will happen to her?"

"She will be a difficult sale. There is never any dispute of ownership if the slave is black. He is black; therefore, he is a slave. White people are not considered slaves. Therefore, her ownership could be brought into question."

"Then why take her as a slave at all if any profit is questionable?"

"There is always the chance that someone will buy her for other reasons."

"Other reasons?" He did not answer but raised an eyebrow at her. "Oh. So the circle continues," she mumbled as she studied the young mother breast feeding the child while she ate her own meal. When she'd almost finished her meal, she stuck her finger into the gruel and finger-fed the baby. It was a tender scene in the midst of such horror and degradation, and it tugged at Françoise's heartstrings. Her gender had been born to provide children, yet it was the one thing Françoise could not do.

Her gaze turned to Dale who was watching the mother feed the baby. A gentle smile crossed her lips at the baby's antics. Françoise could not stop the single tear from sliding down her cheek.

"Don't cry, my love."

"I do not cry." Her voice faltered as her hand came up to wipe away the wetness.

"It's not your fault."

"Fault?"

"I know what you're thinking, Philippe." Dale put her finger under her chin and lifted it. "I know we may never have children."

"You can have children."

"But who will be brave enough to father them?"

Françoise managed a smile.

"Would you let a man come between us?" Françoise's smile widened. "I thought so." Dale leaned in closer. "We have each other. That is enough."

"*Oui*... enough." Françoise's voice faded off into the wind.

\* \* \*

*The bloodied whip hung in her limp hand. "Please, my husband, she can stand no more."*

*"Again," he whispered.*

*"But..."*

*"Again!" he yelled. "I will tell you when she has had enough."*

*Reluctantly, the whip sliced through the air, landing on the screaming whore's back. Françoise cast her gaze at her husband, visibly repulsed by his look of gratification at the poor woman's suffering.*

A hand on her arm disrupted Françoise's reverie. She turned to Dale. It was yet another day, and they were standing on deck.

"Are you all right?" Dale asked.

"There you are, young pup." Honorine shoved two rough-hewn bowls at them, nearly dropping them when the two women were slow to respond. She turned on her heel and walked away without another word.

Françoise was content to hold the warm bowl in her cold hands to allow the heat to seep into joints that hadn't felt warmth for some time.

"What I wouldn't give to feel warm again. An hour. Just one hour."

"I know what you mean. Even the cabin has no warmth."

Dale dipped her finger into the lumpy mixture. She scooped a piece of food onto her finger and slipped it into her mouth. "Hey. That's not bad."

*"Oui,* honey and a touch of…"

"Cinnamon, if I'm not mistaken. How does she do that?"

"Do not complain. Be thankful that she is a good cook."

"I'm not complaining. I'm very thankful." Dale glanced at the biscuit. "Believe me, I am."

Françoise ate the porridge and enjoyed the feel of the hot food sliding down her throat to settle warmly in her stomach. "Where are you going?" Her spoon was halfway to her mouth when Dale walked away. Porridge dropped from the hovering spoon back into the bowl as Dale knelt in front of the white woman.

"Hello there," Dale said as she hunkered down on the deck. Even from where she stood, Françoise could see the suspicion and apprehension emanating from the young mother. Dale slowly handed over her bowl to her. She nodded as she pushed the bowl into shaking hands. "For you and your child." Dale studied the baby and smiled at the little boy. "Aw, aren't you adorable." Her voice was soft and soothing and drew a shy smile from the young child. "Yes, you are." She extended a finger for the baby to grab, while her gaze alternated between the baby and the mother. "I mean no harm." The young child held on tightly and giggled as Dale jiggled her finger up and down.

"Monsieur!" The harsh guttural sound from the captain cut through the air.

Françoise looked up from watching Dale play with the baby. Beaudry scowled at her. "Dale. Enough."

She could tell Dale wanted to stay, but she obeyed without question and returned to her side. Once she was out of range, the mother placed the child on the deck and began to eat the porridge, occasionally dipping her finger into it to feed the boy.

"I do not think our captain is amused, *chérie.*"

"Well, it was my porridge to do with as I wished. No child should go hungry."

It was a noble sentiment. "Still, it would be better not to do that again."

Françoise had noticed the captain's frank looks at Dale ever since she had boarded the vessel. Her presence had not even deterred him.

"He gives me the creeps," Dale murmured.

"The creeps?"

"When he looks at me, it's like he's undressing me with his eyes."

"He probably is." Françoise glared at the captain. "She is mine, old man," she muttered, drawing a quiet chuckle from Dale. But his eyes turned to the mother and child.

"Captain! This was my wife's doing, not the slave's."

"Do not assume to know what I am thinking, monsieur." He trundled down the stairs to stand face-to-face with her. "These are my slaves. They are none of your business."

"*Your* slaves?"

"Do not play this game with me. I would suggest you tell that harlot of yours…" The words died in his throat as Françoise's hands encircled his windpipe.

"Let us pray you do not utter those words again, Captain." She shook him violently. "My wife was showing a little kindness, nothing more."

Rumkey approached quickly and tried to pull Françoise off the captain. "Please, monsieur. Stop! You are going to kill him."

"Anyone who insults my wife deserves nothing less."

"Philippe. Please." Dale's soft melodic voice cut through her anger.

"But he called you—"

"Then it's just as well I don't understand French, isn't it?"

"But I do, and I will not tolerate anyone calling you that."

"Please let him go." Dale gently gripped her arm.

Beaudry clawed at Françoise's hands. Anger and indignation lent strength to her fingers as they dug into soft flesh. Just when she was about to help him meet his Maker, she lessened the pressure until she removed her hands.

He rubbed his throat and glared at her. "You have made a dangerous enemy, monsieur. Give me a reason why I do not toss you overboard."

"For one, Captain, I know you will miss all that coin if we do not arrive at St. Domingue." Françoise was certain she had hit his Achilles heel with that comment.

"But I have to decide whether it is worth the coin I will lose to be rid of you."

Françoise did not flinch at the hollow threat.

"Philippe. Is there a problem?" Sébastien walked over.

"I do not know, my friend. Is there a problem, Captain?" Françoise smiled at his beet-red face. When no sound came out, she spoke on his behalf. "No, Sébastien. It looks like the captain and I have reached an agreement." Her demeanor turned serious. "And that includes no retribution against the woman and child. Understood?"

The captain stomped off. Françoise took a deep breath. "Thank you, Sébastien. I think he finally saw my point of view."

"I do not think it was wise, Philippe."

"No. It was not wise." She shook her head. "This was to be a nice quiet voyage."

"You cannot help that pig of a man's manners."

"True. I think I will not be getting any sleep from now on." She was exhausted enough as it was. Another four weeks of little sleep, and she would be cranky as all hell.

"All you have to do is ask, Philippe, and I will watch the captain." He patted Françoise on the shoulder, buffeting her hard and sending her off balance. "Sorry."

"Do not apologize, my friend. It is nice to know that I have a strong arm at my side if the need arises." She looked past him to Lucette and her group. Lucette studied Sébastien with interested eyes. "I think you may like to join the ladies." He gazed over his shoulder at the gaggle of women, his lips tilting up to a smile when he found Lucette.

"Excuse me."

"Of course."

"You better stop that," Dale told her.

"Pardon?"

"Playing matchmaker are we?"

"I would do no such thing." Françoise tried to sound indignant but failed miserably.

"Monsieur," Rumkey said, "I do not think the captain is happy with you."

Françoise thought that in the captain's present mood, she could easily be keel-hauled in the blink of an eye. "No, he is not, Rumkey."

"So, should I start calling you 'Captain' now?" He chuckled and laughed even harder when she sputtered at the comment.

"I am only trying to protect the innocent."

"Innocent?"

"My wife and the mother and her child. They did nothing wrong but accept what my wife gave them. I do not trust him to keep his word."

Rumkey said nothing.

"And I will never be the captain," she said vehemently. "That is mutiny, Rumkey. I may not know much about the sea, but I do know that."

"Aye, Monsieur Théroux. But you have the captain worried."

"Tell him he has nothing to worry about. I have no interest in his position. I am only interested in protecting what is mine."

"And the mother and child? Are you claiming them?" He smiled at her unease.

"Of course not. I have enough trouble with my wife. Why would I increase my aggravation?"

"No reason. No reason at all."

"However…" Françoise couldn't help but put a provision on her statement. "If he feels a need to vent his anger on someone…"

"Do not worry, monsieur. I will seek you out if he crosses the line."

Françoise now knew at what point Rumkey would intervene, and it wouldn't be before a lash or two had been given.

# Chapter 23

Françoise sat at the captain's desk, her quill hovering over the empty page of the journal. She looked up from her work to observe Dale sleeping, and she smiled. It was at moments like these that she looked her most innocent and most youthful. She dipped the nib into the ink pot before gently tapping the tip on the edge.

*Day Sixteen*

*I have once again made the captain angry. Dale gave one of the slaves some porridge, and he objected. I know he is within his rights to do so, but he seems to want them to suffer as much as possible. It is in his nature. It...*

Françoise stopped suddenly. She had intended to write, "it broke my heart to see my wife playing with the baby," but Dale would read it and be upset. She brushed the feather over her cheek as she thought.

*It... he reminds me of le Comte, and I think that is why he irks me so. Maybe that is why I spoil his plans at every turn. I now have the control. I am now the mistress of my own destiny.*

Françoise slumped back in the chair shocked. She reread what she'd written, and the disclosure was very revealing indeed. It didn't solve the problem of the captain's behavior, but at least she now understood her own actions.

She wrote for a little while longer, trying to put her own perspective on the events she knew Dale would enter in her own inimitable style later. A quiet moan drew her away from her musings, to the bed. Dale rolled over restlessly. The blanket fell away to expose Dale in her undergarments. Françoise was so tempted to find the skin underneath the delicate fabric. Her eyes went to the door, anxiously waiting for someone to enter at a moment's notice.

She leaned back in the chair to watch Dale sleep. As her body rolled and moved, Françoise caught glimpses of what she most wanted to see. She lost herself in a daydream and was not aware of Dale's stare until the dream had come to its conclusion.

"Interesting dream?" Dale asked seductively.

"*Oui*, and it pains me to suggest we go on deck."

"Do we have to?"

"Yes. I have asked Lucette to stop her girls plying their trade on board. How can we expect them to honor that if we cannot control ourselves?"

"But I don't want to control myself. I want to lose myself in you."

Françoise looked at the ceiling and drew a big breath. She stood and uncomfortably adjusted the attachment in her pants. When Dale's gaze followed her hand, she was close to dismissing her good intentions. "Come on. Maybe some fresh air will help your control."

Dale threw off the covers and rolled out of the bunk. Françoise's gaze never left her body. "Can you help with the ties?" Dale presented her back and waited for Françoise to close up the dress.

Finally, they were ready to face the crew, but not before Françoise muttered, "I may just have to kill someone."

They emerged into the bright light of day. So far, they had been lucky with the weather. Most of the days were full of bright sunshine and fair winds. The afternoon sun was slowly sinking in the west, and preparation of the evening meal had started. A metal brazier stood precariously on the slowly rolling ship, its fire slowly being fed until deemed ready for cooking. The ship's cook lifted the heavy pot on top and began adding the day's rations to it.

Françoise couldn't help but wince at what was in store for the crew and the poor slaves, glad that their own grumpy cook could at least make something edible. But Honorine's turn would not come until later. Honorine had finally decided to experiment with her cooking, adding small pinches of the aromatic spices she had bought in Algiers. It took a little getting used to, but now Françoise quite enjoyed the subtle changes in flavor and texture.

Her vision filled with the endless sea, her nose filled with the aroma of salt water, and her mind filled with boredom.

"We have got to get you a hobby," Dale said.

"I seem to recall you said that before."

"Yeah, but that hobby is only available at certain times. Maybe you could borrow one of *Monsieur* Barbineau's books."

"There is a book or two in the bottom of the trunk, but I am not inclined to read them."

"How about you swap them then?"

"Swap?"

"Exchange. You give one to *Monsieur* Barbineau, and he gives you one of his in return. You know, borrow them. Just until you have read it, and then you can return it to him."

She had always wanted to read Marivaux again. It was worth thinking about. Alain mostly had kept to himself, but from time to time, Françoise had drawn the shy young man out for conversation. She realized that his snobbishness was more a defense against his shyness rather than true elitism, if his furtive glances at Rosalie meant anything.

"It's a shame he doesn't have any English ones. I could use something to read."

"Well, *chérie,* if you would learn to speak French, it would not be a problem."

"And if my teacher would take the time, it wouldn't be a problem either." Dale grinned at her.

*"Oui,* I am guilty." But she wouldn't say why. Teaching Dale French always left her with a headache because her American accent painfully ground over her fair language. "If we reach America…"

*"When* we reach America," Dale said.

"When we reach America, there will be no need." Françoise thought about that for a moment. "Your accent will be different there, too. Most people still speak English."

"I speak English."

*"Non.* English… from England."

"Ah. British not American. I don't think I can change my accent at this point. How about you teach me some French anyway just to pass the time?"

"If you wish." She inwardly cringed at the thought. St. Domingue couldn't come soon enough.

* * *

Françoise immersed herself in Marivaux, her eyes gliding over every syllable with loving care. In the background hovered the sound of voices murmuring, laughing, and arguing. The weather had finally turned foul, and a steady drizzle stopped them from spending time on the deck. Françoise sat on the floor with her back against the stern. She chose this particular spot so that the light from the windows would illuminate the pages of her book.

A lantern swung precariously from the rafter, and its monotonous squeak annoyed her as the swell gently rocked the ship. She looked up from her reading to observe the activity in the cabin. Dale was busy adding another entry to her journal. Her tongue peeked out of the side of her mouth as she wrote. A frown crossed her features a second before the quill shifted across the page.

Lucette and her girls, Sébastien, and Alain were playing parlor games in the center of the room. It had taken some prodding to get the young man to join their group, and it wasn't until Lucette promised to introduce him to Rosalie that he relented.

As she watched the group, Alain threw back his head and laughed at something Rosalie said.

Alain had proved that he was nothing like his father. Soft spoken and thoughtful, he reminded her more of Dale's father. Alain seemed to have the same steely resolve. She wondered if, like Dale's father, that resolve would surface when the need arose. Alain had not had the need to express his displeasure forcefully so far.

Françoise smiled as she watched the game unfold, both in the group and between Alain and Rosalie. He cast glances at her often.

There was a loud cough. She turned at the sound to find Dale watching her. Dale smiled, and Françoise returned the smile. She knew Dale was thinking about the match.

She focused on the book once more as she lost herself in Marivaux for a while longer.

\* \* \*

Eventually, the weather returned to warm sunny days.

"Rumkey."

"Yes, monsieur?" He trotted over to Françoise's side.

"How far do we have to go?" She was hoping he would say they'd reach their destination tomorrow, but that was more wishful thinking on her part than actual fact.

"I cannot be exact."

"I am aware of that."

"The captain keeps his own counsel most of the time, but if I had to guess…" His gaze turned out to sea, and his eyes narrowed as he muttered, "How many days have we sailed already?"

"Twenty-five days." She laughed at his look of surprise.

He wandered off toward the wheel to talk to the captain. Moments later, he returned. "According to the captain, we are over halfway, monsieur. Perhaps, with fair winds, ten to twelve more days and we should arrive at St. Domingue."

Ten more days. Surely she could survive ten more days. Dale's French was progressing slowly and painfully. Could her ears survive that long? Perhaps she needed a diversion. At that moment, there was a shift in the wind and the ship. The sudden movement sent a crewman into a female slave, taking both of them over the side.

"Man overboard!" Rumkey shouted.

As Françoise stood by, Dale sprung into action. She grabbed an empty barrel and flung it over the side into the water. Françoise watched as it bobbed in the swell. But the sailor and slave were too far away to grab hold. The sailor clumsily dog paddled to the floating wood while the slave's panicky movements warned of an impending death.

Françoise saw movement out of the corner of her eye. She turned just as Dale jumped overboard. Françoise cried out in panic. She ran to the railing and frantically searched the dark green depths below the hull. "Dale!" The word tore from her throat in a garbled scream. *Oh, chérie, what have you done? Where are you?* As tempted as she was to jump right in after her, she knew she couldn't swim. If her wife didn't surface soon, she might do that anyway, to join her in the hereafter.

A head bobbed to the surface. Dale began swimming toward the struggling woman.

"Turn this ship around!" Françoise said angrily as she approached the helmsman. She was tempted to reach for the wheel herself. "Turn around. We have to rescue them!"

"How many times do I have to remind you that this is my ship, monsieur?" Captain Beaudry smirked at her.

"The same amount of times it will take for you to do the right thing, Captain. Turn the ship around!"

Françoise could see he was considering leaving them behind. "Do not even think about it," she growled. Her hand hovered over the rapier hanging at her side, and she was ready to draw it and beat him into submission if needed.

"He is right, Cap'n," Rumkey said. "We have a bare minimum crew as it is. Losing one of the men will result in prolonging the voyage. And as far as the slave—"

"Rumkey, when I want your opinion I will give it to you." The captain sighed. "All right, prepare to pick them up."

Rumkey was already in motion, barking orders quickly and efficiently. The passengers backed away as the crew literally fell over themselves to perform the maneuver.

Once the captain had agreed, Françoise wasted no time in returning to the railing. "Oh, Dale, do not leave me. Not now…"

\* \* \*

For the tenth time, Dale cursed herself. What an idiot she'd been to leap over the side. Still, she was the woman's best chance of survival, and she was thankful for all those swimming lessons her mother had bullied her to take. Reaching them was not easy. The pull of the tide and the weight of her dress added to her difficulties, forcing her to dig deep for the determination to reach her victim. The sailor had managed to reach the wooden keg but did nothing to aid her.

Stroke by stroke, she inched closer to the rapidly tiring woman who was barely able to keep herself above water. Finally, she succumbed, forcing Dale to dive deep to find her. The water darkened as she swam down, her arms burning with each stroke. It was getting colder, biting deep into her aching bones. Just when she was about to give up, she touched something. It was a hand, but its coolness sent a shiver through Dale's body.

Her lungs were about to burst when she broke the water's surface, her mouth gasping in relief as the fresh air replaced her depleted supply. Dale tugged hard to bring the woman to the surface, and the effort sent her under the water for a moment. She kicked hard to dislodge the wet cloth from around her legs. Exhaustion was calling to her, enticing her with an easier solution to the problem. *Succumb, it whispered. It is easier this way…*

It would have made sense to listen to the seductive words, but she took a moment to look up to see the ship circling to return to them. Although she couldn't make out the figures, she thought the one leaning over the railing was probably Françoise, and she would be begging her to live. She took heed of that silent plea and began to move her arms. With one arm, she pulled through the water. Her other arm grasped the limp form she had so foolishly jumped in to rescue.

By the time she had reached the bobbing keg, what energy she had ran out. The sailor watched the rescue without so much as a word of encouragement. He held onto the wood possessively. It took a stern look on her part for him to relinquish part of it to her.

Dale couldn't lift the unconscious body onto the floating buoy. It was too much. Mentally, she would have swum back to the ship, but physically she could barely keep herself afloat. The world faded out for a time until shouting voices cut through the haze in her mind, alerting her to the ship's arrival. It was strange. One moment she had seen the ship turn, the next it was on top of her. Exhaustion was playing tricks with her mind.

"Dale!" That voice. It called to a part deep inside her, and she dragged her eyes skyward. "Dale! *Mon Dieu*, Dale!" It was a balm to her soul and food for her strength.

The sailor was already climbing the ladder to safety. "I don't think I can make it up the ladder." Moments later a rope appeared next to her with a loop on the end. Dale tied it around the woman's ankle, giving it a firm tug when it was secure. Slowly, the crewmen lifted the woman out of the sea upside down, the water sluicing off her as she rose to the railing. Dale's nerves were on edge as she waited for the rope to return, her mind continuing to play tricks on her. Would they sail off without her? Would the sharks get her before they rescued her? She understood that the thoughts were ridiculous, but her logical mind wasn't working.

"Dale!" The low, husky voice called to her again.

She sputtered as a wave crashed into her face. She shook the water from her eyes and looked up.

"Put your foot in the loop."

She numbly accomplished the task. Again, she faded out, not acknowledging reality until Françoise talked to her. "Dale, are you all right? Speak to me."

She lay on the deck in Françoise's arms. "Yeah, just tired I guess." Dale looked around for the woman she saved. "What about the woman?" She looked up into concerned brown eyes.

"She is dead."

"No, no, not now." Dale pushed Françoise aside and scrambled over to the still body. She felt for a pulse but there was none. "Don't do this to me," she muttered as she commenced CPR. Audible gasps rang out around her when she put her mouth over the slave's mouth. She repeatedly blew air into the lungs. She moved to the woman's chest and began cardiac compression, drawing a wave of mumbling and whispering.

"What are you doing? You are making a spectacle," Françoise said, her voice in a panic.

"No. Trust me."

"Dale."

"Philippe." She looked up at her again. "Trust me."

"Fine." Françoise stepped away and let Dale get back to work.

Dale continued for several minutes without success. "Come on, come on." She was getting frustrated and was losing hope. "Live, damn it!" She pounded the black skin in anger, sending everyone a step back from her. The body twitched in reaction. "Come on…" She sought out the carotid pulse with her shaky fingers, and although it was faint, it was present. The woman was alive. The chest began to rise and fall slowly, gathering strength with each breath.

Dale fell back onto her ass, her arms draped over her knees.

*"Mon Dieu!"* Françoise muttered.

There were gasps of wonder and murmurs of distrust.

"I am not a witch, Françoise. In my time it's common knowledge." She looked at the captain and saw the frown on his face. "Stop complaining. I saved your precious cargo."

"Captain, I think it is time to continue our journey."

He glared at Françoise as if deciding what action to take, before finally turning on his heel and walking to the helm. "Heading west, northwest."

As soon as he left, Françoise turned her attention back to Dale. "How could you do that? Jump into the sea."

"I had to."

"No, you did not. You could have…" Françoise's eyes filled with tears.

"Died? Don't think that didn't cross my mind a time or two in the water."

"It would have killed me."

"I wouldn't have been too happy about it either."

"It is not funny." Françoise's voice was shaking.

"No," Dale murmured. "No, it's not. It's deadly serious." She reached up to cup Françoise's face.

"Come." Françoise helped her to her feet. "Let us get you out of those wet clothes."

"Any excuse, huh?" The only thing holding Dale together was the quips. Anything more serious and she would fall apart.

She sighed with relief when they reached the cabin. While it was still cool, there was no biting wind to cut through her wet clothes. Dale was freezing, aching, and exhausted. She was in desperate need of warmth and a bed.

Françoise offered her own clothes, still warm with her body heat. She rummaged through the trunk for a change of clothes when the door flung open. Françoise's first reaction was to cross her arms over her chest until she realized that Lucette was alone.

"Your wife has caused quite a stir."

"I am sure she has." Françoise continued to find her clothes. Her hand rested on a knitted shawl. Barely in anything at all, Françoise ignored her nakedness for the sake of Dale's comfort and strode across the floor to wrap the shawl around her shaking shoulders. "Into bed, *chérie.*" As Dale did so, Françoise pulled up the blankets to her chin, briskly rubbing the quivering body underneath.

"It may mean trouble," Lucette said.

"Let them think what they want. That is unimportant right now."

"Unimportant to you, but it may start a revolt."

"What's g-g-g-o-ing o-o-n-n-n?" Dale managed through chattering teeth.

"Lucette is worried about your 'miracle.'"

"Miracle? It was a normal procedure."

"Normal for 200 years in the future, but here it is considered witchcraft."

"Well, tell Lucette it's not." Dale left Françoise to fill in the details.

"Dale says"—Françoise prayed that she had understood correctly—"that where she comes from, it is common practice to know such matters. She lived near water. They of course must know how to... to..." What were the words she was looking for? "To save a life."

"Little one, I know she is not some sort of demon, but there are others on this ship who do not know her as I do. The captain could use this as a reason to rid himself of you, perhaps even all of us." There was real fear in her eyes.

Françoise's jaw tightened. "He can try." She would die first before the captain would get his way. As she dressed, she said, "Talk to Monsieur Rumkey and explain everything. He is a levelheaded fellow and a friend. I am sure he will try to reassure the crew." She wrapped her fingers around Lucette's wrist. "Do not worry, Tantine. It is done, and we will have to live with whatever comes next. I will not let anything happen to you or your girls."

"How does she fare?" Lucette nodded at Dale.

"Cold. Very cold."

"I will ask Honorine to see if she can find something to warm her." A sly smile settled on the woman's face. "And no one to warm the bed, either. It seems that is a task for you, my dear." Her smile widened as a blush heated Françoise's face. "In you get and stir the woman's blood."

"Lucette!" How was it that she always made Françoise feel like she was ten years old? Such talk between them always brought out the innocence in her. As Lucette started to leave, Françoise called out, "Keep a close watch on the captain. He may try to take advantage of my absence."

"Yes. Until later."

"Yes." After Lucette left, Françoise made her way to the bunk and perched herself on the edge as she looked down at Dale. "How do you feel?"

"Better. Just cold and tired."

"I can help."

"That's what I wanted to hear." But Dale didn't budge, clearly beyond exhaustion.

"Do you want to move over?"

"No. Do you?" Dale raised an eyebrow. "All right, all right. You may have to push me though." With obvious effort, she moved over to the wall. Françoise crawled in beside her.

"Come here," Françoise murmured, pleased with Dale's immediate response, despite her fatigue. Her arms encircled Dale. She rubbed her hands briskly up and down her back. "Foolishness," she whispered then planted a loving kiss on her cold cheek.

"Yeah, I know." Dale's eyes drooped quickly as she fell into a deep slumber.

*　*　*

"Françoise." The comforting voice broke through the haze in her head.

"*Oui.*" Sluggishly she awoke, her eyes taking moments to come into focus. She suddenly panicked about her appearance. It was too late. She focused her eyes more and breathed a sigh of relief when she saw it was Lucette.

"How does she fare?"

Françoise swept her hand over Dale's brow. "She is a little warm."

248

"Here. All we could manage was some herbal tea. The brazier will not be used until the evening meal."

"I am sure she will enjoy it, even if it is cold." Françoise shook Dale gently. "Dale," she said in a soft voice. "Lucette has brought something warm to drink."

"Hmm." Dale lay where she was and looked up at Françoise with glassy eyes.

"You are hot, *chérie.*"

"If I have a fever, it would explain why I'm having trouble sitting up." With Françoise's aid, Dale sat up in the bunk and leaned forward as Françoise slipped in behind her. As she fell back against Françoise's chest, she sighed. "Oh, that is so much better."

"I... er... 'ope... you... well," Lucette said in her broken English and handed her the cup of liquid.

*"Merci, madame."* Dale's voice sounded sore and irritated. "Damn," she muttered. "Not a cold now."

Françoise fed her the herbal tea under the watchful eye of Lucette. Dale chuckled after the last drop passed her lips.

"What is so funny?"

"I was just thinking how funny it is that we three are together. An aristocrat, a brothel madam, and a furniture restorer. Three classes of people making up a family. Strange."

*"Oui,* strange." Yet it seemed right. It took the lowest class to show Françoise the true meaning of friendship. In the ruling class, there rarely was such a thing as friends.

"What did she say?"

"She was pointing out that we find friends in the unlikeliest of places." Françoise smiled at Lucette.

"That is so true. Who would have thought I could find an aristocrat worth talking to?" She grinned wickedly and held up her hands as Françoise pretended to throw the cup at her. "But it has been worth it, little one. Yes. It has been a pleasure to know you."

Françoise could feel the tears welling in her eyes. She was not going to shed them. "I just wish..."

"No, Françoise. You were a victim as were we. There is no blame to give or take." Lucette tilted her head sideways and in a teasing voice asked, "Are you really an aristo? You certainly do not act like one."

"Only a little one." Françoise held up her index finger and thumb and pinched them together. "It is the ones with a little power that are the most dangerous of all."

"But you did not become one of them."

"No. Having my parents sell me to a madman killed any thirst for power I may have had. Slavery can cross all boundaries of class distinction. Even the daughter of a nobleman can become a slave and understand its subtleties."

"See? There is another good thing to come out of this horror. I would never be friends with a snobby elitist."

"Tantine!"

"What?"

"You know what 'snobby elitist' means?" Françoise leaned back against the wooden wall. "It surprises me that you know the words at all."

"Ahh, my baby. Occasionally the men who come to my establishment talk as well. They tell me what they would not say to their wives."

"You have also become a confessor?"

"Yes, but I do not give absolution, only comfort." Lucette laughed at Françoise's reaction. "It was not always about sex in my establishment—" She stopped suddenly.

"Of course it was, otherwise why would they be there in the first place? But I know what you mean. Everything will be fine, Tantine. If you wish to return, I will arrange it." It would be hard to say goodbye. Her family would be half a world away if Lucette decided to return to France.

"Do you ever wonder what happened to your real family?"

"They lost the right to be my family the day they sold me."

"It was an arranged marriage."

"They sold me!" Françoise yelled, her anger making Dale jump. "I was nothing more than chattel to them."

"They needed the money, Françoise."

"And that gave them the right to sell me to that man as a trophy?"

"But your father was in danger of losing his title."

"No! My *mother* was in danger of losing his title. 'Baron' meant more to her than it ever did to him. She shamelessly manipulated him. And my brother? Oh no, he was too important to sell. But their daughter… she was only worth what gold the count would pay them." Françoise's face reddened with indignation. "They sold me like some prized filly."

"Hey." Dale stroked Françoise's arm that encircled her waist. "What's the matter?"

"Nothing," Françoise muttered.

"Nothing has you screaming in my ear?"

"Not now, Dale." She breathed deeply and allowed her senses to settle. She knew her hands were shaking, even without looking at them. "So how does it fare on deck?" she asked Lucette.

"I talked to Rumkey. He will do his best."

"And the captain?"

"He wanders around muttering to himself. I am not sure what he is thinking."

"Never mind about him. I will take care of it if the need arises." Françoise tugged Dale closer to her. "How is the other woman?"

"The slaves are uneasy around her, thinking she has been bewitched. They do not trust her, but they have left her alone." Lucette hesitated. "It may have been better for her to have drowned, young one. Her life may not be worth living."

"It is not worth living now," Françoise said. "I agree, but Dale is who she is. She did not want to see the woman die if she could help her. For that, I praise her. She has a generous heart and a loving spirit."

"Ah, love overlooks many things, Françoise. It is a wonderful thing to see in you." Lucette shuffled to her feet. "Now I will leave you two alone to rest."

"Before you go, how are your girls?"

"Violette is feeling better with the herbs you gave her. Angelique, Lisette, and Edith are teaching us the games they learned from the crew. Dice, cards, check-ers and something called knoo... nuke... knucklebones, I think. Sabine has struck up a friendship with one of the sailors. She has been sneaking around. I think we need to keep an eye on her. Céleste has taken up reading one of Monsieur Barbineau's books. And Rosalie? Since you introduced her to Monsieur Barbineau, her eyes have not wandered anywhere else."

"Lovesick fools." Françoise gently caressed Dale's hair. "Perhaps Sabine will need a word of warning. Friendship is one thing, but plying her trade on board is not wise."

"If you think so."

"If it were common knowledge that the women were amenable to earning some coin, fights could break out. Jealousy and possessiveness are powerful tools to a man's libido. We cannot afford any more trouble."

"Take heed of your own words, Françoise."

"I know, Tantine. The captain irks me so."

"Now rest. I will return later with dinner." Lucette winked as she opened the door and left.

# Chapter 24

The sounds of the scratch of the quill and the whoosh of the vessel in the waves were hypnotic.

Scratch, scratch, whoosh, scratch, scratch, whoosh.

It was a gentle rhythm that, by now, had become a way of life. Françoise read back over her entry, recalling the last few nervous days.

*Day Twenty-Nine*

*Dale's foolish saving of the slave came back to haunt her, as I suspected it would. The fever finally left her, and she has been sleeping for the last two days. I think our God must be pleased with us because she is getting better every moment. I am trying to keep her in bed, but I think my time is gone. She is eager to breathe the sea air for herself.*

Françoise had added a bit more, but decided to scribe it in French…

*I do not know if love is as wonderful as everyone claims. I was nearly sick with worry as Dale tossed and turned in a fevered state. Every mutter and moan was as if it came from my own lips. Seeing her sick made me sick as well. If love is God's gift, then why does He make us suffer so?*

Françoise dipped the quill into the half-empty bottle of ink and continued her musing in English.

*It was comical to see Lucette and her girls fussing around her, and I am sure that Dale appreciated the sentiment. Sébastien, as a favor to Lucette, would bring in the evening meal for both of us. Maybe he is what Tantine needs. Someone to finally share her remaining years with. I hope I am right. Even Rumkey expressed his concern over her health. It seems my instincts were right about him also.*

Françoise turned her gaze to the mirror that rested against the wall behind the trunk. What she wouldn't give to be back in Dale's time. Dale's illness had scared her. It made her painfully aware of how fragile life was out on the high seas. At least back in Boston, there was a warm bed, hot food, and that delightful steaming waterfall Dale called a shower. Although she had no need before, she was sure she could have found a doctor if Dale had taken a turn for the worse.

She studied the ridges and whorls of the mirror's intricate carving. She had always liked that piece, but she did not fully understand the attraction until a few weeks ago.

"Hey." Dale's voice was hoarse. "What are you up to?"

"Just writing."

"About me, I suppose."

"No."

"There's no point in lying to me."

"Fine. I am writing about you."

"And cursing me, too, I bet."

"How could you think such a thing? I do not curse strangers, and I barely know you since you cannot tell me your family history."

"I thought we had gone through all of this."

"It was about your ancestors, not about you."

"So?"

"So, what do you hide from me?"

"I've got nothing to hide and to prove it, just ask me."

Françoise put down her quill and dusted the page, allowing it to dry while she moved herself behind Dale and rested her back against the wall. She pulled Dale against her chest. "Tell me all."

"Everything?"

"Why not?"

"For one, I don't think I can remember everything. How about the highlights?"

"High… light?"

Dale lightly pinched Françoise's arm. "I will give you the short version."

"As you wish."

"Do you want the story or not?"

"*Oui*, I do."

"I was born in Boston twenty-seven years ago and raised in our family home. But you already know that. I have an older brother, Marcus, and he has two lovely sons." Dale looked over her shoulder. "At least the family name will continue."

"Did you not say to your mother that you were the last in the line?"

"It was an idle threat. She pisses me off sometimes."

"No. I find that hard to believe."

"No more sarcasm, thank you very much." Dale yanked one of Françoise's dark locks. Hard. "Marcus had a falling out with mother, and she disowned him. She was expecting me to be the breeding cow to supply an heir to the fortune."

It seemed family expectations had not changed in two hundred years.

"Now she has to go crawling to him and accept him back into the fold. That's why she was trying so hard to keep me. Eating crow is not on her menu. Ever."

"Americans eat that kind of bird?"

"Oh Lord. I mean my mother finds it hard to apologize. According to her, she is never wrong."

"What about your father?"

"Daddy?" Dale looked back at her with a smile. "He's a sweet man who has a harpy for a wife."

"Tsk tsk. Such a thing to say about your mother."

"Do you think that I'm wrong?"

"Not at all, but to hear you say it is… is… surprising."

"You shouldn't be surprised. You've seen firsthand what she's like. That's why I live in my own place. Boy, that started World War Three."

"World War Three?" Françoise held her breath. "World War?"

"Don't worry about it. World War One is more than a hundred years from now. And it's not literally the whole world, just the major countries. What I mean is that there was major trouble between her and me. It went on and on, and she threatened to cut me off as well. If it wasn't for Daddy, I would have been living in a one-room hellhole."

Françoise was getting lost quickly, but she at least understood part of it. Dale's overbearing mother had tried to force her to conform, and she wouldn't. At least she had a choice. "He had something to say at the dinner."

"True. That was a side of him I hadn't seen before. I suppose he'd have to be tough or he wouldn't have the job he has. I think he's very indulgent of my mother."

"And you became a furniture restorer."

"Do you know that if it wasn't for my job, we never would have met?"

"How so?"

"I was looking for used furniture in a basement and found the mirror frame. There was something about it."

"It was the same when I looked up and saw you in the mirror. It was strange. I opened my eyes, and you were there, looking at me… through me… into me. You had grabbed my soul with one look."

"Yeah, I'm figuring that out now. I was wondering why you were chasing me."

"Chasing? Oh, no, no, no. You came to me, if I recall."

"That was because you were screaming like a banshee half the night."

"It drew your attention, did it not?"

"You were going to wake up the neighbors!"

Françoise's hand came up and covered Dale's mouth for a moment to keep her from shouting more. "Now, about this furniture."

"It was something I was always interested in. Old furniture. Chairs, tables." She smiled. "Armoires."

"What is it?"

"I was searching for an armoire when I found the mirror by accident." Dale dropped her head back onto Françoise's shoulder. "Anyway, I went to a private school. I think that's where my love for old furniture was nurtured. It began at home, but mother was not encouraging. I was to get married and produce an heir."

"And your father?"

"He was the one who sent me away to boarding school. I'm sure he was also the one who put in a good word to my first job after college. He never told me, but I knew it was him."

"See? Perhaps if we return, he will protect you."

"Us. Protect us. He knows what you mean to me."

"We still have a journey to complete." Françoise did not want to express the concerns she had about the voyage. It was better that Dale lived in hope of returning to her home.

"I worked in the back room of a museum, but the politics drove me out."

"It was owned by the government?"

"No, but the lying and back-stabbing was the same. People were trying to get into a better position in the company at the expense of the work. It broke my heart to see such beautiful pieces sacrificed like that. Father bought the loft for me, and I set up my own business."

"Like Lucette?"

"No," Dale drew out the word. "I was not selling myself to the highest bidder." Françoise laughed. Dale tilted up her head to grin at her. She pinched Françoise's thigh.

"Ow!"

"I know that didn't hurt, you baby," Dale said. "I would find old pieces of furniture and restore them. Oil and polish them to their former state. Just the small stuff for families. I had yet to find a major piece that would set me up."

"Set you up?"

"For me to gain a reputation as a quality restorer I needed to find that one piece that would put my name into the papers. Unfortunately, I'm still waiting."

"It is a shame that the mirror will not allow us to transport such things."

"I found something much more valuable." She snuggled into Françoise's embrace. "Does that satisfy your curiosity?" Françoise tightened her arms around her.

"It is enough… for now."

\* \* \*

Dale emerged into the sunlight for the first time in a week. Françoise hovered nearby as she made her way to the railing. She lifted the shawl around Dale's shoulders as the sea spray hit their faces. It was wet and cool. They watched the waves toss the ship up and down.

"How is she?" Lucette asked as her girls surrounded them.

"Good as new." When Dale answered in French, Françoise blinked once and then blinked again. "Don't look so surprised, my husband." Maybe all the hours of grinding syllables and guttural vowels had paid off.

"You understood that?"

"A bit, yeah, but it would be the first thing I would ask in her position."

Françoise sighed and had to sadly accept that there were still more hours of painful lessons to go. She looked over the heads of the hovering crowd to spot the captain. He scowled at her. The crew was busy attending to their normal duties of swabbing decks, coiling ropes, and helping the cook for the evening meal. Rumkey raised his hand and nodded, and Françoise returned the gesture. At least Dale's arrival had not disturbed the running of the ship.

Françoise turned her attention to the slaves, not sure what reception she and Dale would receive. What greeted her surprised her. Instead of the fear and suspicion she expected, the slaves seemed pleased to see her or, more to the point, Dale. They stared at her with something akin to awe.

"Why are they looking at me like that?"

"I do not know." Françoise continued to watch the slaves congregated on the far side of the deck.

"I hate to say it, but God, they smell awful." Françoise had to agree. Even the gentle breeze couldn't dissipate it. "I know it's not their fault, Philippe. Keeping them in that enclosed space is just plain cruel."

"We do not smell much better, Dale."

She slapped Françoise's arm. "Speak for yourself," Dale tried to sound indignant, but Françoise knew better. "Yeah, I know. I want my shower."

"You know my mind." Even with Dale's mother intent on seeing her in jail and separated from her daughter, they had been wonderful days free of worry and strife. Playful days. Loving days. *Perfect* days.

"Rumkey."

"Yes, monsieur?"

"Do you know why they stare at my wife so?"

"I do not know. While you were in the cabin they talked among themselves for quite some time."

Françoise watched the slaves continue to look Dale's way. "As long as they are not hostile. What about the woman?"

"As well as could be expected, for a slave."

Even though the woman sat on the edge of the group, she had not been ostracized, unlike the white woman and child. The baby cried while being held in the limp arms of his mother.

"What about them?" Françoise nodded her head toward the mother and child sitting apart from the group. "She does not look well." She narrowed her eyes and could see a bruise or two around her face and neck.

"She…"

"Never mind. I can see for myself." She looked to the upper deck and glowered at the captain. He only grinned at her.

"I am sorry, monsieur." Rumkey shuffled his feet as if he knew he had failed in his duty to inform her.

"I should never have put you in that position. Your duty is to the captain, even if he is undeserving of the title."

"The journey will be over soon." He returned to his duties.

"Dale." Françoise turned her attention to Dale, but she was gone. She was crossing the deck and now stood in front of the slaves. "Dale, come back!" Françoise couldn't see her face, but the expressions on the slaves' faces varied. Some looked with interest, a few with awe, but the majority looked at her with respect. Dale touched the head of the woman she had saved, as if she was blessing her, before moving over to the mother and child to do the same thing.

Dale eventually sauntered back to stand at Françoise's side.

"What are you doing?" Françoise asked.

"I figured it out. They think I'm some kind of shaman, a priest, a witchdoctor."

"And touching the head?"

"Maybe if it looked like they were in my favor, the woman and child might be accepted by the rest of the group."

"That is a dangerous game you play."

"Yeah," Dale said and sighed. "I know. But what am I supposed to do?"

"I see that you have recovered, madam." The captain had sneaked up behind them.

"Madame." But Françoise knew he deliberately used the word to irritate her. "Yes, she is now well again." *No thanks to you, you son of a mule.*

"Maybe we should dine together in the captain's cabin. What do you think?" His muddy eyes skimmed over Dale like slippery seaweed.

"It is our cabin for the duration of this voyage, Captain, and I am afraid that we are already overcrowded. One more would just not be possible." Françoise's reply garnered no response as the captain's eyes were riveted on Dale. She could see Dale react to the obvious ogling as she tugged her shawl tighter around her shoulders to cover up even further.

"I will have to see what arrangements can be made for an intimate supper." He turned to Françoise, standing nose to nose with her.

"Yes? Do you wish to say something?"

"I am just curious that you do not seem to suffer from the same curse as the rest of us, monsieur."

"Curse?" Françoise felt her voice starting to slide upwards, so she stopped at the one word.

His raised his hand and touched the smooth skin of her chin.

"I beg your pardon." Françoise smacked his hand away. When she could stand it no longer, she took a step back, glad to feel the gentle breeze between them.

"No beard." He dropped his gaze to her chest before continuing the journey to the crotch of her pants. "A very hairless man... monsieur."

"It runs in my family, Captain. I tried growing a beard once, but my wife did not appreciate the bristles." His skeptical look told her she hadn't convinced him yet. "Why do I need to explain myself to you?"

"I could say because I am the captain."

"You always say that you are the captain, monsieur, and I grow weary of hearing it."

Dale touched her arm. "Philippe," she said softly.

"And everything aboard this vessel is my business."

"Very well then, but this will be the end of it. My wife does not like the bristles because it interferes with her pleasure." Françoise did not wait for his reaction, instead steering Dale toward their cabin.

Françoise entered the cabin and closed the door quietly. She took a moment to lean against the wall and watched as Dale put away some clothes. No longer aware of the gentle roll under her feet, she was now at ease with this new sensation in her life. Her anger fueled her desire, but as much as she wanted Dale at that moment, Françoise kept a tight rein on her urges. The captain had made her feel less than she was, but it was not a good enough reason to ravage Dale's body. Dale should not be the solution to her ire.

Françoise left and went on deck to stand at the rail and look out over the swelling ocean. Her thoughts were in as much turmoil as the water beneath her. A rapidly building storm in the distance filled her mind, and her thoughts were tossed around like pieces of paper under the onslaught of the raw emotions swirling inside her.

# Chapter 25

Dale had been putting away her clothes and didn't notice Françoise's departure. A knock on the door went unheeded until a second knock telegraphed urgency in the visitor. *"Entrez!"* She turned around as the door swung open. She tried to hide her unease at who stood there. "What do you want?"

The captain's gaze swept over her. "I see that your husband has left you, little one."

Dale saw the lust in eyes and heard the rough timbre of his voice. But she thought he wouldn't be so foolish as to try anything with Françoise nearby. *"Monsieur, sortez s'il vous plaît."*

He chuckled. "I should not need an invitation, madame. After all, this is *my* cabin." He edged forward slowly, closing the distance between them. He held up his hands in entreaty, as if trying to gentle a horse. "Now, now, little one. There is no need for you to be scared."

He moved closer until he was an arm's length away from her. Whatever he wanted it was not conversation. *Françoise, where are you?* Dale's mind screamed for help. "Stay back, Captain." She had nowhere to go with her back pressed against the wall, her hands in front of her as a feeble barrier against him.

He grabbed her arms with his rough, gnarled fingers as he pinned her in place. When he moved those last few inches to make contact, Dale brought her knee up and found her target. He reeled to the floor as he clutched his manhood. He reached out and grabbed her dress.

"Let go!" Dale tugged frantically at the hem of her dress, trying to dislodge the meaty hand holding onto it. She lashed out again with her foot but to no avail. His muscles flexed as he pulled her toward him, the tattoos on his flesh shifting in a macabre dance with each exertion.

The door flew open, and Françoise stood there. She felt her anger rise with each breath she took. "Let her go!" Her voice boomed through the room and bounced ominously off the wooden walls.

The captain stopped, his attention now drawn to Françoise who quickly approached him. His hands rose in surrender but had little effect as she pounded him with her fists. "Monsieur, please."

"Please? I think not, you sorry excuse for a Frenchman." In a show of strength born from rage, Françoise bodily lifted the rotund man to his feet. She all but dragged him through the door, down the short corridor to the deck, before throwing him the last few feet to land with a thud in front of his men. "Give me a reason not to kill you!" she bellowed to the gusting wind.

"Is there a problem, monsieur?" Rumkey approached slowly.

"This putrid piece of water scum attacked my wife." Françoise paced back and forth, her fury seeking an outlet. She drew her sword and waved it ominously in the captain's face.

"You must be mistaken, Philippe." Rumkey was obviously attempting to diffuse the situation with the use of her first name.

"Rumkey, I know what I saw. That man was grabbing at my wife's dress." But Françoise took some of the blame for the situation. Her arguments with the captain had fueled his actions.

Rumkey looked at his captain lying on the deck. "Is that true, Cap'n?"

"True? You are taking the word of this child over the word of your captain?"

"He was in our room. He was on the floor grabbing at her dress. What more do you need to know?"

"What's going on?" Dale had stood to the side while Françoise handled the situation.

"Nothing," Françoise answered.

"But he attacked me."

"I know, Dale. I am trying to make them see what he really is."

"She invited me in," he said smugly.

"You invited him in?" Françoise couldn't believe that Dale would do such a thing.

"There was a knock on the door. I thought it was you. So I said 'entrez.' When I saw it was him," Dale said and nodded with distaste in the direction of the captain, "I asked him to leave."

"Then what happened?"

"He came toward me, and when he grabbed me, I kneed him in the groin."

"Groin?"

"Manhood."

Françoise winced at the thought, but the man deserved no less. It was comforting to think that Dale would respond if she was in danger. After that first day in the woods, Françoise had her reservations about leaving her alone. It seemed that Dale was capable of taking care of herself.

Françoise turned back to the captain, who was now on his feet. "Answer Monsieur Rumkey's question, Captain. Did you attack my wife?"

"If you have to ask, then you doubt it also."

"Answer, damn you!" Françoise rushed him and pushed his flabby body against the railing. Her sword rested against his neck to emphasize her point. "Admit it. You attacked my wife." He did nothing but smile.

"Why are you wasting time believing this son of a pig?" Lucette asked.

"Shut your mouth, whore," he shouted at her.

"Captain, I would suggest you keep that wayward tongue of yours in your mouth," Sébastien said. "This lady has the right—"

"Lady?" He laughed boisterously. "Has she not told you what she does, blacksmith?"

"Do not lecture me, you piece of crap." Sébastien took a step toward the chubby man, his sheer size moving the captain back a step or two. "Lucette may be a whore," Sébastien said the word but tempered it with a gentle smile at her, "but as far as I am concerned you, sir, are the one prostituting himself here. Taking advantage of this gentle flower in such a way." He swept his hand toward Dale.

"Gentle flower? Look at her and tell me she is not inviting such advances. They all are."

"Why you..." Both Sébastien and Françoise battled for the space that would have put them in front of him, effectively knocking each other to the side.

"I do not know what all the fuss is about. She would have enjoyed my attention had we not been interrupted."

"She is married, you dolt," Lucette yelled.

Françoise doubted that the man could be that stupid, so he must be crazy.

"So you say, woman. A woman is a woman and is here for only one purpose."

"See? He admits it with his own words. Can you deny me justice?"

"I am still the captain. I answer to only one person, and he is not present." His words were met with murmurs from the crew.

"And you hide behind that name, you coward." Françoise yanked him away from the railing and slammed him back against it, drawing a whimper before a quiet chuckle escaped his lips. Françoise was so tempted to run him through to wipe that sick smile from his face.

"You raped those poor women below."

"They are but slaves. They are nothing."

Françoise thought about it. Had she not said the same thing long ago to Dale about Madeleine? No, she was not like that. She'd dismissed the woman's opinions, not her life. Her servants were well looked after and paid. They could have left any time they wanted. She was not a tyrant... was she?

"They are not nothing. My wife is *not* nothing. Do you hear me? She is very precious to me, and I will *not* allow you to go unpunished for this attack."

"Who is going to help you, eh? This is my ship and my men. They are loyal to me."

"You, sir, are not worthy of the title of captain. My father shall hear of this." Alain spoke up. Françoise had not seen him in the sea of faces.

The captain looked him up and down. "What has your father got to do with this?"

"My father owns this ship, Captain, and he owns you."

"You lie. Your father is Étienne Barbineau."

"My father is also known as Marcel Courant."

The captain blanched. Françoise removed the fist she'd buried in the captain's dirty jacket and backed away. The sword in her hand vibrated. She was so, so close to committing murder. She wanted—needed—retribution. Françoise began pacing back and forth again. "Give the captain a weapon."

"Philippe—"

"Stay out of this, Tantine." She stared the captain down. "Rumkey, find him a sword."

"Monsieur, this is not wise." Alain tried to intervene.

"I do not care. I demand satisfaction. This man attacked my wife. It cannot go undefended." Françoise flexed her rapier and made a few cursory swipes.

The captain looked her up and down. "Yes, my sword, Rumkey." He smiled at her as Rumkey slapped the pommel into his hand. "This should not take long." His chuckle drew a snicker from a handful of the crew.

Françoise finally looked at her opponent and the weapon he was swinging. It was far heavier than her own and would easily break through her defenses. Before she could utter a word, Rumkey presented the handle of a similar sword to her. A fresh breeze started to pick up and blew the long tendrils of her plait of hair into wild disarray.

"It must be a fair duel, monsieur," Rumkey muttered as he met her eyes.

"Thank you." Behind the captain stood Sébastien, his trunk-like arms crossed over his barrel chest. She could see from the look in his eye that he would step in and stop the fight if it became necessary.

The cutlass felt heavy in her hand, and it threw off the balance she had acquired with the lighter weapon. Not only was she fighting a man she detested, but she would also be fighting her own waning stamina. Her lack of sleep had sapped her energy. She tried to draw on her anger again to see her through.

The breeze became stronger, flicking wisps of dark hair into her face. Françoise looked up at the sky and noticed the closing cloud. On the far horizon, dark, angry clouds were gathering quickly, illuminated once or twice by a flicker of bright light. A storm was approaching and fast. It was as if everything was working against her need for justice.

"Whenever you are ready, monsieur," the captain said and sneered at her.

He still was smug about the whole situation, like it was his God-given right to assault Dale. With her righteous indignation in place, Françoise stood in the ready position, eyeing him closely for his opening move.

From the first swing of his weapon, Françoise knew she was in for a fight. He obviously had a good grasp of swordplay and superior weight behind him while she had youth and guile on her side. At first, neither of them made much contact, each combatant studying the other for strengths and weaknesses and looking for an opportunity to strike.

She allowed her anger full rein and moved in to engage him, thrusting the weapon directly at his chest. Its weight lay heavy in her palm as she tried to hold the blade steady. He batted it aside and took a swipe at her midsection. Françoise barely had time to react before the blade came perilously close to gutting her. She backed away as her anger settled to simmering hatred and a healthy dose of caution.

The crew formed a circle around them, closing off any means of retreat. Most of the comments supported the captain, but her heart found one voice that was meant for her. Dale had thrown her verbal weight behind Françoise's fight. She took strength from that and launched another attack. Her movements were sluggish and lacked refinement, and she soon realized that what she had learned with a rapier only partly applied here. The quicksilver style of the rapier was impossible with the heavier weapon.

They circled one another, the clang of metal cutting through the sounds of the rising wind and the billowing sail. Françoise pressed her advantage in a series of swings, the blade arcing overhead as she tried to beat the captain into submission. In the last swing of her attack, she felt pain across her brow, unaware that a blade had opened up her skin. It was not possible. The captain's sword was directly underneath her own. How could that be?

Then she noticed a dagger in his other hand, its edge tinged in red. Blood... her blood. He could not even fight fair. Her left hand reached out and grabbed his wrist before he had a chance to strike again. They stood locked together, swords crossed and a dagger hovering close to Françoise's face.

"You cannot even fight honorably, Captain!" She spat out the last word as if it was spawned from the devil.

"On the high seas, monsieur"—his putrid breath in Françoise's face made her gag—"there are no rules. There are only those who live and those who die."

"Cap'n," Rumkey said.

"Stay out of this, traitor."

"Storm ho!"

"Good. That whore of yours had been whining about wanting a bath." He snickered, feeding Françoise's anger.

She pushed away and lunged at him. It was almost too late when she saw that his comments were designed to make her angry and act foolishly. His blade came toward her, and she was forced to arch her back to allow it to pass by. While it was a dangerous move, it gave her the opportunity to swipe her sword in an arc toward his unprotected back.

There was a satisfying cry of pain from her opponent as the blade cut deep. Immediately his shirt became crimson, first as a patch of red then two tracks of blood running down the dirty white material.

"Had enough, Captain?" Françoise put all her menace into those few words as she tried to end the confrontation.

"It is but a scratch."

"But, Captain," Rumkey shouted.

"What?"

"The storm is nearly upon us!" Rumkey raised his voice even more, but it was hard to hear him over the sounds of the approaching squall.

"Captain, see to your duties. Now!" Alain yelled.

He looked at Alain as if he was about to argue with him.

"I will speak to Monsieur Théroux."

"It seems you live another day, monsieur." The captain lowered his sword as the duel came to an end.

Françoise was so tempted just to run him through at this point, but unlike him, she wanted to win this particular fight in the spirit that it began. There would be no justice if she ignored the protocols of the duel.

"Storm ho!"

The captain's decaying teeth peeked out as he smiled. "It seems that I am the one holding all the cards, monsieur. How do you expect to sail out of this storm without me?"

Françoise looked at the crew. "And what do you say, Rumkey?"

"He is right, monsieur. He is our best hope of riding out this gale."

"My father will not be pleased if he hears you killed his only son." Alain's eyes blazed with anger. Françoise silently applauded his stand and hoped that the captain was smart enough to try his best.

Françoise leaned against the railing and watched the approaching tempest. Clouds dark and menacing rolled toward them at terrifying speed. Jagged streaks of lightning hit the water, followed moments later by what sounded like cannon fire as the thunder rumbled with ferocity.

"This is not over yet, Captain." She took a step toward him to stand just inches from his face. "Remember, one mistake from you and you go down with this ship like the rest of us."

"Lower the sails!" the captain yelled. Rumkey scuttled around the deck, directing the crew to pull down the canvas.

Françoise found Dale in the chaos and directed her toward the cabin. "You look after Lucette and her girls. They are a little nervous."

"They're not the only ones." Dale glanced up at the dark clouds.

Françoise smiled. "You? The one who stepped through a mirror to find me? You are one of the bravest people I know. Tie down whatever you can."

"Philippe…"

"No time for talk. I will be there soon. I would never leave you alone in a storm." She raised her index finger to caress Dale's water-spattered cheek. "There is no one but you."

"Good." Dale turned on her heels and ushered the women toward the cabins.

"What can I do to help, monsieur?" Françoise stood there awaiting her orders.

"Find cover, Monsieur Philippe."

"Do you believe that the captain attacked my wife, Rumkey?"

He looked over his shoulder at her. "Yes, I do."

"What about the slaves below?"

"What about them?"

"You cannot leave them chained up down there."

"Is it any worse than being up on deck unprotected?"

"Of course it is. Those poor souls below should not even be here. If this ship goes down, they need a chance to survive. Chained up would mean certain death."

"I do not have time for this. The storm will be upon us shortly. Do what you will." And he was gone, quickly pulling on ropes to lower the sail.

Dale would never forgive her if she did nothing. Françoise had to admit that a few short weeks ago she would not have given the matter a second thought. Now, her present circumstances uncovered revelations that she had never considered before. She had been a slave in a gilded cage.

Françoise climbed down into the hold to the small platform just below the deck. The smell was indescribable. Putrid odors emanated from the dark space that housed the slaves. Barely more than two feet high, the platform lay just under the length of the deck. Here, the slaves lay, chained to wooden blocks running the length of the space.

*"Est-ce que quelqu'un parle Français?"* There seemed to be silence, but she was not sure. The howling wind was buffeting her ears, so she shouted the question again.

A lone male voice cut through the darkness. *"Moi."*

"What is your name?"

"They call me Badoo."

"Badoo, a storm is approaching. Do you want to live?"

"A storm?" There were anxious voices among the slaves as he murmured the words in his own language.

"Listen to me. I will find someone to open these shackles."

"Why? Why do you do this?" Françoise could hear the suspicion and fear in his voice.

"Why? I want you to have a chance to survive."

"He did not care. Why do you?"

"Because I know what it is like to be a slave." Françoise did not wait for an answer, instead searching for a sailor to free them.

It took several minutes of arguing before Rumkey relented and allowed one of the crew to undo the locks. One by one, the slaves emerged on deck. The rain had started to fall and was picking up intensity. When the one called Badoo stepped onto the deck, she drew him aside.

"We can use some help."

"Why should we?"

"Because I will free you of him." Françoise pointed to the stern and the captain. "And because we will all die if you do not."

She gave him time to translate what she had said and helped Rumkey with the sail while Badoo tried to encourage the slaves on deck. When she returned, five men were present. "Badoo, where are the others?"

"They will not come out, monsieur."

"We have to cover the hole to stop water flooding the ship."

"No matter. They are frightened of punishment. They will not move."

Françoise sighed. She could not blame them. "Tell them that the hole will be closed, but only for the length of the storm. Tell them everything will be fine."

As the black man spoke in his native tongue, Rumkey approached them.

"I have found you a few extra hands, Rumkey. Badoo here can speak French. Use them as you will." As she spoke, the hatch was covered, blocking out all light to the platform below. There were a few anxious cries as the darkness came. It sounded like Badoo tried to settle them with soothing words.

"So... Monsieur Philippe." The strange tone of Rumkey's voice drew her attention away from the work.

"Pardon?" Françoise watched his gaze drop to her shirt, her own eyes following. He had caught her. The rain had soaked her clothes and made her shirt nearly transparent. *Stupid, stupid, stupid.* Even though her chest was still bound, it was obvious she was a woman.

A wide grin split the man's face. "I think you should go see to your wife's needs. Do you not think so, monsieur?" His eyes danced in amusement. He let her worry for a moment longer before giving her a wink. Then, he grabbed Badoo's arm and guided him toward the slaves cowering on the deck.

# Part Five: Destiny

# Chapter 26

Françoise didn't know what to think. What would happen now? In a perverse sort of way, she was glad the charade was over. The bandage and the leather piece had been slowly driving her insane. Her breasts were sore and rubbed nearly raw from all the constant chafing. She just wanted to be done with it. With her mind contemplating these questions, she didn't even knock, instead entering the captain's cabin without much thought or conscious direction.

"There you are. I was about to send a rescue party. Come here and let me take care of that cut you have."

"What cut?" Dale touched her forehead. She showed the blood to Françoise. "'Tis but a scratch."

"I would feel better if I looked at it."

"There is no time."

"We'll make time. Now sit." Grudgingly, Françoise sat down in the captain's chair while Dale busied herself gathering herbs.

Dale applied the herbal paste she'd mixed, liberally covering the cut with the ointment. "Keep that clean." She tore off a piece of the cotton in the trunk and tied it around Françoise's head before she could object.

"Is that really necessary?"

"Yes." Dale leaned down and placed a kiss on Françoise's injury. "You can go play with the kids." It was then that Dale noticed the state of Françoise's shirt. "Um." She waved a finger at the buttons.

"I have been discovered."

Dale didn't say anything for several seconds. "So, now what?"

"Now?" Françoise unbuttoned her shirt and began to remove the bandage. "There is no need to wear this any longer." She reached for the buttons on her pants. "Or this. I am glad." She stood there after she had removed the offending items to allow the breeze to flow over her naked body. "*Oui*. That is better."

271

"It sure is." Dale's gaze skimmed over the uncovered flesh. Françoise stared down at the skin that had reddened and chafed from the constant contact.

"You are incorrigible."

"Huh?" Dale looked up at her.

"Never mind." Françoise rummaged through the trunk for her spare shirt. The soaked cloth she had been wearing hit the floor with a slap and a gentle sigh left her lips as the dry shirt touched her skin. "Heaven."

"And we're sailing right into hell."

"True." Her eyes scanned the room for somewhere to hang out the wet cloth, but besides the window, there was none.

"You want a laugh?"

"A laugh?"

"Sure. Look up. Sébastien helped me."

Françoise did as asked. "*Incroyable.*" There sitting between two rafters was the mirror. "We both got our wish."

"Oh no. Not quite. I want you naked, my love. All skin and muscle, thank you very much."

"Skin and... *Mon Dieu!* You have such an imagination." She couldn't help but chuckle at Dale's erotic picture.

"I love the way you move, and no amount of clothes is going to stop me watching you make love to me in any form I so desire." Dale smiled as Françoise's fingers twitched. "But that's for another time." A knock at the door interrupted their conversation. "That'll be the others."

"It is going to be very crowded in here, Dale."

"No different from any other night."

"But we will all be wide awake. And there will be *Monsieur* Barbineau."

"I'm sure Rosalie won't complain."

"I am sure you are right. No cuddling?"

"Oh, cuddling is allowed. Just nothing else."

"I have never made love on a storm-tossed sea," Françoise said in a dreamy voice.

"Another day and another time. We have the rest of our lives."

"That we do." Unless, of course, the rest of their lives ended at nightfall.

Lucette and her girls entered the cabin, closely followed by Sébastien. Françoise felt a hand slip inside her own, and she looked into Dale's trusting eyes. If things turned bad, she knew she wasn't alone.

No one spoke as slack jaws and wide eyes stared at her chest.

"Well, that is a surprise."

"The rain revealed me, Tantine. I am glad the hiding is over."

"You knew?" Rosalie asked Lucette.

"Yes, I knew." Lucette seemed to be gauging the reaction of the others as her gaze swept the room.

"And you, Sébastien?" Somehow what the man thought was of importance to Françoise.

"It answers some questions."

"Like what?"

"When you came in that first day, you looked too... too... pretty to be a man. Now I know why, Madame Countess."

Françoise gasped. She felt her hand squeezed, and she gazed once more at Dale. What could she say?

"It was obvious you were hiding, madame, so that marked you as aristocracy."

Lucette stepped in between them, facing Sébastien. "You must make a decision, monsieur. Who will you reveal this to, eh? The captain? Or maybe you will wait for the authorities at St. Domingue?"

Sébastien held up his hands. "One moment, Lucette. Did I say anything about revealing her secret? Please, let me finish." He looked over the top of Lucette's head to Françoise. "Madame Countess..."

"Please, Sébastien, that is all gone now. Call me Françoise." She was still coming to terms with that despite everything she'd said. It was hard to erase over ten years of one's life without at least a bit of resistance, even if that existence was nothing more than slavery. "How did you know who I was? Did Gérard confide in you?"

"No, madame. It was simple deduction. I knew where Gérard lived and who the local aristocracy were. He talked about them often. You were obviously held in high regard by him. He does not give away that trust readily."

Her heart beat a little faster at the compliment. Her own love for the old man she left behind rose another notch.

"And of course what happened at Lucette's when the count was visiting was a juicy tale." He looked at the madam with interest and obvious affection. "Do not dismiss what you did for these women, Françoise. Your generosity did not go unnoticed."

"A little money..."

"No, madame, not the money. The concern. The care you bestowed. One does not easily forget that. Am I right, Lucette?"

"Yes, Sébastien." He glanced her way, and she batted her eyes.

Sébastien smiled at her before turning back to Françoise. "I can see why Gérard loved you so much. Your secret is safe with me."

Françoise released her pent-up breath in relief. She grabbed his hand and pumped it hard. Maybe she had more effect on these people than she had originally thought. She had never considered what she did as anything special. It was more a penance she felt she had to do after what her husband had subjected them to.

The ship lurched as the storm hit. "Everyone find somewhere to sit. It may be awhile." Françoise turned her attention to Rosalie. "Would you please find Monsieur Barbineau and ask him to join us. I am sure he would prefer to be with company during this tempest."

"Stop playing matchmaker," Dale murmured. When Françoise looked at her in question, she said, "Just because you're speaking in French, don't think I don't know what you're doing."

"Maybe it was destined to be. Did you ever think of that?"

"If it was destined to be, you don't need to interfere."

"I cannot have you. What else is there to do?"

"Kick that son of a bitch at the wheel."

"Son of a... what?"

"You heard what I said. Son... of... a... bitch. I'm sure you've heard swear words before."

"Not ones so colorful as that. Son of a bitch. *Fils d'une chienne.*"

"One day, you'll have to teach me some French ones."

"Not today."

"No, not today."

The heavens shook and the sea rebelled as the storm pounded the small vessel. It was as if God himself was testing their mettle as seamen to see if they were worthy to travel across his domain.

They looked around the cabin at the others cowering there. The storm had been raging for some time now, pitching and rolling the vessel with monotonous regularity. Violette had already succumbed to the storm, heaving energetically into a bucket.

"Dale?"

"Yeah?"

"How are you feeling?"

"Besides my stomach?"

"Does that mean you are ill?"

"Not as bad as her." Dale nodded toward Violette, whose bloodshot eyes rose to meet them. "I'll manage."

"It should not last much longer," Françoise predicted. The roar of the wind had dropped to a howl, and the blinding flash through the window had become less frequent. It looked like they were going to survive. Her gaze swept the room, and a smile touched her lips when she saw Lucette and Sébastien. She nudged Dale and nodded in the direction of the couple.

"Well, well." Lucette was tucked under Sébastien's brawny arm. They were quietly talking and oblivious to their scrutiny. "Aw. That is just so damned cute." Dale chuckled. "It seems lots of things are going right. If we can reach America, I'll be happy."

"I will do my best."

"I know you will. I'm just happy to be where you are."

Françoise felt that tickle around her heart again. It always seemed to strike whenever Dale said something sentimental.

"What about them?" A gentle nudge in her side drew Françoise's attention to the other couple. Rosalie was asleep in Alain's arms.

"It is making me sick," Honorine mumbled.

"You have no romance in your soul, Honorine."

"I have plenty of romance, young pup, but you will not see it."

A knock at the door drew everyone's attention. "Monsieur... uh... Philippe. May I have a word with you?"

"Enter, Rumkey."

"Out here, please."

Françoise disengaged herself from Dale's arms, rising in one fluid motion from the bunk.

"What's going on?" Dale asked.

"I do not know yet. Rumkey has asked for a moment of my time." She held up her hands as questions began to flow from the dozen people in the room. Her legs took a moment to adjust to the sway, her walk more a stagger as she made her way across the room. "It seems the storm is abating."

"Close the door please, madame, so the others cannot hear." The serious look on Rumkey's face caused her to step back. When she shut the door, he murmured, "We have lost a handful of the crew overboard."

Françoise shifted uncomfortably. "Should you not be discussing this with the captain?"

"I am not sure who the captain is."

"Then we must include Monsieur Barbineau in this conversation." Françoise opened the door and nodded her head at Alain. He lifted Rosalie off his body and moved her onto Lisette's shoulder. He closed the door behind him.

"Is there a problem?"

"Rumkey wishes to know who the captain of this vessel is."

"He should be on deck at the wheel." Alain looked from Françoise to Rumkey.

"That he is, monsieur, but after the fight, I was not sure whether he was still considered the captain."

"It is your decision, Alain."

He looked uncertainly at Françoise, and she held up her hands. "This was supposed to be a quiet journey to St. Domingue," he said.

"Sometimes things do not turn out the way you think they will. If it had been the voyage that you planned, you would not have met Rosalie." He blushed. "For now, let the captain be. You can think on it until tomorrow."

"What shall we do with the slaves?" Rumkey asked.

Alain's mouth opened and closed but no sound came out. Françoise stepped in and made a decision. "When it is safe to do so, remove the cover. Allow them to come above deck for fresh air." When Alain nodded, Rumkey left.

Françoise reached for the door handle, but Alain stopped her entering. "Can we talk?"

She directed him to the small storage room next to the captain's cabin. Françoise sat on a sack of grain while Alain perched himself on a barrel and stared at her. "I do not like being made a fool of... madame."

"It was never my intention, monsieur." Françoise winced. She didn't know what to call him at this point.

"Yet, you did. What am I to do?" He rubbed his face with his hands. "When the captain hears of this—"

"I do not care what he thinks. I only sought to protect those he would prey on." Françoise tempered her voice. "Monsieur... Alain, Dale and I were setting out on a dangerous journey. I had to do this to protect us both. Please understand."

"I do understand the need for protection." He made a face and waved his hand to encompass her body. "But you are still a woman."

"Indeed, but I am the same person you had called 'friend.' Does what you see here really matter?"

"It should, but—" He dropped his head. "If my father knew," he muttered.

"Your secret is safe with me." Françoise patted his shoulder. "I will have to take up the disguise soon enough, but for now, it is nice to be myself. About the captain…"

"I do not know anything about being captain of a ship. I hate ships."

"And you are here because…"

"When my father says go, I go. He is not one to accept no."

"Maybe he was trying to get you out of France quickly."

"No, my father wanted a messenger boy, nothing more. I am his son in name only."

"You are not interested in following your father?"

"Not even his legitimate business."

"What do you want to do?"

"Me?" Alain smiled. "I do not know. No one has ever asked me that."

"Are you two going to sit around all night and chat?" Dale stood in the doorway with her hands on her hips, while her body swayed with the rolling ship. "Rosalie has woken up."

"Rosalie?" Alain said only the name.

"Dale asked if we had finished talking. Rosalie is awake and wondering where you are." Alain jumped to his feet and left quickly.

Françoise laughed. "It seems he is eager to get back to his cuddle."

"I am, too," Dale said suggestively.

"Then how can I deny you that?" Françoise looped her arm in Dale's and led her back to the captain's cabin and their bunk.

The room was alive with chatter when Françoise and Dale returned. It came from everyone in the room.

"What is the verdict?"

"What is going on?"

"We will all die!"

"I told you, you young whippersnapper."

"Quiet!" Françoise yelled. "It is nothing important. The captain is still at the wheel, and the storm will be over soon."

Dale pulled on Françoise's sleeve. "Are you going to tell me or do I play charades?"

"Rumkey wanted to know if the captain was still in charge."

"He's still alive? Damn."

"My my, such bad thoughts."

"An hour ago you were ready to run him through."

"It is not over yet, Dale."

"Do you know something I don't?"

"We will find out tomorrow." She glanced at Alain who was smiling at Rosalie while she snuggled into his shoulder. "Can we discuss this later?"

"Why? They don't understand." Dale swept her arm to indicate the others in the room.

"I do." A distinctly male voice spoke up.

"All this time we have been together and now you tell me?" Dale poked her finger in the air at Alain. "I've been all alone, and you didn't even bother to come up and talk to me?" Her voice continued to rise. "What is the matter with you people, huh? She doesn't speak French so don't talk to her, is that it?" Françoise put her hand on her shoulder, but Dale shook her off. "You arrogant, self-centered—"

Françoise covered her mouth with her hand before anything more was said. "Watch what you say, Dale. Remember, I am also French," she murmured with a touch of anger. "We have been taught not to trust the English."

"I'm not English, I'm American."

"For us, it is all the same. We speak French, you do not. That makes you different." Françoise pulled Dale into a strong embrace and whispered into her ear, "But not to me. You are my life." She felt Dale relax at the words. She spoke a little louder so Alain could hear her. "He knows now, and I am sure he will make every effort to engage you in conversation. Am I right, Alain?"

"Of course, madame."

"What is going on?" Lucette asked.

"My wife is upset that none of you have shown any effort to talk to her."

"Why bother?" Rosalie spoke up. "She cannot understand us."

"Exactly. What I said to Alain is between us. Now you know how she feels." She slyly smiled. "Of course, if we land in America, you will know that feeling more. I would suggest that you get my wife to teach you some English. You may need it."

"I thought we were going to St. Domingue?"

"We should have stayed at Nantes," Honorine mumbled.

Françoise had enough of her grousing. "Maybe you should have. You ungrateful—"

"They would not have killed us," Lucette said.

"Of course they would. To them you are just someone in the way of their enemy. You would have died on those docks, Tantine." Françoise took a shaky breath. "I could not let that happen."

"Maybe you are right. We will never know." Lucette took Françoise's hand and patted it. "This ship will be returning to France, will it not?"

"Eventually. Do you want to return to your life there?"

"It is all I know, little one."

"Have you ever thought that what we are traveling toward may be better?" Françoise glanced at Sébastien leaning against the wall. "A chance to start anew?"

Lucette looked over her shoulder to smile at him, which he returned. "It is worth thinking about, little one."

"So now what happens?" Dale asked.

"Alain will let us know his decision tomorrow."

"Alain?"

"Of course. He is the son of the owner of the ship."

Dale looked at Alain. "So will he throw the captain overboard? Put him in chains with the slaves?"

"We wait," Françoise said with some finality. To stop Dale from speaking, she pulled her into her chest and patted her hair. "Get some rest."

Dale looked like she was about to object but must have noticed Françoise's frown. "Okay."

Françoise closed her eyes and hoped that the conversation had ended. Tomorrow would be long enough without endless chatter.

\* \* \*

Alain called a meeting in the captain's cabin. Françoise had been asked to attend, although she was not sure why. When the captain arrived, Alain had already taken his seat. Rumkey stood near the door.

"What is the meaning of this, sir?"

"Captain. The matter of your inappropriate behavior toward Madame Théroux is over."

The captain waved a hand toward Françoise. "So what I heard is true." He looked at her with disgust. "A woman?"

"Yes, and my being one saved your life," Françoise spat out.

The captain laughed. "You? Saved me? Ridiculous. How could you possibly have saved me?"

"If I had a man's strength in that duel, you would already be dead."

"Yet, as a woman, you could not best me."

"How pathetic, you miserable excuse for a man. Seeking your victories on those weaker than you."

"Women will always be second class, you whore!"

Francoise lunged at the captain, but Alain held her back.

"Enough!" he yelled. "This matter is settled."

"Monsieur," Françoise begged,

"It is settled," he repeated. "However, there is the matter of theft."

"Theft? What theft?"

"You, Captain, accepted paying passengers without the permission of my father, and you did not pass on the coin that exchanged hands. My father dislikes thieves. In fact, I know he has killed men for less."

"Here is the money." The captain reached into his pocket.

"Too late. You knowingly brought these people on board without permission. You will stand down. I will take over as captain, and Monsieur Rumkey will assist in performing the captain's duties."

"And what am I supposed to do?"

Alain smiled. "I am sure that Madame Théroux will have something in mind to occupy your time." He glanced at Françoise. "Did you not mention something about helping the slaves?"

"Slaves?" Françoise looked at him, perplexed. "Oh, slaves. Yes. With your permission, monsieur, I would like to clean the slaves' quarters. If they are fed and cleaned up, they will be worth more to you."

"True," Alain said. "What did you want the crew to do?"

"Rumkey, have the men clean out the slaves' quarters tomorrow. Cut another hole in the deck if needed to rid the smell. The captain allowed this to happen, and it has led to the loss of human life. I am sure he will be more than pleased to help out in this endeavor."

"The slaves?" Beaudry asked in an incredulous tone.

"The slaves," Françoise said. "They are human beings." She could see the look of surprise on Alain's face. "I know, monsieur, it was the last thing you expected from me, but a certain young woman showed me the error of my ways." She looked over to Rumkey who nodded with approval. "They will have the... what do you say, Rumkey? The part below the deck?"

"The 'hold,' madame."

"They can sleep in the hold," Alain said. "Move what cargo you can onto the platform once it has been cleaned. They will be allowed free access to the deck."

Françoise addressed Rumkey. "Please talk to Badoo. He must ensure that there is no trouble, you understand me? It is for all our own safety that there is order."

"I will do what I can, madame."

"No. You must do it. Otherwise, we will all be doomed. Tell him his people can come on deck in the morning. They can wash. Any injuries will be treated then. In the meantime, I have arranged for some hot food to be available tonight to everyone."

"Beaudry, you are now relieved of duty. Your belongings will be moved into the hold," Alain said. "You are dismissed."

Rumkey left quickly. Beaudry glared at Alain before leaving without a word.

"Did you see his face?" Françoise nearly laughed with glee. "Alain, you did very well."

"We cannot let them near the cargo, Françoise."

"And why not?"

"It is my father's business."

"What are you hiding? What is so important that you will not share it with us?"

"There are some things in the cargo I am escorting to St. Domingue for my father. The problem is, I do not know what is in the chests. He told me to ensure that it reached the Colonies. That is all."

Françoise doubted that Alain was ignorant about what he was escorting. He was a smart young man. "Well, if a chest or two happens to break open when they are moved tomorrow, do not come to me."

"You would not dare."

"Of course not, but accidents happen, do they not?"

There was a knock on the door.

"Enter!"

Dale poked her head in. "Are you finished?"

Françoise smiled. "Come. How goes it on the deck?"

"Some of the slaves are missing. Rumkey indicated to me he thought we had originally fifty. I counted twenty-eight. We had lost ten to sickness, so I guess we have lost about twelve to fifteen slaves, including the young mother and her son."

"That is so sad. Just as she has the chance to be free of the captain."

"Yeah."

Françoise approached Dale and ran her hands up and down her arms soothingly. "She is in a better place now. Her suffering is over."

"She should never have been here in the first place."

"I know." Françoise kept her voice low and gentle. "I know. But we all have to accept the cards we have been dealt." She held Dale's gaze. "Even the child."

Dale sighed deeply. "So now what?"

"We try to get to the Colonies. St. Domingue or America... whatever land we can find. We will worry about where after that." She leaned in close. "I have something for you to do tomorrow, s'il te plaît."

"What do you have in mind?"

"First, check what food and water we have. See if there is enough left for the journey. Hopefully Alain can find out where we are by then. Second, the slaves are to bathe in the morning. Can you organize the herbs for any infections?" Dale nodded.

"Does this course of action meet with your approval, Alain?" Françoise made sure to include Alain in the decision-making. He had made concessions to her. She felt it only fair to do the same.

Alain looked at her in confusion. "Fine," he eventually said.

"Good man." Françoise felt her spirits lift. She pulled Dale into an affectionate hug. "Thank you, chérie. Did you see any charts or maps in the cabin earlier?"

"I put them in the chest. Hang on." Dale slipped her hand down her bodice, forcing Françoise to step in front of her to stop the young man ogling her wife. "Damn it." She delved deeper into the bodice as the key remained elusive.

"Do you need some help?" Françoise asked in amusement.

"May I?" Alain was quick to jump to Dale's rescue, only to back away quickly at Françoise's venomous glare.

She was relieved when Dale lifted out the key. "Thank you. You may like to find somewhere else to hide that."

"I was in a hurry, all right? What are you complaining about? I didn't lose it."

"True, but I would prefer that it was just you and me in this room when you do that." Françoise opened the trunk and began searching. "They are not here."

"Wait. I think the captain took them at your last meeting."

"Alain, check with Rumkey. He will know where the charts are. You will need to meet with him to plot your course."

"You seem to have the situation in hand." Alain couldn't keep the smile off his face.

"You can step in at any time."

"No, no, no. I have enough to worry about."

"I think we deserve some dinner," Dale said.

# Chapter 27

Françoise stood on the upper deck while Dale carried out the duties she'd been assigned. The language barrier caused frustration for all concerned—especially Dale. She flayed her arms about in reckless abandon as she tried to make her wishes known.

"Aw, Jesus. Why won't you listen?" Dale stomped her foot in aggravation. "If I can give up my precious soap, you can damn well use it." There was a snicker behind her. "Don't you laugh, Alain. You're next."

"Me?"

"Just because you've got money doesn't mean you don't stink." Dale handled her duties with zeal. "And don't think I didn't see you smile either, missy." She stared up to Françoise. "You'll bathe, too."

"Fine." Françoise began to reach for her shirt buttons.

"You want to come down and do this then? I'm quite happy to give you the job."

"But, Dale…"

"Oh no, don't 'but, Dale' me. They're as stubborn as mules."

"Almost as stubborn as you."

"What did you say?"

"Nothing. Nothing at all. I am afraid that I have other matters to attend to."

"Yeah, I can see that. Standing up there watching the day go by." Earlier that morning, Dale inspected the food supplies while Françoise used the cabin for her meeting with Alain, Rumkey, and the former captain. She had absolutely no idea how long the supplies would last, so she found the cooks, both of them. With a lot of charades and ranting and raving, she was able to ascertain they could survive for about another week with some creative cooking.

Now, every single person on board had an aversion to soap and water. She had to practically strip off and show them how to use it before someone volunteered to be first. Thank God for Rumkey, who plastered on his wide grin and grudgingly washed off the weeks of sweat and grime. When they saw that he had not melted from the wash, and with the threat of no food, one by one, the crew stripped off filthy clothes before taking soap to their bodies.

It took a lot of prodding and pushing by Badoo to convince the slaves. Badoo finally volunteered and vigorously used soap and water in an effort to finish the job quickly. Dale treated cuts and abrasions with an herbal mixture and allowed them to dry in the sun. The whole process seemed to go on and on and drained most of Dale's patience.

* * *

Françoise stood on the upper deck overlooking the bathing fiasco while she thought ahead to the next few days. Alain and Rumkey had studied the map and calculated they were close to reaching St. Domingue. The man in the crow's nest had not called land yet, but the news should be good soon.

"Ho, madame!" Rumkey's urgent call drew her back to the hole in the deck. The cleaning of the platform had proved difficult, back-breaking, and suffocating, but she was pleased with the progress. In the middle of the task was Beaudry. She was certain he cursed her with every movement of his brush. She wondered how the slaves had ever survived in such a poisonous environment.

"Monsieur Rumkey," she called back. "Is there a problem?"

"You must look." He stood over the hole they had cut in the foredeck in an effort to air the space.

Françoise moved down the stairs quickly. "What did you want me to—" The words died in her throat as she looked into the hole. One of the crew picked up a small cloth-wrapped package and was in the process of handing it up to Rumkey. "My God!" It was the white woman's child, lying deathly still. "Dale!"

"What's wrong?"

Without speaking, Françoise handed the child to Dale.

"Oh, God."

"That is what I said." Françoise took a step backward, as if the movement would help.

"What do you want me to do?"

"What you always do. Make it better."

"Me?" Dale's voice cracked.

Françoise noticed the slaves were staring at Dale. "They expect you to perform another miracle. How you say? You are the witch *docteur?*"

Dale took a deep breath and examined the child. "He's alive... barely. I think he's weak from dehydration and hunger." He lay still in her arms. "Water," she whispered, the word caught on the wind and blown away. Dale cleared her throat and repeated, "Fresh drinking water. Just a cup. And something soft to eat, like porridge. Warm, if Honorine can manage it. And a blanket, or my shawl if you can't find a spare."

Françoise turned and delivered the orders. "What do you want me to do?"

"I don't know. I have no idea what I'm doing."

"Dale, follow your heart."

"I know," she said and sighed deeply. "It's going to be touch and go."

"Touch and go?"

"He may or may not survive."

Dale had confirmed her suspicions. Françoise scanned the assembled crowd all hovering around to watch what would happen next. "Do you not have something else to do?"

"Wait," Dale said as the milling throng began to dissipate. "Can they stay here for a moment? I want to sponge him down, and they can block the sea breeze."

"Stay where you are." The looks of confusion she could understand. Go. Stay. She must have sounded a bit addled in the brain. Dale removed the swaddling clothes to gently wash the baby's skin with a soapy cloth.

"You know, he really is a gorgeous child."

*"Oui,* I can see that. He could easily pass for white."

"No, not that. Black or white, he is well proportioned and has fine features. He is a very handsome boy." As she finished, a hand appeared through the mass of bodies holding out her shawl.

Dale wrapped up the boy. Françoise saw the instant attraction. "Oh *non, non, non.* Our lives are hard enough without a baby."

"I know, but who's going to look after him?"

"We need someone to look after the baby," Françoise said loud enough for all to hear. But she suspected they would be alone in this endeavor. The only sound was the rustle of the canvas overhead. "Lucette?"

"I am too old to be worrying about a child. After all, I have a big child to keep an eye on."

"What about…"

Lucette looked over her shoulder at her girls. Their heads dropped one by one. "What about you then, child?"

Françoise tensed. "We do not need a child."

Lucette looked at Dale as she cuddled the infant. "I think you do."

"I am not ready for this, Tantine."

"This may be your only chance, Françoise. And what about Dale, eh? Have you discussed children with her?"

"A little. She said she was happy."

"That could be to allay your fears, my dear."

"I know." Françoise's attention returned to the sight of Dale rocking the baby. She contemplated their future. Dale cooed to the baby as she gave him water one drop at a time. "I know." She had resigned herself to their fate.

"Do you want to die and be forgotten? He could be your legacy for the future."

"Maybe one of the slaves." Françoise was running out of options.

"No. They ignored him before and will ignore him now. Why do you fight this?"

"So much has changed in too short a time, Tantine. I cannot think."

"Do not think, Françoise. Let your heart be your guide."

"I told Dale that."

"That is it!" Lucette replied triumphantly.

"I will think about it."

"But…"

"No, Lucette. Leave it be. The child may not survive yet."

Honorine arrived with a bowl of porridge and stood back to watch with the others. Dale tested the food before feeding the boy. "Where have you been hiding the honey, Honorine?" She dipped her finger in the mixture and fed it to the infant, constantly returning to the warm food. "Are we going to give him a name?"

"Is that wise?"

"Why? What do you mean?" Dale looked up in alarm.

"What if he…" Françoise couldn't bring herself to utter the word.

Dale held her breath. "Then he shouldn't go to the afterlife without a name."

"Do you have a name?"

"How about..." Dale furrowed her brow in thought for a few moments before making a decision. "Jacob."

"Jacob? Who is Jacob?"

"He was the son of Elizabeth and Joshua Wincott."

"Why that name?"

"I don't know. It just popped into my head. It's got to be an old name."

"Old?"

"Well, old for me. It's rather fashionable in this time. Lots of biblical names were used in the Colonies."

"Fine, he is Jacob." Françoise leaned down to the wrapped bundle and introduced herself. "Hello, Jacob. My name is Françoise." The baby's lips twitched. "Aw." The gesture grabbed at her heart. Maybe this was meant to be.

Dale smiled at her. Françoise felt in her heart this connection had guaranteed his survival. It looked like they now had a son.

* * *

The next few days had been busy while establishing a routine that was acceptable. Now free of their chains, the slaves spent most of their time on the deck.

While the evening meal was prepared on the lower deck, Françoise leaned on the railing of the upper deck and looked out to sea as she contemplated their next move.

"Land ho!" She looked to the horizon in reaction to the call. She could barely see the speck of land. Anxiety spiked through her. The last few weeks had been a respite from their flight, despite Beaudry's actions, but now... now she had to find new transportation.

"Françoise!" Lucette approached her.

"Yes?"

"Are we there?"

"Nearly." She pointed in the direction they were heading.

"St. Domingue?"

"I think so, but we will not know until we arrive." She wished it was Boston Harbor and their journey was at an end.

"Still, it is land." Lucette stretched her body and there was an audible crack.

"Yes, that it is," Françoise murmured absently.

"Then why do you look so sad?" Lucette asked, her expression laced with concern.

"Me? We are nearing the end of our journey. Why would I be sad?"

"You tell me, little one."

Françoise hesitated telling Lucette what she had withheld up until now. "Dale and I will not be staying. We will be moving on to the Colonies, to Boston."

Lucette looked surprised. "But why?"

"I promised her, Tantine. If I can, I will keep my promise. And you? What will you do?"

Lucette turned around to rest her elbows on the railing. Françoise glanced over to where Lucette's attention was drawn. The girls were laughing and chatting with the sailors. "I do not know."

"Maybe we should see what St. Domingue is like before making a decision. Monsieur Rumkey!"

He trotted up to them. "Yes, madame?"

"How goes it in St. Domingue?"

"Last time I heard, everything was fine."

"When shall we reach land?"

He looked at the sky. "It should be on the morning tide." As he trotted away, Françoise's gaze fell on the ex-captain, who stared back at her with some animosity.

"I would still watch out for that one," Lucette said in a low voice.

Françoise agreed. She turned around and looked back at the approaching land. "If he succeeds in whatever he is plotting for my demise, please look after Dale."

"Pardon? You are not seriously—"

"It is just a thought. With some luck, I will not have to look at his ugly face after we reach St. Domingue."

"How is the child?"

"Jacob? It is slow. Dale has been at his side all day and night, which has done nothing to soothe her mood."

"Now you know what motherhood is like. She will do what is necessary to ensure the child has a chance."

"But he will survive."

"That is good news."

"Yes, good."

"Then why does it sound like it is anything but?"

"I..." Françoise stopped and sighed. She rubbed her hands together. "I am afraid she will forget me."

"For… you are talking like a crazy woman." Lucette laughed. "Even these old eyes can see the love between you and her. She may be nursing the child, but her thoughts are always of you."

Françoise touched Lucette's arm. "Do you see why I need you? Your pearls of wisdom stop me from going crazy."

* * *

That night, Françoise tried to remember Lucette's advice when Dale turned her back to comfort Jacob. As she had told Lucette, she had not been used to sharing Dale's attention and she did not like it.

The next morning, the ship approached the island. On their way landward, they met a rowboat leaving the shore.

"Ho! Are you in need of assistance?" Rumkey called out.

"Take warning, there is an uprising on St. Domingue," one of the men in the boat called out.

"Uprising? By whom?"

A crowd had gathered at the railing to hear the news.

"The slaves revolted. Anyone white is killed on sight."

"When did this happen?"

"About a month ago, I believe. I did not stay to ask questions." The rowboat continued on its way, slowly heading out to sea before turning left and disappearing behind the point of land.

Françoise heard a splash of water and ran to the other side of the ship, shocked to see Beaudry swimming toward shore. "Are you insane, man? They will kill you! Come back!"

He laughed at her. "Better than put up with you!" His stroke was clumsy but effective.

"Can we stop him?" Françoise asked.

"No, madame. Not unless you want to send men into danger," Rumkey replied.

Alain joined them on deck. "What happened?"

"Beaudry has jumped ship and is heading to shore."

"And?"

"St. Domingue is in the hands of the slaves. There has been an uprising."

Alain watched for a while until Beaudry crawled onto the sand. Within moments, he disappeared into the undergrowth and out of sight. "It is too late to chase him now. He has made his choice."

"What are his chances?" Françoise asked.

Rumkey shrugged his shoulders. "Some may know him from his previous voyages. They will not look kindly on him."

"You finally got your justice, Françoise," Alain said.

"Yes, that I did." Surprisingly, Françoise did not enjoy the victory.

* * *

Alain stood at the desk, his balled fists resting on the roughened wood. Françoise made eye contact with him to try to gain some insight into what he was thinking. As far as she was concerned, she was focused on Boston. That was their ultimate destination. Anything less was unacceptable.

"So, how goes it on land?" He addressed the question to Rumkey who had spoken at length with the two men who had returned from scouting the mainland.

"The uprising has settled for now."

"So it is fine."

"It is far from peaceful, monsieur. The slaves roam free and in power. It would not be safe for the women to go ashore."

Françoise glanced at Badoo to watch his reaction. "But the slaves would be accepted."

"Maybe. While there is no open hostility at present, there are many scuffles and skirmishes. It would be a risk to send anyone."

"Any news of Beaudry?"

"They did not find him, but the slaves were cheering about something. They think he may have been caught."

"What do you want to do?" Françoise asked Alain.

"It would be foolish to try to rescue him. He may already be dead. We grow short of food and water."

"Perhaps we should send a couple of men ashore to find supplies. Not the port though. Try the local area. Do you agree?" Françoise asked.

"Agreed."

"Aye, Cap'n."

"Alain, we will have to sail on farther. We cannot stay here," Françoise said.

Alain's face was lined with concern. "Yes. But my father…"

"Your responsibility is to those on this ship. Once we have found port, you can send a message back to him."

Alain lifted the map onto the table. "Where do you suggest?"

"You are the one to decide, Alain. Your father owns this ship."

"You wish to go to Boston." He found the city on the map and rested his finger on the point. He placed his second finger on their present location and looked at the distance.

"That is my wish, not yours. But you will be able to take on fresh supplies and new crew for the ship's return journey."

"What about us?" Badoo asked in a quiet voice.

"Yes, what about you?" Françoise said. "Monsieur Barbineau?" It was a decision she did not want, nor was she in a position to make it. "You are the rightful owner of them. What do you want to do?"

"What am I to do with thirty slaves?"

"You could sell them," Françoise said, and Alain winced at the word. "Or you could set them free."

"Free?"

"Badoo, talk with them," Alain said. "We will not be staying here. Those that wish to leave the ship will be taken to shore. They will have to survive on their own. Anyone who stays on board will end up in slavery. That cannot be avoided." He hesitated for a moment before continuing. "We will be moving on to Boston."

"Boston? Are you sure?" Françoise asked.

"From what I have heard about the city, it is civilized enough for the women but not for the slaves. The Colonies have slavery. There will be nowhere they can hide there."

Françoise was exhausted contemplating what decision would be best. "For now, we all have a lot of thinking to do. I suggest we meet back in the afternoon to decide our fates."

\* \* \*

That afternoon, they gathered again.

"Have you made your decision?" Alain asked. He looked at each person in turn.

Rumkey took the initiative. "We will sail wherever you want to go, Cap'n. If you wish to go to Boston, then so be it. Some of the crew will be leaving when we are in port and will be replaced with new crew."

"Why so?"

"They are loyal to Beaudry, Cap'n."

Françoise turned her eyes to Badoo. Here was where their problems would arise.

"Some want to go ashore, Captain." Badoo gazed at Alain with concern.

"How many?" Alain asked.

He tried to hold up fingers to show how many, but he grunted in obvious frustration.

Rumkey came to his rescue. "A bit more than half of them, Cap'n."

"What about the rest?"

"Can we go home?" Badoo asked. Alain didn't answer.

Finally, Françoise answered for Alain. "I am sorry, Badoo, but it would be a matter for the new captain to decide. Do you want to risk capture again once you land in Ouidah? Next time you may not be so lucky."

"Yes, I know. But I wish…"

"I understand. Do they know that if they continue on it will mean slavery?"

"Can we come with you?"

Françoise pointed at herself. "With me? You mean to Boston? That is what we are talking about."

"No. With *you*. Can you look after us?"

"Me? Why would I want slaves?"

"But you said slavery was in Boston. Why can we not be your slaves?"

"Because I do not want any slaves." Françoise's mind flew in a hundred different directions. Did these people think she was their *Jeanne d'Arc*? Their savior? What if this was her destiny all along?

"But, madame, if you will forgive my impudence, would it not be better to have slaves that know you and will protect your secret?"

Françoise considered this option. As much as she wanted to be herself in America, she knew that the charade would have to continue. Two women living together would be unseemly and frowned upon.

She rubbed the rapidly tightening muscle in the back of her neck. She thought that it would come to this. No one wanted to make the decision, and she would have to be the devil's advocate. "Let me think on this."

* * *

"Well, look who sucked on a lemon today," Dale said as Françoise approached her on deck. "What's wrong?"

Françoise sighed. "The slaves want to come with us."

"You thought they might want to do that. What's the problem?"

*"Non.* With *us.* You and me. They want to be *my* slaves."

"Your slaves?"

*"Oui.* Mine. Well, yours and mine."

"Are they nuts?"

*"Non,* they are slaves."

"Nuts... certifiable... crazy."

Françoise leaned on the railing and hoped that the water held the answer for her.

"I can see a problem with that."

"Only one? I can see at least twenty."

"No, wait. This might work."

"That would make me responsible for fifteen slaves, plus Lucette and her girls and Sébastien. We have enough to start a new village. Why is life so... "

"Complicated? Difficult? Confusing?"

*"Oui,* and more. I do not know if I can do this."

"Maybe this is our destiny all along. Cause and effect, Françoise. Cause and effect."

"Cows and effet?"

Dale smiled. "No, we don't need cows. Cause and e-ff-ec-t."

"Caws and effect."

"If I hadn't come through the mirror, you might possibly be dead." Dale shivered. "If we hadn't come to Nantes, Lucette, her girls, and Sébastien might also be dead in the scuffle on the waterfront. The slave woman would have drowned if I hadn't saved her, and that made the other slaves think I'm a miracle worker. Cause and effect." Dale pursed her lips. "I wonder how much I've changed history. Damn. Why didn't I think about that before?"

"Make sense, Dale. What are you talking about?"

"I do not belong here, Françoise, so my very presence here will change history. How much, only time will tell. Anything I do, such as saving that woman from drowning, has ramifications later on. Maybe she was meant to die after all, and my saving her has changed everything. Do you understand?"

"I think so."

Dale blew out a breath, obviously frustrated with Françoise's inability to fully understand. "What I'm saying is that if we don't help them, it may change the future. Then again, it may not. Who knows? Maybe this is our destiny... to save these people."

"Badoo said it would be better to have slaves that know us and will protect our secret."

"He has a point. Unless we want to live in the city, but that would be stressful for us both. People around you would watch you closely." Dale's eyes lit up. "But if we built a house out in the country somewhere, and you became a 'gentleman farmer' with the slaves, you could spend a lot of the time being yourself."

"Being myself? What am I now?"

"I mean, you wouldn't have to dress up as a man so much. Wouldn't that be easier?"

"But this still does not explain why they want to be my slaves."

"Because you would be a fair mistress. You would protect them, feed them, and look after them. In return, they would protect your identity and help with the illusion you wish to create. I'm going to think of them as paid employees, because if I think about them as anything else, I'm going to puke." Dale swiped her hand over her brow. "I can't believe I'm even considering this. I know, I know. We're saving them from a fate worse than death, but…"

Françoise lost the thread of conversation somewhere in the middle, but what she said sounded good. "Two kings' ransom," she muttered.

"Sorry?"

"That is your worth, Dale. Maybe I should sell you to solve all my problems, *n'est-ce pas?*"

"Why you… you…"

*"Oui."* Françoise laughed. *"Ah, merci, ma chérie.* I needed that." She turned to the small group of women huddled in the corner. Dale followed her line of sight. "Now I must decide about them."

"I'm sure they can make up their own minds."

"But I will not like what they say. Lucette talked of returning to France."

"Not a wise move. They won't stay in Boston?"

"Perhaps if there was something to stay for."

"Not even for you, Françoise?"

"I will not ask her to stay for me." But she was so tempted to do so. Lucette was her last link to her heritage. "I have said that she could start again but she has no…" Françoise hesitated as she sought the word she was looking for.

"Experience? She is a brothel madam and knows nothing else."

*"Voilà!"* Françoise smiled as she watched Sébastien tossing young Jacob into the air and then catching the giggling child. "But she should not have to turn back to that life."

Dale looked at the women. Her lips drew into a slow grin. "I think I have a solution."

\* \* \*

"Finally." Lucette said as Françoise approached.

"Pardon. I am sorry it has taken so long."

"So what is to become of us?"

"It is not my place to tell you."

"Child, just tell me."

"It is too dangerous here. The slaves have control of the port and will target anyone white. There is nowhere for you to hide, Lucette."

"So?"

"So, we will move on to Boston as soon as we can obtain fresh food and water."

"Honorine will be pleased to hear that. She has been nagging me about trying to make sawdust edible." Sébastien came up behind her and placed his hands on her shoulders.

"I see that you two have not wasted time, eh?"

"No. Just get to the point, Françoise. What is to happen?"

"What do you want to happen?"

"Stop these games, young lady. What are you afraid to tell me?" She gently squeezed Françoise's shoulder and gave her the support she needed.

"Nothing. Not really. I wanted to know if you are returning to France."

"That will depend on what you are trying not to tell me."

"Dale has made a suggestion, and I agree that it might work."

"Your little wife, eh? Well, out with it."

"I do not want you to go back to your old life, Tantine."

"I know nothing else."

"I know that. Dale has suggested a 'gentlemen's club,' as she calls it."

"You mean a brothel."

"No. No sex. What did she say? A 'sophisticated establishment.' Fine wine, fine food, beautiful women as dinner companions. It could be a place where the elite of society could spend time with their kind to discuss business or find a dinner companion whom they did not have to take home and live with." Françoise wasn't sure she had conveyed the idea well. It was a strange idea when she heard it herself, and by the look on Lucette's face, she was confused as well.

"I do not have that sort of coin, my dear. You know that."

"I will lend it to you. I can become, as Dale says, 'a silent partner.'"

"You do not talk?"

"No, she said it means that while I own it, no one knows that I do. It is a secret."

"Ah."

"Do not decide yet. Give it some thought."

"What about Sébastien?"

"Now, Lucette, I can look after myself."

"I thought your future had been taken care of, my friend. But I am sure a man of your obvious size and strength would be a discouragement for any trouble."

"I am a guard?"

"Sébastien, I know that time grows short for you as a blacksmith." She grabbed his much larger hand and ran her finger over the gnarled knuckles. "How much longer, my friend? You have served well. Now is the time to reap the reward of such servitude."

"That is a pretty speech, Françoise, but I am still a guard."

"And husband to the madame of the premises." She laughed. "Do not look so shocked, you two. Get married and be done with it."

"And when are you going to make an honest woman of Dale, eh?"

"Who will marry two women, Tantine? Such a union is frowned upon by the Church. I do not think so."

"A captain of a ship may do it," Sébastien said.

"A captain?"

"Think about it just as we will think about your offer." He turned Lucette to face him. "She does have a point. Will you marry me?"

"Finally," Françoise muttered.

# Chapter 28

St. Domingue had been left two days behind them. The crew was sailing in unknown waters, their normal trade route of Nantes, Ouidah, and St. Domingue now broken. Dale did prove useful in filling in some of the gaps on their rather scant map of the Americas. They had crossed the open sea, and they now followed the coastline north.

Supplies were scarce, but two crewmen found some fresh water and a small amount of fruit. The variety was bewildering, and Françoise was hesitant to try the more exotic types. With the thought of more fish and sea biscuits, and Dale's badgering, she tried them. Some were to her liking, and others were more an acquired taste.

On deck, Alain walked over to her.

"Alain. It will not be long now."

"Yes, I know."

"Have you made a decision?"

"I have, but I fear taking the course I have to follow."

"Returning to France?" Françoise suspected as much. His father was his father, and he owed it to him to make sure he was safe.

He nodded.

"Is that wise?"

"I have to know, Françoise."

"But you saw what was happening."

"If it were me, I would be pleased to know my son thought enough of me to return."

"But if I were your father, I would want you to be somewhere safe, not returning to danger. The journey will not be easy."

He gazed out over the turbulent water to the distant land, narrowing his eyes as if trying to focus on something. "The sea voyage will again be difficult."

"I am not talking about that, Alain. You are returning to a land that has become a stranger to us. You will not know whom to trust or whom to fear." She hesitated. "Your father may be dead."

"I cannot return thinking that, Françoise. I cannot."

She rested her hand on his shoulder and gently squeezed. "You are right. He is probably fine and just looking for an opportunity to depart." Françoise certainly hoped, for Alain's sake, that the man was indeed plotting his escape from the war-torn land and not taking advantage of it. "What of Rosalie?"

"She will be staying with Lucette."

"And she has no say in this?"

"No. As my future wife, it is not her decision to make. As the head of this family, I have told her what to do."

She glanced over at Dale. Françoise was glad her French was still poor, otherwise Alain would have felt the full wrath of her biting tongue on the matter.

"Future wife is it? I must have missed that."

"You were busy with the slaves, my friend."

"So will there be another marriage on this ship?"

"Marriage? Who?"

She almost laughed at the shocked look on his face. "It seems I am not the only one remiss of what is happening aboard this ship." The confusion remained. "Sébastien has asked Lucette to be his wife."

"Well, well. That wily old fox."

"Has Rosalie informed you of where she will be working?"

"I do not want her to be drawn into such an endeavor."

"Oh no, no, no. It is a gentlemen's club."

"That is bad enough, Françoise."

"I would not allow Lucette to return to her old profession, Alain. It is companionship, nothing more. It is a place to talk and meet, and perhaps acquire a dinner companion if one wishes it."

"And you are a dumb companion?"

She chuckled. "A silent partner."

"You are able to do this?" he asked.

"Yes." She still wasn't totally convinced. It was going to take most of her resources to accomplish what she had promised, but she was not going to tell Lucette that.

Alain shifted a little closer to Françoise, his voice lowering in secrecy. "I ask a favor of you, Countess." The title surprised her. "The chests below…"

"Should be kept in a bank, Alain."

"There is a chance I may not return." He held up his hand as Françoise prepared to dispute him. "If I do not return, I do not want it to be handed over to a total stranger. There is a real possibility that I may perish, we both know that."

"Yes, I do."

"Hold the chests for me until I return or until two years have passed. If I have not appeared in that time, then it is yours." A look of relief crossed his face. "I know that you will take good care of my Rosalie. This would help in her... in *their* care."

Françoise nodded. She could not deny his last wish, if this was indeed just that.

Alain's face hardened. "I want you to make me the, how you say... dumb... quiet...?"

"Silent?"

"Silent partner. Your coin is better spent on looking after Dale and the group of slaves you now seem to own."

"Oh, that."

"Yes, that. You attract waifs like fleas to a dog, Countess."

"I am so tired of it, Alain."

"Truly great people keep going even in adversity."

"I am not—"

"Françoise, there are fifty people on this vessel who would disagree with you, including Dale I am sure."

Françoise flushed. "I do not feel great."

"Of course not, my friend. If you were full of self-importance, then your efforts would have been for naught."

"Self-importance?"

"Yes... Countess. Are the aristocracy not the epitome of arrogance and self-gratification? Who are you, young woman?"

"I am who you see, young man," she tossed back at him.

"Good retort. But that does not answer my question. You are not like any aristocrat that I know."

Françoise chuckled.

"What?" Alain said.

"Lucette said the same thing not long ago."

"Well?"

"Now is not the time to drag up the past."

"Oh. Pardon. I did not mean to cause affront."

"No, you are not at fault here, Alain. It is a past that is better left where it rests. In the past."

"Then it is a story for another day."

"Yes, another day." As far as Françoise was concerned, another day would be many years in the future.

Alain abruptly steered the conversation in another direction. "On my return to France, is there anything you would like me to find for you?"

"Find?"

"Françoise, the coin you brought with you is not all that you own. I am not stupid."

"It is going to be dangerous enough traveling through France. Do not risk your life over a few gold coins."

"A few? I doubt that a few are involved. I am well aware of what the count was worth. At least let me try to recover some for you. I am sure that it will be sorely needed."

The offer was tempting. "I cannot in all good conscience allow you to do this."

"I am sure I will be transporting more of my father's fortune anyway. What is a chest or two more?"

"You will need an army to protect it, Alain. The countryside is rife with thieves and killers."

"Do not worry about me. I can take care of myself. I will have *Le Renard* at my disposal, and my father has the odd friend scattered through the port. My 'army' as you call it will be at my command from the moment I step foot back on French soil."

"You so sure of yourself, Monsieur Barbineau."

"Naturally. I inherited that from my father. Arrogance, I think he called it."

"I know that word well."

"The count was full of it. You, on the other hand—do not confuse arrogance with confidence."

"I do not feel very confident, or arrogant for that matter." What was she? Scared as hell? Confused? Tired of it all?

"Still trying to come to terms with your loss, Countess? This has not been a gradual loss of social status or wealth. This has come with the force of an act of God, and you are hanging onto the one thing that is anchoring you to the ground. Dale. You will do what you need to do to accomplish this, and it is very admirable. Despite your claims to the contrary, my friend, you have changed the lives of everyone onboard this ship."

He held up his hand and began ticking off his points. "Lucette and her girls now have a chance to start anew and leave their prostitution behind them. Sébastien has found love, as have I, and I know I would never have approached Rosalie without your subtle push. You are giving these slaves a chance at a better life. Something, I am sure, that they could not have even hoped for."

"It is nothing. I just wanted to get to Boston."

"And in doing so, you have accomplished much."

"And in doing so, I have to listen to you wax lyrical about me. Have you finished?"

"Have I convinced you to let me try to recover some of your fortune?"

"If it will keep you quiet, then yes."

There was silence for a moment or two. "Françoise, you have to help me, or am I supposed to divine for it?"

"Oh." She was reluctant to reveal such a secret even though the coin had been given up as lost. "The first spot is in the fireplace in the main bedroom on the top floor. There are some loose bricks at the back."

"Fireplace, main bedroom, loose bricks. Yes. First spot?"

"There is a well in the far corner of the estate…"

* * *

Françoise found Dale on deck with the journal in her hands. "Where is Jacob? What have you there?"

"Lucette has him. This is the diary." That was all she said before seconds later throwing it overboard.

"Why did you do that?" Françoise wasn't quick enough to grab it as it flew over the railing into the sea.

"It's the best place for it."

"In the sea?"

"It served its purpose. It occupied our time aboard this ship, and it gave us a place to air our grievances. We could write what we wanted in it, Françoise. It was a haven for our thoughts, our sorrows, and our joy, even though there was not a lot of that on this trip."

"Then why throw it overboard?"

"I've been thinking about it the last day or so, re-reading a lot of what I had written. There's too much 'twenty-first century' in it. I can't risk it being revealed to the world."

"What on earth did you write? Something that is to come?" Françoise had taken the time to read some of Dale's entries, and while her turn of phrase was quaint, she didn't think it was dangerous.

Dale glared at her. "No, of course not. I'm not that stupid. But if it fell into the wrong hands, maybe people would question it. I speak differently from anyone on this planet right now."

"I do not need a journal to know that."

"I'm just thinking of cause and effect."

"Not the cows again."

"Yep, I've probably done more than enough damage as it is. No, better for it to be fish food, I'm afraid."

Françoise gazed into the watery depths. She sighed. She had wanted to keep that journal as a memento of both their journey and her lover. Dale had splashed her innermost thoughts across those pages, but now the ink would be long gone, dissolved into nothingness by the salty water.

Françoise noticed Alain's arrival on deck. "My friends, a moment of your time!" she shouted. "Let us gather together." Françoise remained silent while everyone moved closer. Her mind was racing as she tried to put words together in some sort of order.

"Tomorrow we should reach Boston Harbor." Françoise expected a loud cheer to erupt, but it was more a relieved sigh. "The captain has been asked to perform a marriage ceremony." A low murmur flowed around the assembled crowd like a wave. Badoo's deep voice rumbled as he translated for the slaves present. "Lucette. Sébastien. Step forward please." She smiled as Lucette handed Jacob to Rosalie, and the two lovebirds moved to stand in front of her. "Monsieur Barbineau, as captain of this ship, will perform a wedding at sea. Does anyone object?"

All that could be heard was the billowing of sail, the whoosh of sea spray, and Badoo's ever-present murmuring. "Fine." Françoise hesitated. She had wanted to say something before the ceremony began. Should she use too many words or too few? As she clamored for the right words, someone touched her. She turned to Lucette who gently nodded.

"I have known Lucette for a long, long time, and we have experienced much together. Despite her former life, she is a woman of great character and honor. Sébastien I have known for only a short time, but he is someone I gladly call friend."

Jacob whimpered. Tiny fingers waved frantically in the sea air. Dale closed the few steps between them and reached for him as he tried to get out of Rosalie's arms.

"Just get on with it, little one. None of us is getting any younger."

Françoise didn't need to search for the owner of that voice. The tone and sentiment told her exactly who it was. "Some of us are younger than others, old woman." Laughter flowed across the crowd, but drew a disgruntled harrumph from Honorine.

Françoise stepped out of the way and motioned with a flourish for Alain to take her place.

He cleared his throat before speaking. "Lucette... Sébastien... do you wish to become husband and wife?"

"Yes, I do." They spoke as one.

"Then as captain of *Le Renard,* I pronounce you man and wife."

"That is it?"

"What more need be said? Short and sweet." Everyone jostled around to congratulate the newly joined couple. Françoise searched for Dale, who bounced Jacob in her arms. Jacob's palm landed on her lips as she blew on them. He giggled when Dale nipped his fingers.

How could she deny Dale this? Even Jacob was at his happiest in Dale's loving arms.

Lucette sidled up beside her. "I think you have to surrender, Françoise."

She sighed deeply. "Yes, I think I do."

"One moment, madame. There is one more thing to be done."

Françoise looked at Alain in confusion. "Is there? I do not think so, Captain. Tomorrow, we—"

"Not that. You and your wife please come forward."

Françoise looked at Dale, wondering what it was that she had done wrong.

"You cannot arrive in Boston under false pretenses."

What was he saying?

"Françoise... err... what is your full name, madame?"

"Françoise Marie Aurélie de Villerey."

He turned to Dale. "And you, madame. What is your full name?"

"Dale... Dale Wincott."

"Dale Wimcutt?"

"No, Wincott. W-i-n-c-o-t-t."

*"Ahh, bien."*

"What is going on?"

"We must know the names of those getting married, do we not?"

"Married? Us?" Françoise's heart beat wildly in her chest. Married? Could they? Should they?

"You do not wish this?" Alain asked in surprise.

"I…" Françoise turned to Dale and looked into her eyes. *"Mon amour,"* she whispered, "will you marry me?"

"Marry you?" Tears spilled down Dale's cheeks. "Of course I will marry you, my love."

"Get on with it."

Lucette slapped Honorine's arm. "Shh. Let them be."

"Is there anything you want to say to each other?" Alain asked.

Françoise nervously ran her hand down her pants leg. "I…er…" But then Dale took her hand and gently squeezed.

"You don't need to say anything. You are shaking like a leaf, Françoise. All through this voyage you have told me what was in your heart. You have loved me, protected me, and nurtured me. You never have to say another word because you have said it in the way you look at me." Dale caressed Françoise's cheek. "And here." She placed her hand on Françoise's chest. There was a low murmur accompanying the words as Alain translated the conversation for the witnesses.

A lone tear trekked down Françoise's cheek. "I love you, Dale Wincott, with all my heart."

"Then, as captain, it is my duty to declare that you two are married."

Jacob must have sensed something and wriggled in Dale's arms before launching himself fearlessly at Françoise. She was lucky she had good reflexes because the little boy was seconds away from hitting the deck.

"That has got to be the quickest marriage ceremony I've ever attended," Dale said in amusement.

"Oh twaddle. All this gushing is making me sick to my stomach."

"Then go and start the evening meal, Honorine," Françoise told her. "You do not have to participate in all this celebration." Nothing was going to spoil their unexpected wedding, not even a grumpy old cook.

# Chapter 29

"You should have offered the bed to Lucette." Dale lay in the crook of Françoise's arm that night, relaxing with the gentle sway of the vessel.

"I did. It seemed that she preferred the privacy of Alain's compartment."

"Privacy or comfort. Tough choice."

"You mean you would make love in front of everyone in this room?" Françoise was surprised. If there was one thing she was sure of, it was Dale's shyness.

"Of course not, but Lucette isn't me."

"I am sure she was protecting Sébastien's sensibilities, *chérie*." Françoise was amused to watch the two newlyweds dancing around each other. She suspected that Sébastien was prepared to wait until they were on dry land. But Lucette—her Tantine—was acting like a virgin on her wedding night. It was adorable.

Dale caressed her face. The gentle touch was addictive. Her fingers stopped above her eyebrow to feel the slight ridge she knew was there.

"Looks like you're going to have a scar."

"Does that bother you?"

"It will destroy your perfect face, but I can live with it." Dale snickered. She gazed up at Françoise. "Don't worry. I think it will give you a rakish look. It's going to be so sexy."

"I am glad you approve. Maybe I should go out and get a tattoo." She didn't see the slap coming, but she reacted quickly by wrapping her long arms around Dale's wriggling body. Dale's head nestled into her chest, and they were content to listen to the familiar sounds of the sea.

She heard a faint noise that was foreign to the room. A noise that she hadn't heard in what seemed like a lifetime ago. Françoise's breath caught in her throat, and she waited to see if it happened again. There it was… a faint car horn. Was she going mad? "Do you hear that?"

"Hear what?"

Françoise waited a moment to see if the sound would repeat itself. It took longer, but it was definitely a sound out of place. "That."

"A car horn," Dale whispered.

Françoise untangled herself from her wife and shuffled over to the far wall where Sébastien had put the mirror after the storm. There was barely any light to navigate around the sleeping bodies, but the sparse moonlight gave her glimpses of the room. She reached out and touched wood. She blindly tapped along the wall until she found the familiar frame.

Françoise didn't know what to expect when her hand hovered over the glass. She was almost fearful to touch it in case the magic was finally gone, that Dale was bound to live in a time that she was not born to.

She touched the surface, and it took a heartbeat before it bent, giving way like the surface of water. Although she could not see it, she knew that the glass rippled outwards, her touch with the magic being the epicenter of the disturbance. Despite herself, Françoise smiled. It seemed that Dale's father had understood after all.

She made her way back to the bunk, tip-toeing around the sleeping women on the floor.

"So?" Dale said in an urgent whisper. "What did you find?"

Françoise heard the hope in her voice. "It seems that your father had the foresight to fix the mirror. You can go home anytime you want to." She tensed, afraid of what Dale would say.

"Not now. Still, it's nice to know there's a way out if we need one."

"Way out?"

"If life gets too hard for us, we can always go forward."

"So true." Françoise wrapped her arms tightly around Dale and pulled her close to allow Dale's scent to fill her nostrils.

Jacob cooed. He was lying in the bunk also. He was snuggled into Dale's back, while his new parents enjoyed the closeness of a slumbering couple.

As drowsiness started to overcome Françoise, Dale whispered the words she'd longed to hear.

"I'm not leaving you, so stop worrying. We're here for a reason, my love."

Françoise smiled as the words slurred with sleep. Tomorrow was hopefully the final day of their voyage. Tomorrow their lives would begin anew.

* * *

Dale still hadn't gotten used to having someone in her bed besides Françoise, but she also had a hard time waking alone. She'd turned during the night, surprised not to feel the presence of little Jacob. The fading heat of the blanket told her Françoise had risen not long before her waking, taking their child with her. Their child. *That* was taking some getting used to.

She rose quietly and tried not to disturb the sleeping women who were in various stages of snoring, mumbling, and rolling over. The smell was indescribable, and she sought the clean air out on deck. She emerged to a new day and spotted Françoise at the railing with little Jacob sitting in the crook of her strong arm. She seemed to be pointing out something to the child on the nearby land.

Despite what Françoise had told her, it was obvious Jacob had a strong hold on Françoise's heart. She watched Alain approach Françoise and hand over a sheet of paper. Françoise took one look at the paper and laughed.

They talked for a moment before Alain excused himself.

She approached Françoise. "What's so funny?"

"We should reach Boston Harbor today." Françoise looked out over the water to the slowly approaching city.

"That's not what made you laugh. What's on that piece of paper?" She was about to snatch it out of Françoise's hand.

"It made me realize that no matter what we do, what will happen, will happen."

"That's rather philosophical of you. How do you come to this conclusion?"

Françoise didn't respond. Instead, she handed over the paper in question. "It is about our marriage."

"A marriage certificate?" Dale glanced at the page.

"Look at the names." As Françoise watched for a reaction, a smile crossed her lips.

Dale's mouth gaped open.

*"Oui."*

"This… this is some joke, right? I wonder where he came up with those names?" Dale shook her head as she felt the cosmic tumblers click into place to reveal their destiny.

*"Non,* no joke. Alain wished for us to start a new life with a new name. It is, as you say, our destiny."

Dale reread the page in disbelief. "But those particular names? How did he know? Did you tell him?"

"I swear I said nothing. Perhaps he felt a French name would not be accepted."

"But you have a French accent."

"It could be explained. I was born in London but raised in Anjou. Your accent, however…"

"Not now," Dale said. "It's too beautiful a day to worry about such things."

Françoise handed over the squirming boy to Dale and placed the precious piece of parchment in her pocket. She pulled them against her chest and wrapped her arms around Dale's waist as they faced the harbor. "Welcome to America, Elizabeth Wincott," she whispered. "I love you."

# About the Author

Erica Lawson was born in Sydney, Australia, and has lived there all her life. Her writing career didn't begin until 2005. Her first novel, *Possessing Morgan*, was accepted for publication by Blue Feather Books in 2007. In 2010 her debut novel won the Golden Crown Literary Society Award for Mystery/Thriller. Her second novel, *The Chronicles of Ratha: The Children of The Noorthi*, was published in December 2011, and was a finalist in the 2011 Golden Crown Literary Society Awards. *Soulwalker*, her third novel, published in 2012, won the Golden Crown Literary Society Award in the Science Fiction Category. Her most recent novel is *Miss-Match*, co-written with AC Henley.

Erica is currently working on more novels, among them a sequel to the successful first installment in the *Chronicles of Ratha* Series, *A Lion Among the Lambs*.

Make sure to check out these other exciting
Blue Feather Books titles:

| | | |
|---|---|---|
| Clandestine | Cheyne Curry | 978-1-935627-78-4 |
| Pulse Points | Barbara Valletto | 978-1-935627-79-1 |
| Cresswell Falls | Kerry Belchambers | 978-1-935627-95-1 |
| Rebellion in Ulster | Angela Koenig | 978-1-935627-76-0 |
| Survived by Her Longtime Companion | Chris Paynter | 978-1-935627-88-3 |
| The Midas Conspiracy | Jennifer McCormick | 978-1-935627-84-5 |
| Lesser Prophets | Kelly Sinclair | 978-0-9822858-8-6 |
| Right Out of Nowhere | Laurie Salzler | 978-1-935627-60-9 |
| Appointment with a Smile | Kieran York | 978-1-935627-86-9 |
| Flight | Renee MacKenzie | 978-1-935627-73-9 |
| And a Time to Dance | Chris Paynter | 978-1-935627-64-7 |
| Arnica | I Christie | 978-1-935627-82-1 |
| No Corpse Is an Island | Gato Timberlake | 978-1-935627-74-6 |

**www.bluefeatherbooks.com**

CPSIA information can be obtained at www.ICGtesting.com
Printed in the USA
BVOW08s0904041113

335273BV00003B/121/P